With Wine Comes Wisdom

Book 1 of the With Wine Series

JE Johnson

JE JOHNSON AUTHOR LLC

Contents

For those like Alex, who have lost their faith and feel the silence where God once was.
And for those like Roman, who hold onto Him like a lifeline, even when the waters rise.

This is for every heart caught between doubt and belief, still reaching for something greater than itself.

This story is yours too.

—JJ

Chapter 1

ALEX

"Good morning, sun," I muttered, dragging the covers over my face, trying to block the light stabbing through my skull. Another night. One too many drinks. Again.

Insanity, they say, is doing the same thing over and over and expecting a different result. By that definition, I'm textbook. At least I hadn't dragged anyone home. I'm good at the preemptive disclaimer—*not looking for anything serious*. Divorce will do that to you.

A year out from the paperwork, I still can't decide if I'm relieved or just numb. I married too young, right out of college, and four years later I was signing papers I never thought I'd touch. No kids—thank God—but the emotional fallout was enough to make me question whether I'd ever try again.

I was raised by two loving, attentive parents—at least when my mom was sober. When she wasn't, I couldn't get out fast enough. Still, there's always been something between us, invisible and undeniable. Maybe it's just a mother–daughter thing. Maybe it's deeper. We always seemed to feel each other, especially when it hurt.

The youngest of three, I arrived after Patrick and Edward. Mom finally got her girl, but I wasn't the princess she pictured. I was a scrappy tomboy, fierce on the field, grass-stained jeans and hand-me-down cleats my uniform. Barbies and tea sets made me cringe. Even the thought of Mary Janes turned my stomach.

Before I left home, Mom told me, "You don't need a man to be happy or to have a baby." Which was rich, considering she's been married to Dad for thirty-five years.

Now, at twenty-eight, I'm stuck—not romantically, but existentially. Business degree. Successful real-estate career. Downtown condo. A life that looks perfect on paper. Something's missing, and I can't name it.

Most of my friends have swapped girls' nights and career goals for playgrounds and PTA meetings. I'm the odd one out—the aunt who shows up with sugary treats and wine-stained lips, spoiling your kids and then disappearing.

Their lives are picture-perfect—the husbands, the kids, the cul-de-sac homes. And here I am, groaning into my pillow, reaching for Advil and praying the pounding will ease before brunch.

I roll toward my nightstand and grab my phone. One message:

MAGGIE: *Hey jerk, you gonna be on time for brunch today?*

I can practically see her—hair perfectly tousled, one manicured hand wrapped around a mimosa, the other firing off sass like it's an Olympic sport.

I tap back a thumbs-up emoji and drop the phone on the nightstand.

After chugging a bottle of water and downing two Advil, I stumbled into the bathroom and twisted the shower knob. One glance in the mirror stopped me cold—mascara streaked like war paint under my eyes, lips cracked, hair a tangle of curls around my face. The guy from last night had a good smile and smooth rhythm on the dance floor...but I left before the night turned into a mistake. I always do.

Every Sunday at 11:30, Maggie, Abby, and I meet at Sunny Side Up—our sacred ritual. Same table. Same waitress. Same ridiculous laughter that makes the world feel tolerable for an hour.

Sunny Side Up is a polished blend of white linen and French Provincial charm. Sunlight filters through striped yellow awnings framing the wraparound porch, casting soft shadows over whitewashed floorboards. Delicate French doors, open to the breeze, carry hints of lavender from the garden and the sweetness of baked brioche from the kitchen. Inside, the air smells of citrus zest and rosemary undercut with the creamy richness of hollandaise. Each table gleams with heirloom silverware, vintage glassware, and fresh-cut blossoms in porcelain bud vases. Soft conversation hums between the quiet clink of cutlery and the hiss of a champagne cork. It's like stepping into a southern Parisian morning—refined but easy.

The walk clears my head. My navy sundress sways below my knees, catching the breeze. My hair is piled in a loose knot, curls slipping free like little rebellions. No makeup—just moisturizer and sunglasses.

Inside, the hostess greets me with a warm smile. "Ms. Kennedy, right this way. The ladies are already here."

"Thank you."

Maggie and Abby sit at our usual table, Mimosas in hand. Maggie—flawless blonde waves and oversized sunglasses—looks every bit the politician's wife: chic, composed, a little too perfect. Abby is petite, with a sleek chestnut bob and meticulous makeup. Always elegant. Never a hair out of place.

I order my own Mimosa before they can call me out for being late and pull them both into a quick hug.

"You two look amazing, as always," I say, sliding into my seat. "So tell me—how are my sweet little monkeys?"

Maggie sighs theatrically. "Cameron and Sophia Grace? Still trying to break everything I own. When are you coming to kidnap them?"

I laugh. "I'm sure you're exaggerating. No way those angel-faced devils could be so destructive."

Abby grins. "Jax keeps asking when Aunt Ali is taking him to the park again."

"I'll check my calendar," I promise.

Cameron is five and a half—restless, curious, all elbows and energy, but somehow angelic when he's with me. Sophia Grace, four and a half, is her mother's mini-me: blonde curls, bright eyes, a pint-sized shadow in a tutu with sass that rivals reality TV stars. One sticky summer afternoon she climbed into my lap, popsicle juice on her fingers, and whispered, *You smell like sunshine and cookies, Aunt Ali.* My heart cracked open. She wasn't planned, and Maggie's world tilted for a while, but Sophia Grace brought a kind of joy that softened even Maggie's hardest edges.

Abby's son, Jax, is four—wide-eyed, dinosaur-obsessed, a wild child with me. I wouldn't trade a minute of it.

By our third round of mimosas, the conversation shifts—as it always does—to my nonexistent dating life.

Maggie leans in, eyes glinting. "So...what was last night's flavor? Chocolate, vanilla, or something new? Maybe rocky road?"

I arch an eyebrow. "What the hell is rocky road?"

She shrugs. "I don't know. Bald, maybe?"

Abby, ever the cautious one, tilts her head. "Are you being careful? Protection, regular checkups?"

I pause. The truth? I haven't been with anyone in months. One drunken mistake post-divorce and a few rumors later, and I've got a reputation I don't deserve.

"Let's not," I say, sharper than intended. "I'm not in the mood."

They both retreat. I flag the waitress. "Vodka martini, straight up. Dirty. Extra blue-cheese olives."

Their eyes follow me—concerned, curious, but quiet.

Abby shifts the subject. "How's your mom? Still drinking, or has she dried out again?"

I sigh. "Same as always. Just waiting for the other shoe to drop."

Maggie leans forward. "And Peckerhead? Still bugging you?"

Luke. My ex. Still texting. Still clinging.

"Nope. No word."

Lie.

I close my eyes and sip my martini, letting the briny sting and sharp vodka burn away the conversation.

"Everything's fine. Nothing new to report."

The vibe has shifted. Or maybe I've shifted—restless, hungover, maybe tipsy, definitely not in the mood.

"I've got a lot to do today," I say, grabbing my purse.

Maggie narrows her eyes. "Sure you do."

Abby smiles. "Don't forget about Jax."

"Never. I'll text you."

Back home, I collapse onto the couch still in my dress, too tired to care. Later, I trade it for leggings and an oversized tee, pour a glass of wine, and order vegan pizza with a salad to blunt the guilt.

My apartment is soft chaos—white walls, dark hardwood, jewel-toned velvet pillows, and a fuchsia throw that feels like cashmere. A weathered photo frame sits on the bookshelf near the window, holding a sun-faded snapshot of my brothers and me at the beach the summer before high school—Dad behind the camera, Mom's laughter frozen mid-giggle in the background. A memory caught before everything fractured, sealed in a time when the sun was warm, the water was endless, and life still felt safe—pain-free, untouched. One wall is glass—floor-to-ceiling windows with a reflective tint—bathing the space in a muted afternoon light.

The kitchen is bright and modern: white cabinets, stainless appliances, quartz counters lined with candles, fruit, and protein bars. Vanilla and lemon drift from the candle burning beside the coffee maker.

I sip wine, half-watch a rom-com, and scroll through my phone. My mind drifts.

Tomorrow is big. Three showings and a closing on a seven-figure invest-ment deal—the kind of deal that could catapult me to a corner office, maybe even the firm's shortlist for partner. Months of work, coaxing wary clients into trust. If I land this, it's not just a win; it's validation. I've got the dress. The heels. The manicure. The confidence.

But still no answer to the bigger question: *What am I doing with my life?*

Just before bed, I set my alarm and click the coffee maker on for morning. A memory arrives—sharp, uninvited.

"Ali Marie, sweetie," my mom once slurred, wineglass in hand. "It's a good thing you're pretty, because you're really not very bright."

That one stuck, a splinter under the skin. Maybe that's why I work so damn hard to prove her wrong.

Chapter 2

ALEX

The sun and my alarm made a ruthless tag team. I groaned, dragging a pillow over my head. With no curtains, the early light spilled through the untinted window and stretched across my sheets like an unwanted guest. My bed was too comfortable, my body too tired, but the gym won—as usual.

High-waisted black leggings, cropped racerback tank. My go-to armor for mornings like this. Cross-trainers waiting by the door, laces already loosened as if they knew the ritual. I tied them tight, feeling the support wrap snug around my arches. In the kitchen, a scoop of watermelon pre-workout fizzed in my shaker. Tall water bottle. Earbuds. Phone lighting up with unread texts I ignored. This was my sanctuary hour—the one slice of time I didn't owe to anyone but myself. No emails, no clients, no family drama. Just the sound of my breath, the beat of my playlist, and the rhythm of my feet pounding against the treadmill—the only time I could outrun the noise inside my head.

The first-floor gym buzzed—Monday mornings always did. I skipped the pool and headed straight for the treadmill, but walked in long enough to smell the chlorine. That sharp scent hit something nostalgic—childhood summers, hair stiff with salt and sunblock—a simpler time in my life.

The Pitbull remix thumped as I ran until my legs burned. My muscles screamed while my mind slid back to last night's wine. I hated admitting it, but maybe I was drinking for more than social reasons. Genetics weren't on my side. My mom was an alcoholic. I wondered if I was heading there too.

I wiped sweat—and the thought—from my face. Switched to weights. Twenty-pound dumbbells felt heavier than usual. Playlist pulsing, inner voices louder. I couldn't seem to lift those, no matter how many reps I did.

Yoga helped. Sort of. On good days, it felt like a quiet conversation between my body and my breath. On others, like today, it was more of a negotiation. Downward dog, warrior two, pigeon—my limbs stretching and shaking, trying to release tension I didn't even know I was holding. Each inhale was a tiny rebellion against the anxiety crouched in my chest; each exhale, a release I didn't quite trust. In savasana, palms open to the ceiling like an offering, the cool air kissed my damp skin. Tight hamstrings. A knot near my shoulder blade. Calves still humming from the treadmill. Eyes closed, thoughts blurred at the edges. For a minute, maybe two, it almost felt like peace.

The sauna came next—my final ritual before facing the day. I peeled off my damp clothes and wrapped a thick white towel around my waist, still warm from the dryer. Earbuds switched to ocean waves—slow, rhythmic, familiar. Opening the cedar door, a wave of heat hit me like a blanket thrown straight from the sun. I stepped inside, sealing the door with a soft hiss.

The wooden bench burned against my thighs as I leaned back, spine melting into the wall. The humid air clung to my lungs—thick and velvet, each breath a slow push. My pores surrendered instantly, beads of sweat gathering at my hairline, rolling down the slope of my back, tracing my collarbone like a silent prayer. It was uncomfortable but oddly comforting—proof my body still functioned, still detoxed, still fought for something. Each drop of sweat whispered: *You're still here. Still alive. Still trying.* The heat softened my muscles and, for a few quiet moments, even the ache behind my ribs—the hidden bruise I carried—began to ease.

Lying back, I thought of our annual family beach trip. I always showed up solo—even when I was married. Luke had never come. Too busy, or so he said. Later I found out it was just other women and not wanting to face my brothers.

A text pinged.

LANDON: *Owen's looking forward to meeting you tonight at Sebastian's.*

My stomach flipped. I hadn't expected that. Until now I'd only admired Owen from afar, handled our company's dealings through his secretary or a partner named Stewart. Flattered or wary—I couldn't tell. I didn't reply.

By the time my phone rang again, I was stepping off the elevator, arms loaded—gym bag, almost-empty water bottle, damp towel, shaker cup I hadn't rinsed yet. Of course it was my mom. I sighed and hit *accept* with my pinky while digging for my keys at the bottom of my tote.

"Good morning," I said, breathless.

"Ali Marie, is it too early?" she chirped, far too cheerful for anyone who hadn't just slogged through cardio, weights, yoga, and a sweat bath. Her mornings came with coffee and baileys, not pre-workout and existential dread.

"Nope, just got back from the gym," I replied, clamping the phone between my shoulder and ear as I finally found the key fob. My towel slipped out from under my arm and landed with a wet splat. The water bottle followed, clattering across the tile and rolling under the entryway table.

"What in the world was that racket?" she laughed. "You moving furniture?"

"Just dropped something," I muttered, bending to retrieve the bottle while holding the door open with my hip. "No casualties."

"Well, I've got the vacation dates!" Her voice glowed with excitement.

Relief eased my shoulders. "Great. I was starting to think it was canceled."

We always rented the same two houses on the Florida Gulf—pool in the backyard, big lawn, private beach access. As she rattled off dates, I smiled. Time enough to close a few deals before we left. When we hung up, I held on to the rare warmth of a pleasant exchange with her.

After a quick shower, I pulled on a fitted black dress, styled my hair in soft waves, dabbed on natural makeup. Heels clicked across the floor as I headed to the kitchen for coffee. Purse, keys, leather tote—check.

The elevator hummed down to the parking garage, cool air heavy with motor oil and concrete. I skipped valet today—some mornings I needed the ritual of opening the door myself.

My black Lincoln Navigator waited in its corner spot, gleaming beneath the overhead lights. Betty. Sleek, powerful, elegant. My first big post-divorce purchase—a declaration that I'd survived.

Opening the door, the scent of fresh leather wrapped around me. I slipped into the driver's seat, the cabin cocooning me in quiet luxury. Stitched leather, polished wood trim, buttery steering wheel—all of it whispering: *You've got this.* I adjusted the mirrors, touched the dash like a good-luck charm, and exhaled the last of the morning's tension.

I tapped my "Consciousness Cleanse" playlist and let soft instrumental tones fill the car. Light traffic. Cloudless sky. Just me and Betty, gliding toward the day with a kind of freedom I used to think I'd never feel again.

I called Shay at the office.

"Everything's on time," Shay said. Relief slid through me like a breath.

Johnson Realtors sat on the city's edge, surrounded by trees and a narrow stream. I'd chosen this office over the downtown one for its quiet and for the people. Grant, my broker, was more father figure than boss—kind, steady and real.

My office was my sanctuary. Floor-to-ceiling windows overlooked the woods, filtering golden light across plush beige carpet. A stately glass desk with polished brass legs anchored the far wall, topped with a leather blotter, gold pens, and a crystal lamp casting a soft glow. Family photos framed one side—me with Maggie, Abby, Sophia Grace—beside my sleek laptop and a delicate vase of white roses and blush carnations on the other.

In front of the windows sat a tufted emerald-green velvet sofa draped with a cream throw, a glass-and-gold cocktail table in front bearing an antique tray, a sandalwood-vanilla candle, and a bowl of sugared almonds. Matching green-and-gold swivel chairs added whimsy, while two cognac leather wingbacks grounded the space opposite my desk. Built-in bookshelves behind me held real-estate manuals, design books, framed certificates, and a few odd treasures from past retreats.

The room smelled faintly of chamomile and lemon oil. A hidden Bluetooth speaker played low ambient jazz. A gold-framed mirror bounced enough light to make the room feel more boutique than office. Elegant. Intentional. Like me—at least on the surface.

Today's deal: a 500-unit apartment complex. Seven-figure commission. Huge.

I paced. Checked the flowers. Switched the music. Tried to breathe.

Grant appeared in the doorway.

"You ready?" he asked, pulling me into a hug.

"Nervous," I admitted. "But good nervous."

"You've got this. And vacation?"

"Booked."

He smiled. He was one of the few who knew the full story—my mom's relapses, the divorce, the hospital stays. During the darkest days, this office had been my refuge.

I did my best to keep my private life from bleeding into work, but my marriage, the divorce, and nights in hospital corridors left their mark. Despite Grant's shield, the scars showed.

The meds the doctors prescribed dulled me into a ghost, so I quit and started self-medicating. Alcohol felt easier, faster, more familiar. The next day was never great, but nothing ibuprofen and water couldn't blunt.

I rubbed at my temple, staring out the window at the trees swaying in the breeze. *Ugh. I might need a drink now just to shut off my brain.*

On my way to the conference room, I stopped at Shay's desk and tapped gently. "Good morning, Shay."

"Morning, Alex! Ready for today?" She beamed, stepping around her desk to hug me.

I'm a hugger—always believed human contact boosts serotonin, and I needed every drop. Shay felt like a little sister. In a couple weeks she'd shift from receptionist to my assistant and start her real estate licensing journey. I planned to mentor her hands-on—the only way to learn.

"All set," I said, releasing her and heading for the conference room.

Inside, I greeted the title company reps, laid out paperwork, and checked the agenda. With thirty minutes to spare before the investors arrived, I slipped outside to the picnic table. Meditation, music, coffee—the perfect trifecta. Earbuds in, face tilted to the sun, I breathed deeply, letting the warmth blur my edges.

Five minutes in, a tap on my shoulder jolted me. I flinched, squinting up against the light—and froze.

Tall. Blond. Built. Sharp in a tailored gray suit. Cobalt eyes and polished shoes catching the sun. White shirt, blue-and-silver tie. He looked like he'd stepped out of a window display at Macy's.

"Hi," I said, slipping out my earbuds. "Are you early or did I get the meeting time wrong?"

"Hi. No, I'm early." He shifted nervously, hands in his pockets. "I wanted to introduce myself before things got formal."

That smile—dimpled, lethal. "I'm Owen."

I smiled back, suspicious of this private chat.

"I'm actually kind of intimidated by you," he admitted. "I'm used to women...well, throwing themselves at me. But you've never even said hi."

I raised an eyebrow. "Where's this coming from?"

He rubbed the back of his neck. "We have a mutual friend—Ryan. He said you were excited to meet me at Sebastian's tonight. I figured I'd get the nerves out early."

Ugh. Ryan. Oversharing again.

Pivot. "Absolutely," I said, taking his hand in both of mine. "I've heard great things about you. I was hoping to pick your brain about investing. I'm trying to find a path that truly excites me."

I adjusted my posture, ankles crossed. No need to feed a fantasy.

"You're close to my age, successful. That's what drew me to you. I hope that's okay?"

His cheeks flushed, but I needed him to think he'd misread the vibe—because he really hadn't.

"I'm such an idiot," he muttered. "Of course we can brainstorm."

And just like that, the possibility of a fling turned into a safe, productive meeting. Probably for the best.

We talked and laughed a little more before heading back inside. It actually calmed my nerves. Owen was sharp, thoughtful—someone who deserved a partner who wouldn't steamroll him.

Angel on my shoulder: one. Devil: zero.

As we neared the conference room, I caught Shay gazing at Owen like he was a Hallmark hero come to life—freckles glowing, lip caught between her teeth.

I cleared my throat. She jumped.

Leaning close, I whispered, "He doesn't like women who throw themselves at him. I'll introduce you tonight. He's sweet. You'll like him."

She blushed scarlet. "No! You don't have to do that!"

I laughed softly. "Oh, but I do. Just be there. He's not scary, promise."

She hid her face as I pushed into the conference room. The investment team followed close behind.

Stewart, the oldest of the group, tapped my shoulder. "You're Alexandra, right?"

"Yes—Alex is fine. Nice to see you again."

His tone was off. "Before we begin, I want to know who I'm dealing with."

My brow lifted. "Excuse me?"

"You were whispering to that receptionist earlier. She looked embarrassed. I thought she was going to cry—and you were laughing. Please tell me that wasn't as bad as it looked."

I bit back a smile, steadied my expression. *Intimidating much? I need to work on that.*

"Come with me." I guided him to Shay's desk. "Stewart, this is Shay Pierce—soon to be my assistant. She's like a little sister to me."

He shook her hand. "Miss Pierce, a pleasure. Are you well today?"

She nodded, a little awkward. "Doing wonderfully, thank you." She glanced at me for reassurance. I winked.

Back in the conference room I whispered, "She has a crush. I was boosting her confidence."

Stewart chuckled, slipping an arm around my shoulders. "Okay, I'm definitely in the right place. Sorry for the misunderstanding." He turned to Grant. "Do you pay this one for counseling too?"

Grant and I both lost it laughing. Truth be told, I probably needed therapy more than anyone.

The meeting ran three hours. We shook hands, agreed to meet at the bar later to celebrate. When they left, I finally exhaled.

"Should I break out the bourbon?" Grant teased.

"Nope—three showings still to go." I spun in my chair, adrenaline still buzzing.

"You sure? I can send someone else so you can savor the win," he said, lifting the bottle.

I threw my hands up. "Holy shit, that was intense." I declined the drink, though briefly considered it. "No, I've got this."

He hugged me, and I floated out of the room.

Applause echoed down the hall. I bowed and curtsied dramatically before darting into my office. One hour until my first showing. Still needed to research the property. *Why hadn't I done that last night?*

Then Landon appeared—timing flawless, as always. Tall, effortlessly handsome, mocha skin glowing against a crisp white shirt and navy sport coat. He moved with the kind of relaxed confidence that turned heads. Warm brown eyes locked on mine, full of mischief and just a flicker of protectiveness.

Piper, his girlfriend, was his mirror in all the right ways—cool, composed, stunning. Together they looked like a luxury-lifestyle ad, but it was the way he treated her—gentle and attentive—that made me believe in partnerships again. Landon loved playing matchmaker. It was like a sport to him—nudging me toward someone he thought could crack the code of my heart.

"No, I'm not telling you the commission," I said without looking up.

He laughed. "We already know—and yes, you're buying tonight. But that's not why I'm here."

I looked up. "Oh? Why then?"

He rested his hands on his hips. "Why'd you tell Owen you wanted to pick his brain?"

I gave him a look. "Because after five minutes I knew I'd eat him alive and spit out the carcass. I wasn't going to wreck a good guy—or a solid business connection. Besides, Shay has a crush. I'm playing matchmaker."

He shook his head, grinning. "You scare the shit out of me sometimes—glad we're friends."

It was a joke—but maybe I did need to practice softer looks.

I stood and gave him a side hug. "Same. I'm lucky to have all of you. You keep me sane."

He started, "If I didn't have a girlfriend..."

I cut him off with a playful glare. "You'd be a carcass."

He backed away, laughing nervously. "Yeah...good thing we're friends."

I smiled and waved him out.

Chapter 3

ALEX

I hadn't done much research on the penthouse—just enough to know the location. A video tour played through my car speakers as I drove, feeding me bullet points and square footage, enough to fake confidence if I had to.

Then my GPS rerouted me through a rougher stretch of town and doubt crept in. Once-grand architecture stood sagging under rusted chain-link fences and overgrown yards. Windows wore iron bars like scars. Porches drooped under the weight of forgotten time.

This couldn't be right.

I pinged my location to Grant and Shay—our unspoken SOS. If one of us felt uneasy on a showing, the others would call within ten minutes.

Just as suddenly, I crossed an invisible line into manicured streets and million-dollar townhomes. The contrast was whiplash sharp. I texted Shay a quick *All good* but tucked the moment away. How could something so neglected sit shoulder to shoulder with something so pristine?

Inside the marble-clad lobby, Mr. and Mrs. Carter waited by the concierge desk—polished, punctual, every inch the banker couple relocating downtown.

"Hello, Mr. and Mrs. Carter. So nice to see you again. Ready to take a look?"

"Absolutely," they said, smiles bright.

We shook hands. I led them to the elevator, swiping the temporary key card for penthouse access. On the ride up, I filled the silence with listing highlights, reciting them from memory like a seasoned tour guide.

The doors opened onto six thousand square feet of show-stopping luxury: floor-to-ceiling windows, polished marble tile, a sweeping glass-paneled staircase curling up to the second level like a ribbon. The upper floor, a partial mezzanine, looked down into the great room, kitchen, and dining space beneath soaring vaulted ceilings.

Four bedrooms. Four and a half baths. Bonus rooms for offices or guests. Wraparound balconies with panoramic views—city skyline, river, sunrise, sunset. Asking price: three million.

"Is this a pet-friendly building?" Mrs. Carter asked.

"Yes," I nodded, recalling that from the video. They either had kids, planned to, or loved a fur baby. These days, it was all the same.

When I opened the rooftop garden door, their faces lit up like Christmas morning. That was it. The moment they mentally moved in. The offer was coming—I could feel it.

There's something deeply satisfying about watching a couple fall in love with a space. I don't dream much about that for myself anymore, but seeing it through their eyes still hits me in the heart. Maybe domestic life will sneak up on me someday. Or maybe not. Let's not get carried away.

I still had two more showings—both large estates up north for the Santoros, a family of six, newly arrived from Italy. Cagey about why they were moving, especially to this area. I didn't press. People value their privacy. I just hope they're not laundering anything. I've cut clients loose for less.

The market was moving fast. I needed to get the Carters' offer submitted before anyone else swooped in.

Standing by the massive windows overlooking the city, I called Shay.

"Hey," I said into the phone. "I'm emailing the offer for the penthouse. Can you draft the contract and send it to the listing agent?"

"Got it," Shay replied. "Heads-up—the seller's agent said they're in no rush. Seller's on vacation for the next couple months, but I'll get the paperwork started."

I updated the Carters. They were understanding, appreciative even. We shook hands at the door, and I headed back to my car.

Halfway through checking my email, I nearly tripped off the curb. Distracted Alex—one misstep at a time. My gas light blinked on. Fifteen miles to empty.

Damn it.

I must've ignored it earlier while focusing on the video tour. My SUV didn't exactly sip gas, and I had no clue where the nearest station was.

I called the office. "Grant, can you cover my next showing? I don't think I'm gonna make it."

Then, "Hey Siri, find the nearest gas station."

Three miles away—just past that run-down neighborhood. Perfect.

As I eased the car up the incline out of the parking garage, the fuel estimate plummeted: fifteen miles...eight...five. I shut off the A/C and the music—pointless but it made me feel like I was trying.

I didn't make it.

Right before the last house on the block, my dashboard lit up: every light blazing. The steering went stiff. The engine died.

You've got to be kidding me.

I smacked the wheel and called the office again. Purse in hand, I stepped out—more carefully this time—and smoothed my dress.

An older woman rocked on her porch, sipping something from a glass. She waved, shaking her head.

"Hello!" I called.

She said something I couldn't hear, so I approached the gate. "Sorry—what was that?"

"You shouldn't be out here alone. It's not safe for you people."

I blinked. "Oh yeah? And what kind of people am I?" expecting her to call me an airhead or a lost tourist.

"Fancy rich ladies," she smirked.

Not what I expected.

I raised an eyebrow, caught off guard. Her house—weathered but charming—was a Victorian with pink and mint trim, iron bars over the windows, and a sagging chain-link fence. Worn, yes, but cared for.

"I don't know about fancy," I laughed. "But I've got my own set of problems."

She smiled, and I took a chance. "Mind if I wait here until help arrives?"

She nodded.

I opened the gate and climbed the steps, gripping the iron rail to steady myself. "Sorry for parking in front of your house. I hope I'm not causing trouble."

She waved me off. "Ain't nobody messin' with Big Mama."

I smiled. "I'm Alex Kennedy."

She shook my hand—strong, warm. I sank into the wicker rocker beside her, its cushion faded but surprisingly soft.

"How long have you lived here?" I asked.

"Sixty-five years. Raised my kids here. And their kids too."

"Wow. Do you still like it?"

She stopped rocking, eyes sharp. "Wouldn't still be here if I didn't."

"I didn't mean it like that," I said quickly. "It's just... some of the homes look like they've seen better days. The architecture's beautiful. I was wondering what changed."

She softened. "Used to be safe. Then it wasn't."

Ryan pulled up with a gas can. She glanced at him, then back to me.

"I'd love to visit again Saturday, if that's okay."

She nodded. "I'm Ella. And I'm glad you're not like the others."

"Miss Ella, I'm not like anyone else." I promise, I thought to myself.

We exchanged numbers. Just as I stepped off the porch, a group of young men rounded the corner. Their eyes locked on me.

Ryan caught my look. "Time to go."

I nodded, mouthed "Yes," and pointed to my car. He got into his, waiting for me to get in mine—but one of the guys stepped in front of my door. Another blocked Ryan's. His face went tight with worry. My pulse thudded in my ears but I kept my expression neutral.

Big Mama rose from her porch. "I don't want no trouble in front of my house," she said loudly. "You start somethin', I'll call the police."

The guy closest to me squinted at her, then leaned in until his breath brushed my cheek. "What's an uppity bitch like you doin' in my hood talkin' to Big Mama?"

Seriously?

I plastered on a smile I didn't feel. "Ran out of gas. While I waited, this nice lady said hi." I gave Ella a small wave. She smiled back—barely—and shook her head.

"We just talked about the neighborhood," I added, one hand on my hip with more sass than sense.

His eyes dragged down and back up. "What the hell you want to know about my hood for?"

"Curiosity," I said evenly, matching his stare.

He smirked. "You know what curiosity did to the cat?"

"Yeah. But cats have nine lives."

He barked a short, cold laugh. "Watch yourself. Stay the fuck out of my hood."

"Can't do that. I've got lunch plans with Big Mama on Saturday." I glanced up at her, trying to summon backup energy. She smiled at me like I was a fool she'd reluctantly grown fond of.

The guy stepped in again, close enough for me to taste his breath. "What the fuck you comin' back to talk to her about?"

"I just want to be friends. I need all the friends I can get." My arms crossed—defiant even as my heart hammered.

"She don't need no more friends."

Heat climbed up my throat. I dropped my arms, fists curling at my sides. "I didn't say she did. I said I did."

He finally stepped back. I inhaled hard, my nails leaving crescents in my palms.

"I like the homes here," I added quietly. "They have history. Character. And Big Mama? She's a treasure."

He didn't answer, but his eyes stayed hard.

Then police sirens split the air.

A squad car rolled up, lights flashing like a nightclub strobe.

"Everything okay out here?" an officer called from behind his rolled-down window.

The guy next to me didn't even flinch. No fear. Just cool, practiced calm. That unsettled me more than anything.

I stepped toward the cruiser. "Yes, officers. I ran out of gas. These young men were helping."

The passenger officer narrowed his eyes, then barked at the group: "Let's clear this side of the road."

He turned back to me. "You got gas in the tank now, ma'am?"

"I do," I said evenly. "Enough to make it to the station."

The guys drifted back. I signaled Ryan I was okay and pulled away as the cruiser followed me like I'd just robbed a bank.

At the gas station, I parked next to the pump—relieved, until I saw the cruiser still idling behind me, lights still flashing.

Why?

I rolled down both windows, hands on the wheel.

One officer came to the driver's side, the other circled to the passenger door. Instinct made me thumb the lock.

"License," the one at my window said.

I handed it over. "Sure."

"What are you doing in this neighborhood?"

"Ran out of gas," I repeated. "And you are?"

No answer.

"Those men are known drug dealers," he said. "You looked pretty friend-ly."

"I assure you, no one was selling me anything. I'm a realtor. Showing at The Towers."

"And you just...ran out of gas?"

"I was distracted. Busy day."

He scoffed. "That was dumb. You shouldn't be here."

There it was—the condescension, the threat wrapped in concern. Not here to protect. Not here to stop the men they'd just labeled dealers. Here to interrogate me.

"That's funny," I said coolly. "They told me the same thing. But I've got lunch with Ella on Saturday. I'm keeping it."

"It's your funeral," he said. "People like you cause trouble in neighborhoods like this."

People like me.

"What kind of trouble? Talking on a porch? Or not looking scared enough?"

He crossed his arms. "You better watch your mouth."

"You know who's dealing—you even said it. But instead of doing something about that, you followed me here like I'm the problem."

He handed me back my license with a smirk. "Stay out. That's your only warning."

They pulled away, lights dimming as if nothing had happened.

I got out of my car and stood at the pump, still gripping my ID, staring after the retreating cruiser. The injustice of it sat heavy with me. That wasn't protection. That was power-tripping on a woman alone at a gas station.

I threw my hands up and spun toward the empty lot. "What the actual hell? I ran out of gas. How did I end up the villain?"

Five missed calls. Grant, Ryan, Shay. I called Grant.

He answered mid-panic, having already heard Ryan's version. I gave him the watered-down one—left out the part where I nearly went to war with a drug dealer and a cop. No need to give him a heart attack.

By the time I pulled into the office parking lot, I was emotionally fried.

When I walked in, every eye swung toward me. Concern. Worry. Fear.

I raised my hands. "I'm fine! Nothing happened—I just ran out of gas."

I shut my office door a little harder than necessary, grabbed a water from the mini fridge, and collapsed onto the couch, fingers raking through my hair.

Did that really just happen?

A knock. I jumped.

Grant stepped inside holding a bottle of Weller and two glasses. No words, just that look: *calm down, drink this.*

He poured two fingers. I stared into the amber, let the scent soothe my nerves, then took a slow sip.

"Before you begin," he said, "give me your glass." He refilled it and sat down. "You weren't telling me everything."

I exhaled. "Still processing. But...I think I found my purpose."

That got his attention.

"I met this woman—Ella. Everyone calls her Big Mama. She's lived there forever. That neighborhood's falling apart. The cops have given up. The dealers run things. But she hasn't left. She hasn't given up."

Grant stayed quiet, listening.

"I want to start small. Talk to people. Fix what's fixable. Help clean things up. Raise property values. Maybe gentrify just enough to make it livable again—without pushing people out."

He nodded slowly. "Most people would've driven away and never looked back. I always knew your fearlessness would find the right target. You want to help. That's rare."

"Thanks," I said softly. "I think I just need to be careful. Might be time to talk to my brother about how to protect myself."

"Good idea," Grant said, smile fading. "Those cops...they went after the wrong person." I wasn't sure if he was referring to me or him as far as who they should be worried about, though.

We drank in silence for a minute.

Shay peeked in. "Is it safe to come in?"

"Yeah," I said. "I'm better now. I learned something important today."

They waited.

"Get gas?" I joked.

Nothing.

"Tough crowd," I muttered. Laughter finally erupted.

"It's five o'clock somewhere—and that somewhere is Sebastian's!" Rang out from the hallway.

Outside, a Cadillac Escalade limo idled at the curb.

I turned to Grant. "What's this?"

"You deserve it," he said, patting my back. "And I don't want anyone driving tonight. You can Uber tomorrow."

Grant never joined us, but he always paid. This time, drinks were on me.

Chapter 4

ALEX

I flipped open the tiny mirror tucked inside my purse and checked my reflection—smudged eyeliner under tired eyes, lipstick faded to a ghost of itself. The day had wrung me out and it showed. I retouched my lips, smoothed my hair, drew a steadying breath, and stepped out of the car.

First stop: the bar. Open a tab. Priorities.

The place pulsed—shoulder to shoulder bodies, music threaded through clinking glasses and low laughter. I slipped between two suits, bumping one hard. He shot me a look. I didn't apologize. Not tonight.

Steve, the bartender, lit up when he spotted me. "Alex," he said with a grin.

I shook his hand, leaning in. "Tab's open under 'Team Alex.' Anyone who says it drinks on me."

This had become my go-to—maybe a little more than it should have. But it had good wine, flattering lighting, and an endless parade of cocky, commitment-phobic men. All swagger and surface. Perfect for a night out. Perfectly forgettable the next day.

No harm. No foul. No heartbreak.

After a quick chat with Steve, I spotted the investors I'd closed with earlier—Stewart and his crew—hovering at the far end of the bar. I wove through the crowd.

"Alex, good to see you again," Stewart said, raising his glass. "What are you having?"

"Cab," I said.

He motioned to Steve, who glanced at me for confirmation. I nodded. He knew what I drank—it wasn't on the menu, you had to buy it by the bottle—but I'd already ordered one when I opened my tab. Steve poured from the stash, no questions asked. Stewart wouldn't know the difference.

We made small talk for a minute before I caught a glimpse of Shay and Owen by the outdoor bar. They were deep in conversation, her cheeks flushed like she'd been brushed with rose gold.

I tossed Shay a wink. She lit up like a lantern.

Mission accomplished.

Outside on the patio I made the rounds like a politician at a fundraiser—smiles, nods, hugs on autopilot. My feet were screaming, my skin felt tight, and no amount of professional charm could make this socializing feel natural tonight.

At the edge of the patio bar I stopped, gripping the counter for balance as I reached down to adjust my shoe straps—first one, then the other. Gorgeous shoes. Absolutely not designed for twelve hours of being on. I gave myself a silent pep talk, squared my shoulders, and slipped back inside through the crowd, angling for the one place I might find peace: the front bar, end stool

I slid onto the stool and exhaled, finally alone.

The last sip of wine went down sharp and sweet. I tapped a finger on the rim. Steve caught the signal and poured another without a word—he knew my tells.

I didn't want conversation. Didn't want company. Just stillness. I thumbed open my phone, texting with family and friends to fill the space. Not ready to leave, but not in the mood to be anyone's entertainment either.

People at the office saw me as some kind of unofficial team lead. Maybe I earned it on paper, but half the time I was tuning out or turning up just to survive the room. Still, I played the part.

Besides, I'd already clocked a few men worth a second glance. Maybe I'd snag a number before the night was over. Maybe not. Tonight, didn't feel like one of those nights. I'd be going home alone—and I was okay with that.

I leaned back, crossed my legs, and started typing. The group chat lit up like a pinball machine after my message.

ME: *You would not believe what happened today. Definitely a brunch chat. Ran out of gas, got punked by drug dealers, and scolded by cops.*

MAGGIE: *WTF are you kidding me?? Are you okay??*

ABBY: *Alex, what the hell? Where were you?? Why were you near drug dealers??*

ME: *Long story. I wasn't buying anything. I didn't do anything wrong. Promise. I'll fill you in later.*

Then Mom, blissfully unaware:

MOM: *Hey honey, do you need anything for vacation? It's supposed to be really hot in Florida. Want me to grab some sunblock or a new hat?*

ME: *I've got all that. As long as the ocean's still there, I'm good. Love you.*

MOM: *Okay, love you too. Can't wait*

And Diana, my favorite family member:

DIANA: *Ali girl! You get the dates for our trip yet?*

ME: *Hi, Auntie. Got 'em. I'm already mentally on the beach. Wouldn't miss it for the world. Love you.*

DIANA: *YAY! Love you too!*

I smiled faintly at the screen. My life felt split—half adrenaline-fueled chaos with my friends, half beachy family chats. Somewhere in between, I existed.

Quiet, exhausted, wine in hand...still searching for something that felt like peace.

***

ROMAN

Sitting in this bar felt like a chore. It was crowded, noisy, and thick with desperation—the kind of place where everyone was trying too hard. I wasn't here for fun. I was here to mark the ink drying on a massive renovation contract.

Stewart and Owen—two of the investors I worked with—had closed on a five-hundred-unit apartment complex that afternoon. Not exactly light work, and that's how I liked it. I didn't take small projects. If my name was on the plan, it meant the scope was big, the money was good, and the outcome would be unforgettable.

The neighborhood had been decent once, before time and neglect gutted it. Now it was clawing its way back—upscale developments creeping in, one block at a time. "Weeding out the weak," one of the investors had joked earlier. He meant the poor. He'd said it with a chuckle like it was clever.

Now the property was prime. Once King Construction finished, it would be unrecognizable—in a good way. Luxury condos. Green spaces. Panoramic windows. Rooftop bars. Indoor-outdoor pools. A state-of-the-art gym. A clubhouse. Maybe even a wine cellar if I had my way. We were turning decay into opportunity, and I liked being the man behind that transformation.

Just down the street, we were expanding an entire district along the river to make room for shops, restaurants, galleries. Stewart's team had vision. Working with him made sense—he'd been my father's friend since before I was born. I'd still had to fight for the bid, but I knew it was mine. I wasn't the cheapest. I was the best. If you wanted it done right the first time, you called me.

And yet, sitting here with a drink sweating in my hand, I couldn't shake the feeling that something about this project—and tonight—was about to change everything.

Which is why I said yes to tonight's celebration—out of obligation.

Sebastian's was the kind of white-collar watering hole where ambition came poured into every glass. Deals were inked here, egos polished and retold until they gleamed. The air smelled of leather, whiskey, and quiet desperation. I respected it for what it was. I even liked the design: black leather barstools lined up against a mahogany bar with a polished copper top, low lighting glinting off glassware like muted starlight. Not my favorite—felt too sleepy—but it made the place feel expensive.

Not a wife-finding spot. But perfect for a solid bourbon, a one-night stand, or a business lead. I should know. I'd done the renovations.

A loud thud and a bump on my shoulder broke my focus. I turned, ready to brush it off—and then the scent hit me.

Lavender and vanilla. Warm and dangerous.

I turned sharply, catching sight of a long-legged woman slipping past. Olive skin, dark hair, a dress that moved like it had been sewn for her alone. She brushed my shoulder without a glance or an apology.

Did I walk into her space? I didn't think so.

I leaned back slightly, annoyed, then watched her longer than I should have. Gorgeous. The kind of woman who looked better in motion than standing still—like confidence and command had learned to walk on heels. For a second my imagination went places it shouldn't, and I cleared my throat.

She handed her credit card to the bartender—Steve, I'd heard—and stifled a yawn behind her hand. My mouth twitched. She looked exactly how I felt—like she'd rather be anywhere else, yet still here, opening a tab and telling Steve that anyone who said "Team Alex" drank on her.

I didn't know who Alex was, but I liked her already. Loyalty like that stood out.

She vanished into the crowd, and I made a mental note to find her later.

Eventually, I spotted Stewart and made my way through the crush of bodies.

"Stewart. Congratulations," I said, gripping his hand and pulling him in for a quick one-armed hug.

"Roman, good to see you, son. Thanks for coming out," he said, clapping my back. He scanned the room. "There's someone I wanted you to meet, but she seems to have vanished. Maybe later. How's your dad enjoying retirement?"

God, please don't be trying to set me up again.

"He's bored out of his mind. Keeps calling to give me unsolicited advice. Won't stay out of the office." I smirked.

He laughed. "That sounds like him."

We spent the next hour talking shop and catching up, but my mind drifted more than once—wondering if "Team Alex" had already left. She didn't seem like the type to linger. If she slipped out the back, I couldn't blame her. I hated these events too.

Eventually I drifted back to the bar, scanning the room one last time. Pretending at small talk, really just trying to spot her again. Pathetic. If I didn't leave soon, I'd end up bribing the bartender for her number—something I'd sworn I'd never do.

I drained the last of my bourbon, set the glass down, and there she was.

Alone.

Still gorgeous. Still unreadable.

She was multitasking—texting with one hand, sipping wine with the other.

Ambidextrous. Efficient. I wondered—then stopped wondering—what else those hands could do.

Focus.

Was she texting a boyfriend? A husband? I hadn't seen a ring, but that didn't mean anything. People lied. People cheated. I had no interest in being collateral damage.

But I was interested in her.

I leaned toward Steve. "Excuse me—Steve, right?"

He turned, smiled. "That's me."

"Roman." I shook his hand.

"What can I do for you?"

"The woman in the black dress," I said quietly. "Is her name Alex, or is she just sponsoring someone named that?"

He grinned. "That's Alex. Great girl. Real sweetheart. Why?"

His arms crossed, a little protective. Interesting.

"I'd like to buy her a drink. Do you know what she's having?"

He smirked. "Our most expensive cabernet. We don't sell it by the glass. Gotta buy the whole bottle."

Challenge accepted.

"That's fine. I'll take the bottle—and her tab, too."

He blinked. "You sure? That tab isn't just her drinks."

"I'm sure." I handed over my black Amex. "And let's keep this between us. There's a generous tip in it for you."

He gave a slow, impressed nod. "Got it."

It wasn't about showing off. She seemed like the kind of woman who took care of everyone else. I wanted to do the same—for one night, at least.

Steve delivered her refill and pointed down the bar toward me. Before she could get a good look, I moved through the crowd and tapped her gently on the shoulder.

She turned, eyes tired but polite. I braced for that flicker of awe I usually saw when women met me up close—not arrogance, just pattern recognition.

Instead, she offered a small, friendly smile.

"Hi. And thank you, I presume?"

She raised her glass, then turned back to her phone, finishing her text.

Unimpressed. Unbothered. Completely, completely captivating.

***

ALEX

Steve set the glass in front of me and tipped his head toward the far end of the bar. "Courtesy of the gentleman."

My eyes flicked up. "From the bottle?" I mouthed.

He shook his head.

I let my forehead dip toward the bar with a slow exhale. Of course. I picked up the glass—along with my composure—and pasted on my best *thank you but please don't talk to me* smile. When I glanced toward the end of the bar, it was empty.

Thank God.

Maybe it was someone from the downtown office. Maybe just another guy flexing. Either way, I wasn't in the mood to navigate an awkward exchange where I thank someone I plan to turn down, only to get called a bitch. Not tonight.

Then came the tap on my shoulder.

Here we go.

If this wasn't "from *my* bottle," then technically he'd bought the whole thing. That wasn't just a drink—that was a commitment. I braced myself for the ego, the line, the inevitable eye roll. Inhale. Turn slowly. Sweep hair over one shoulder like armor.

And there he was.

Oh. Hell.

The man behind me wasn't what I expected. Absolutely jaw-dropping. Tall, tanned skin, dark eyes with a spark of something dangerous. Five o'clock shadow that made me want to lean in just to feel it scrape my skin. Hair messy in the best way—like it belonged to someone who knew how to sin and still look good doing it.

"Hi—and thank you, I'm presuming?" I murmured, lifting the glass with a nod like it was no big deal, even as my brain short-circuited.

I turned away quickly, pretending to text. Anything to stop myself from visibly drooling.

"Hello. And you're welcome," he said. "I'm Roman King."

Roman King.
Is that a name or a title?

I blinked, trying to refocus in the dim bar light. Normally the low light helped me stay unreadable—good for maintaining distance—but now I wished I could see him more clearly. No one should look that good in a room this dark.

"Alex Kennedy," I said, my voice flat with exhaustion.

"May I sit down?" he asked, that gleaming smile looking too damn good to be legal.

Yes, please. Or I could sit on you. Either way works.

I motioned to the stool beside me, hoping he didn't notice how tightly I crossed my legs. "This one's empty."

He slid onto the seat, his knee brushing mine—a shiver traveling up my spine. I was hanging on by a thread.

"Do you come here often?" he asked, teasingly casual.

I squinted. "That's a terrible pickup line."

It slipped out—no filter, too tired to dress it up.

He laughed, unfazed. "Fair. But I meant it honestly."

His voice was pure velvet—low, smooth, with just enough rasp to make me lean in despite myself. And those eyes... they could convince me to do things I hadn't even considered tonight.

"Yes, I'm a regular. I like the staff," I said.

I didn't add that I mostly couldn't stand the crowd. Everyone here served a purpose—networking, sometimes a one-night number to forget the week.

"Not the patrons?" he asked, amused.

"Not all of them. Too many frat-boy vibes for my taste."

He nodded, scanning the room. "Desperate crowd tonight."

His shoulder brushed mine as his gaze swept the bar. I followed his line of sight to a man cornering a woman with smooth lines and strategic flattery. Her laughter rang out like a bell. I didn't need the audio. I knew the script by heart.

"The women are looking for that guy," Roman said, nodding toward the pair. "And the guys are hunting for the one woman who doesn't want a guy at all."

I laughed. I *was* that woman.

He smiled at my reaction, settling back in his seat, more relaxed now. He crossed an ankle over his knee and rested an elbow on the bar like we'd been talking for hours.

Then Stewart walked up, planting a hand on each of our shoulders.

"Well, I was wondering when you two would meet."

Roman and I glanced at each other, then back at him.

"And the plot thickens," I muttered.

"You know—he's a builder, you're a realtor. Makes sense," Stewart said, as if we should've known. "I figured you'd get along."

We both started laughing. We hadn't even made it that far in conversation. Just two strangers at a bar—and I'd been enjoying the simplicity of that. Now things were getting complicated. I didn't mix business with pleasure. *Ever.*

"What's so funny?" Stewart asked.

Roman looked at me for a long beat, then said, "I didn't know what she did. I just thought she was the most beautiful woman in the room."

Okay, not bad. Still not smooth. But sweet.

"Thank you," I said automatically, then took a sip of wine and—God help me—giggled. Giggled. What was happening to me?

He clinked his glass against mine. "You're welcome."

"Alex," Stewart added, "Roman's doing the renovations on those apartments you sold me today. He's the guy I wanted you to meet."

Oh. Really.

My hand instinctively touched his shoulder—just lightly—but something sparked under my skin, and I pulled back fast. Butterflies. Everywhere.

"Would you have time this week to meet about a project I'm thinking of starting?" I asked, hoping to reset the mood. "I'd love your insight. Even just advice."

"I've got an opening at noon tomorrow. Come by the office. I'll grab lunch."

He didn't sound thrilled, but I couldn't tell if it was indifference or something else. My words started to ramble.

"That works. I usually block out noon to two unless I have a big closing or last-minute showing, but I keep that time open for impromptu meetings..."

Stop talking, Alex. Practically begging him to memorize my schedule.

I shifted in my seat to ease the pressure—mentally, emotionally, physically. All of it was catching up to me, and the heat between us wasn't helping.

"I'll have my assistant set it up," he said smoothly.

An assistant. I sighed into my wine, almost moaning at the thought—of both the assistant and Roman.

"Sounds like a plan. Do you have a card?"

He held out a hand for my phone instead. That smirk, those eyes... I was done for.

I handed it over without a second thought. He typed in his info, sent himself a text, and handed it back. His fingers brushed mine and every nerve ending in my hand went live. What was this sorcery?

"Steve, can I get some water, please?" I asked, turning back to the bar.

"Sure, Alex. Anything else?" Steve's glance at Roman carried a knowing smirk. I didn't like it. What was that about?

I popped two ibuprofen and chased them with the water.

Roman tilted his head, amused. "I'm impressed."

"For what?"

"Your self-control."

I nearly spit out my water. If only you knew.

"Am I missing something?" he asked.

Everything, I thought. I had never been this physically affected by someone so fast.

"You are," I said, standing abruptly. "But it's for the best. If you'll excuse me..."

I slipped away to the restroom, weaving through the crowd, desperate for cool air and a mirror. Once inside, I locked the door, braced my hands on the sink, and stared at myself.

Gloss intact. Hair still decent. I looked good. But my heart was racing like I'd just sprinted a mile in stilettos.

I reapplied lip gloss, smoothed the flyaways, and exhaled slowly—long, deliberate breaths, just like my counselor taught me after the divorce.

I had no idea what just happened at that bar.

But it felt like the start of something I wasn't sure I was ready for.

***

ROMAN

She jumped up from her barstool like someone had pulled a fire alarm. I watched her go, wondering if she felt what I did—tight heat, restless energy, that magnetic pull to get closer. And if she did, then yeah... I understood the sudden need for space.

Still, I hoped she was coming back. Her purse sat untouched beside her water. Good sign.

I caught Steve's eye and nodded toward it. "We'll be right back. Mind watching her things?"

He gave me a thumbs up.

The hallway near the restrooms was quieter—just far enough from the crush of the bar to soundproof the noise. Across from the women's room was a small VIP lounge I'd used before: dim, tucked away, the kind of room where deals got made or lines got crossed. Empty tonight. Perfect.

I leaned against the wall, one hand in my pocket, thumb flicking across my phone screen though I wasn't reading anything. My mind wasn't on notifications. It was on her—her laugh, her perfume, her mouth. The way she'd looked at me like I wasn't quite real.

Then she appeared.

She stepped out of the restroom, surprise flickering in her eyes when she saw me. She tried to slide past, casual but tense, the kind of walk you do when you're trying to outrun your own heartbeat.

I stepped forward, slow, deliberate, and placed a light hand at her elbow. Just enough to stop her without trapping her.

"Hey," I said softly. "You okay?"

"Come with me," I said quietly, guiding her toward the private room.

She didn't object. Didn't even ask why. Her eyes flicked to the door, then back to me—nervous but curious. I could feel her pulse under my fingertips. Or maybe it was mine. Either way, I wasn't going to push.

I closed the door behind us, muting the hum of the bar.

"I just wanted to steal you away for a second," I said, hands up in mock surrender. "Not planning an ambush. Promise."

She raised an eyebrow, wary. Her breath caught, and God—standing this close, I could feel it against my collarbone. I tried to play it cool and failed.

"You're pretty popular out there," I added with a half smile. "I don't like being interrupted."

"I don't think I'm all that popular," she said, almost breathless.

"You are to me."

It came out softer than I intended—honest, uncalculated. She looked up at me, unsure. I stepped closer. Her perfume wrapped around me again: lavender, vanilla, and something else I couldn't name but would never forget.

"I don't usually do this," I said. "Come on to someone."

"Well," she murmured, "now you're just like everyone else."

I smiled. "Touché."

My hand went to her hip without thinking. She didn't move away. I leaned in, speaking low near her ear.

"I'd love nothing more than to kiss you right now... but we've got a meeting tomorrow. And I think the less awkward, the better."

Her eyes fluttered shut, head tilting slightly, like she'd been caught in a spell. She swayed.

I caught her instinctively, my arm sliding around her back. Her body fit against mine as if we'd rehearsed it. She could definitely feel how affected I was—hell, I wasn't hiding it.

She exhaled, deep and shaky.

I laughed softly, not to mock her but because I understood. Whatever this was, it wasn't casual. It didn't feel like another bar flirtation. It felt dangerous—in the best way.

But I wanted more.

I brushed a hand lightly down her back, guiding her toward the door. "Let's go before I forget why I shouldn't kiss you."

She nodded, eyes wide, lips parted like she was still catching her breath. That made two of us.

Back at the bar, Steve had guarded her seat like a pit bull. Alex slid onto her stool, reaching for her water as though it were the only solid thing in the room. I gave her space, finishing my bourbon while her scent still lingered on my skin—lavender and temptation.

Eventually, she signaled Steve to close her tab. He leaned in, handed her card back while shaking his head and said, "Already taken care of."

She looked confused and rightfully so.

"What do you mean someone paid my tab? This isn't a coffee at Starbucks," she said.

He just made a lock gesture at the corner of his lips and went back to pouring drinks. Good man.

She scanned the room, clearly trying to figure it out. But I'd already slipped into the background. I didn't need the credit. I just wanted to do something for her—for once, not to impress anyone but because I wanted to. That alone was unusual.

When the group moved toward the valet stand, I walked out with them. A limo idled at the curb. I opened the door for her. Her hand slipped into mine—warm, delicate, slightly trembling.

"Goodnight, Alex," I said, holding her gaze. "I'm looking forward to our meeting tomorrow."

I didn't let go until the last second. She rolled down the window as the limo slowly pulled off, her voice soft and unguarded.

"Good night, Roman."

The window slid up asl they disappeared down the road.

And I was left standing there... completely wrecked.

I waited for the valet to bring my car, thumb hovering over my phone.

ME: *It was nice meeting you. Hope you made it home safe. Looking forward to our meeting tomorrow. Good night.*

I slipped the phone into my pocket, confident she'd respond. They always do.

By the time I pulled into the garage and rode the elevator up to my penthouse, nothing. Huh.

My jaw clenched. Was she ignoring me?

I rubbed my palm along the stubble on my jaw, smirking to myself. Either she was asleep, or I'd just been given a taste of my own medicine. I didn't like it.

I tossed my keys and wallet onto the counter and poured a bourbon—neat. The burn was welcome. I needed something to take the edge off. Because the truth was, I couldn't stop thinking about her. About that damn moment in the VIP room. The way her eyes fluttered shut when I leaned in close. The way her whole body shifted toward mine like gravity had rewritten itself.

She was affecting me in a way no one had, *ever.*

I set my glass in the sink and left my phone on the island—out of reach. If she wasn't going to text me back, so be it. I didn't need to obsess. I didn't need to know why.

...Except I did.

I headed into the bathroom, stripping down and turning on the shower. Hot. Full blast. Steam rose, curling up the glass as I leaned forward, bracing one hand against the tile. The water hit my skin like a slow cleanse.

But there was no rinsing her out of my head.

In my mind she was still there—close enough to touch, perfume wrapping around me, her voice soft, her mouth just inches from mine. That look in her eyes. That sway in her hips. The way she'd tilted her head like she was daring me.

I dragged a hand over my face and let out a harsh breath. "Jesus Christ," I muttered to the empty room. "I don't even know you and you've got me losing my mind."

I shut off the water, staring at my reflection through the fogged mirror.

Who the hell are you, Alex Kennedy?

Chapter 5

ALEX

I should have been grateful just to be waking up—and honestly, I was. The sheets were still warm, sunlight stretched across the hardwood in golden slats, and for once, my body didn't ache the way it usually did after a night out. No hangover. No pounding headache. No regret gnawing at the edges of memory.

Just energy. A low, electric current under my skin. Restless. Buzzing.

I blinked at the ceiling, trying to name it. Adrenaline? Hope? Nerves?

Maybe it was because I actually had something to look forward to today—a meeting that might matter. An investment opportunity that wasn't just business. It felt personal. That forgotten neighborhood still had a heartbeat, and I wanted to be part of bringing it back.

And maybe—just maybe—the buzz had something to do with Roman King.

The man from last night who looked like he'd stepped out of a dream and smelled like confidence and trouble. The one who smiled like he already knew things I hadn't admitted to myself.

At least, he had in the moody shadows of the bar. But shadows could be liars. So could wine. What if I walked into his office today and found someone ordinary—aloof, disappointing?

That would almost be a relief. If he was underwhelming, I could focus. Pitch my idea. Stay sharp. I wouldn't be sitting there trying not to get lost in his voice, his eyes, or the scent of whatever cologne had lingered in the corner of my mind like a bad idea I wasn't ready to let go.

The alarm threatened to blare, but I reached for my phone first. The second I unlocked it, his name lit up the screen.

ROMAN: *It was nice meeting you. Hope you made it home safe. Looking forward to our meeting tomorrow. Good night.*

The butterflies in my stomach didn't flutter—they dive-bombed. I hovered my thumb over the reply button, exhaled, then rolled my eyes as I dropped the phone onto the comforter.

Nope. I was not going to be that girl. The one refreshing her messages, heart hammering over a man she barely knew. I wasn't sixteen. And I wasn't drunk anymore, either.

Roman King was too good to be true. Tall. Smooth-talking. Successful. The whole trifecta. A perfect gentleman.

Well—gentleman, my...

I knew exactly why he'd pulled me into that side room. And I knew that if we didn't have a meeting scheduled today, I probably would've woken up beside him... then left without ever saving his number. Just another story I'd never tell. Another choice I'd regret in the morning.

Instead, I threw on workout clothes and tried to sweat him out of my system. Thirty minutes of cardio. Twenty of yoga. Still no peace.

In the sauna, steam curled around me, blurring the memory of his mouth close to mine, the way his voice had dipped when he said my name. I rested my head against the wall, eyes closed. *Get a grip.*

This city swarmed with good-looking men who wore expensive watches and used the word *empire* too often. Roman wasn't special. Not really.

I sent a quiet prayer toward the ceiling. *Please don't let me drool. Or trip. Or sound like I'm twelve with a crush.*

Back in the apartment I let the shower run until steam billowed past the door, then stepped in and stood there for long minutes, skin flushed from heat, thoughts looping in endless circles. When I finally emerged, I wrapped myself in my plush white robe and checked the calendar on my phone.

I'd taken the day off.

Past me had probably assumed I'd be nursing a hangover. Cute. Smart. Real classy.

With a few hours to spare before the meeting, I toyed with the idea of swinging by Abby's or Maggie's, after, to see the kids—maybe pick up little surprises from that boutique they loved downtown. But first: lunch. With Roman. Strictly business. Professional cap firmly on.

I dressed clean and simple—classic lines. High-waisted tan linen trousers, a sleeveless white mock turtleneck, brown wedges. Delicate gold hoops, a thin bangle. Just enough makeup to look polished. Sleek low pony-tail. Nude gloss. One last glance in the mirror. I gave myself a pointed thumbs-up. *Pull it together, Kennedy. You're not a fangirl.*

After breakfast, I ordered an Uber to the office. Betty to pick up my beloved SUV

I stopped by Jason's desk to follow up on the showings he'd handled while I was busy running out of gas and dodging cops. The Italian couple was intrigued—no offer yet, but they wanted to speak to me personally. I made a mental note to follow up later.

As I headed toward my office, I thumbed through emails. No update yet on the penthouse offer—not a surprise. Those sellers weren't motivated.

I was halfway down the hall when I heard Ryan's voice.

"Alex! What the hell are you doing here? Didn't you say you were off today?"

I waved him off with a half-smile, but of course he fell into step beside me—sharp suit, designer shoes, that cocky grin women either loved or hated.

"I'm not really here," I said, unlocking my office. "Just checking in and grabbing my car."

He leaned on my desk like it belonged to him. "What are you so dressed up for?" He wiggled his eyebrows like he was auditioning for a sitcom.

I raised mine right back. "Just a contractor. Investment talk."

Before I could shoo him off the furniture, Shay walked in, arms crossed, expression stern.

"Ryan, get your ass off her desk. When I'm Alex's assistant, I'm not cleaning your butt print off her workspace."

He stood up like she'd burned him. "Damn, Shay. You wound me."

I shook my head, laughing under my breath. Then I added a follow-up task for the Santoros to my to-do list before turning back to her.

"You have fun last night?"

Her cheeks bloomed pink. "That obvious?"

"You two were adorable."

"Thank you for pushing me," she said, shy but sincere.

"You didn't need me. But I hope he's treating you right."

"He is. We're going on a real date this weekend."

I meant it when I said I was happy for her—even if watching her navigate something sweet and easy poked at a soft, unsettled spot inside me. I didn't want easy. I didn't even know what I wanted. Just... not vanilla. Not predictable.

With time to kill, I stopped by the coffee shop near Roman's office. I called the Santoros, left a voicemail, then noticed the unopened message I'd ignored.

Shoot.

ME: *Sorry for the delayed reply. Thank you—and I look forward to our meeting at noon.*

Short. Friendly. Neutral. Business. Definitely not a date.

I ordered a green tea and a blueberry muffin, settled into a quiet corner, and opened my laptop. My go-to playlist hummed in the background as I built out a clean, compelling PowerPoint—maps, data, projected ROI, key demographics. This wasn't a vanity project. It was personal. It was about Big Mama's street, about dignity, about rebuilding something that mattered.

That's what made me nervous.

Not Roman.
Not the memory of his hands on my hips.
Not the way he'd looked at me like a mystery he wanted to read cover to cover.

Purpose. That's what this was about.

When the slides were finished, I packed up and slid into the car. Classical music hummed on the radio. I drew a few grounding breaths, reminding myself for the hundredth time—this was just a meeting.

Then I pulled up to the building.

A high-rise of steel and glass shimmered in the sun like it was alive.

I blinked.

No way.

Etched in clean, elegant letters across the front: *King Construction, Inc.*

My jaw slackened.

He didn't just run a company.

He owned this.

The *whole damn building.*

A drop of sweat rolled down the back of my neck, and I took a long, steadying breath—suddenly very, very grateful that I'd remembered deodorant this morning.

***

ROMAN

I took the private elevator from the penthouse down to the office—early, for once. The corridor lights were still half-dimmed, the space quiet except for the low hum of HVAC and the occasional creak of settling steel. No Amelia yet. She usually beat me here.

I pulled out my phone, not expecting anything, but wondering all the same if Ms. Kennedy was going to ghost me after last night. Women like her didn't usually vanish without a trace—but they didn't linger long in my world either. That kind of heat never lasts.

Just as I unlocked the screen, a new message slid across the top of the display.

ALEX: *Sorry for the delayed reply. Thank you—and I look forward to our meeting at noon as well.*

There she is.

I smirked, thumb hovering over the screen a beat longer than necessary. Better late than never.

Still, I wasn't used to waiting for women like her. Truth was, I wasn't used to women like her at all.

I'd met hundreds of potential investors—developers, buyers, eager first-timers. Most wanted a fast flip. Shopping centers, condos, urban builds with fat margins. They came in talking ROI and left bragging about cash flow.

But this wasn't that.

At least, it wasn't why I'd said yes.

I'd agreed to this meeting for one reason only: I wanted to see her again. Simple.

The plan was straightforward—refer her to someone I trusted to handle the small-scale construction and then ask her to dinner. Quick, clean, professional. That's how I liked things.
Except nothing about her had felt quick or clean or remotely manageable.

My morning was stacked—two meetings before noon. One, a status update on the shopping center we were halfway through building out in Northside. The other, a waterfront proposal that had real potential: upscale restaurants, boutique shops, art galleries. A chance to breathe life into a forgotten slice of the riverwalk.

Only snag? A stubborn residential block right in the middle. No matter how much we offered, those homeowners hadn't budged. But I knew how this game played out. Give it time. Incentive. Leverage. They'd fold. They always did.

The primary investor on the project?
My brother.

Harrison King. He'd never cared for sawdust, scaffolding, or the grind of a job site. Construction wasn't his side of the world—numbers were. When Dad retired, I took the bones of the company and kept building. Harrison came on board to handle investors and finance.

Bringing him in turned out to be the move that solidified our business into an empire. Same blood, different instincts. We share the name, but not much else.

I spun my chair toward the picture window, letting my eyes rest on the steady flow of the Ohio River. The surface shimmered in the morning light, fractured silver shifting with the current. Towboats passed slow and quiet beneath the bridge, their wakes trailing like long, lazy exhalations. The city buzzed behind me, but out there, everything looked calm.

My thoughts drifted inward—to the greenspace I carved into the heart of the building. I'd gutted the entire central core, reworking the layout so offices now wrapped around the perimeter, giving every floor a view straight down into what we built: real trees, stone paths, and a waterfall wall that stretched two stories high at the base and could be seen from every floor up to the fifteenth. The open atrium brought in natural light, filtering down through glass panels and bouncing off the water in a way that made the whole place feel alive.

It was designed for the staff, a wellness feature or whatever the consultants called it. But I was the one who used it most. That space was mine. My sanctuary. The only part of this empire where the pressure didn't reach.

I thought about heading down there to clear my head. But back-to-back meetings left no time to breathe.

The first dragged—long-winded updates, overcomplicated questions. I nodded, answered, half-listened. My eyes kept drifting: watch, phone, door. Every ten minutes.

The second meeting was worse. Numbers blurred. Charts turned into wallpaper. Projections washed over me while my mind replayed her—her voice, her mouth, the way she looked at me like she wanted to argue and kiss me in the same breath.

I checked my watch again. Ten more minutes.

"Roman, your thoughts?"

Lease rates. Something I'd already reviewed twice.

"I'll run the numbers myself," I said evenly. "If anything needs adjusting, I'll follow up before close of business."

Before another question landed, I stood and wandered to the coffee station. Technically, I hadn't left the meeting—I'd just stepped out of it. They could keep talking. I needed caffeine.

Half a cup in, I felt him at my side.

Harrison. Of course.

He leaned against the cabinet with that all-knowing grin, arms crossed like he'd been waiting for me.

"You good?" he asked, casual as hell.

"Peachy."

"You haven't heard a word in forty-five minutes," he murmured, amused. "We're literally reviewing your numbers."

I stirred my coffee with deliberate calm. "I like to verify in real time. Keeps me sharp."

He gave a short laugh. "Right. That why you keep checking your phone. Who is she?"

I didn't answer.

He tapped the counter once, twice. Irritatingly pointed.

"Knock it off before you lose a finger," I muttered.

He held up his hands, smirking. "Just making sure you're alive under all that brooding. You're twitchy today."

"I'm fine." Too quick.

His eyes lit with satisfaction. "Sure you are."

With a nudge to my arm, he turned back toward the table. "Alright, back to work. Time to turn paper into profit."

I followed, body present, head already gone. Five more minutes.

Five more minutes, and I'd see her again.

Alex wasn't just another client. Not just another beautiful woman I wanted to impress. She made me hesitate.

And I never hesitated.

Last night replayed on loop—her laughter, her sharp tongue, the flicker in her eyes when I touched her waist. The almost-kiss. I could still feel the heat of her against me, hear the breath she caught when I leaned in close.

Five more minutes.

Five more minutes, and she'd be in front of me.

And for the first time in a long time, I had no idea what I'd say.

Because this didn't feel like business.

It felt like the beginning of something I knew I wanted.

Chapter 6

ALEX

I pushed the front door open and nearly gasped. I *almost* said "Wow" out loud—but thankfully, I caught myself.

This place was... incredible.

It looked more like the headquarters of a luxury investment firm than a construction company. Wide open, sleek, and humming with quiet energy. Nothing about it said hard hats and job sites. No loud machinery, no steel-toe boots. No slovenly dressed laborers in sight. More like a scene from *The Devil Wears Prada*—all glass, marble, and confidence. And here I was, worried about looking *too* dressed up for a business meeting with a contractor.

The floors gleamed black, polished so perfectly they reflected the light from above like water. In the center of the building was what looked like an indoor park—real trees, soft grass, winding stone paths. A full ecosystem under glass. Offices ringed the perimeter, all enclosed in transparent walls. I could see silhouettes of people inside—presenting, pacing, writing on whiteboards. Deals being made, ideas becoming blueprints.

I moved instinctively toward the green space, needing a better look, but was quickly intercepted by a voice with a razor-sharp edge.

"Excuse me, miss. Can I help you?"

I turned, startled, and spotted the massive reception desk just to the right of the elevators. Behind it sat a trio of women so stunning they could've been plucked from a Milan runway. Behind *them* was a wall of cascading water—an actual waterfall inside the lobby. I stared at it for a moment too long.

Smooth, Alex. Real smooth.

I forced myself to the desk, suddenly hyper-aware of every inch of my outfit. "Hi. I'm Alex Kennedy. I have a meeting with Roman King at noon."

The one in the center looked up with a smile that didn't quite reach her eyes. She scanned me from head to toe like I was a suspicious package left in a luxury boutique.

She nodded. "Yes. I see your appointment here..." She reached for a lanyard and scribbled my name on a badge with all the enthusiasm of a DMV clerk. "You'll need to wear this while in the building. Your meeting is on the fifteenth floor. Please check in with the receptionist up there—she'll escort you to the meeting room."

She handed me the badge without another glance.

"Thanks," I said, forcing a smile and heading toward the elevators with the badge dangling awkwardly in my hand. As soon as I was out of her line of sight, I shoved it into my bag. The handwriting was so bad I could barely read my name anyway.

The elevator bank was made entirely of glass—walls, floor, and back—except for the front panel and buttons. As I stepped inside, the doors closed behind me with a whisper, and the elevator began to rise, revealing the full scope of the building's interior.

It was breathtaking.

From up here, I could see it all: the park at the core of the structure stretched all the way up through the fifteen-story atrium. Real grass. Real plants. Even birds flitting between branches. The greenspace was surrounded by brushed nickel railings and floor-to-ceiling glass half-walls, so each level looked down into the heart of the building.

It wasn't as massive as I'd imagined from the outside. But the space was used so brilliantly, so intentionally, that it felt enormous. Light streamed down from skylights far above, bouncing off every reflective surface. It was a world within a world. And Roman King had built it.

My stomach twisted. Nerves. Wonder. Something between awe and panic.

I tried to focus on the architectural design to keep my brain from spiraling. *Thoughtful of Roman,* I told myself, *to create something like this. To prioritize beauty, fresh air, and mental wellness in a corporate space.*

And then the elevator climbed past the tenth floor.

I gulped. My grip on the handrail tightened.

I was terrified of heights. *Why didn't I take the stairs?* Still, as the numbers ticked up, I slid farther from the window until I was practically pinned to the front panel by the time it hit fifteen. The doors opened, and I nearly tripped forward, relieved to be on solid ground again.

To the left was another reception desk—sleek, minimalist, and bathed in soft light from the open atrium. Another woman sat behind it. If the team downstairs looked like Vogue models, this one was the cover. Tall. Effortlessly poised. Radiating confidence in a silky blouse that probably cost more than my car insurance.

I stifled a chuckle at my own expense.

She stood and walked out from behind the desk, smiling warmly. "Hi, I'm Amelia," she said, offering her hand. "You must be Alex."

Her handshake was confident, but kind. She had straight platinum blonde hair, blue eyes, and the kind of skin that glowed from a million-dollar skincare routine. I instantly wanted to know what moisturizer she used.

"Hi, yes," I said. "Thank you for having me."

She gestured for me to follow. "Let me take you to the conference room. Would you like coffee? Tea? Sparkling water?"

I shook my head. "No, thank you." I don't think I could keep anything down right now.

She glanced at me and smiled. "Don't worry. He's been just as on edge all morning."

Before I could ask what that meant, she winked and turned away, disappearing down the hall.

I blinked after her. *What way? What did she mean, 'just as on edge'?*

Inside the conference room, I set my bag on one of the chairs and took it all in.

The table was a long slab of black glass, reflective and pristine. The chairs surrounding it were sleek black leather with chrome arms—definitely not cheap. The walls were bright white, creating a clean contrast with the gray tile floor. A giant screen hung on one wall, and framed photographs of buildings they'd completed lined the rest. Awards, too. So many awards.

I felt very, very small.

This wasn't just a construction company. It was a legacy. A polished, high-functioning, wildly successful machine. And I was a woman with a dream and a PowerPoint. I was officially out of my league.

As panic threatened to close in around me, I turned toward the door—maybe I could get some air, collect myself—and froze.

He was already standing there.

Roman King. Larger than life. Brooding and magnetic as ever, wearing tailored black slacks and a gray shirt rolled at the sleeves, every inch of him screaming composed confidence.

And then he looked at me.

That slow-burning stare locked in, and I swear I forgot how to breathe.

My pulse jumped. My stomach twisted tighter.

Get it together, Alex.

I smoothed my palms down the front of my pants and resisted the urge to check for sweat marks. Please, God, don't let there be sweat marks.

"Hello, Mr. King," I said, voice slightly too high. "It's good to see you again. Thank you for taking this meeting. I know you're busy, and I really appreciate it."

I held out my hand.

Instead of shaking it, he took it gently in his and brought it to his lips.

"It's Roman," he said, his voice smooth as silk and warm as bourbon. "And the pleasure is mine. I'm happy to help in any way I can."

He let my hand go, and I stood frozen for half a second longer than I should have.

A spark. A real one. Like static and fire and warmth all at once.

Was that normal? Is that how he greets *everyone* in meetings? Or had I just stepped into a whole new kind of negotiation?

***

ROMAN

What the hell did I do that for?

Real professional, man. And there you have it—I'm screwed.

She gently pulled her hand away, either unfazed or being polite. "I was just about to run to the restroom before we get started, but I'll be right back. Don't start without me." Her voice pitched on the last word.

Don't worry, I thought, *there's not much I want to do without you right now.*

"Do you need coffee or anything? I can have one here before you get back," I offered, desperate to do something useful.

"I would love one, thank you. Black is fine," she said over her shoulder, already halfway out the door.

I watched her disappear down the hall and exhaled. I needed a minute, too. Hell, maybe ten. I had no idea what was happening to me.

I called Amelia to bring us two coffees. She showed up a minute later, grinning like she'd just read my mind.

"And what the hell is that look for?" I grumbled, already knowing she was dying to say something.

Amelia could get away with murder. She was sharp, loyal, and fearless—which is probably why she's lasted so long working directly for me. She had a sense for reading people that bordered on psychic.

"What look? I'm just smiling because it's a beautiful day," she said, all innocent. "Also, lunch will be here in fifteen minutes."

I narrowed my eyes. She was definitely messing with me, but I didn't have time to get into it. Alex was already coming back.

She returned to the room, her energy completely different. A little flushed, slightly guarded, like she'd just had a full argument with herself in the hallway. As she passed me, I stepped aside to let her through, then quietly closed the door behind us.

Click.

She thanked me for the coffee without looking at me. She took a sip, inhaling deeply, then set it down and tried to pretend she wasn't unraveling.

"I just wanted to thank you again for this meeting," she said, voice taut with nerves.

"Of course. I'm looking forward to hearing your ideas."

She hesitated, then cleared her throat. "I put together a short presentation if that would be alright, to kind of guide you through what I'm thinking."

I nodded, gesturing toward her laptop. "Whenever you're ready."

She turned the screen toward me and launched into her pitch.

I sat beside her, trying—really trying—to focus on her words, not the perfume clinging to her skin, not the soft curve of her mouth when she spoke, not the flicker of nerves in her voice. I needed a distraction. And then she showed the first slide.

And I couldn't breathe.

The image on the screen hit like a sucker punch to the chest.

That neighborhood. *That* neighborhood.

The one we were already bidding on. The one I was helping Harrison tear down.

Not flips after all. Not a vanity project.

She wasn't looking to make a quick buck. She wanted to save it.

My throat tightened instantly, and I tried to swallow it down. I couldn't take my eyes off the photo. She kept talking—about the architecture, the residents, the potential for restoration, her nonprofit idea. But the words washed over me like white noise. Because I was already ten steps ahead in a different direction, trying to figure out how the hell I was going to tell her.

She finished with, "What do you think?" and turned to me, hope practically radiating off her.

But I had nothing. I was frozen, staring at the screen, begging for an emergency to break the tension—a fire drill, a phone call, anything.

Nothing.

Then I felt her hand on my arm.

"Roman, did you hear me? Is something wrong?"

I jumped slightly, blinking myself back into the room.

Time to break the news. And there was no easy way to do it.

"I love your idea," I said first, because I meant it. "I think it's amazing. Your heart's in the right place wanting to help people. But... we already have a bid on most of that property."

I leaned back in my chair, crossing my ankle over my knee to hide the tension crawling up my leg.

Her lips parted slightly. Her eyes narrowed.

"A bid? A bid to do what, exactly?"

Her entire face changed in an instant—from open and hopeful to cold and sharp. Like a storm rolling in over calm water.

"To tear it down," I said carefully. "Condos, restaurants, shopping, a waterfront complex. Make it like everything else around it."

She didn't speak, but her entire body stiffened. Her jaw clenched. Her nostrils flared.

The disappointment in her eyes hit harder than I expected.

I'd seen that look before.

But it was never personal.

Until now.

***

ALEX

I stared at him. My heart pounded in my ears, drowning out everything else. Did I hear him right? Did Roman King—the man who kissed my hand and served me coffee like some reformed fairytale villain—just say he was tearing down the neighborhood I wanted to save?

No. *No, no, no.* This couldn't be happening.

I slammed my laptop shut. The sound snapped through the room like a gunshot. I stood up slowly, squaring my shoulders even though my legs felt like they might give.

"I cannot believe what I'm hearing right now," I snapped, trying to keep control of my voice and failing miserably. "Did you just say you were tearing that neighborhood down? What exactly are you planning to do with the people who live there?"

He looked at me calmly—relieved, even. Like this was the easiest question he'd had to answer all day. The arrogance in that expression made my fingers twitch.

"We're planning on offering them fair market value for their homes so they can find another place to live."

Fair market value. Like that made it okay.

"And what if they don't want to move?" I asked, my voice shaking with fury. "What if that's their home, their life?"

"We can make it worth their while," he replied, emotionless. "The economic value of the area is the most important thing, making anything they may want—or not want—immaterial."

It felt like the air was being sucked out of the room.

"You are a greedy, compassionless bastard!" I shouted, right in his face.

The door creaked open. Amelia stepped in slowly, a bag in her hand.

"Lunch. Is. Here...?" she said, placing it on the table and wisely retreating.

I started shoving my things into my bag, every movement sharp and jerky. My hands were shaking.

"Look, Alex, this meeting didn't go as planned. I'm sorry—"

My phone screen lit up.

Mom. Five missed calls. Three texts.

My breath left me in a single gasp.

I sank into the nearest chair, eyes fixed on the words: *Your dad had a heart attack. We're at the ER. Please come.*

"Alex, what's going on? Are you okay?" Roman's voice was softer now, cautious.

I couldn't speak. I handed him my phone.

He glanced at the screen. His whole demeanor changed.

"Oh my God. I'm driving you to the hospital right now."

That snapped me out of it.

"Like hell you are. I'm not going anywhere with you." I stood up, snatching my phone, but it slipped from my hand and hit the floor. We both reached for it, but the look I gave him stopped him cold.

"Don't come near me right now," I said, my voice flat and cold.

He backed off.

"You're in no condition to drive," he said, more gently. "I'm not the bastard you think I am. Let me take you to your family. After that, I'll leave you alone."

I nodded. I didn't want to. But I couldn't think straight.

Chapter 7

ALEX

My head pounded. My heart wouldn't stop racing. I stood at the elevator with my hands over my face, barely breathing. Amelia glanced at me, then at Roman.

"Cancel the rest of my meetings today," I heard him say. "I'm taking Ms. Kennedy to the hospital. If anything can't be rescheduled, direct it to Harrison."

She nodded. "I hope everything's okay."

When the elevator opened, Roman reached to steady me. I didn't have the strength to resist. I turned into him and cried against his chest. His arms came around me. It felt safe. Infuriatingly, shamefully safe.

What the hell was wrong with me?

By the time we reached the garage, I pulled away. "Thank you. I'm so sorry for crying on your shirt."

"No need to apologize," he said.

"I can't lose my dad. My mom can't lose him. This would destroy our family."

"You seem strong," he said gently. "No matter what happens, I think you'll be okay."

I didn't respond. I didn't have it in me to argue, but I didn't believe him.

He opened the passenger door of his black Mercedes GLE Coupe AMG. I hesitated. Distracted by the thought that his car was one of my choices to purchase before I bought Betty, then got in. The classical station that was playing caught me off guard—my favorite kind of background music—I started to feel like this was a sign until he quickly changed it to country. *Why?*

I gave him the name of the hospital, and he plugged it into the GPS.

We didn't speak. I stared out the window. Then I felt it—his hand reaching across to take mine. I should've pulled away.

But I didn't.

His touch was steady. Warm. Grounding. I looked down at our hands, intertwined on the seat. His thumb traced small circles against my skin.

God help me, it felt good.

But it didn't make any sense. This was the man who just told me he was wiping out a neighborhood. How could something that wrong come from someone who felt so right?

The ride was too quiet, except for the noise in my head.

As soon as he parked, I jumped out, racing to the reception desk. They directed me upstairs. I didn't wait for the elevator—I ran the stairs two at a time. I couldn't risk being alone with him again.

I burst onto the floor and spotted my family in the waiting room. Hugs, questions, tears. I barely heard them. I just needed to see my dad.

He was sleeping. Mom sat beside him, holding his hand, eyes glassy with exhaustion.

"Oh, Mom. I'm here. Is he okay?"

She stood and wrapped me in her arms. "He's stable. They're still running tests. But he's resting."

I stayed there with her a few more minutes, then slipped back out to the waiting room.

Everyone was there—my brothers, their partners, Abby, Maggie. I felt surrounded, loved, grounded. And then I felt it: a tap on my shoulder.

Roman.

"Roman," I said, keeping my voice even. "Thank you for everything today. You were right—I wasn't in any shape to drive. But I'm good now. I've got plenty of people here to take care of me."

He nodded. "Would you mind doing me a favor and letting me know how your dad's doing? Just a quick text would be fine."

Do you a favor? I wanted to laugh in his face.

"Sure," I said, smiling sweetly. "That's the least I can do for you."

Venom. Pure and undiluted. I hoped he felt every drop of it.

I turned my back before he could respond.

I watched him walk away for a split second over my shoulder. Any longer, and someone would've caught me staring—and I'd never hear the end of it.

Everyone else had been here longer and already ridden out the worst of Dad's heart attack. I was the one playing catch-up. Now that things felt more stable, I finally exhaled and sat down with Abby and Maggie.

"I was going to swing by both of your places after my meeting," I said, trying to sound normal, "but... well, Dad had other plans."

They exchanged a look. I knew that look. It wasn't about Dad. It was about Roman. I ignored it, hoping we'd move on to safer territory.

Maggie leaned in, taking both of my hands. "I'm having a BBQ Saturday night. Starts at seven. I get it if you can't make it, but... I'd really love for you to be there. It's not the same without you."

I didn't have much going on besides lunch with Ella that day. "I'll be there," I said with a small smile.

Abby looped an arm around my shoulders. "I'll be there too. Bringing coleslaw and mac and cheese."

That made me smile for real. Mac and cheese was my weakness—and they knew it. My girls had been comforting me since elementary school. Through every mess with my mom. Every heartbreak. They'd always been my safe place.

"Well, that's shocking, since you live one street over." I smirked and leaned into them.

Their laughter grounded me. Familiar and steady.

"I'll bring the wine," I said, teasing. "In fact, I could use a glass right now."

Their laughter faded into silence. A loaded glance passed between them. That unspoken "Are you okay?" kind of judgment that hits you harder than any words.

I suddenly wanted to be anywhere but here.

Dad was stable. Mom was with him. And since she couldn't drink, I didn't have to worry about her disappearing down a bottle. My brothers had already left. I was done for the day. Over it.

I reached for my purse so I could say my goodbyes, but my fingers came up empty. I stared at the floor beside my feet.

Only my laptop bag.

"Damn it," I muttered, louder than intended.

Maggie's head tilted. "What is it?"

A nightmare. That's what it is.

"I think I left my purse... at Roman's office. Or his car. I don't remember grabbing it."

Maggie raised an eyebrow. "Well. That's convenient."

"What's that supposed to mean?" I snapped, defensively.

Abby raised both hands. "C'mon, Alex. If the man who drove you here was your mystery meeting, I'm just saying—he's hot. Like, hotter than anyone we've ever met. And I've seen your type."

"I didn't *plan* to leave anything behind."

Maggie shrugged, completely unfazed. "I'd have left a lot more than a purse."

I groaned. "It wasn't a good meeting. It was a total disaster. The only reason I'll ever see him again is to get my stuff back."

They exchanged glances, smug and annoying.

"Okay," they said in unison.

I rolled my eyes. "What?"

"Nothing!" Abby said, all innocence.

Maggie put her hands on her hips. "So, what happened that has your panties in a knot?"

"I beg your pardon?"

"Well?" Maggie poked.

I glared at her. "This conversation is over."

My phone buzzed in my back pocket. I pulled it out.

Roman.

***

ROMAN

Twice in one day, this woman managed to verbally slap the hell out of me. Once with fire, and now with a smile. And somehow, the smile was worse. It was composed. Calculated. Dagger-sharp. And I just stood there like a jackass, taking it.

What the hell is wrong with me? Why am I still thinking about her? She'd probably shove me into traffic without blinking—and yet, I can't stop wondering what's underneath all that rage.

There's something more to her. I feel it. And for some stupid reason, I want to find out what it is.

I don't know how the hell I'm going to do that after today. But I'll figure it out.

The elevator ride back up proved oddly calming. Quiet. Reflective. I leaned against the handrail, tapping my fingers against my thigh, trying to sort through the mess in my head. I had her number. I could text her. But not yet. She needed space—and I probably needed my head examined.

Her car was still in the garage. That gave me an excuse to see her again. A casual "hey, just happened to be here." Maybe Amelia would have advice. She always did.

Back in the garage, I stepped into the private elevator just as Harrison stepped out. Great.

"Shit!" he muttered, bumping into me. He patted his pockets, then caught the door before it shut and stepped back in.

Fantastic.

He leaned against the wall, arms crossed, already in a mood. "Where the hell did you run off to?"

"The woman in my noon meeting had an emergency. I drove her to the hospital."

His eyebrow jumped. "You gave her a ride?"

I nodded. "Yes."

"Why didn't you call her a cab? Or let one of the drivers handle it?" He was watching me way too closely.

I exhaled. "Weren't you on your way home?"

"Forgot my keys." He smirked. "Don't change the subject."

"I drove her. That's all I'm saying."

I pulled out my phone to avoid looking at him. He scoffed, but didn't press further.

"Amelia rescheduled all your meetings," he said. "So I didn't have to play boss today. Lucky you."

He peeled off toward his office as I headed to mine. As I passed Amelia's desk, she stood.

"Mr. King, I hope everything's alright with Ms. Kennedy. I just wanted to let you know—she left her purse." She held it out. "It was still in the conference room. Her keys are in there."

I stared at it. My answer.

"Thank you," I said, taking it from her and heading into my office. Door closed.

A second later—"Knock knock."

Harrison again, hands in his pockets, leaning in the doorway.

"You want to grab a drink?" he asked, like he hadn't been suspicious two minutes ago.

"Not today. Another time."

He nodded, gave a lazy wave, and disappeared.

I sat down, stared at the purse, and reached for my phone.

ME: *Hi Alex, I hope your father is doing better. I just wanted to let you know Amelia found your purse in the conference room. Your keys were in it. I didn't know if you'd like me to or not, but I could drive your car to your place and give you your things, then grab a cab home. Let me know if that works for you.*

I included the part about her dad first—to keep her grounded in what actually mattered.

A minute passed.

Then two.

The three little dots popped up.

My heart started racing.

This was either going to end in another verbal assault... or the beginning of something I hadn't planned on at all.

I was surprised she was texting back—pleasantly, cautiously surprised. She didn't seem angry. Or if she was, she was hiding it better than earlier. Maybe she just wanted her things back. Still, I'd take progress where I could get it.

ALEX: *Thank you. That would be great. I'm guessing you know the address.*

ME: *Yes, Amelia checked the ID to see who the purse belonged to. If that's the same address on your license?*

ALEX: *Yep, that's the one. I should be there in ten minutes.*

ME: *Do you need your keys to get in?*

ALEX: *Nope. I'll let the concierge know you're coming up. You'll need a code for the elevator.*

ME: *Sounds fancy.*

ALEX: *Not really. Just safe from lunatics.*

ME: *Anyone I know?*

ALEX: *Not referencing anyone in particular. Just lunatics in general.*

ME: *See you in about twenty minutes?*

ALEX: *That's fine. You can leave the car with the valet.*

ME: *Thanks. Was just about to ask.*

ALEX: *It's the black Navigator on the second floor of the garage.*

ME: *Perfect. That'll save me the trouble of trying to locate the beeps.*

I grabbed her purse and keys and headed to the second floor of the garage where she said her SUV was parked. When I stepped out of the elevator, I spotted it immediately—a sleek black Lincoln Navigator, polished to a mirror shine.

Not what I expected. Nothing girly about it. This thing looked like a Secret Service detail vehicle. Presidential. Serious. Powerful. Kind of like her.

I got in and started the engine.

Classical music poured through the speakers, filling the cabin with warmth and calm.

Huh. She listens to the same station I do.

Well, well. We have something in common. I can work with that.

According to the GPS, her building was only ten minutes from the office. I took my time. Used those ten minutes to think. To puzzle her out.

Who drives a tank like this solo? Was she afraid of something? Over-compensating? Or just practical? Maybe she liked feeling safe. Maybe she needed to. She lived in a secure building with a valet. Definitely not the picture of modest living, yet here she was trying to save a neighborhood nobody wanted to touch. A contradiction in heels and ambition.

Most women I knew who lived like her didn't have the first clue about compassion. But she'd sat across from me today, practically trembling with purpose, and laid out a plan to change lives. I couldn't stop thinking about it.

She was a puzzle. And for the first time in a long time, I wanted to solve someone.

I pulled up to the valet stand and stepped out, handing the key fob to the guy in the vest. Then I headed straight to the concierge desk.

"Roman King," I said, placing her purse on the counter. "I'm here to return something to Alex Kennedy."

The concierge gave me a once-over. Then a look I couldn't quite place.

"I believe she's expecting you," he said, though his tone suggested he didn't approve. As he scribbled something on a notepad, I heard him mutter under his breath—something that sounded suspiciously like *flavor of the month.*

Interesting.

He handed me a four-digit elevator code and instructions to press twelve and enter the code on the keypad. I nodded, keeping my expression unreadable. "Thanks."

I took the elevator up, heart pounding more than I wanted to admit. When I reached her floor, I stepped out, turned right, and walked three doors down. I paused outside her unit. Took a breath.

This could go either way.

I didn't know what was going to happen next—but I knew I wanted to find out.

And I wasn't going anywhere just yet.

***

ALEX

Today had been such a whirlwind. This morning, I was optimistic, energized—even a little excited. Now? Drained. Exhausted. And dangerously close to spiraling. The only thing I'd managed to grab from that meeting was my computer bag, which I dropped beside the entry chair. I made a beeline to the kitchen.

The wine cooler practically sang to me. I opened it and grabbed a bottle of cabernet, twisting off the cork and letting it breathe while I set a glass on the counter. Then I headed to my bedroom, peeling off the remnants of my day in exchange for black yoga pants and a gray tank that read *Namaste Away*—a small rebellion in cotton form.

I poured a healthy glass, almost to the rim, and had barely taken my first sip when a knock landed on my door.

"Seriously?" I muttered under my breath, checking the camera on my phone. Roman. Of course. Early.

I took a long sip of wine—bold, velvety, a little too honest for what I was about to face—then set the glass down and shuffled to the door.

"Hi, Roman. Come in, please." I stepped aside quickly before any of my nosy neighbors caught a glimpse of him.

"I didn't mean to sound so nasty at the hospital earlier," I said as I closed the door behind him. "I know you were just trying to help. Today's just... been a rollercoaster, and I need a second to process."

He gave me that unreadable expression—half patient, half practiced. "No need to apologize," he said. "You were going through a lot. I'm sure my being there didn't help. How's your dad?"

He looked maddeningly good standing there—hand in his pocket, my purse in the other, perfectly relaxed while I tried not to fall apart. "He's okay. My mom's with him now," I said, reaching for the purse.

Our fingers brushed.

And just like that, the air shifted.

Sparks. Real, undeniable ones.

I moved quickly, setting the purse on the island, pretending I didn't feel a thing. I could almost convince myself it didn't happen... almost.

There was a pause—quiet enough to notice. I thought maybe he was going to say goodbye and head out. Perfect. But then—

"Alex, there's something I need to say about our meeting today."

My stomach sank.

"Your ideas were good. Noble. I used to be like you. I believed in things. But I learned it's better to separate business from personal matters—it makes things easier."

I stared at him, blinking. He didn't just say that.

He started to walk towards the door. Nope. Not today.

"Whoa," I snapped, my voice sharp and rising without permission. "You do *not* get to say that to me and just walk out like this."

He froze, one step away from retreat.

My hands were fists at my sides, shaking. "Who the hell do you think you are? You don't know a damn thing about me."

I took a step toward him, and he took one back.

"I don't give a damn about this project as some sterile business transaction. Those are people—human beings. You might be able to write them off as a line on a spreadsheet, but I can't. I won't."

I threw up my fingers in air quotes. "'Just business,' right? That's the kind of language people use when they bulldoze homes and sleep like babies afterward."

He stood there, speechless. Maybe stunned. Maybe annoyed.

Didn't matter. I was done.

I opened the door wide. "Goodnight, Roman."

And slammed it shut before I could talk myself into anything else.

Chapter 8

ALEX

The next few days were blissfully uneventful. Peace and quiet—finally. Blocking Roman had been the right move. No texts. No calls. Not that I expected him to reach out after the scene I caused in my apartment.

I focused on work, booked an appointment with the Santoro family, and did my best to keep my head down. The Santoros were an intriguing bunch—elegant in speech and manner. Their Italian accents made everything sound like a toast. They owned wineries around the world and, oddly enough, were looking to start one in Ohio, of all places. I found myself actually looking forward to that project. It might just become my new favorite hangout.

Still, despite my better judgment, I kept checking my phone—half-hoping, half-dreading. Then I'd remember I blocked him. For sanity's sake. I considered deleting his number altogether. The last thing I needed was to drunk text a man who could turn my spine into jelly just by looking at me.

By Friday night, I needed a distraction. Everyone from work was heading to Sebastian's to blow off steam, and I was fully on board. I raced home to get ready—maybe I could find someone, anyone, to keep my mind off the Greek God I was trying to forget.

After a long, hot shower, I slipped into a red satin dress that hugged my curves like it was designed to take no prisoners. Spaghetti straps. A thigh-high slit. Just enough cleavage to flirt with danger. My long, dark hair fell in thick, glossy waves. Smokey eye. Bold contour. Red lips so bright they might as well have come with a warning label. The devil was definitely dressing up tonight.

Shay was bringing Landon, Piper, and Ryan over so we could pregame—our tradition. We always hosted "Happy Hour" in my apartment before going out. Tonight, Ryan picked the drink: dirty martinis with blue cheese-stuffed olives.

I grabbed my go-to stiletto sandals—the broken-in ones that didn't completely murder my feet—and headed to the kitchen barefoot to prep the drinks. Heels were a last-minute ordeal. Torture devices invented by a man, no doubt.

I needed a pedicure, I thought as I looked down at my bare feet.

Despite being the oldest in the group by just a couple of years, I always felt like the mom. Maybe it was all those years of helping my own drunk mother home. Maybe it was the failed plan to have a family of my own by now. Or maybe I just liked taking care of people. That said, my behavior once we hit the bar? Not exactly maternal.

They showed up right on time, and the second they saw me, the reactions were loud.

"Is that new?" Shay's eyes widened as she circled me like a stylist on set.

"Not new—just haven't had the right moment." I gave a dramatic spin.

"Is this the moment?"

"Damn right it is. I survived this week."

Laughter erupted as I poured the martinis. We clinked glasses. To survival.

Ryan, never subtle, leaned closer. "Alex, since Landon has a girlfriend, what about me?"

I smiled and looked straight at Piper, who gave me a knowing grin. "Landon, you want to take this?"

Landon didn't miss a beat. "Ryan, ever heard the term 'maneater'?"

Ryan blinked, sipping slowly.

"You wouldn't survive," he said. "You should consider yourself lucky."

Shay chimed in. "Alex, I'd be terrified to be on your radar."

My eyebrows shot up. Wait. Were they serious?

Piper added softly, "You seem really nice to me."

I blinked. Wow. This took a turn.

"You guys make me sound like a serial killer," I muttered, suddenly self-conscious. "I've hurt feelings, maybe, but I've never destroyed anyone."

Landon tilted his head. "That might not be true..."

"What?"

"There was a guy from the other office," he continued. "You brought him home one night and never texted him back. He said he's never been the same."

My stomach dropped. I couldn't even remember the guy's name. "Wait... Todd's friend? The one Grant smacked for talking trash about me?"

"That's him."

I winced, finishing my martini. I didn't even sleep with the guy—he was too clingy. Still, that didn't justify ghosting him like he didn't matter. The guilt crept in, fast and heavy. I sat at the island, drink in hand, and stared at the counter.

"Why didn't anyone tell me I was doing this to people?"

Shay shrugged. "Guys do it all the time."

Piper backed her up. "Exactly. Women can play this game too."

Maybe. But it didn't sit right. "I never thought I was doing damage," I murmured. "I just didn't want anything serious."

I remember Grant saying I'd grow out of it.

Maybe I was.

They all came over for a group hug. Ryan slipped an arm around my waist.

"So... does that mean I have a chance now?" He tried to whisper.

"No," we all said in unison, laughter breaking the tension.

***

At 9:30, the line outside Sebastian's was already snaking around the block. But Bruce, the bouncer, spotted me and waved us in the second I hopped out of the cab. I slipped him a fifty and hugged him like always. Six-five, muscles for days, ex-MMA fighter turned bar bouncer—he could crush a man with one hand but always turned to putty around me.

Inside was packed. Hot, loud, chaotic.

I held onto Shay's hand as we made our way to the bar. Landon, Piper, and Ryan were already out back on the patio. Steve, our regular bartender, saw me and nodded. I held up two fingers. Shots. It was tradition.

Just as I reached between two patrons to grab our drinks, someone grabbed my ass.

Hard.

I turned to Shay, voice tight. "That better be your hand."

She held up both hands, eyes wide and confused.

I downed the shot, handed her the other, and turned slowly.

There he was. Six feet of arrogant audacity, standing like the world owed him gratitude just for showing up. His brown hair was freshly cut, not a strand out of place—military sharp with a designer edge. His blue eyes were the kind you'd call striking if they weren't busy undressing you without permission. The smirk on his face wasn't charming—it was calculated.

Slick and practiced. The kind of smirk that made my skin crawl, like he'd gotten away with this kind of behavior more times than he'd been called out for it.

"Hi," I said sweetly. "Did you just put your hand on my ass?"

He smiled like he'd just done me a favor. "As a matter of fact, I did. Hope you don't mind. I was hoping to grab a few other places later."

I handed my purse to Shay and took a breath. "This might be a bad idea..."

"I'm with you," she whispered. "Do what you have to do."

I straightened, smoothed my dress, and turned to the jackass. "Actually, I *do* mind. You think you can just grab women whenever you feel like it?"

He rolled his eyes. "Lighten up, bitch. What are you, a fucking prude?"

The switch flipped.

I didn't hesitate. I reached out and grabbed him by the balls—hard. My fingers curled with precision and rage, squeezing until I felt the resistance in his knees give out. He buckled, collapsing in front of me like a puppet with cut strings, his mouth open in a silent scream. I braced myself with one hand on his shoulder to keep my balance in the heels, using him like a human railing. My body was steady, but my blood was boiling.

I leaned in slowly, my lips close to his ear, voice low and razor-sharp. I wanted him to feel every word sink into his skin.

"How does that feel? Being grabbed without permission?" I whispered. "Next time, keep your fucking hands to yourself."

I let go. He stumbled back, calling me a psycho bitch before disappearing into the crowd.

The bar erupted in cheers.

Mortified, cheeks blazing and adrenaline still buzzing in my veins, I turned back toward the bar like I could outrun what just happened. My heels clicked sharply against the floor as I made my way to Steve, who was already watching me with a raised brow and the ghost of a grin tugging at his mouth. I didn't say a word—just held up two fingers with a shaky breath, my hand trembling slightly from the rush of it all.

"Round two, please," I said, my voice steadier than I expected. My other hand was pressed against my chest like I was trying to hold my heart in place. The crowd behind me was still murmuring, buzzing with the aftershocks of the scene I'd just caused, but I couldn't face any of them. Not yet. I needed something strong, something fast. Something that would help me forget the weight of every eye that had just watched me take back control in a dress that suddenly felt too hot, too tight, and too revealing.

Patrons at the bar offered to buy me a drink, but I politely declined. I just wanted to disappear into the night and forget it happened. We took our second shot and escaped to the patio where the air was cool, the lights were soft, and I could finally breathe again.

***

ROMAN

My brother said he needed a night out. I didn't want to go, but he wore me down like a toddler asking for candy. His final pitch? Sebastian's. The overcrowded yuppie bar where I'd first met Alexandra Marie Kennedy—information I'd gleaned from her license, of course.

We got there around 8:30, and the line was already forming. Harrison knows everyone, so we walked right in. There were open seats at the bar, thank God. I wasn't about to spend the night elbowing through drunk idiots or getting groped in a crowd. Bars weren't my thing, but Harrison thrived in this chaos.

Too loud. Too packed. Too much of everything. I wanted conversation, not lip-reading. But I was here now. Maybe I'd get lucky and meet someone worth taking home—someone who could get Alex out of my head.

Eventually, Harrison got bored of listening to me complain and announced he was off to "make the rounds." Translation: soak up every ounce of attention the room had to offer like the narcissistic sponge he was born to be. He adjusted his shirt, flashed that effortless smile, and disappeared into the crowd.

I stayed exactly where I was—planted on my barstool like a statue with a bourbon. I had zero interest in elbowing my way through a sea of drunk finance bros and perfume-soaked twenty-somethings pretending to be interested in each other. Instead, I decided to strike up a conversation with the bartender, Steve—the same one who looked like he might spit in my drink the last time I was here.

Tonight, I needed answers. And maybe a little redemption.

"So, Steve. I feel like we got off to a bad start the last time I was here." I extended a hand.

"Who are you again?" he asked, deadpan, but the smirk gave him away. He wiped his hands and shook mine anyway.

"Roman," I said, playing along.

"Ah yes. You're the guy who was hitting on Alex Monday night. What can I get you, Roman?"

"Woodford Reserve. Neat."

He reached for a glass. "Start a tab?"

"Yes, please." I slid him my black Amex.

He glanced at it and laughed. "Anyone else's tab tonight?"

"Not tonight." I smiled, remembering the $200 bottle of wine from earlier in the week. Team Alex, indeed.

Steve returned with my drink, but before he left, I leaned in. "Hey, you got a second?"

He raised a brow. "Barely. What's up?"

"Alex. Are you two a thing?"

That made him laugh. "No. Great woman, but I'm married. Not the cheating kind. Alex is just a regular. Good tipper. Good people."

"Anything else you can tell me about her?" I asked, keeping my tone casual. Just a guy making conversation. Nothing more.

Steve shrugged, grabbing a towel and wiping down the bar with practiced boredom. "She went through a bad divorce. That's all I know."

Divorce?

Interesting.

She didn't strike me as someone who'd been through a marriage—much less a messy one. There was no bitterness in her voice, no scarlet letter of resentment stitched across her smile. If anything, she seemed... polished. Calm, collected. Like she'd already walked through the fire and come out on the other side with her head held high.

Kids? No clue. She hadn't mentioned any, and there hadn't been a trace of that particular kind of tired in her eyes—the kind parents wear like permanent luggage.

I leaned back, taking a sip of my drink. "Doesn't add up," I muttered, mostly to myself.

She was a contradiction in heels. Cool on the outside, but I'd caught that flicker—the way her jaw clenched when she thought no one was watching. There was something under the surface she didn't want people to see.

And now, I wanted to know what.

Steve left to tend the growing crowd. The noise was getting worse. If I didn't see someone worth staying for soon, I was out. Then—

A flash of red caught my eye.

Red satin. A toned frame. Long dark hair. I couldn't see her face yet, but my body reacted before my brain could catch up. I shifted uncomfortably on the barstool. That dress wasn't fair.

I kept my eye on her as I scanned the room. It was packed—shoulder to shoulder, drinks sloshing, elbows flying. Definitely over fire code. One exit? Maybe two, if you counted the barely-visible side door by the bathrooms. A place like this was a lawsuit waiting to happen. I clocked the exit signs out of habit, and tucked it away in the back of my mind.

Then I caught a flash of movement from the red dress at the bar.

A woman raised two fingers—confident, like she owned the place. There was something in the fluidity of the gesture that tugged at the back of my brain. Not just familiar. Intentional.

Steve caught it too. He grinned, flipping the towel over his shoulder like he'd just been proven right. "Speak of the devil."

I stepped onto the footrest of my barstool and leaned forward, eyes skimming the crowd. And there she was—Alex Kennedy, in that red dress that had no business being worn by someone trying to keep a low profile if that's what she was trying to do. The fabric clung to her curves, her dark hair spilling down her back like something scripted. I didn't have a good angle, but even from here, I could feel the ripple she caused just by existing in a room.

Then she turned, sharp and sudden, toward someone behind her.

My body tensed.

There was a guy—too close. His energy was off. I couldn't hear the words, but I didn't need to. Her posture tensed—shoulders stiff, chin lifted, hand coming up not in flirtation, but defense.

And then he dropped.

To his knees, yelling something I couldn't make out over the music.

What the hell was going on?

My hand tightened around my glass, the air between us charged now. It wasn't just that she was in trouble—it was the way she didn't flinch. The way she stood there, calm, like this wasn't the first man she'd brought to his knees.

I pushed off the stool.

Because whatever this was, it didn't feel like a scene. It felt like a threat.

And whether I liked it or not, I wasn't about to stand by and let her face it alone.

I stood, ready to step in, but the crowd was too thick. It didn't matter any way because she handled it.

Within seconds, it was over, and the whole bar applauded whatever it was that happened. Whatever that asshole did, she made sure he regretted it. I admired her from afar, impressed, curious, and thoroughly turned on.

The guy slinked toward me, cradling his ego and his groin. "Psycho bitch. Fuckin' prude. Like she hasn't been with half the guys in here."

I elbowed him square in the nose. Hard. Feigned it as accidental. No apology.

Steve caught the move and gave me a wink. I pushed past the bleeding jackass, eyes fixed on Alex, but she was already moving toward the back patio.

Harrison intercepted me. "Did you see that chick in the red dress? Holy shit, she emasculated that guy."

"What did he do?"

"Grabbed her ass."

I smiled, proud of my elbow. "Yeah, I could see her reacting like that."

Harrison said, "I think I'm gonna marry her."

I rolled my eyes. "Do you remember the emergency I had Tuesday?"

Realization dawned. "No shit? That was her?"

I nodded.

"You're the luckiest bastard in the world."

"She told me to get the hell out of her apartment and called me a compassionless bastard."

He laughed so hard he nearly fell. "Awesome. So I *do* have a chance." He slapped my back and headed after her.

"Don't tell her we're brothers."

"Understood," he grinned.

I followed him to the patio, keeping a safe distance. Alex was surrounded—laughing, radiant, entirely in her element. I veered toward the outdoor bar for another drink, watching as Harrison made his move, all GQ charm and swagger.

She smiled when she saw him. Relaxed. Lit up. It stung more than I expected. I watched from behind my glass, sipping slowly, trying not to care. But I did.

When Harrison returned, I motioned for him to stand in front of me, just in case she was looking.

"She's not interested," he announced, sipping his beer.

"What'd she say?"

"She's taking a break from losers. Or something to that effect."

I laughed, almost choking on my bourbon. "You're losing your touch."

Then someone tapped him on the shoulder.

Alex.

She stepped around him, eyes locked on mine. Those green eyes were even more dangerous under smoky eyeshadow and red lips. She was glowing.

"Hi, Roman," she said, calm as ever.

I barely had time to respond before she looked at Harrison. "Is this your brother? You two look alike."

He looked guilty. "Yes, ma'am. Guilty as charged."

She cut him off mid-sentence with a gentle touch. "Harrison, may I have a second alone with your brother, please?"

He didn't hesitate. "Of course. Please, take my seat."

She sat gracefully, crossed her legs, and stared right through me.

Before she could say anything, I asked, "Can I buy you a drink? Since both your hands are empty and I'd rather you be holding a glass... and not, you know, my balls."

Chapter 9

ALEX

The look in his eyes was intense. "Hi, Alex."

God help me. That voice. That low, velvet-wrapped-in-smoke kind of tone that slid along my skin like a secret. It sank deep, coiling somewhere low in my belly and blooming heat in its wake. Goosebumps rippled down my arms, fast and traitorous. And in this damn satin dress—with its clingy fabric and plunging neckline—I had nowhere to hide. My body was doing all the talking, and every message it was sending felt dangerously close to a confession.

"Did you put your brother up to all that?" I asked, aiming for composure, though my voice came out breathy—too calm, too soft. Like I hadn't just forgotten how to function.

He shook his head slowly, a smirk tugging at his mouth. "No. In fact, I warned him not to bother you, but he has his own ideas about what that means."

Of course he did. Harrison seemed like the kind of guy who thought women were parties to crash. Roman... Roman was something else entirely.

"Did he know who I was before he started talking to me?" I asked. His eyes hadn't left mine. Not once. The rest of the room was still moving, still buzzing with conversation, but I couldn't hear a damn thing over the pulse in my ears.

"Not at first," he said. "I didn't even know it was you until the bartender told me."

I tilted my head, narrowing my eyes. "Why would Steve tell you who I was?"

Roman blinked—slowly—and for the first time, looked a little guilty. "He remembered me talking to you on Monday."

He asked about me?

The flutter in my chest wasn't subtle. It was a full-body quake, something between shock and—God help me—delight. That shouldn't have hit as hard as it did, but there it was. A breathless little ache expanding in my ribs.

"Then the altercation happened at the bar earlier," he continued. "I didn't realize it was you until Steve came over and said so. I was going to give you a hand, but clearly, you didn't need one."

I groaned, dragging a hand over my face. "Oh God. You saw that?"

"I did," he said, a glint of amusement in his eyes.

"I thought I was going to get thrown out."

"Why would you get thrown out?"

I dropped my hand, exhaling sharply. "It was a pretty violent retort."

He smiled, and something low and heavy rolled through my stomach. "From what I heard—he deserved it."

"Two wrongs don't make a right," I murmured, already knowing I sounded unconvinced.

"I bet he thinks twice before putting his hands on another woman without consent."

"That was the goal. I hope he listened."

"Let's just say... his reaction didn't exactly inspire confidence in his ability to grow."

I gave him a look. "What exactly did you hear?"

Roman shifted, leaning back, one arm draping lazily over the back of his stool. The other rested on his thigh—strong, casual, and maddeningly close. The movement was slow, controlled, confident. It made me hyper-aware of every inch of space between us—and how little of it I wanted to keep.

"He said some unflattering things about you," Roman said. "But he had to leave right after that."

My stomach tightened. "What do you mean he had to leave? Did he get thrown out?"

"He may have... accidentally gotten his nose broken."

I blinked. "Someone punched him?"

"No." His voice dropped just a notch lower. "It was an elbow."

My eyes widened. "Oh my God. You broke his nose?"

He shrugged, unbothered. "I really didn't mean to. But the things he was saying about you... they set me off."

Heat crept up my neck. A flush bloomed across my chest that had nothing to do with embarrassment. There was something primal about a man who didn't hesitate to defend you—especially a man like him.

"What did he say?" I asked. My voice came out too soft.

"I really don't want to repeat any of it."

"Roman, please." I reached for his hand before my brain could stop me. The moment our skin touched, the air between us cracked. Electricity. Raw and immediate. I snatched my hand back like I'd been burned, but the spark still buzzed under my skin. His gaze dipped to where our fingers had brushed, then returned to mine—darker now, more intense.

"If you really want me to, I will," he said. "But I've probably already pissed you off enough for one lifetime."

"It's okay," I said gently, though nothing about me felt okay. My heart was beating out of sync. "I just... I need to know. For me."

His jaw flexed. Something stormy passed behind his eyes. A pause. Then he said it.

"He didn't understand why you weren't interested in him. Then insinuated you'd been around the block."

The words landed like a slap. Sharp. Cold. Unfair.

"Roman... thank you. For telling me. And for stepping in. That was... rare."

He shifted in his seat like the compliment made him itch. "Seriously, it's none of my business."

He took a drink, and I watched his throat move as he swallowed. My lips parted, and I barely noticed. Everything about him was pulling me in. Every glance, every pause, every restrained bit of tension—it was all unraveling me, thread by thread.

"Maybe someday I'll want to talk about it," I said softly. "Today's not that day."

He nodded, slow and solemn. Understanding without pity. That mattered more than I could say.

Then he looked at me and said, "Can I ask you something?"

"Go ahead." My hands landed in my lap, a little too eager.

"Will you unblock me?"

I blinked. "You knew?" I should've known he'd try to contact me to smooth things over, given who our mutual contact is.

He grinned, the kind of grin that should've come with a warning label. "Come on, Alex. Give a guy a break."

"Fine." I sighed, reaching for my clutch. "Can I trust you not to abuse the privilege?"

"No promises," he said, amused.

I pulled up his name and tapped the unblock button. "There."

He took out his own phone, one brow raised, and began typing one-handed while sipping his beer.

A second later, my phone buzzed.

ROMAN: *You look absolutely amazing tonight. I still want to kiss you, and I'd love to start with those RED LIPS.*

I inhaled sharply. Heat rushed to my face, my chest, my thighs. My hand trembled slightly as I typed back.

ME: *Name the place and I'm there.*

His eyes snapped up to mine, that cocky grin faltering for half a second before something hotter took its place.

And just like that, the air between us turned molten.

So much for staying sober.

In more ways than one.

***

ROMAN

That text hit me below the belt—literally. No metaphor. Just blood rushing south with a vengeance, and no time to disguise the aftermath. I shifted in my seat, slow and discreet, praying she didn't glance down and realize the exact effect her words had on me.

I'd once told her I was impressed with her self-control. Now? Mine was unraveling by the second.

What the hell do I do now?
Ask her to leave with me?
Yank her off that stool and press her up against the nearest wall just to hear her gasp against my neck?

Before I could move, she spoke.

"I'm sorry. I shouldn't have said that," she murmured, eyes flicking downward. "I'm in the middle of some lifestyle changes, and that might not have been the best response."

Lifestyle changes.
That could mean anything. Sobriety. Celibacy. Emotional rewiring.
Maybe she was just trying to rewrite the part of her that trusted men like me.

I didn't want to guess. And I sure as hell wasn't going to push. Not with her.

"I'd love to get the hell out of here," I said, lowering my voice so only she could hear it. "But I'm not going to ask you to do anything you're not ready for."

It wasn't a line.
I meant it.
I just wanted to be alone with her. Somewhere without the noise and the bodies and my insufferable brother buzzing around us like flies.
I didn't care if we talked, sat in silence, or just breathed the same air—
I just needed her near me without a thousand distractions pulling her away.

She smiled then—small, hesitant and beautiful.
It was the kind of smile that didn't come easy. Like it had fought to survive.
And God, the way it hit me—right in the gut.

"Thank you. I really hope you understand that it's not you."

I exhaled slowly. "The classic 'it's not you, it's me,' huh?"

She laughed—tilting her head back just enough to show the curve of her throat.

Jesus. That sound was sunlight after a storm. It was everything warm I hadn't let myself want in a long time.

Her neck arched slightly, the soft slope of her collarbone peeking out from the satin edge of her dress, and I had to grip the edge of the bar to keep from leaning in. Just to taste that skin. Just to hear what she sounded like when she whispered my name with want instead of caution.

"I told you once," I said, my voice coming out lower than I intended, "I was impressed by your self-control. You made me feel like I was the one losing mine."

She blinked, caught off guard. "I remember. Not sure I believed it then or now."

I let my eyes drift—slow and unapologetic—from her eyes, down the line of her neck, across the satin drape of her dress, then back to her mouth. "Well," I said quietly, "you might now."

She inhaled like she felt it too.

Her voice was barely above a whisper. "It does feel like I'm the one losing control tonight."

A muscle in my jaw ticked.

This woman was driving me insane—and I liked it.

This wasn't flirting. This wasn't foreplay.

This was a match held to a fuse that had been burning between us from the start.

And then she said it.

"I really want to get out of here."

I didn't hesitate.

Didn't let logic or caution win.

I just extended my hand.

"Can I give you a ride?"

She nodded, quiet and certain, and I swear the earth shifted under my feet. When she stood, she placed her hand in mine.

Warm.
Soft.
Undeniable.

My other hand found the small of her back, and she leaned into me—not much, just enough to let me feel the heat of her body and the way it fit perfectly against mine.
It took everything I had not to close the distance, not to pull her fully into me and kiss the last bit of reason out of both our heads.

But I didn't.

Not yet.

Harrison could call his own damn Uber.

I had something infinitely more important to do.

Chapter 10

ALEX

I don't know what came over me, but suddenly I needed to get out of that bar.

Everything I'd been trying to escape lately was swirling around in there—loud voices, careless hands, too many eyes. I loved my friends. I really did. But the vibe tonight? It was off. Stifling. Like I was stuck under the weight of something to heavy to hold.

Roman kept insisting I had all this self-control, but I'd never felt less in control of myself than I did in that moment. My skin buzzed with awareness, my heart pounding in a way that had nothing to do with alcohol.

When I told him I needed to leave, I saw the flicker of understanding in his eyes—like he got it without me having to explain.

Then came the question. "Can I give you a ride?"

I should've hesitated. Should've made up an excuse, played it safe, said I'd call an Uber. But something in me leaned toward him. Something quiet and persistent that whispered, *He's not like the others.*

"There," he said, pointing across the street. "That's me."

He kept one hand on my lower back, guiding me gently through the crowd. His other hand laced through mine, firm and reassuring. It wasn't showy. It wasn't possessive. It just felt... steady.

And I liked it.

He opened the door for me, and I climbed in carefully, trying not to think about what I looked like doing it in heels and a satin dress. He lingered for a second, watching me—his expression unreadable—and then shut the door.

The car was clean, comfortable. The classical station was still playing softly through the speakers. He didn't change it.

"Okay, Ms. Kennedy," he said with a half-smile, turning slightly in his seat. "Where to?"

I stared out the window for a second, letting the music settle my nerves. Then I said it. "Lookout Park."

His brow ticked upward, but he didn't question it. Just plugged it into the GPS and pulled away from the curb.

We drove in silence at first. Not the awkward kind, but the kind that made me feel like I could finally exhale. The further we got from the city, the more my thoughts began to untangle.

I had no idea why I'd invited him along. I'd never taken anyone to the lookout before—not friends, not exes. It was mine. My little patch of sky and silence.

Maybe it was the way he hadn't tried to impress me. Maybe it was the fact that he'd stepped in earlier, without hesitation. Or maybe it was the way he listened—really listened. Like I wasn't just noise to him.

Whatever it was, I didn't feel unsafe. Not even a little.

The road stretched out ahead of us, the stars just starting to show through the inky sky. I pressed my forehead lightly to the cool glass and tried to breathe through the knot in my chest.

I could feel Roman glance over a few times, and eventually he spoke. "Does this place have some significance to you?"

"Yes." It was all I could manage. My voice barely above a whisper.

There was a pause. I could feel him waiting for more.

Then, teasing: "Do you want to share what that is, since you're basically kidnapping me?"

That earned a laugh out of me. It caught me off guard, bubbling up unexpectedly. "You're the one driving," I said, glancing over with a smile.

His answering grin was crooked, boyish in a way that didn't match the sharp lines of his jaw or the way he filled out the driver's seat.

"What's at Lookout Park?" he asked.

"Absolutely nothing." I exhaled, hugging my arms around myself. "That's the point."

He didn't push. Just nodded like he understood. And for some reason, that made me like him even more.

When we finally exited the highway and turned onto the long stretch of road that led to the overlook, I felt my chest loosen for the first time all day. The trees were tall and close together here, lining the road like quiet sentinels. The moonlight filtered through them, casting silver shadows on the asphalt.

I guided him to my usual spot—right at the edge, where the land opened up and you could see the city lights scattered in the distance like spilled glitter.

The car stopped. The music kept playing.

"Wow," he said quietly. "You're right. There's nothing here."

There was something uncertain in his voice—maybe surprise, maybe caution. Maybe judgment.

He got out first, walked around, and opened my door like a gentleman.

I stared at his hand for a second before taking it. It was warm. Strong. The kind of hand that made you feel like if the ground gave out beneath you, he'd keep you steady.

"Would you care to dance?" he asked, voice soft but certain.

My heart skipped.

I nodded, and before I could second-guess it, he pulled me gently toward him.

His hand found my waist. Mine landed on his shoulder. And just like that, we were swaying. Slow, quiet, steady. The music wrapped around us like fog, the stars above glowing like tiny watchful witnesses.

I tipped my head back, just for a second, to look at the sky. Then I rested it on his chest. His heartbeat was strong and steady beneath my cheek—like he was in full control of everything, including my traitorous pulse.

His cheek rested lightly against the top of my head, and I could feel his breath against my hair—warm, it grounded me.

We fit together in a way that made something inside me ache. Not the usual ache for attention or approval or escape. This was different.

It was peace.

And that terrified me.

I didn't open my eyes. I didn't want to break the spell. Because in that moment, I could see it all: a perfect life, a partner who stayed, a quiet house with laughter in the corners, a future that didn't hurt.

But none of that was real.

Not for me.

I was the girl who smiled through the noise, who worked until she broke, who drank too much to forget the pain and wore nice clothes to convince people she wasn't falling apart.

And now here I was, dancing with a man I barely knew—who saw too much and didn't look away.

A tear slipped down my cheek. I didn't mean for it to. But he felt it. I could tell.

Because a moment later, he wrapped both arms around me, pulling me in tighter. Like he knew I didn't want to talk. Like he knew the storm was still there, even if the sky was clear.

And I let him.

Just for a little while.

Well, that was unexpected.

I hadn't planned to cry. I hadn't planned to bring Roman to my most sacred place either, but here we were—at Lookout Park, the one patch of ground where I could usually breathe.

He released me long enough to bring me a sweatshirt from his car and a tissue without saying a word. I muttered a choked "thank you" and turned away, trying to recompose myself. The sweatshirt was big on me, hanging almost to my knees, and it smelled like him—clean, warm, something faintly woodsy. I wrapped it around myself and inhaled deeply, the scent settling something shaky inside me.

This wasn't something I was used to. Closeness. Kindness. Being looked after with no agenda. And especially not from a man like Roman—one I'd pegged as composed, sharp, maybe a little cold. But what he gave me tonight... wasn't any of those things.

It overwhelmed me.

I thought I could sit here quietly and let the night swallow the moment whole, but I knew I couldn't leave it hanging like this. Still, to come right out and say *You should probably stay away from me if you don't want to get hurt* felt like a threat, and I didn't want to scare him off. A low, bitter chuckle slipped from the back of my throat.

"You must be feeling better."

I flinched at the sound of his voice—startled that he was so close. I hadn't even realized he'd returned.

I glanced at him, then back out toward the glittering city below, hoping the lights might have answers I didn't.

"I'm definitely feeling something," I said, my voice soft and uncertain. The kind of answer that wasn't really one at all.

He didn't push. Just stood beside me in silence and then, slowly, reached for my hand. His fingers laced through mine, and I closed my eyes.

I almost let myself believe I deserved this—deserved him.

But that illusion cracked the moment my mind betrayed me with the memory of Luke—drunk and mean, coming home hours late, reeking of someone else's perfume. *You know if you gave a bj like my assistant, I might actually come home once in a while.* That line would haunt me forever.

Or the events I pretended to enjoy, where everyone pitied me behind fake smiles while my husband disappeared into bathrooms and coat closets with a busty blonde who looked nothing like me.

Even more recent moments piled up behind my eyes—the guy at the bar accusing me of being used goods. My coworkers joking about me being a maneater, like I was some threat to every man within arm's reach. Grant telling me I'd *"grow out of my extracurriculars."*

I pulled my hand away before he could feel the tremble. Clenched my fingers into fists.

I wasn't falling apart—I was unraveling.

What the hell was I thinking, bringing him here?

Maybe I thought the quiet would silence the demons in my head. But tonight, they were louder than ever.

I turned to Roman, studying the lines of his face, trying to find something to ground myself in. Anything that would keep me from crumbling completely.

"So," I said, forcing a note of casual curiosity into my voice, "what do you think of my secret retreat?"

He exhaled, his shoulders slumping in what looked like relief.

"Do you want my honest opinion?"

"I would like to hear both, please," I said, managing a small smile. Assuming if there's an honest one there's also a dishonest one.

His lips curved as he turned to face me fully. "Of course you would."

He gestured toward the view. "Well, my not-so-honest opinion is that this place is a hidden gem. Absolutely stunning. The view is to die for, the silence is therapeutic, and the air smells like fresh beginnings."

I laughed, shaking my head. "That sounds like a tourism brochure."

He grinned, then shifted slightly. His expression grew more serious. "My honest opinion?"

I nodded.

"I was just... wondering if you come here alone. At night. And how unsafe that really is. There's no one around. No lights. If something ever happened—no one would know."

His words caught me off guard. I looked around like I was seeing the place for the first time—not as a peaceful haven, but a void where anything could happen and no one would hear you scream.

"Well," I said after a pause, "that's food for thought." I laughed quietly, hollow and self-aware. "Guess I'm not as concerned about my safety as I should be."

He didn't laugh with me. Just kept watching me, brows slightly drawn.

I nudged him gently with my elbow. "It's okay. I'm just... thinking."

"What exactly are you thinking about?" he asked, tilting his head like he was genuinely curious.

I panicked slightly, trying to find a detour from the minefield inside me. "Oh, I don't think you'd be interested in that."

He started walking toward me, slow and deliberate, his eyes darker now—something between playful and devastatingly focused.

"I wouldn't have asked if I wasn't."

His nearness made my breath catch. The look on his face... I couldn't tell if he was in the mood to tease me or taste me. Maybe both.

I swallowed hard. *Oh God. How do I get out of this with my heart intact?*

And then I felt it—that shift. The one that said I was about to either run or fall.

And I was so tired of running.

***

ROMAN

As I moved closer to her, I said, "I wouldn't have asked if I wasn't interested," not taking my eyes off her for a second. I knew they had some kind of power over her. I figured it out back at the bar when she looked at me like she could see straight through me. No one had ever looked at me like that before—like they weren't just seeing a man but something deeper, something buried. When our eyes met, it wasn't just attraction. It was connection. And while she seemed to be fighting it, I was trying to welcome it.

She looked wary, like she thought I was about to pounce. I was tempted. God, I was tempted. But I softened my stance, gave her some space. "So tell me, what are you thinking right now?"

She opened her mouth, then stopped. Bit her lip. Tapped her chin. My eyes dropped to her mouth, that full lower lip caught between her teeth.

"Well, I was thinking that I was hungry, at first."

Me too, I thought, but not for food. I smiled, half hoping she couldn't read the very vivid image playing in my head.

"Then I thought about what you looked like in those pants you have on tonight..."

That look in her eyes? Predatory. Devouring. It sent a bolt of heat through me so fast it made me dizzy. She kept going, and I let her. Let her drag this torture out.

"How I can literally see the definition of all your muscles right through them. I was thinking the same thing about your shirt and how your chest felt against my face and then..."

And then. Christ, I was already halfway to losing it.

"...and then, yep! I realized I just wanted a cheeseburger."

I blinked, thrown completely off course. And then I laughed—hard. So did she. The spell was broken, just like that. I walked over, swung my arm around her shoulder, and kissed the top of her head.

"Come on, let's go get you a cheeseburger."

She tucked herself into my side, arms wrapping around my waist. "Okay," she mumbled.

We drove to an all-night diner downtown, found a booth off to the side, quiet and tucked away. She ordered a cheeseburger. So did I.

I couldn't stop looking at her. In my sweatshirt over that satin dress, she looked like she'd wandered off the cover of some old Hollywood film—ethereal and out of place in a way that felt oddly right.

"So, Roman," she asked, arms crossed, eyes locked on mine. "Did you think this is how your night was going to turn out?"

"Most definitely not," I said without hesitation. "I thought I was going to have to drag my brother out of the bar before he found some crazy chick to take home."

She laughed. "Is that something he does often?"

"More than I'd like to admit. This time, I had to stop him from going after the craziest chick in the bar."

She paused. Her eyes narrowed. "Anyone I might know?"

I raised my brows.

"Is that a serious question?"

Recognition flickered across her face. Then she laughed again. "Oh, right. Harrison... of course. Wait, what? Are you calling me crazy?"

"If the shoe fits," I teased, kicking her foot lightly under the table.

She tipped her head. "Well, I'm here with you, so who's gonna save *your* dumb ass?"

"Good point," I said, raising my water glass. We clinked and drank.

She leaned in a bit, more serious now. "So, how are you feeling about this evening?"

I sobered. "Honestly? I'm concerned about your well-being. You have a total disregard for your safety."

She brushed it off with a joke about getting eaten by sharks. I didn't laugh.

"You really don't see anything wrong with going to a deserted overlook in the middle of the night? Or walking through neighborhoods you know are dangerous?"

She blinked, like it had never even occurred to her.

"No. Not until you pointed it out. In fact, I'm going there tomorrow for lunch with a nice lady I just met."

I couldn't believe it. "That just blows my mind. I've never met anyone who wasn't scared of anything."

"That's not what I said," she corrected. "I just don't worry about things that *might* happen. Worrying is being afraid of something in the future that hasn't happened yet."

It was so simple the way she said it. So sure. I stared at her, trying to make sense of this woman who defied logic and stirred up every buried instinct I had.

"You're not cautious," I concluded.

"I'm not careless either. I care a lot. About everything. Everyone."

"Except yourself," I said quietly.

She went quiet after that, and I could tell she was tired. This whole night had been a slow unpeeling of armor, and I didn't want to push her any more.

"Roman," she said finally, "thank you for a very fun night. You've given me a lot to think about. But I have a long day tomorrow."

I slid out of the booth and reached for her hand. "I hope I didn't offend you. I just wanted to be honest. Because I care."

She nodded and took my hand. "I appreciate it more than you know."

I paid the bill, walked her to the car, and drove her home. I made sure she made it inside, and kissed her cheek goodnight. Just a light brush of lips, but it lingered.

Back in my car, I sat for a moment, staring up at her building.

Was that a date? Hell if I knew. But I wanted to see her again.

Later, back in my apartment, I cracked open a beer and dropped into my leather chair, letting some jazz calm me down. I kicked off my shoes, stretched out, and let the quiet wash over me.

One text from Harrison lit up my screen.

HARRISON: *You good?*

ME: (thumbs up emoji)

It was after 1 a.m. when I finally let myself close my eyes. And when I did, I dreamed about her.

She was safe. And that was all I needed.

Chapter 11

ALEX

I woke to the familiar smell of Roman King.

It was disorienting at first, my brain still foggy with sleep, but unmistakable—clean and woodsy. I knew he hadn't come in last night. I'd left him at the door, kissed on the cheek, thanked him, and sent him away with my sanity still intact.

But that scent lingered.

I rolled over and realized I was still wrapped in his hoodie. In my dress, no less. Jesus. That's a first. I've never slept in my clothes, much less someone else's. But there I was, fully tangled in the fabric that still held his warmth.

This man is getting under my skin.

It was Saturday—rest day from the gym—but perfect for a morning run. I threw on some running shorts with pockets, a tank top, and pulled my hair into a high ponytail while brushing my teeth. I sat on the edge of the bed to lace up my shoes, grabbed my earbuds, and hit the pavement by 6:00 a.m.

Downtown was quiet, still sleeping off the sins of Friday night. The music blared in my ears—my "focus" playlist, a genre-hopping mix that helped my restless brain find rhythm. Focusing on one thing at a time had never been my strong suit. I was a multitasker by nature. I started projects and forgot them halfway through. I once forgot I was showing a house to a client until they texted me asking where I was. That's when I hired an assistant.

Deals? I could close them.
Follow-through? That was another story.

Selling that apartment complex had been a huge win, mostly because I actually finished the job. It had taken me over a year, but I stuck with it. That's rare for me.

Ten minutes later, I made it to the river—already a sweaty mess, lungs burning, hair clinging to my neck. I ducked into a coffee shop for a large iced coffee, a water refill, and a blueberry muffin. I sat at one of the outdoor tables, letting the breeze dry the sweat and watching the muddy brown water roll by.

I tried not to think about Roman.
I failed.

Would he think this morning jog was reckless? Was I supposed to be scanning for suspicious characters now? I looked around just to satisfy the ridiculous voice in my head and crumpled the muffin wrapper in frustration.

Damn him.
He's in my head now.

His eyes. His hands. His concern.
His ridiculous, insufferable, overprotective concern.

I dropped my face into my hands and groaned internally. This man was already interfering with my day-to-day life, and I didn't even know what we were yet.

After finishing my snack, I tossed the trash and took the long way back to the apartment, walking slowly, soaking in the greenery. The city had done a great job cleaning up the park areas—green, vibrant, and beautifully maintained. I should've been proud of the progress.

But all I could think about was the neighborhood Roman's company planned to tear down to build more of this.

Why did we fix what was already thriving, just in a different way?
Why did everyone seem so comfortable with erasing communities instead of investing in them?

I picked up my pace again, letting the rhythm of my feet drown out the thoughts. When I got home, I stepped into the shower and stood there, letting the water do what it always did—clean more than just my skin.

By the time I stepped out, I felt human again. Maybe even hopeful.

Today was about Ella. I needed the right mindset.

I slipped on black joggers, a striped oversized tee, and black sneakers. No frills. I tied my hair in a wavy ponytail and added a swipe of mascara and tinted lip gloss. No need to draw extra attention in that neighborhood. My car would do that enough by itself.

"Fancy rich lady," I muttered, laughing at Ella's voice in my head.

As I made my way to the kitchen, I pulled out my phone and called Edward. Time for some big brother wisdom—sprinkled with a healthy dose of judgment.

"Well hey there, if it isn't my favorite sister!" he answered cheerfully.

"Only sister. Thank God," I shot back, hopping onto a barstool.

"You got that right."

Edward was my favorite sibling to spar with. He was the calm to Patrick's fury, the cool to my chaos. Martial artist. CEO of a security company. Always the one telling me I needed to stop tempting fate.

He once tried to teach me self-defense in high school to keep boys away. Didn't work, but the effort was sweet.

"To what do I owe the pleasure?" he asked.

I sighed. "Apparently, I have a death wish and need advice."

"That bad?"

"I guess provoking serial killers and hanging out in high-crime zones isn't safe." I grinned. I was being dramatic, but not totally.

He chuckled, but the laughter died quickly. "What the hell does that mean? Where have you been hanging out?"

"Well, I've been stargazing at Lookout Park alone at night. And I've made some friends in Burrow Township."

Silence. Then: "What part of Burrow?"

I braced myself. "You know where the old Victorians are? Between the high-rises and condos?"

A beat. Then: "Please tell me you're not seriously hanging out down there."

"Not hanging out. My car ran out of gas. I met some people. I'm having lunch with one of them today."

He groaned audibly. "You do know they're tearing that place down, right?"

"Yes, Edward. But one of the residents is trying to save it. I'm just going to see what I can do to help."

"You're not a superhero, Alex. You sell houses. Help them relocate. Don't try to save a place that's already a lost cause."

I clenched my jaw. Why did everyone talk about that neighborhood like it was garbage?

I exhaled. "Okay, fine. What do you suggest I do to stay safe?"

"Well, short of learning self-defense in the next five minutes—yes, you should take some classes. And maybe be a little more careful where you go."

That wasn't a terrible idea. "Got it. Self-defense classes. Perfect." I spun on the stool, mentally penciling in the MMA gym Sebastian's bouncer owned.

"And what about who you hang out with?" he added.

I grinned. "You know me. Trouble finds me. I don't look for it."

He laughed. "Just... don't make yourself a target, okay? You're the only sister I have and I kinda like you."

"Aww, big bro. I kinda like you too. See you at the beach."

We hung up, and I made myself a quick breakfast, finally feeling grounded again. I stared at my phone, wondering if I should text Roman.

And just as I reached for it, his name lit up my screen.

ROMAN: *Good morning, Ms. Kennedy. I hope you slept well.*

My stomach flipped. My heart stuttered.

God help me.
I am in *big* trouble.

***

ROMAN

I got up early, checked my phone. No messages.

Figures.

I went to the gym and pushed harder than usual, hoping to sweat out the worry still clinging to my chest. Part of me wanted to ask if I could go with her today—to meet the woman in that neighborhood she keeps talking about. But the irony wasn't lost on me. She's heading into a place I'm actively tearing down. Probably not the best guy to bring along. Still, I wish she weren't going alone.

After the gym, I took a long shower, trying to rinse her out of my thoughts. No luck. Even breakfast had her name on it—every scenario I imagined involved her sitting across from me, hair still damp from a morning run, teasing me over eggs and coffee.

I dried off, grabbed my phone, and sent a message before I could overthink it.

ME: *Good morning, Ms. Kennedy. I hope you slept well.*

I stared at the screen, wondering if she was even awake. She didn't get home until after midnight. But then—there they were. The typing dots. I smiled like an idiot. That answered that.

God, she could still be lying in bed. My mind wandered—to her hair messy from sleep, her skin warm, the curve of her spine under my sheets. Wrapped up in me.

And then, her reply lit up the screen, yanking me out of the fantasy.

ALEX: *Good morning. I slept great, how about you?*

I would've smiled at anything she said, but the fact that she asked? Yeah, that hit different.

ME: *Me too, thanks for asking. I was wondering if you were interested in having breakfast with me this morning?*

So much for easing into it. I sounded overeager, like I'd forgotten how to play it cool because I probably had.

ALEX: *I would've said yes, except I already had a muffin after the first half of my run, then breakfast after the second half.*

Wait—what?

She'd already been out on a run? It was barely seven.

ME: *What time did you go for a run this morning, and where did you run to?*

I hit send, immediately regretted it. I sounded like a worried boyfriend. Which... I wasn't. I was just impressed. And maybe a little protective.

Her reply didn't disappoint.

ALEX: *I've been up since five. Thought I'd take a nice run through crack town, maybe do some ding-dong ditching.*

I laughed, shaking my head. Smartass.

ME: *LOL. Good for you for being so dedicated to your physical fitness.*

I could picture her reading that, proud of her sass.

ALEX: *Thanks. Today's one of my days off from the gym, so I like to run down by the river and sit outside Brew HAHA, eat some carbs, drink some coffee... get the motivation to run back home.*

That gave me an idea. Maybe I could get her to give me her workout schedule and casually run into her some day.

ME: *You take days off from the gym? Who does that?*

ALEX: *I'm a weekday warrior. Only time I need to focus is during the week. Weekends are for relaxing.*

Relaxing? Running at six a.m. didn't sound like relaxing to me.

ME: *You consider running relaxing?*

She didn't hesitate.

ALEX: *I don't just run. I walk along the river, listen to music, sit at the coffee shop and chill. Then I run home and do whatever I'm doing that day. So yes, six a.m. runs are very relaxing.*

She had a rhythm, a ritual. I liked that about her.

ME: *Next time you go running at six a.m., would you like some company?*

Probably overstepping. She seemed like someone who prized her solitude. But I had to ask.

ALEX: *Maybe sometime.*

Not a yes. Not a no. That was something.

ME: *I understand. No worries ;)*

ALEX: *I like that. Very cute.*

That was her way of saying I wasn't going to see her this morning. She had that neighborhood visit. She was going, and I wasn't invited.

ME: *Well, if I'm not going to see you today, would you mind texting me after lunch?*

I wasn't proud of how much I cared. But the thought of her wandering those streets, even with her confidence and sharp tongue, didn't sit right with me.

ALEX: *I'll talk to you later.*

That was it. That was all I was getting.

Normally, I made it a rule not to work weekends—for my sanity—but not today. Today I was going to bury myself in files and project maps and anything else that kept me from tracking her location like some kind of lunatic.

I could wait.
But I wouldn't be patient about it.

***

ALEX

Boy, this man is good.

How in the hell did he get me to give him so much information about my weekend? I bet he starts showing up at the coffee shop now. Why is he so adamant on spending time with me? Yes, I wanted to see him too. I wanted him to stay last night, and I wanted to see him this morning, but that's exactly the reason I had to say no. I don't need the distraction. I'd never get anything accomplished with him around, clouding my better judgment. I wouldn't get out of bed at five a.m. if he was in it next to me, that's for sure. It would be a miracle if I made it out of my bed by noon.

Why can't he understand my life was fine without him in it? Because that's just not true. *He's amazing.* My shoulders slumped and I felt myself about to start pouting. He seems to genuinely care about me and he's respectful. He didn't try a damn thing with me, and we have, mostly, good conversations. I enjoyed spending time with him last night, but my life was going so well before he came into it. In fact, I feel like the minute he came into my life is when the shit started hitting the fan. Now he has me second guessing who I am and what I should be doing with my life, not to mention how I should be doing business. That thought got me fired right back up. I snapped out of the sappy mood and sat up straight with a glare on my face. Remembering the conversation in my apartment the day my dad had his heart attack was starting to build that wall up even higher and thicker. I don't know if anyone is going to be tough enough to penetrate it. It's made from some pretty strong historical bullshit.

Around noon, I called Ella and told her I was leaving home shortly. I offered to stop and pick up lunch for us and she told me that she already made us something to eat and was looking forward to our chat.

I grabbed my things and headed out to the car. As much as I wanted to help everyone in the neighborhood, I realized I may only have one friend there. From my previous interaction with the police, I have a feeling they wouldn't be too happy running into me again either.

This was out of my element, but it didn't mean it always had to be that way. I genuinely felt a connection to Ella. I didn't know what it was, but every fiber of my being wanted to be her friend and help her.

The ride over gave me time to think about what I wanted to accomplish. I needed to tell her what was about to happen to her neighborhood then come up with some way to save it. Maybe a historical preservation petition. I really had no idea what I was going to do, and I may not be able to do anything. Maybe my brother was right, and my job was to help them relocate. This was not a relaxing drive, I had too much going on in my head. I turned up the radio as loud as I could stand to drown out the mental noise.

I pulled up to Ella's house and parked in her driveway around the back where she told me to so that we didn't draw unwanted attention to my presence.

I hoped Ella was looking forward to my visit, but I knew that others here didn't feel the same way. In fact, from what Ella told me on the phone, most of the residents thought I was part of the revamping project. I went in through the back door as Ella instructed, and I was greeted warmly with a big hug. We proceeded to the living room—arms linked.

"I knew I liked you," I said as I took a seat and crossed my legs to make myself comfortable.

"How did you know that?"

"That hug you gave me. I knew you gave hugs like that— I could just tell." She laughed as she reached out, patting my arm gently.

"Yes, I'm a hugger. My grandson thinks it's embarrassing, but I do it anyway."

"Good! Never let anyone tell you what to do or how to hug."

Her laughter was so genuine and lit up her whole face. Somehow, I knew that no one told Big Mama what to do.

"Never have, never will."

I felt a connection I couldn't yet pinpoint.

"So, Ella, tell me a little about you. I really want to understand your connection to the neighborhood. I think that will help me help you more."

"Like I said before, I've been here my entire life. This is my home. I don't know any other place. I don't want to lose it. My kids grew up here and their kids grew up here." I felt a tug on my heart as tears welled in her eyes— she blinked them away trying to be strong. It's a reaction I'm very familiar with.

"Do you have boys, girls, both?" Her smile looked strained and uncomfortable.

"I have a daughter that I haven't seen or spoken to in ten years, and I have, I mean, had a son." She paused as sadness filled her eyes. "He passed away a few years ago." My hand flew up to my mouth automatically.

"Oh, Ella, I'm so sorry. You don't have to talk about it if you don't want to." I felt so bad for drudging up old painful memories.

"It's okay. It was an overdose. He was never into drugs but when he lost his job a few years ago something changed. He moved in with me and brought his three boys with him." I wanted to commiserate with her by telling her about my mom's struggles with alcohol, but I refrained letting her story be my focus.

"Ella, are you raising three young boys on your own?"

"No, Alex, they're not that young. But they are good boys, and I don't want them to end up like their dad. I made sure they have plenty to keep them occupied. My oldest grandson, Darius, is twenty-two, Isaac and Dante are teenagers in high school. They're all out now. The younger two are at sports camp and Darius is hopefully staying out of trouble." She smiled and her eyes lit up with pride speaking of *her boys*.

I shook off the thoughts of my mom wanting to steer the conversation back to the reason I was here. "Ok, now what about the good stuff?" I continued, "Ella, is there anything I can do for you?"

"What can a sweet little girl like you possibly do to change any of the evil around here?"

That didn't sound good. *Evil?*

"Good question, my friend. I first need to know what sort of evil you speak of." This is the first time I felt a little worried about this area.

"Well, it seems there's more going on around here than people really want us to know."

"Tell me what you do know." I clasped my hands on my lap and listened intently.

"This stretch of street has been built up on either side because everyone left. I heard they got paid a lot of money. This section took so long because none of us wants to give in to their extortion." What the hell was going on around here?

"Who are you talking about? Who's paying all this money?" My worry was building.

"I was told they were just investors and to mind my business..."

Does Roman know who bought all this property? I work with investors. Is it Stewart and Owen?

"...and then when I said I didn't want to accept the offer all of a sudden the offers were more like threats, and I started to see a particular politician in the area chatting with people across the street."

Politician? I took a deep breath to try and relax. I was getting worked up, I could feel it.

"Well now that's interesting." I tried to stay calm as best I could. "How have the police been since all this came about? Do you know which politician it is?"

"Well, it's like the police no longer do their jobs. The politician is the one all over the TV all the time." She was waving her hand around trying to think. "You know who I'm talking about don't you?" She asked.

I nodded. "Like they're letting the street go, so people want to leave?" I was pretty sure I knew of only one politician that loved being on TV, and that was Marcus Ellington. I met him years ago at one of those schmoozing parties with Luke. Gave me the creeps. I sighed deeply. "Yeah, I know the guy you're talking about." He had a horrible reputation for being cruel. I might be biting off more than I could chew but damn it if I didn't hate people being taken advantage of.

"Exactly. The crime and the drugs have gotten so much worse."

"When did all this start?"

"Maybe a couple of years ago."

"And where do things stand now?" *How far along is this project?* I wondered.

"I have thirty days to sell my home and another thirty to find a place and move out."

Oh my God, I'm too late. My heart stopped. They were just stealing her home to make money. This was making me sick to my stomach, especially knowing that Roman was a part of it. Does he know Marcus too?

"Ella, I don't know what I can do if anything, but you can damn sure believe I'm going to try to do something. If nothing else, I'll help you find another place to live. I'm a realtor, but I'd really like to do more. Sixty days may not be enough time to figure something out, but I promise you that I will try." I took both of her hands in mine. "Please call me if you need anything and don't accept any deals without me present, okay? I am, as of right now, your realtor and anyone wanting to talk to you about your house has to go through me." I was fired up and my hands were shaking with adrenaline pumping through me.

I let go of her hands and started rummaging through my purse for a pen and paper then wrote down a bit of information to seal the deal and had her sign it. I took a picture of it and emailed it to myself and Shay so that on Monday morning we could write up a contract.

If I couldn't save her house, I was going to get her the best deal I could. I made a note to make an appointment for her to come to the office this week and we would get all the information together. I saw tears welling up in her eyes as she signed that piece of paper. My chest squeezed.

"I don't know what to say. I thought I was going to have to do this by myself. The boys don't know everything about what's going on and they don't know we may have to move." She swallowed, shaking her head as her face fell. "I thought my son's death was hard and then having to raise the boys, but at least I still had my house. What am I going to do now?" Her head bowed as her hands squeezed the sofa cushions on either side of her legs.

"First thing we need to do is find out how far along this project really is. Next thing I want you to do is make sure you let your grandsons know. You don't need to go through this alone. I'll be here to help as well. We'll just have to play it by ear after that." She reached out, pulling me into a tight hug.

"Thank you so much." I gripped her tight and squeezed my eyes shut containing the tears that were threatening to spill over. I needed to be strong for her right now.

I'm also going to find out what was going on around here. You don't treat people like this. I could feel my hands begin to tremble. I don't like seeing people scared. She doesn't deserve this. I could just scream. How sick is it that people take advantage of other people this way? Threatening them out of their homes? Well, they messed with the wrong woman this time. I guess running out of gas was for a reason after all.

We said our goodbyes and I left out the back door. I was putting my purse on the passenger seat when I felt a strong hand grip me around my upper arm then I lost my footing as I spun around into the side of the car. It hurt but the shock kept me from reacting-it all happened so fast. I pushed myself away from the car and two hands rammed into my shoulders, shoving me back against the door. That knocked the wind out of me with a loud grunt. I opened my eyes to see it was a young man, maybe eighteen, at most. I'd never seen him before. He was at least six inches taller than me, but I was ready to defend myself. He started screaming at me that I didn't belong here and that I was destroying their homes.

"I am not a part of that," I said through gritted teeth. I tried to be as calm as I could while also heaving to get the air back in my lungs.

"You're a lying bitch." He spit the words into my face, and I turned my head. There was no sense in trying to argue with him— he was out of control.

Ella came running out when she heard the commotion, "What do you think you're doing? You leave her alone, right now!"

He yelled back at her without taking his eyes off me, "Shut up and go back inside old lady."

I motioned for her with my hand that I was okay and shook my head lightly so she wouldn't come out any further, and that's when he stepped away from me. I thought he was leaving but he gave me an evil little smirk, pulling a large knife out of his pocket. *Oh shit.*

"Bitch, don't think you got no control over no one in this neighborhood. I will slit your fucking throat." I swallowed and a calm came over me like I was stepping out of my body and someone else was taking over, and she was really pissed.

"I told you I'm not part of what's going on around here." I kept my voice controlled and steady too. This is the voice that I remembered hearing when my mom and Luke got verbally abusive with me. This, however, wasn't verbal abuse. This felt like life and death.

I yelled to Ella without taking my eyes off the knife wielder in front of me. "Please call the police." She immediately ran back into the house.

The kid laughed at me, making whatever was happening to me worse.

Whatever this was taking over summoned my courage. "Why don't you put the knife down so this doesn't end badly for anyone." My fists were balled at my sides and rage was flooding my veins.

Just then the man I had a confrontation with on Monday strolled up. *Just what I freaking need—a drug dealer.* My eyes scanned back and forth between the men not wanting to lose sight of either one. My heart was beating out of my chest.

"Grams you alright?" *Grams?* This was a revelation. I held my gaze on Ella's grandson in surprise and my lip twitched, but smiling in front of this other young man was probably a bad idea.

Ella replies, "Yes honey I'm fine, but Alex here may need some assistance." She looked at me and winked. I couldn't help but smile when I heard that exchange and felt a little better about my situation now and started to calm down.

Ella's grandson yelled at the boy, "You need to get outta here, right now." I heard the sirens coming down the road.

The kid looked between me and Ella's grandson with that same evil grin on his face. "I'll be seeing you." He tipped his head at me, pointing the knife in my direction.

I returned his evil grin. I couldn't show fear. I won't let him win. "I look forward to it."

He took off out of the yard. I let out the breath I was holding and placed both hands on my knees as I bent over to catch my breath— trying to control my overactive heartbeat.

As I stood up, I looked over at Ella's grandson with a curious smile. "I'd really like to have a word with you." *Why didn't she tell me this was her grandson to begin with?*

He smirked back, but there was no bite to it this time. "I bet you would, but right now you can enjoy the company of your friends." He pointed in the direction of the police cruisers coming down the road.

He left me to deal with the officers on my own. I looked at the cops pulling into the driveway and rolled my eyes, hoping to get this over without incident. It was the same two cops from Monday. Sweat was beading on my forehead as the thought of another confrontation with the police seemed imminent and probably worse than last time since they didn't seem too thrilled with me.

Ella stepped outside on her back porch as the cops were pulling in, squinting her eyes at me. "I may have underestimated you."

"Everyone does," I winked at her and mentioned, "I'll be in touch," waving her back into the house. I wanted to keep her and her family out of this as much as I could. There was something off about these cops.

I turned toward my car door and the officers got out and approached me from both sides. I closed my eyes, taking a deep breath willing this exchange to be over quickly.

"Ms. Kennedy, is it?" I rolled my eyes in the most exaggerated fashion realizing they kept me on their radar.

"How nice of you to remember. I was just leaving." I went to grab the door handle of my SUV but the officer to my left reached out, keeping me from opening it.

He said angrily, "I thought we warned you about bringing trouble here." I felt alarms going off in my head and needed to reign in my temper that's still fresh to keep this from going south.

"What trouble did I bring?" I mumbled. I crossed my arms over my chest to keep them from visibly shaking and firmed up my stance.

"Considering we were called to this house by the owner because a young lady was being threatened with a knife by some punk kid, it seems to me like trouble." *You sound so utterly concerned for me. How nice.*

I looked for his badge since he was reluctant to give me his name last time and he wasn't wearing one. That's not good.

"Thank God you got here so quickly, but maybe you should be chasing after the kid with the knife?" I pointed in the direction the kid took off hoping maybe they'd go after him. No such luck.

The officer had a really pissed look on his face and I thought my attitude was about to get me in trouble. I couldn't seem to keep my mouth under control regardless of what I told myself needed to be done. Something about these two was really prickling my senses.

"Ms. Kennedy, what exactly are you doing here?" Now he was leaning against my car with his arms crossed and the other officer was standing just where I couldn't see him. I turned and glared at him to let him know I knew where he was, too. I checked his chest for a badge quickly and he wasn't wearing one either. Great. I doubt it would be a good idea to ask them if I can take their picture.

"Trying to figure out why no one cares about this place." I felt a little threatened but figured they wouldn't do anything in this driveway. I took a step to angle myself where my back was to my car, and I could see both of them clearly.

"Well after this little incident and the band of thugs from Monday, don't you think that could be a good reason?"

I laughed in frustration thinking that these cops were a band of thugs.

"Seriously?! How do you think they get that way? These kids or men whatever you want to call them didn't come out of their mamas this way. They were innocent babies. I'm sick of everyone being reactive instead of proactive. Why do we wait until things get out of control to try and fix them?" Now my hands were on my hips, and I was standing up a lot straighter. I might want to back this down a bit. Going on some bad parenting tirade might not be the best idea.

"What are you, some kind of therapist or reporter?"

"No, I'm a concerned human being, what are you?" I said as resting bitch face became don't mess with me face. I could tell that he was getting mad as his face started turning red and his eyes turned to slits. He stood toe to toe with me, glaring down at me. I didn't move a muscle— clenching my hands around my shirt tightly so I wasn't tempted to push him.

"Why do I get the feeling you're just trying to annoy me into leaving this place alone?" I asked to distract him.

"Is it working?" he glanced at the other officer quickly then back to me.

"I'll let you know next time." I took a step back to get some more space and was stopped by my car. I felt trapped and nervous now.

"What's with you? Don't you know they're tearing this place down?" I whipped my head to the other officer in utter disgust as he chimed in.

"Yeah, I heard."

"Then why do you care? You don't even live here."

"Are you planning to help everyone relocate and move?" I took a step between the officer and my door, cautiously, hoping he wouldn't try to stop me from getting in my car. I looked him up and down when he didn't move as if to say, *"excuse me."*

"No, why would I?" After what felt like an eternity he moved away from my car.

I shook my head in awe of his less than helpful public servant attitude and silently thanked God neither of them put their hands on me. "That's exactly why I keep coming back. Because I would." They looked so baffled by me, like most people do.

"After that little asshole pulled a knife on you, you would still come back here and help?"

I was exasperated with this guy. It was like he couldn't hear a word I was saying, or he just didn't care.

"He's a freaking kid. Clearly, he has no guidance, no structure and no one seems to give a damn. I feel sorry for him, but if people were more willing to help these kids you wouldn't have these issues." I threw my hands in the air and grabbed the handle of the door, hoisting myself in.

He just smirked and rolled his eyes.

"Please find a different place to try and save the world. You don't know what you're getting yourself into here."

"I'll keep that in mind." Then I shut the door. I had a death grip on the steering wheel as my knuckles turned white and I was actively holding my breath. *What am I getting myself into here?* That's a good question.

The officers got back in their cruiser and left. I put my head back and screamed at the top of my lungs "AAAAHHHH." Seriously, what is happening, why is this happening?

I sat there for a minute in silence then I turned the car on, cranking up the radio as loud as I could stand. I noticed from the display on the console I had a bunch of missed calls. I'll have to deal with that when I get home. I'm not in the mood and I cleared the notifications from the screen.

The phone rang again. I was planning to ignore it too but noticing it was Ella— I answered it. She was laughing when I said hello.

"My grandson likes you."

I laughed back, almost deliriously. "Are you serious?"

"He called you white girl Rambo!" I lost it. *What?*

"Why would that make you think he liked me?"

"Because he gave you a nickname."

Oh geez, a nickname? I've been called worse.

"Well, I want to feel flattered about that, but the cops told me he was a drug dealer." I heard a pause and the laughter stopped.

"My boy ain't no drug dealer." I had a feeling I already knew that.

"I know, I just wanted to see if the cops were lying to me."

"They ain't no good, you need to watch yourself with them." Her light mood seemed to be gone now. She sounded worried.

"I've recently been told I have personal safety issues, so I doubt I'll watch myself too closely, but I appreciate your concern, nonetheless."

She chuckled and I was glad to lighten the mood again.

"We need to talk more because I see something in your grandson that could help me. Why didn't you tell me he was your grandson the last time I was here?" I had a really good feeling about him.

"You're right, I am concerned about you, and the last time you were here I didn't know you, and I'm very protective of my grandchildren. You're a good person, Alex, and I don't want to see nothing bad happen to you."

"Thanks, Ella." It was nice to know an almost complete stranger could see things in me that I couldn't see in myself.

"So, what do you think my grandson has that could possibly help you?" she asked curiously.

"Leadership skills." I'm good at reading people and developing latent talents. I just need to uncover them.

"Yes, he does." I could hear the pride in her voice. It made me feel hopeful that this was the right decision.

"Put in a good word for me that I'd really like to have a serious conversation with him."

"I most definitely will."

That was productive, I think.

Chapter 12

ALEX

I pulled into my apartment building, grabbing my purse as I hopped out of the car and handed the valet my key. There were missed calls and texts from Maggie, Abby, Roman, and Mr. Santoro. I'll have a longer discussion with Mr. Santoro later when I can be in front of my computer.

I guess Roman's freaking out from the three-minute voicemail he left. He knew where I was going to be this afternoon and it seemed to have worried him so I decided to call him in the elevator so he wouldn't send out a search party or call the police. He picked up on the first ring. I wondered if he was staring at his phone, he picked up so fast.

"Are you okay?" He almost sounded frantic.

I responded in my usual sarcastic way, "Well, hello to you, too."

"I'm sorry. Hello. I guess that answers my question, you're alive."

"Of course. Why wouldn't I be?" I mean seriously, this guy is a little intense.

"I don't know, because you didn't pick up your phone or respond to texts and you weren't exactly in the best part of town. Plus, we both know that you have safety issues."

I laughed as I flipped my hair out of my face.

"I need you to take a breath. Geez, you sound like my dad. Thank you for being concerned but I'm a big girl, I can take care of myself. There may have been a small incident with a knife, but no big deal." With that the line went completely silent and I started giggling.

Why do I have to push people? I didn't have to tell him about the incident.

"Roman, are you still there?" I giggled more.

He finally spoke, "That isn't funny."

"Which part wasn't funny?"

"What part do you think?" he snapped and I held in the laugh trying to escape. Ok, so I may have pushed too far with that one.

"I don't know, I didn't even tell you what happened yet."

"The part with the knife, Alex."

"Oh, yeah, that wasn't the funny part. The funny part was your reaction."

"You think me having a heart attack is funny."

"I don't think you can actually have a heart attack that way and yes, a kid may have pulled a knife on me..." I was about to say more but he had a complete freak out.

"Are you freaking kidding me right now?" he yelled so loud I had to pull the phone back from my ear.

I decided to give him a few details of the events to hopefully calm him down. "No. I told Ella to call the police and her grandson stepped in to help me diffuse the situation before the cops got there. I did get chastised by the police again and treated like I'm just some dumb woman, though." It seemed like he wasn't really listening anymore. I stood next to the counter and leaned against it placing my elbow on top while I rested my face in my hand waiting for his next reply.

After about a minute he asked, "Where are you right now?" His tone was much more subdued.

"Home," I simply stated. I didn't appreciate his reaction at all.

"May I please come see you?" I could hear the caution in his tone. I think he understood that with one more outburst, I would hang up.

"I have to get ready for Maggie's BBQ." That was the last thing I was truly thinking of right now, but I didn't want to escalate things.

"Please, I just need to see you, see that you're alright. I can be there in ten minutes."

I sighed loudly. *Why does he care so much?*

"If it'll make you feel better, sure."

"I'll be there shortly," and the line went dead.

I went straight to the liquor cabinet, grabbing the vodka. I really hadn't had time to process any of what had just happened to me, and I was afraid that it was going to hit me hard when it did, so I needed liquor back up right now.

I grabbed a shot glass from the cabinet, taking a shot of vodka then putting the glass in the dishwasher and the vodka back in the cabinet, so there's no evidence of my true state of mind. As fine as I was telling myself I was, I couldn't stop shaking. I held my hand up, watching the tremors as I used the other hand to try and rub the shaking out. *Yeah, my nerves were shot.*

My heart was pounding, and I couldn't calm my breath down. I felt like I was going to hyperventilate. I probably wouldn't be feeling this as much except Roman had a way of twisting my reality to something much scarier than it was, and it was affecting me.

The vodka wasn't working fast enough either. I needed to calm down before he arrived.

I walked quickly down the hall to my room. I needed to do something to pull me out of this. *I know, I'll change clothes.* I put on a cute short sleeved one shoulder fuchsia shirt and paired it with white shorts and black flip flops. I needed a pop of color to make me feel less stressed and relaxed. *"Color therapy"* was what my mother called it. I didn't feel like doing my hair, and knowing we'd be outside anyway, I just threw it up in a messy bun. No need to fight the humidity too.

I called Maggie on my way out to the living room.

She picked up the phone with a quick greeting, "Hey Jerk, where the heck have you been?" I laughed because that was just what I needed to hear right now to take my mind off the events of the day.

"Avoiding my haters!"

She laughed. "You can come over whenever you want."

"What should I bring?"

"How about chips and dessert of some kind?"

"Ok, I'll stop on the way." I was thinking about how to ask the next question, that just popped into my head without warning, and I'm not even sure why.

"Everything alright?" she asked knowing the three of us can always tell when the other has something going on.

I snapped out of my daydream and mumbled, "Yeah, um, I just wanted to know if I could bring someone?"

"Do I know this someone?" Her voice was higher pitched and curious.

"I think you may have seen him the last time we saw each other."

She squealed with excitement.

"Oh my God, yes of course. But wait, when did this happen?" At that moment there was a knock at the door and my eyes darted in that direction.

"Details tomorrow at brunch. For now, I'll just see you soon."

She squealed again.

"You're damn right you will." We hung up on that very high-pitched note and I opened the door.

He was standing there holding flowers and if I wasn't so mad, I would have swooned.

"Hi," he said with an apologetic smile on his face.

"Are the flowers for my grave?" I raised an eyebrow, crossing my arms over my chest. He was totally taken aback.

"Excuse me? Why the hell would you say that?" He looked outraged but then again, so was I.

"Because you seem to think I'm going to get myself killed. Look, my mind just doesn't work like that, and I don't like it when you point out everything you think I'm being careless about. It freaks me out."

His face fell and I wanted to comfort him, but refrained, instead, waiting for what he had to say for himself. "I'm sorry, I didn't realize I had that effect on you. I just worry about you. I've never met a woman who would literally run into danger."

What? I'm not some damn thrill seeker.

"I don't put myself in danger. I understand that the neighborhood I visited today has its issues. It's why I announced to the police and the locals that I would be there today. The dude with the knife was a dumb kid. I have more issues with why the cops don't care and what you and your people are doing to that neighborhood than being afraid of the residents." He couldn't even bring himself to look at me at that point, letting out a woosh of air as he turned his head away.

When he finally did look at me, he admitted, "I feel like a total creep right now. Would you like me to leave?" My guard lowered after that.

No, I don't want you to leave—the opposite actually.

I smiled, looking thoughtfully into his eyes still feeling that undeniable connection that grounded me.

"Actually, I'd like you to join me at Maggie's BBQ." He smiled. What a beautiful smile it is too. It melted my frozen heart.

"Really, are you being serious?"

"Yes. Don't think this is going to be fun." I pointed out. "I'm doing this so I can enjoy the party while you get interrogated. My friends will want to know everything about you, and you'll have to be uncomfortable and figure out what to call whatever this is between us. I'll be off the hook."

He laughed. "And what should I call us?"

I shook my head and smiled. *No earthly idea.* I'm as confused by that as he must be.

"You aren't getting any help from me."

In truth, I just didn't want to be alone, and he made me feel safe. He didn't expect anything from me, and he seemed to know what I needed. I just didn't feel like letting him in on what's behind the wall yet. I wasn't ready for the whole boyfriend thing either because he was already kind of territorial towards me, and I don't know how much of this closeness I can handle for too much longer.

"Can I make something up then?" *I'm not really a fan of lying.* I had enough of that with my ex.

"You can say anything you want, as long as it's true." I wiggled my brows and smiled, wondering how he was going to maneuver that.

He frowned and even that was cute, I thought. "What if I don't know if it's true or not?" *Good question.* I'm not too sure what I want out of this relationship right now anyway.

"Then you better find out the truth." He looked puzzled, like he was really contemplating what I had said, as if there was some way to actually figure it out.

"Is there some place other than your grave I can put these flowers?" It seemed he had resigned to giving up on our little game. I smiled when I realized he was still holding the most beautiful bouquet of purple and yellow flowers, so I ran and got a vase out from under the sink.

"Yes, they can go in here. They're beautiful, by the way. What kind are they?" I'd never seen flowers like that before. They looked like daisies, but they had yellow petals and sort of faded to purple with a dark yellow center.

"The lady at the counter told me they were African daisies." *Huh, so they are daisies.* I may have to start ordering those for the office instead of the roses and carnations.

"I'm sorry for lashing out about that."

"Yeah well, I guess I'm just not used to your quips yet." *Yet? He's planning on sticking around, I take it.*

"What makes you think you'll be around long enough to get used to them?"

He bowed his head while slowly shaking it and I could feel the enormity of his eye roll.

"Stop, now you're just hurting my feelings."

I held in my laugh as long as I could while watching the smile on his face grow wider and we both started laughing. He pulled me in for a hug and I felt a calm wash over me. He gave the best hugs. They make you forget there's evil out there in this world and I wrapped my arms around his waist, absorbing as much of his calming energy as I could before releasing him.

"Are we ready? I have to stop and get some chips and a dessert to bring."

"Do you need to bring drinks or anything?"

"Nope, they'll have plenty."

"Sounds good."

"I have some questions for you while I'm thinking of it, so you're driving." I needed to figure out his relationship to Marcus Ellington.

"Okay, I can handle that."

I grabbed my things as he put his hand on my lower back, leading us toward the elevator.

I was leaning against the back wall of the elevator like I normally do to keep from feeling too much of the height dizziness, and he started scooting closer to me. I side eyed him trying to figure out what he was doing. He was being nonchalant and sly then he turned in one swift movement, putting his hands next to my head on the wall, pressing his body gently into me. I wasn't sure what he was trying to do but I didn't want to move. I wanted to feel every inch of his body touching every inch of mine. I was drawn to him like he was a magnet. At this moment I couldn't even feel the usual sensations I got from being up too high. It was something completely different. He didn't try to kiss me or anything, he was staring at me, straight into my soul. All of a sudden I felt lightheaded, like the air was being sucked out of the elevator. He leaned his head down and I felt his lips barely brush against my ear and volts of electricity shooting through me everywhere. My eyes closed automatically— transporting me somewhere else entirely.

He whispered, "I just wanted to see if you felt the same way I do."

I barely had enough breath to get words out. "And how do you feel?"

Before he could respond, the elevator stopped to let someone on, and he casually returned to the spot next to me. I followed him with my head, taking inventory of him from head to toe since I was too mad to do it in my apartment. His white linen shirt was rolled up at the sleeves, showing his very tan muscular forearms with his trademark top two buttons undone. *I think I might be drooling.* I ran my tongue over my bottom lip to casually check. His khaki shorts landed mid-thigh, fitting snugly around those lean muscles. I looked him over thoroughly. I swear there wasn't an ounce of fat on him. He was wearing tan and brown leather boat shoes with no socks, yet again, and somehow I found that sexy as well.

I didn't seem to care that there was another person on the elevator watching me look him up and down, like I was going to devour him whole. Roman finally broke the silence and politely said hi to her. That brought me out of it long enough I slowly turned my head to acknowledge and smiled at the woman. She smiled back, raising her eyebrows, as she turned away abruptly as if saying *"Get a room."*

When the doors opened before we stepped out, he took my arm in his hand, gently pulling me to him. He whispered to me seductively, "Now you know how I feel." I gasped and he let go of my arm, taking my hand, almost possessively, to usher me to the car. But if he hadn't escorted me this time, I would've gotten hit crossing the street.

Chapter 13

ROMAN

Alex was quiet. That wasn't unusual—but this was a different kind of silence. Tense. Heavy.

"Alex," I said gently.

She turned to me like she hadn't even heard me speak. "Huh?"

I smiled, but I wasn't convinced she was okay. "What's going on in there? I thought you had questions for me."

She looked at me, a slow smirk tugging at her lips. "Oh, I do. A lot of them. But they can wait. Let's just get going."

She pulled one leg up on the seat, rested her elbow on the window, and tucked her chin into her hand. She was shutting down again, pulling away when things got too close, maybe. I didn't push. I just drove.

The longer we sat in the car, the thinner the air felt. She was wound tight, and whatever she'd been through earlier hadn't left her yet. I didn't blame her—someone had pulled a knife on her. And even though she played it off like a joke, I knew it rattled her. It rattled me.

When we pulled into the neighborhood, I raised a brow. "Nice place. What do your friends do?"

"They're housewives," she said, smiling like that was a punchline.

I waited.

She continued, "Their husbands are lawyers. One of them's also a politician."

I caught the faintest shift in her expression—guarded.

"Ah. So this is where the lawyers and politicians live," I said with a chuckle. Maybe there was a jab in there. Maybe not.

She shot me a glance. "Looking for any in particular?"

There it was—that edge. I held her gaze. She was fishing for something. Maybe she suspected something I wasn't aware of.

"Nope," I said easily. "Just making small talk. You seemed quiet."

"Oh yeah," she said, almost too quickly. "Nothing to worry about."

Not yet, I thought. But I let it go.

I don't know what kind of barbeque this was but there were a lot of cars parked everywhere. We had to walk from down the block. By the time we made it to the back gate, she looked tense. The house itself was white brick, black shutters—classic political ambition on display. Her friend Maggie's husband definitely had his eye on more than city council.

Alex punched in a code and led us through the side gate instead of going through the house. I heard music and splashing and kids screaming before we even rounded the corner.

She grinned like a little kid and snuck up behind someone and yelled, "BOO!"

The woman jumped a foot in the air.

"You jerk!" The woman shouted, then spun around and pulled Alex into a massive hug. She seemed familiar, but I couldn't put my finger on where.

Then her eyes fell on me, and she gave me the kind of once-over that made me feel like I was about to be cross-examined in open court.

"Roman, is it? Maggie" she said, offering her hand.

I returned her smile and shook it. "Hi Maggie. Thanks for having me."

Her eyebrows arched with interest as she glanced at Alex. I was definitely about to be interrogated.

Before I could even step away, another woman with sharp eyes and an even sharper voice called out, "Well, hello Alex, where the heck have you been?"

Then her eyes locked onto me. She looked familiar as well and it dawned on me these women were at the hospital the day of her father's heart attack.

"Oh no, mister. Get your butt over here. Who are you, and how did you manage to talk to our girl before we did?"

I walked up behind Alex and slipped my arms around her waist, leaning close and resting my chin on her shoulder. I needed something to ground me.

"I'm Roman," I said, then reached around to shake her hand. "I used my superpowers on her."

Abby snort laughed and looked to Alex whose whole body stiffened as she tilted her head to let me know the woman's name was Abby in a breathless whisper. Maybe she wasn't so grounding after all.

"That's only if your superpowers involve dumb luck." Alex said as she slipped from my arms, giving me a look that was half exasperation, half... something else. Desire, maybe. I'd seen that look before. I wonder...

"I ran into him at the bar last night," she said to Abby and Maggie. "He gave me a ride home. And broke some guy's nose for me."

I gave her a look. Really? You're opening with that? The last thing anyone needs to remember about me is a temper that sometimes I have trouble controlling.

She smirked with a tilt of her head, like a cat who'd just knocked over a vase on purpose.

Before I could say a word, she bailed. "I'm going to get a drink. You want something, Roman?"

"Something tall," I said, gesturing with my hands far apart insinuating very tall.

She winked and gave me two thumbs up before vanishing into the crowd.

Maggie ran off yelling at someone by the pool. Abby, however, stepped closer. Her expression had shifted. The teasing was gone.

"This isn't going to be the interrogation she warned you about," Abby said coolly. "But let's pretend you know anything about Alex. Why the hell did you break someone's nose for her?"

I crossed my arms and tried to keep my tone calm. Alex had told me earlier I could say anything—as long as it was true and these are her friends—there was going to be questions.

"I overheard some guy talking about her," I said. "He said some awful things. Whether or not they were true didn't matter. I didn't like it. And I acted. It wasn't my proudest moment."

"Were the things he said true?" she pressed, shifting her weight with her arms crossed tight.

I shrugged. "I don't know. Didn't ask. Didn't care. It wasn't my business. She made me tell her, and it made me sick just to repeat it."

Maggie had come back, watching quietly. Abby gave her a little nod—some kind of silent message passed between them.

Before I could figure it out, Alex reappeared with drinks—white wine for her, cold beer for me.

"Well," Maggie said, placing a hand on my shoulder, "this one's not so bad."

Alex raised an eyebrow. "We're definitely talking about this at brunch tomorrow, aren't we?"

They shrugged in unison. With a look that said, definitely.

I needed a diversion fast.

"Well, ladies," I said, "since I haven't made it inside yet, how about you introduce me to your husbands? Let's knock out all the scary interactions in one go."

They laughed, linking arms through mine and dragging me toward the grill while Alex wandered in the opposite direction, toward the pool and the screaming kids. I watched her kneel down as three little ones tackled her with hugs.

It caught me off guard how natural she looked with them. How happy. It stirred something in me I hadn't expected. A thought I wasn't quite ready for. *Family.*

We made it to the grill, where two guys were talking about sports—which I could not care less about.

"This is Jack," Abby said. "My husband."

I reached out to shake his hand and introduce myself. "Nice to meet you Jack. I'm Roman King."

"Matt," Maggie added. "Mine."

"Roman King," Matt said, his eyes narrowing slightly. "As in King Construction?"

I nodded. "Yeah. You're...?"

"Matt Stevens. I'm the rep for District 5—next to Burrow Township. I've been trying to work with Marcus Ellington to relocate residents from his district into mine. He won't even return my calls. But I saw your name on some of the development paperwork, alongside your brother's, Harrison, I believe. He part of the investor group?"

I tightened my grip on the beer bottle. Not the time. Not the place. And not the conversation I wanted to have with Alex ten feet away.

"Well," I said carefully, "it sounds like you have more info than I do. Honestly, I need to get caught up before I can speak to anything with confidence."

Matt backed off immediately, raising his hands. "Totally fair. Sorry, that was out of line. I've had a few drinks."

Abby and Maggie looked nervous, but I'm not sure why unless they all know something I don't.

Jack jumped in. "Roman, I heard you protected Alex last night?"

I laughed. "Have you met Alex? She can handle herself. Probably didn't even need me."

They all nodded and laughed.

"She wasn't always like that, ya know." Matt said, and Maggie shot him a glare.

"Wasn't always like what?" I asked.

"Angry," Abby replied. "Confrontational."

"Geez," Maggie muttered.

"Did something happen I should be aware of?" I asked, watching Maggie's face fall.

"Growing up with an alcoholic mom... a messy divorce... yeah. That'll change a person," Maggie said softly. "Okay, that's enough." She shook her head. "No more talking about Alex behind her back."

They moved on from there, keeping things light. But my mind lingered. That's the second time someone has mentioned Alex's divorce. I wonder what happened that was so traumatic.

Later, I asked Matt for his number. I'd have Amelia set up a meeting. He knew things I didn't, and I needed to get ahead of this. Not just for the sake of business...

...but for Alex.

***

ALEX

While Maggie and Abby carted Roman off to meet their husbands, I made a beeline for the kids—my godchildren: Cameron, Sophia Grace, and Jax. Seeing them always made my heart ache a little. I loved them more than I could explain, but sometimes I couldn't help but wish I had kids of my own. A husband. A house full of chaos that belonged to me. I hated that little twinge of loneliness, but those three always filled the void, even just for a few hours.

I took a seat on the lounger and all three jumped into my lap. They were all talking at once, telling me about nothing and everything. Riding bikes, sleepovers, movies, board games, coloring. Ordinary stuff that somehow felt sacred.

I glanced over to see where Roman had ended up and spotted him in the thick of it, right there with Abby, Maggie, and their husbands. Laughing, talking. He looked like he belonged. Relaxed, like he fit in. I watched him for a second too long. He only looked over once, probably to check if I was coming to rescue him. I almost laughed. This is what I thought I wanted. To relax and hang with the kids while he braved the interrogation.

So why did it twist something in my stomach to see him fitting in so well?

Why was it so hard to let myself have this? This version of life. Of peace. Why did I keep telling myself I didn't want it when my heart clearly did?

It had to be the ghosts. My mother. My ex-husband. The weight of their voices still echoing through my thoughts, even years later. Maybe I needed to talk to someone. Or maybe this was just how I was wired now—always bracing for the next emotional earthquake.

Still, I felt better next to the kids. I didn't want to rejoin the adults just yet. I pulled the three of them into a hug, letting their joy soak into me.

"Let's ask your parents if you can have a sleepover soon," I said, grinning. "Pizza, movies, ice cream. The whole deal."

They screamed "YES!" in perfect unison, and I reluctantly made my way back to the grown-up corner of the yard.

I snuck up behind Roman and gave him a quick pat on the back. He looked down and wrapped an arm around my shoulders, pressing a kiss to the top of my head. Sweet. Comfortable. But I still slipped out of his embrace—carefully—and went to greet Matt and Jack with hugs.

As I hugged Matt, he leaned down and whispered, "This guy really likes you. Hope you know that."

I smiled softly. "I do."

He gave my shoulder a gentle squeeze.

Jack murmured, "The kids really miss their Aunt Ali." He lifted his glass to me in that warm, brotherly kind of way.

"I miss them too," I said, looping an arm around him. "Just told them I'd ask if we could do a movie night sleepover. Pizza, games, the works."

Maggie lit up. "Absolutely. Just pick a day."

Abby nodded, practically bouncing. "They're all yours."

That perked me right up. I needed that. Needed *them*.

As the night stretched on and the kids went to bed, the firepit took center stage. Roman hadn't had anything to drink since his first beer, probably because he was driving—and maybe because something was sitting heavy on his mind after talking with Matt and Jack. I didn't push. I figured I'd get the details either from him or more likely, from Maggie and Abby at brunch tomorrow.

We laughed a lot. Told stories. Teased each other like siblings. It felt good—normal. And just like that, hours slipped past without us even noticing.

Eventually, I leaned toward Roman and whispered, "We should probably head out. I've got brunch in the morning, and I wouldn't mind some alone time. With you." I felt like there was something awkwardly happening between us.

I hugged everyone goodbye, and they made it very clear how much they liked him. Great. Now I had *that* bouncing around in my head the whole ride home. Does that mean I have to see where this goes? I don't know if I'm ready for a *"boyfriend"* right now.

He held my hand as we walked to the car, and I still didn't hate it. He opened the door for me, like he always did. Like a damn gentleman.

What the hell is my problem?

Why is this so hard for me?

I don't want to be the overly emotional girl I've been lately. I feel like a walking Pinterest quote about vulnerability. God, I've been such a whiner.

The ride home was quiet. I leaned my head against the window, eyes half-lidded. I wasn't sleepy, just—processing. Everything.

"Thank you," I finally said, voice low. "For being so great with my friends. They really like you." I wasn't lying. All that was perfect. It was me who was having the issues.

"It was fun. You have good friends," he said, glancing over at me.

I smiled, resting my head back against the glass.

When we pulled into the valet, he was already out of the car, walking around as the valet opened my door. He didn't say goodbye. Just looked at me with those unreadable eyes.

"You don't have to come up if you don't want to," I said quietly. Which was code for *please come up but don't make me say it out loud.* I wasn't sure how much of a gentleman he really was.

His voice was soft. "Mind if I at least ride the elevator with you? Just want to make sure you get in safe."

I nodded. He took my hand as he handed the keys off to the valet, walking with me toward the building.

In the elevator, I leaned into him, head resting on his shoulder. I felt safe there—something I wasn't ready to admit to him yet.

We got to my door. I walked inside without saying a word thinking he would just follow.

But he didn't so I didn't close it.

I turned and looked at him, smiled and asked cautiously, "Would you like to come in?"

He followed, shutting the door gently behind him.

***

ROMAN

An invitation.

I hesitated for half a second—long enough to be sure I wasn't misreading it then stepped inside.

"Would you like a glass of wine?" she asked, already heading toward the kitchen.

"Sure, if you're having one," I said, watching her move—easy, fluid, like she was trying to hide the slight buzz she probably had from the drinks earlier. But it wasn't drunkenness, instead maybe tired with a side of tipsy. Vulnerable in a way that didn't scare me but made me want to handle her with care. There was something about her behavior tonight that I wanted to discuss with her.

She returned with the wine and curled up next to me on the couch. She clinked her glass against mine and tucked herself into me. Then she reached for the remote and turned on soft classical music.

"I guess we have this in common," she said, glancing up at me through her lashes. She was trying not to make direct eye contact. It was like she was keeping a barrier in place, even as she pressed her body against mine. I know how looking into someone's eyes makes me feel. I wonder if she feels the same way. Overwhelmed and intrusive.

"Yeah," I said, nodding. "I found out the day I brought your car back. I didn't know you liked classical music when I drove you to the hospital that day. I wasn't sure how you'd feel about it—it's not for everyone and we weren't exactly on good speaking terms."

"I listen to it to relax."

"Same here." I hesitated, steadying myself. If I didn't say this now, I knew I'd lose the nerve.

"Alex, can I ask you something serious?" I quickly added.

Her body stiffened slightly, but she said, "Sure." Then added with a smirk, "I made you tell the truth tonight. Least I can do is return the favor."

I took a breath, steadying my thoughts.

"Today, Maggie and Abby mentioned some things—about your mom being an alcoholic. And your divorce. Have you ever...seen anyone about that?"

I knew the question could go wrong in a hundred ways. I wasn't trying to analyze her. I wasn't trying to play shrink. But I needed to know how she processed her pain. If she'd ever been allowed to. I think she's got more feelings than most.

She went still beside me. Not defensive. Just quiet.

Then she started talking slowly, almost calculated.

"My mother is an alcoholic, yes. Right out of college, I married my college sweetheart," she said with a bitter little laugh. "He was also an alcoholic. Cheated on me. Emotionally abusive. We divorced after four years." She shook her head. "Sometimes I wonder what kind of pathetic idiot stays in a marriage like that for four years—but I guess that was me. Maybe I didn't think I deserved better. Hell, maybe I was getting what I deserved."

Her voice cracked a little, but she kept going.

"He was friends with Matt and Jack. They don't speak to him anymore, but that probably kept me tethered longer than I should've stayed."

She took a long sip of wine, then continued.

"The divorce devastated me. It was never supposed to be an option." She paused and the look on her face was as if the divorce just happened. "And it broke my mother, too. She started drinking more. Almost died. In and out of the hospital." Her voice dipped, softer now. "I felt like I had to pull it together—to save her, if nothing else. I went to the doctor. Got prescribed a cocktail of meds. I turned into a zombie. So I stopped. Tried alcohol instead. It helped. Or maybe it didn't. I don't know."

She glanced at me, as if gauging my reaction.

"I don't drink like my mother," she added the excuse as if she thought I were judging her. "She drinks because she needs to. I drink because I want to. I can go days, weeks without it. But I like it. I like the atmosphere. I like celebrating things. It doesn't feel like I'm out of control. Most of the time."

Her eyes flickered with something—fear, maybe. Self-doubt. I could see the exhaustion in her shoulders.

I gently took both our glasses and set them on the coffee table. Then I picked up her hands, resting them in mine. Her fingers were warm, slightly trembling. I studied them for a moment, then looked back at her.

"I'm not judging you," I said thoughtfully because I wasn't sure if I was or not at this point. "Or your mom. I know stuff happens and it can suck. I don't know if you're an alcoholic either, but that's not really for me to say either way."

She watched me closely, waiting.

"What I *am* going to say might sound a little weird, but... I think you're an empath."

Her expression blanked. Then she blinked a few times. "That's not what I was expecting you to say. Like someone who feels empathy? Wouldn't that just make me... caring?"

"You're definitely that," I said with a soft smile. "But it's more than that. Do you ever feel like you care more about other people than you do yourself?"

She straightened a little. "I care about myself. I go to the gym, I work hard, I'm successful—" and defensive.

"I know," I said, cutting in with intention to simmer things down. "You do all of that. But do you ever feel overwhelmed by emotions you can't explain? Like you're absorbing the energy around you without even meaning to?"

She paused. Her eyes widened slightly. "Yes." simple answer that she must've thought about more than once.

I nodded. "That's what I mean. Empaths feel everything. We absorb it—carry it—sometimes even when it's not ours to hold. It can be overwhelming. Paralyzing, even."

She was fully alert now, curiosity replacing her wariness.

"Does that happen to you?"

"All the time," I admitted. "Actually, the night I gave you that 'it's just business' speech—when I left your apartment—I was feeling something strong from you. But I didn't want to make it worse, so I shut it down. I didn't tell you the full story about me."

She let out a soft laugh, easing the tension between us. "So I'm crazy, and you're crazy. Perfect."

I grinned. "No. Just different. My mom figured it out about me. She's a psychologist. She taught me how to manage it. How to stop letting other people's pain take me down."

I hesitated, then asked, "Would you have dinner with me tomorrow night? At my family's place?"

That got her attention. She sat up, alarmed almost. "That's kind of serious, don't you think?"

"I just want you to meet my mom. She's the one who helped me. And I think she could help you too. She's not going to shrink you. This isn't therapy."

Alex squinted at me, clearly unsure.

"I don't know. It all sounds a little... magical. Like we're talking about voodoo or something."

I laughed. "I know. I thought the same thing. But it's real. And I think it might give you some peace. That's all I want for you."

She exhaled slowly, then nodded. "Can I think about it?"

"Of course."

She smiled and picked up our wineglasses, handing me mine. "Here, Yoda. Drink up."

I laughed, taking the glass from her. We finished our wine in silence, the soft music wrapping around us like a blanket.

When I finally stood to leave, she looked up at me with sleepy, unreadable eyes.

"Will you stay, please?"

I didn't hesitate.

I sat back down and pulled her into my arms. She nestled into my chest like she was meant to be there.

And for the first time in a long while, I felt like maybe I was right where I was meant to be too.

***

ALEX

The calm I felt with him didn't make any sense. Not the kind of calm you get from wine or a hot bath. It was something deeper—something that made me wonder if he really did have some kind of power over me. Maybe not a superpower, exactly, but still... it was enough to make me want him to stay. Just so I could feel like this a little longer.

It was like my words yanked him back to the sofa. He nodded, pulling me into his arms, settling us back into that same comfortable silence where I felt safe.

That did it. Decision made. I was going to dinner with his family tomorrow. If his mom really did understand whatever *this* was... maybe she could explain what was happening to me.

Because I wasn't used to this. I wasn't used to wanting someone to stay just to snuggle. I didn't want to rip his clothes off. I mean, I *could*—he was ridiculously hot, a total specimen—but that wasn't the urge tonight. I just wanted to be close. To laugh. To talk. To *be*.

And it scared the hell out of me.

When I usually brought someone home, it was with one goal in mind. Distraction. Escape. But this wasn't that. Roman wasn't that. This was something deeper. Something that might unearth feelings I'd buried so deep, I forgot they were there.

"So," he said softly, "do you want me to sleep on the couch? I'd be more than happy to do that."

"Nope," I replied, then tilted my head. "But I do want to know if you're using your superpowers on me right now."

He let out a soft laugh. "I don't have any superpowers."

I smirked at him, not buying it for a second. "You said you did at the BBQ," I teased, wiggling my brows.

He gave me that disarming smile again—the one that made me want to melt. "I'm pretty sure you know that was a joke. Superpowers are for movies, right?"

"I'm not so sure anymore."

He studied me for a moment, then said, "Why don't you tell me how you feel?"

Expressing feelings. Great. My lease favorite activity.

I paused, letting a deep breath fill my lungs before answering, which came easier than I expected.

"I feel like all the anxiety I had about you before is just... gone. Like *poof*." I flicked my fingers. "I feel like I've known you longer than I have. And that I'm safe with you."

Even as I said it, I questioned it. Do I really feel safe with *anyone*?

His voice was soft and gravely. "You are safe with me. I have no desire to take this faster than you're comfortable with. And I'd never take advantage of you in any way—except maybe to get you to go to dinner with me tomorrow."

He pulled me tighter, and I felt something inside me ease. I flipped myself around on the couch so I could face him fully.

"I want to go to your family's house for dinner. I want to meet your mom."

His eyes lit up, full smile breaking across his face. "Yeah?"

I nodded, grinning.

"See? I *do* have superpowers," he said smugly.

I laughed and gave him a playful shove, which only led to him grabbing my arm and pulling me straight into his chest. For a second, we just stared at each other. His eyes found mine, and I felt my gaze drift lower—to his lips. I wanted to kiss him. God, I *wanted* to. But something hit me, all at once—a wave of something hot and tight in my chest.

Overwhelmed.

I dropped my forehead to his chest and used his shoulders to push myself up. "I need to get ready for bed. Brunch with the girls tomorrow... which means the third degree."

He stood, but before I could slip away, he cupped my face gently in both hands, keeping me there.

"I told you I know how you feel," he whispered, leaning close to my ear. "I think we should go to bed and *sleep*."

He emphasized the word *sleep* in a way that made my chest unclench.

Thank God because I wasn't ready for more of anything else.

If he had tried to kiss me just then, I might've spontaneously combusted. Or worse—fallen for him.

I grabbed his hand and led him down the hall. I showed him the guest bathroom and told him which side of the bed I slept on in case he beat me there. I was trying to keep it casual, but inside, my heart was thrumming like a warning bell.

In the bathroom, I washed my face, brushed my teeth, and threw on a long shirt. No lace, no frills. Just cotton and comfort. I tied my hair up in a messy bun—not because I cared what I looked like, but because I didn't want to wake up next to him wearing mascara like a raccoon.

When I came out, the room was dim, lit only by moonlight seeping through the blinds and the low light of my bedside table lamp. He was already in bed, on *his* side, shirtless, with the blanket pulled low around his hips. My eyes flicked to the curve of his back, the line of his jaw in profile.

God help me.

I climbed in as quietly as I could and turned off the light.

I laid on my back, stiff as a board.

"Are you going to do that all night?" I asked after a beat feeling the wait of his eyes on me.

"Do what?" He said.

"Stare at me."

"Only if you don't turn and look at me so I can say goodnight properly."

I slowly turned to face him.

He smiled, inching closer, careful and slow, like I was something fragile. He wrapped his arms around me, and I melted against him.

"Goodnight," he whispered into my hair, the low rumble of his voice vibrating in my chest.

I hummed in response, already sinking into the feeling of him—warm, solid, safe. My cheek rested against his bare chest. One of my arms wrapped around his waist without even thinking. His grip tightened in response, pulling me closer until our bodies were pressed together. His leg hooked over mine, and instinctively, I let mine slide up over his hip.

The contact made my breath hitch. I could feel him—*all* of him. And there was no mistaking what my body was doing in response.

He didn't move. Didn't press into me. Just rested his hand low on my back and held me steady, like he *wanted* me to feel safe. Like he meant it.

No pressure. No game. Just presence.

And in the silence that followed, with only the sound of his breathing and the soft rhythm of my own, I realized something terrifying and beautiful.

I could get used to this.

I could *need* this.

And that scared me more than anything else.

But for now... I let it happen.

I let myself fall asleep in his arms.

Chapter 14

ALEX

I opened my eyes to a calm, overcast morning—no sun beaming in, no alarm blaring, just peace. Holy cow, that was the best night's sleep of my life. I flung an arm across the bed to stretch and realized I was alone.

He did stay the night, didn't he?

I rolled over and inhaled deeply. Yep. His scent—clean cologne and something distinctly him—still clung to the sheets. Best aphrodisiac on the market. Thankfully, it wasn't actually on the market, or women everywhere would be in trouble.

After brushing my teeth, I padded down the hall, assuming he was in the guest bathroom. But as I passed, the door was open and the light was off.

Did he leave?

It was new for me—being disappointed someone *wasn't* still here. I smiled to myself, a little embarrassed.

Then I stepped into the kitchen and froze. There he was—in just his boxer briefs and my hot pink apron that read: *Hot and Spicy (and the Food's Good Too).*

He hadn't seen me yet, so I stayed at the corner of the island, admiring the view. Somehow, I knew he could feel me. He confirmed it when he said, without turning, "Good morning," while pouring coffee.

"I made fruit and yogurt if you want some. I know you're going to brunch with the girls," he added, turning around and handing me a cup.

I wasn't hungry for fruit. My mouth watered for an entirely different reason.

"Thank you for the coffee—and good morning to you too. I think I'll pass on breakfast," I said, winking at the apron. He smiled, made a plate for himself, and joined me at the island.

"Mind if I change? This apron isn't my color."

I tried not to laugh. Failed. His face flushed as he walked down the hall to change. I shamelessly watched him go.

When he returned in last night's clothes, I grinned. "So *this* is what a walk-of-shame outfit looks like on a dude."

"I think that was the apron," he quipped, his face still pink.

"Dinner is at six, but we do cocktails first, so I'll pick you up around four?" he asked, changing the subject, casually popping a strawberry into his mouth.

"Four works great." I stared at his mouth. He caught me. I smiled, stole a strawberry from his plate to save face.

"Okay, it's a date. Have fun with Abby and Maggie—and don't forget to tell me everything they say."

He leaned down to kiss me, but with my mouth full, he landed on my cheek instead. *Man, I kind of wanted that kiss.*

"Absolutely not," I mumbled with food in my mouth. He laughed all the way to the door.

After cleaning up and taking a long, hot shower, I wrapped myself in a robe and wandered into the living room. A text buzzed in.

MAGGIE: *Hey jerk, you gonna make it to brunch on time today or did Mr. Perfect wear you out?*

ME: *I think I'm going to be on time today.*

MAGGIE: *Wait, what? Are you saying nothing happened?*

ME: *I'm not saying anything. Just that I'll be there on time.*

MAGGIE: *Boring!!!*

ME: *LMFAO.*

MAGGIE: *Ok, see you at 11:30.*

ME: *See you then, xo.*

I read a few chapters of the thriller I'd started, setting an alarm so I didn't lose track of time.

When the alarm buzzed, I stared at my closet like it might do the work for me. I finally chose a long, flowy green skirt with white and yellow flowers, a tight white tee, and black low-top Converse. My hair went up in a messy bun, a few pieces left loose. Minimal gold jewelry. No sunglasses needed with the clouds outside.

On my walk to the restaurant, a strange chill crept up my spine. Nothing obvious—just a weird sense of being watched. Probably my new paranoia, courtesy of Roman King and his empath talk.

I arrived early and spotted Abby and Maggie climbing out of their Uber. Their jaws dropped dramatically.

"Told you I'd be here on time," I smirked, flipping them both off before hugging them.

Before we even sat down, the interrogation began.

"Can we please sit first?" I groaned. "One at a time."

Abby dove in. "You can't go from that hospital scene to bringing him to our BBQ like it's no big deal."

"Exactly!" Maggie added.

"Okay. This is going to sound insane—but he feels like my soulmate. It's like... we couldn't stay away from each other even if we tried."

They blinked at me.

"Are you serious?" Abby asked.

"Deadly. It's overwhelming. Sometimes I think I want space, but then I need him. He gets it more than I do. I'm seeing his mom tonight to try and understand it."

"His mom? Understand What? Is she into voodoo or something?" Maggie asked.

"I thought the same thing! But no—she's a psychologist. A doctor. Roman says she helps people who feel a lot."

"You mean, like you?" Abby asked.

"Yes. Have you noticed how emotional I get sometimes?"

Both girls answered at once: "YES!!"

"He thinks she can help me manage it."

"So... you're seeing a shrink?" Abby and Maggie stifled laughter.

"Apparently." I shrugged. "No idea what it'll be like."

"This is way over my head," Abby said. "Now I need something stronger than a mimosa."

We ordered dirty martinis and food. I gave them the bare minimum—told them Roman stayed over, wore my apron, and that was it. They were visibly disappointed.

For once, brunch felt easy. No one trying to fix me. I even switched to soda water after one drink. The girls gave me a look, but I had plans—I wanted to visit Bruce's MMA studio.

After we said our goodbyes, I strolled aimlessly before heading back to my building. I still felt that weird sensation, like someone was watching me, but tried to ignore it. Just hypersensitive now, I guess.

Bruce's gym was fifteen minutes away. I sat in my car out front for a few minutes before heading in. Just as I reached for the door, my phone buzzed.

ROMAN: *Hey, just checking in. How was brunch? Can't wait to see you at four.* He reminded me like I could forget.

ME: *Brunch was great. So much fun. Can't wait either. Running errands—will call when I'm done.*

I walked inside. Bruce was on the phone at the front desk but lit up when he saw me, motioning for me to wait.

While I stood there, I let the scene hit me from all around—deep grunts cutting through the air, bodies slick with sweat straining against one another, the floor thrumming beneath the steady rhythm of fists and feet. A faint haze of chalk dust hung in the light—sharp and dry against the tang of sweat and rubber mats. The sheer force of effort in the room was electric, like static crawling across my skin, and instead of intimidating me, it sent a rush straight through my veins. Something about the raw grit and discipline settled my nerves in a way I hadn't expected—it made me feel alive.

He ended his call and swept me into a hug.

"To what do I owe the pleasure?"

"I want to start self-defense classes."

He laughed. "Heard about that bar incident. Steve texted me. Said, 'Never mind, she's got him by the balls.' Then something about a guy getting his nose broken?"

I groaned. "I'm mortified."

He gave me another quick hug. "Don't be. Let's find the right class. Next time, you'll break the guy's nose yourself."

We headed to his office. My weekends were open, so I signed up for Saturday self-defense followed by kickboxing.

"Is this just about the bar?" he asked gently.

I hesitated. "No... I've been working on something in Burrow Township. It's gotten dicey."

"Dicey how?"

"Someone pulled a knife on me."

His eyes widened. "Damn. How'd you get out?"

"I had help. But it scared me."

Alex's throat tightened as the words left her mouth, the memory flashing hot in her chest. She rubbed her damp palms against her thighs, not sure if she wanted him to notice her unease or not.

Bruce nodded slowly, the set of his jaw hardening, the weight of her confession settling in. His gaze sharpened, protective, but measured. "These classes will teach you the basics. If you stick with it, we'll level up. Maybe even get you into MMA training."

"I'll think about it," I said, buying my gear on the way out. I had a date to get ready for—and a whole lot to think about.

On my way home I called Roman. It was about 2:30, so I expected to get home a little bit before three. I asked him what I should wear to dinner tonight and he said just something casual and comfy. I was getting a little nervous about meeting his mom and dad. I may have sounded a little panicked on the phone too.

I went straight to my closet, picking out an off-white tank top, dark blue skinny jeans, and a lightweight caramel colored jacket. I grabbed a pair of nude, patent leather heels from the rack then took my hair down from the bun, shaking it out. It wasn't half bad in long messy waves. I did a quick touch up on my makeup, adding some lip gloss for a pop of color.

There was a knock as soon as I finished. I scanned the room jokingly for a camera. He always seemed to have perfect timing.

I opened the door and, as usual, I got butterflies and little heart flutters. He looked all nice and refreshed—it took my breath away. I smiled as my greeting breathlessly fell from my lips.

He returned my smile and reciprocated my "Hi." He leaned in kissing my cheek, his lips lingering longer than usual this time. He was the epitome of a gentleman, and I was starting to feel spoiled. That's not something I was used to.

He was wearing tailored black pants, a white short sleeved polo shirt, a brown belt and casual brown dress shoes with no socks. I couldn't help but admire the way his clothes fit like a glove and accentuated every muscle as they drape exactly right. He placed both hands on my shoulders, giving me a little shake. "Hey there, would you like me to put the apron back on?"

I blinked myself back into the moment, "Um, yeah, nope, that didn't help a bit, now I'm remembering breakfast." I hadn't even realized I was staring so dreamily at him. He laughed pulling me into one of his amazing embraces.

"Are you ready to go or would you care to have drinks first?" he casually asked.

I pulled away nervously, "Oh no, I don't think I should drink before I meet your parents."

He chuckled. "It'll be fine. Let's just go and we can have drinks when we get there." My eyes got big as I thought about the conversation I was preparing to have with his mom and the thought of mixing that with alcohol did nothing to help my nerves. I was trying not to change my mind and have a drink before we left when Roman grabbed me.

***

ROMAN

After breakfast, I went home, showered, and tried to reset. The hot water loosened my muscles, but it couldn't wash away the memory of the night before—lying next to her, the heat of her body pressed against mine, every rise and fall of her breathing steady and even while I lay there wide awake. I'd wanted nothing more than to pull her into me, but I forced myself to stay still. She needed to know I could be trusted—that I wasn't going to take advantage of a moment that belonged to her comfort, not my desire.

By dawn, the restraint had burned me raw, and I'd gotten up early, pacing just to shake the ache of it.

I toweled off, dressed, and sat down at my desk, the glow of my laptop cutting through the quiet. I skimmed emails with one hand and, with the other, thumbed out a text to Matt Stevens—something ordinary, something to keep me grounded when my head was still full of her.

Maggie's husband—the representative of District 5—bordered the area we were getting ready to tear down and rebuild. Burrow Township. The whole thing made my stomach turn.

ME: *Hey Matt. It was a pleasure to meet you yesterday. You have a beautiful family. I appreciate you allowing me to join in*

I wanted to keep the conversation friendly. Something about last night left me uneasy—maybe it was how quick he was to bring Harrison into the discussion. I needed to keep my tone light until I understood what I was walking into. Especially since this involved Alex's friends.

MATT: *Hey, man. It was great to meet you. We were glad to have you.*

The next text arrived almost immediately:

MATT: *Sorry about last night. I just have some things I'd like to discuss with you, and I'm a little fired up because the other rep isn't even trying to cooperate.*

ME: *I get it. Don't worry about it for a second. If something weird is going on I'd like to know. I've never met the district rep about this project—no idea what part he plays.*

This back-and-forth wasn't going to cut it. I called him.

"Yeah, I'm not much for texting either unless it's my wife. Helps avoid tone issues, if you know what I mean." He laughed.

I chuckled, remembering Maggie's tone vividly. "No, I get it."

We talked about the BBQ a little. About Alex. He respected her. Protective of her, in that older-brother kind of way. It made me like him more.

"You should be getting an email from my assistant, Amelia, tomorrow morning," I said. "She organizes my work life."

"Perfect. Talk soon."

The call ended and I felt better, if not entirely settled. Harrison would need to be looped in. No more surprises.

***

I dipped my head and pressed my mouth into her hair, just above her ear, breathing her in. The faint scent of her shampoo—something soft, clean, threaded with warmth—wrapped around me until I could almost taste it. My breath fanned across the delicate skin there, and I felt her shoulder brush mine, light and unintentional, but enough to rattle the thin line I'd been holding.

Every instinct screamed to close the gap, to let my lips trail lower, to claim the spot I'd only grazed with air. My jaw tightened, teeth pressed hard against the urge, but my self-control slipped all the same. The heat of her body seeped into me, steady and constant, until it felt like the room itself had tilted toward her.

"You ready?" I asked, my voice a low rasp against the shell of her ear—half a question, half a dare.

She nodded, but her body betrayed her. Her spine arched—barely, just a whisper of movement—but enough for me to feel the shift ripple through the air between us. The invitation was subtle, instinctive, the kind of unspoken pull that made the fine hairs on my arms stand on end. Heat radiated off her skin, brushing against mine in currents I could almost taste—warmth laced with something sweeter, sharper, impossible to ignore.

I bit the inside of my cheek, grounding myself with the sharp sting of it, a quiet act of restraint against the surge pressing to break free. Her perfume—faint, vanilla, threaded with the salt of her skin—curled into my lungs, winding me tighter with every breath. One more second and I'd lose the battle. If I didn't step back, we weren't making it out of this apartment. Hell, we weren't even making it to the door.

Reluctantly, I shifted my weight and put a sliver of distance between us. My palms still burned from the shape of her hips, lingering for one last heartbeat before I forced myself to let go.

"Let's go," I said, though the words scraped out of me rough—low and weighted with everything I was swallowing back.

She turned to grab her bag, and that small, ordinary movement turned merciless. The hem of her blouse shifted, brushing against the curve of her back, while her shorts rode just enough higher to remind me how close I'd been to losing all control. Heat coiled low in my stomach. Her cheeks were flushed, her lips parted slightly, as if she'd just broken the surface after being held under too long—breathless, undone.

I opened the door and stepped aside, letting her pass. The scent of her—warm, clean, threaded with something soft and feminine—curled into me like smoke, making it damn near impossible to steady myself. I forced my lungs to work, pulling air in and out like a man trying to prove he still had discipline and restraint.

She walked ahead, hips swaying with unconscious rhythm, every step dragging my gaze like a tether. I followed, adjusting myself discreetly, the imprint of her body still burning against my hands, the pulse of her heat refusing to fade.

Yeah—there was no doubt about it now. I was the one who needed that drink.
Badly.

Chapter 15

ALEX

We pulled up to a massive house tucked into a private neighborhood just north of the city—one of those enclaves where the ultra-wealthy quietly tucked their lives behind gates and long driveways. I'd sold a home here once, a few years back. Grant had handed me that lead, said he didn't have time. I didn't mind. It had closed fast and brought in my first five-figure commission check. I remembered feeling unstoppable.

Roman's parents' house sat a quarter mile off the main road, surrounded by manicured acres and draped in quiet luxury. The circular driveway looped around a fountain that sparkled under the soft light of early evening. Over the grand entryway was a covered porte-cochère, making the whole place feel like a private resort.

Roman came around to open my door, looking effortlessly casual despite the grandeur around us. Normally, I would've hopped out the second we stopped, but I paused this time—partly to gather myself, partly because I liked the way he did this. Opening the door. Offering his hand. It wasn't showy; it was deliberate. I used to think being treated like a lady meant weakness. Now, it felt like a power move—one I didn't have to perform to earn.

I slipped my hand into his and tried not to blush when his thumb brushed mine. We walked up the stone steps and through the front door, which he opened for me as well.

And then I saw the inside.

White marble floors stretched across a soaring entryway. A spiral staircase curved like something out of a fairy tale. Rich, dark wood lined the ceilings and parts of the walls. A massive chandelier dripped crystal from the second floor, casting prisms of light across every surface. The art on the walls—bold strokes, gilded frames—looked museum-worthy.

My heels echoed as we walked, each step reverberating like I was being announced. I found myself trying to step quieter, as if the house expected me to behave a certain way.

Apparently, cocktail hour was the first order of business. Which, suddenly, didn't sound too bad.

We passed through a showpiece of a kitchen—bright and expansive, every surface gleaming under recessed lights. Not a smudge of oil or crumb in sight, as if the space had been staged for a magazine spread rather than lived in. Stainless-steel appliances reflected our movement, the faint scent of lemon polish lingering in the air. I glanced around, half-expecting a chef in crisp whites to appear, hands busy slicing hors d'oeuvres or arranging trays with military precision.

Roman gave me a sideways look.

"What are you looking for?" he asked, stopping just enough to face me.

I gestured toward the gleaming countertops. "The chef. Or house staff?"

He laughed—a deep, amused sound that rolled through me like velvet.

"You mean my mom?"

I blinked. "Bulls..." It didn't seem right to use profanity in here. Almost as if the house would scold me then kick me out.

He grinned. "Nope. She does the shopping. The cooking. She loves it. They have people to clean, sure—but this place is massive. It would be impossible alone."

I stared at him, surprised by how unaffected he sounded, like it was the most natural thing in the world. His mom, who clearly lived in luxury, still did everything herself. There was something humbling about that.

As we approached the glass doors to the patio, my nerves started prickling again. Roman must've noticed, because he let go of my hand and slid his arm around my waist. His touch grounded me. Warm. Present. Possessive, but not in a way that stifled me—in a way that said *I've got you*.

Outside was another world entirely.

Twinkling lights hung from trees. The stone patio sprawled across the backyard, partially covered to shade the outdoor kitchen. The furniture was stunning—sleek and modern, but cozy enough to curl up in. A massive fire pit flickered at the far end, surrounded by built-in seating, cushions tailored perfectly, layered with vibrant throw pillows.

And beyond it all—water. A pool that looked like it belonged in a resort, complete with a rock waterfall that trickled down into turquoise stillness.

I didn't realize I'd stopped walking until Roman leaned in, his voice brushing just behind my ear. "Alex, did you want to say hello?"

Heat bloomed in my cheeks. I snapped my mouth closed and straightened, smiling sheepishly. "Hi. Sorry, I got completely lost in this backyard. It's like something out of a dream."

His mother approached first. She took both of my hands in hers—warm, soft and sure.

"Alex, it's such a pleasure to meet you. I'm Lisette," she said, her voice graceful, thoughtful. "This yard was our sanctuary project—something to balance out the noise of the world."

She was beautiful. Mid-sixties, maybe, with striking hazel eyes threaded with gold—just like Harrison's, though Roman clearly favored her more. Her shoulder-length hair was a luminous shade of platinum that must've once matched the dark brows and lashes framing her eyes.

"It's wonderful to meet you too, Lisette," I said, meaning it. "Roman speaks so highly of you."

I exhaled slowly. I could already tell I'd end up telling this woman every-thing. Which meant I'd better hire her properly if I wanted my secrets kept. Therapist or not, she was still his mom. And moms always knew. The idea made my stomach flutter—for more reasons than one.

Next came Roman's dad. He gave me a handshake that felt a little too formal at first—like he was trying to size me up.

"Ms. Kennedy, is it?"

I smiled, polite, the corners of my mouth pulling tight while my jaw ached from holding it there. It was the kind of smile that never reached my eyes, more reflex than warmth, but smooth enough to pass without question. "Please, call me Alex. It's nice to meet you, Mr. King."

"If I get to call you Alex, you have to call me Fitz," he replied. That made me smile—Roman's full name flashed in my mind. Roman Fitzgerald King. Definitely more Roman than Fitz.

"Nice to meet you, Fitz."

His expression softened immediately. "You as well, my dear."

He released my hand and, just like that, the formality faded. I could see where Harrison got his charm now—same swagger, different shade.

And speak of the devil—Harrison appeared, swooping in like a scene-steal-ing Broadway star.

"Yep, my brother, the lucky bastard!"

I laughed, unable to help it. "And hello to you too, Harrison."

Roman shot him a warning nudge. "Hands off."

We all settled into the patio furniture—two large sofas facing each other, cocktail table in the middle, and two armchairs framing the edges. Fitz took drink orders and headed to the fully stocked bar. I asked for a glass of white wine—no martinis tonight. My nerves didn't need the extra fuel.

Roman never let go of me. Even once we were seated, his arm stayed wrapped around my back, his palm resting low, a quiet tether that kept me grounded.

His family was warm, gracious, and relaxed. That made it easier to breathe. Cocktail hour unfolded with wine and appetizers, followed by a three-course dinner that felt like something off the food network. Roman told me they did this every weekend.

Every weekend? This was their *normal.*

Just before dinner, Roman turned to me and asked if I wanted to walk the grounds. The timing felt uncanny—like he sensed I needed a moment away from the eyes. A moment to breathe. I nodded, grateful, and when he reached for my hand, I took his without hesitation. His fingers curled around mine, steady and warm, and something in me softened as we stepped quietly into the golden hush of the evening.

***

ROMAN

I offered my hand, and she slid hers into mine, fingers lacing like we'd done it a hundred times before. I guided us toward the pool, wanting a moment with her away from everyone else.

Once we were out of earshot, I let go—not because I wanted to, but because I needed to see her. All of her. My fingers slipped from the warmth of her arm, leaving a faint echo of heat on my skin. I stepped in front of her, close enough to catch the rise and fall of her breathing, close enough to catch the soft trace of her perfume threaded with the salt of her skin.

Her eyes caught mine, luminous and guarded, and I searched them, trying to catch the flicker buried just beneath the surface. Her lashes trembled once, betraying her steadiness, and the corners of her mouth tightened as if holding words hostage. She was holding something back—something I could almost feel pressing against the silence between us.

She smiled, a little shy. "Your family's really nice."

"Yes, they are," I said, watching her closely. "Pretty normal, wouldn't you say?"

A delicate flush spread up her neck and over her cheeks, like a soft sunrise blooming under her skin. God, she was beautiful when she blushed.

"Yes. I feel silly about that," she admitted.

"What do you feel silly about?" I asked, eyes flicking to her mouth, the way it curved when she was trying not to be too honest.

She tilted her head back and let out a breathy laugh, her neck arching just enough to make my thoughts veer completely off track. I had to resist the sudden urge to taste her right there, to find out what kind of "silly" she really was.

"Well," she said, "I was actually waiting for monkeys to fly out of some-one's butt."

I blinked.

What?

I laughed—because how else do you respond to that?

"Um... okay. Could you elaborate?" I asked, dragging my gaze back to her face, away from the tempting curve of her throat.

She started laughing, the kind of laugh that crinkled her nose and brought color rushing to her cheeks.

"When I was married..." she began.

Ah. The shadow.

"...my ex-husband used to take me to all these ridiculous client parties. Everyone was constantly name-dropping and pretending to be impressed by each other's connections. I couldn't stand it. So I'd say, 'If they can make monkeys fly out of their butts, I'll be impressed.'"

That caught me off guard. I burst out laughing—genuine, full-body laughter.

"Are you telling me... you're impressed with my family?"

She grinned up at me, nodding, her expression so earnest and sweet I felt something shift in my chest. A puff of air left her lips that sounded like a quiet, breathy "yes." And for a moment, I forgot how to be cool. Forgot everything but the feel of her hand in mine, the heat of her body pressed to my side.

I tugged her in close, her frame sliding into mine like a puzzle piece. My arm wrapped around her again, my palm splayed over the dip of her waist, thumb brushing just under her ribs. She looked up at me, those long lashes fluttering slightly, eyes full of something soft. Curious. Dangerous.

"That has to be the best thing I've heard all week," I murmured, leaning in just enough to feel her breath catch.

I wanted to kiss her. Right there in the middle of the garden, under the string lights and stars and the faint hush of falling water behind us. to try and get a taste of how much danger. But instead, I smirked and let my hand slide a little lower—just enough to make her feel it.

"Come on," I said, needing the distraction, "let's finish up our walk and head back to the fam. Gotta keep an eye out for those flying monkeys."

She groaned, playfully, burying her face against my shoulder. "Okay, guess I'm not living that one down."

I shook my head, smiling. "Not a chance."

We walked the rest of the yard like that—hand in hand, shoulders brushing, hearts beating just a little too fast. And when we returned to the patio, something between us had changed—quieter now, but deeper.

And I wasn't sure I wanted it to shift back.

***

ALEX

we finished walking the yard and headed back to the house for dinner. The weather was perfect—cool enough for comfort, warm enough to stay out all evening.

We ate beneath the trees at a rustic wooden table, the wood worn smooth from years of use. Candles flickered in glass jars, their flames bending in the soft evening breeze, while wildflowers spilled color across the center like they'd been gathered fresh from the field. The air carried the scent of rosemary and garlic from the meal, rich and comforting, and the cicadas sang in steady rhythm all around us.

His mom was an amazing cook—every bite layered with warmth and care, the kind of food that lingered on your tongue and made you feel at home. When I offered to help clean up afterward, she only shook her head, waving me off with a kind smile, her hands still busy stacking plates.

"They've got this," Lisette said, gesturing toward the house as she grabbed our wine glasses and started walking toward the pool. She paused and looked back, a twinkle in her eye.

I glanced over my shoulder and found Roman watching me, smirking as he gathered dishes.

Uh oh. I had a feeling she was about to corner me—and I wasn't sure if I was ready or terrified.

Lisette's gaze lingered on her son before returning to me. "Alex," she said gently, "I think my son really likes you."

Here we go.

"Yeah, I'm starting to get that vibe from him too." I kept it light, but her expression didn't shift.

Her eyes narrowed, amused but pointed. "Are you trying to tell me you're just now starting to get that *vibe*?" Her tone said she already knew the answer—and that my downplaying wasn't fooling anyone.

I winced. "I may have known he was attracted to me," I admitted, "but I did my damn best to push him away."

My hand flew to my mouth. Great. I'd just casually cursed in front of Roman's mother like we were two friends having brunch.

"Sorry," I blurted, lowering my hand.

She laughed, completely unfazed. "For what? Knowing my son liked you and trying to fend him off? Or the word 'damn'?"

When she said it like that, I felt ridiculous. "Both?" I squinted at her sheepishly. "Am I really that much of a jerk? One of my friends tells me I am... regularly."

Lisette chuckled, clearly entertained by my spiraling. "Alex, you're not a jerk. And I'd bet your friend says that with love." Her tone softened. "Roman has a tendency to pursue what he wants—sometimes relentlessly. It's one of his greatest strengths... and one of the hardest things to manage if you're not ready for it."

She looked back toward the house, where Roman was still clearing the table, and then smiled at me again. "And as far as profanity goes, I'm no stranger to it. Sometimes it's just a tool people use for emphasis or as a defense mechanism. Especially those who've had to build walls around themselves."

Her words struck something in me. She wasn't judging. She was seeing. And for once, that didn't make me uncomfortable.

"Thank you," I said softly. "I appreciate you taking the time to talk with me."

She tilted her head. "Roman told me he thinks you're like him. An empath. Do you know what that means?"

I shook my head slowly. "Not really."

She reached out and took my hand. "Come with me," she said. "I want to show you my favorite place to think."

She led me to the edge of the property where two hammock swings hung side by side beneath a canopy of trees. We set our glasses down and each sank into one. The gentle sway was immediately calming.

"I find it easier to talk when I'm not looking directly at someone," she said, staring out toward the trees.

I let out a quiet breath of relief. Maybe I wouldn't have to guard every facial expression after all.

"So, Alex," she began, "why do you think Roman wanted me to talk to you?"

I hesitated, reaching for the right words. Last night, Roman had said something—something that struck a chord I didn't understand at the time.

"I feel this... connection to him," I said slowly, "and it's not just attraction. It feels deeper. Different. It's overwhelming sometimes, and I don't know what to do with it."

Lisette rocked gently in her hammock, facing straight ahead.

"That's not unusual," she said. "But did he say anything that made you feel like it was more than just emotion?"

I tilted my head back, watching the wind rustle the leaves overhead. The way they shimmered in the light reminded me of water—calm and glittering. The memory returned suddenly, clear as crystal.

"He asked if I ever got overwhelmed by feelings that didn't feel like mine."

She stilled. "And what did you say?"

"Yes," I whispered. "Absolutely yes."

She nodded slowly, then asked, "Do you feel anxious in groups of people? Do you struggle to get comfortable?"

I nodded again, my voice caught in my throat. "It's the worst."

Her questions came gently, one after the next—simple yes or no prompts, no pressure to elaborate. Just... clarity. And when she stopped, I felt something inside me ease, like I'd been holding a breath I didn't know I'd taken.

She stood, brushing off her hands. "Come on. Let's get another glass of wine."

I followed her, my body light and grounded all at once. The quiet in me matched the peace in this place, the way Roman made me feel. I glanced over at her and felt my lips pull into an easy, genuine smile.

I stopped and turned to face her.

"It's a superpower, isn't it?" I asked. "You and Roman—you both have it."

She laughed, her whole-body relaxing. "Oh, he told me you'd call it that. No, it's not a superpower... but maybe it should be. I think it's one of yours, too."

She touched my arm gently. "I didn't want to overwhelm you tonight. I just needed to see if he was right."

I raised both eyebrows. "So... was he?"

She nodded, her smile unwavering.

"Great," I muttered, "now I have to go tell *Mr. Perfect* that he was right."

Her laugh was loud and unfiltered. "Mr. Perfect?" She mocked lightly.

I felt my face go hot. "Oh my God. I can't believe I said that out loud."

Lisette was practically glowing with amusement. "I assure you, no one's perfect. Not even Roman."

I peeked at her through my fingers, embarrassed, but she just looped her arm through mine, still chuckling.

"Come on," she said, "let's get you that wine."

***

ROMAN

As I cleared the dinner table, my eyes drifted toward the trees—toward the hammocks where I knew Mom was leading Alex. That spot had always been sacred in our family. When we were kids, Mom would take us out there to talk. Not lecture. Not discipline. Just talk. It was her way of pulling things out of us without pressure, like she was peeling back the layers until the truth came out. Then she'd save the real advice—or the consequences—for her office.

Dad trained us in business. Mom trained us in life.

I watched them disappear into the trees and wondered what she'd find. Harrison slapped me on the back, dragging me out of my thoughts.

"Another one bites the dust," he said with a grin.

"How do you figure?" I pushed him off.

"We both know what she's doing. She'll stay sweet until she hears the one thing she's looking for to cut the girl loose."

It was true. That had been her pattern. Calm, charming conversations that ended in us suddenly realizing things wouldn't work out with whoever we were seeing. But this time was different.

"I asked her to talk to Alex," I said.

Harrison blinked. "Well then, that makes you an idiot."

I laughed, mostly because he wasn't entirely wrong. "Me being an idiot is irrelevant."

Dad's voice boomed from inside. "Boys—clean first, argue later!"

We got back to it, but Harrison couldn't resist humming "Another One Bites the Dust" as he wiped the counter. I tossed a napkin at him and tried not to think about whether I'd just sabotaged the best thing I'd found in a long time.

When they finally reemerged, both of them were heading straight for the bar, smiling. That was a good sign. *Wasn't it?*

Mom poured Alex another glass of wine, and I moved quickly to intercept.

"Hello there," I said. "How did you like the swings?"

Alex looked up at me, dreamy and soft. "That was the most relaxing swing I've ever been on."

"Delightful, Roman," Mom added, and I caught the tone. It was subtle—but I knew her well enough to hear the approval in it.

"So... was I right?" I asked, glancing between them.

Mom laughed. "You'll have to ask her, *Mr. Perfect*."

Wait—what?

I stared, confused. She'd never called me that before. Not even close. Then I looked at Alex and caught the telltale flush of embarrassment creeping up her neck.

"Oh, so I'm *perfect* now?" I teased. "But was I right?"

Alex groaned. "Yes, you were right. But *perfect* was clearly used in an exaggerated, sarcastic way... started by Abby and Maggie."

"I can almost live with not being right," I said, "but if you're telling me I'm not perfect, we have a problem."

We all laughed, and for the first time all night, everything felt easy. Natural. My mom liked her. Alex was glowing. This thing between us—whatever it was—was starting to feel real.

And then Mom turned to me, her smile shifting slightly. "Can I talk to you for a minute?"

Of course she wanted a follow-up. I glanced at Alex, hesitant to leave her alone with Harrison and Dad, but she seemed fine—already laughing at something ridiculous my father had said. Probably one of his terrible dad jokes.

I followed Mom down a stone path toward the garden.

"She likes you," she said simply.

I smiled. "Yeah, I know. But... she's fighting it."

"She is," Mom agreed. "And if you want this to work, Roman, you're going to need a lot of patience."

"Do I have your seal of approval?" I asked, only half joking.

Mom smiled that knowing smile of hers. "You've never needed my approval. I just wanted to make sure you were thinking clearly. Divorce isn't like breaking up."

I nodded. I understood what she meant.

"Are you going to work with her?" I asked.

"Do you want me to?"

"I think I do... but that's up to Alex."

"We'll talk more later," she said. "If I agree to work with her, I can't talk to you about her anymore. You'll have to trust me."

"I can do that."

We returned to the patio, and I was relieved to find Alex still smiling, glass in hand, chatting with Harrison. She looked at ease—more so than when we'd arrived. That tension she carried in her shoulders was gone.

We stayed another hour, the night growing more relaxed by the minute. Dad was in full comedy mode, cracking ridiculous jokes. Harrison was his usual mix of charming and relentless. Alex held her own with both of them, laughing easily—present.

When we finally got in the car to head home, the silence between us wasn't awkward. It was charged—heavy with everything we hadn't said yet.

"How did you enjoy dinner?" I asked, my voice low.

She squirmed slightly in her seat, and it made me wonder if she was thinking what I was thinking.

"It was nice," she said, but her voice gave her away. The pause. The softness. The way she swallowed afterward like she was holding something back.

I let the corner of my mouth lift. "I think my family really likes you."

"They're great," she said quickly. Then she laughed.

"What's funny?"

She shook her head. "This reminds me of swinging with your mom. She asked a question, I gave a short answer, and it kept going until I had no answers left."

I smiled. "That's her process. She doesn't rush people. Just keeps asking until the silence says more than the words."

Alex looked thoughtful, almost shy.

"How many times did you have to talk to your mom to... cure you?" she asked.

"Who says I'm cured?" I chuckled. "But seriously, she taught me how to manage things—especially how to separate my emotions from everyone else's. There's no 'fixing' people. You just get better at knowing who you are and how to protect it."

She was quiet for a moment. Then: "Do you think it's a good idea for me to talk to her again? What if it messes things up between us?"

I glanced over and gave her a slow smile. "Is there something *between* us to come between?"

Her lips parted slightly. I could see the war inside her, but she didn't back away from it.

"I don't know," she said quietly. "Maybe. And if there isn't now, I'm kind of hoping there will be."

That hit me low in the chest. A quiet victory. A door cracked open.

I didn't say anything right away. I didn't need to. The warmth that settled between us said enough.

Whatever this was—we were both feeling it now.

***

ALEX

"I have an early day tomorrow, so I think I'm just going to say goodnight at the valet, if that's okay?" I asked, hoping I sounded more composed than I felt.

The night had gone surprisingly well—better than I could've hoped—and I didn't want to overthink it. What mattered now wasn't whether he came upstairs again, but whether I could trust myself to make the right choices. To keep my head clear when everything in me wanted to blur the lines.

Roman nodded. "Yeah, I guess I can handle that. I'd rather walk you up, but I understand."

He pulled into the valet, and I stepped out, the night air brushing cool against my bare arms as I smoothed the hem of my dress. My pulse quickened as I rehearsed the exit—quick goodbye, polite handshake, maybe, if I was lucky, the warmth of a brief hug.

What I wasn't prepared for was Roman coming around the car, his strides unhurried, deliberate. He stopped so close I caught the clean spice of his cologne and the faint warmth of his breath in the cool night air. Then his hands were on my face, large and steady, cradling me like I was something fragile, something worth protecting.

And then he kissed me.

Slow. Soft. Unhurried.

His mouth brushed mine, light at first, just enough to rob me of air. Heat surged through me as he lingered, then his lips closed over my bottom one, sucking gently before his tongue traced across it with a languid sweep. The world blurred, the valet, the street, the cool night—all of it dissolved until there was only him. And then, just like that, he let go.

Before I could speak—before I could even catch a thought—he pulled me into his chest, his arms folding me into a hug so warm and unshakable it nearly undid me. "Goodnight," he whispered against my ear, his voice low, steady, vibrating through my skin.

And then he was gone—slipping back into his car with the same quiet control, leaving me rooted to the sidewalk, my entire nervous system lit up like he'd rewired it with a single kiss.

I stood there frozen. Then blinked.

And somehow—I don't know how—I ended up in the lobby of my building. Alone. Buzzing.

What the hell just happened?

I glanced around, trying to remember how I'd gotten here. One second, I was standing by his car, and the next I was staring at the elevator, disoriented and humming with electricity.

That man had ambushed me with a kiss... and then disappeared. Who *does* that? What kind of dangerous, bourbon-laced trick is that?

He was smart to leave when he did. If that kiss had happened upstairs... he wouldn't have been leaving. Not tonight.

Back in my apartment, I checked my phone. A few texts from the girls asking how the evening went with *the Kings*—but I was too wrung out to answer. I'd deal with that tomorrow. Right now, I just wanted sleep.

Before I plugged in my phone, I sent Roman a message.

ME: *I had a nice night. Thank you for inviting me to meet your family.*

The three dots popped up immediately.

ROMAN: *You're welcome. And next time, I won't run away. ;)*

Goosebumps raced across my arms.

Next time I won't run away.

Translation: *Next time there'll be more than a kiss.*

Fantastic. Just the kind of thought I needed in my head while trying to fall asleep.

I smirked, deciding two could play this game.

ME: *Thanks a lot. I was trying to go to sleep. Now I'm going to have to take care of something first. ;)*

I was totally going to sleep. But he didn't need to know that.

ROMAN: *I'm game. What do you need to take care of*

Oh, no. Not tonight.

ME: *Goodnight, Mr. Perfect.*

My phone immediately lit up with his name. I laughed and hit *decline*, sending him straight to voicemail. A few seconds later, a final text popped up.

ROMAN: *Payback's a bitch. Goodnight, and sweet dreams of me, Mr. Perfect. ;)*

If only he knew.

I silenced my phone, checked my alarm, and climbed into bed—my skin still warm, my heart still thumping a little too fast.

And as I closed my eyes, the only thing in my mind was him.

Roman King.

Mr. Perfect.

Chapter 16

ALEX

Five a.m. always came too fast, but I managed to drag myself out of bed and into my workout clothes. I hit the gym by 5:30, determined to stay focused. There was a lot on my plate today, and I was motivated to knock it all out.

A sweet text from Roman came through at seven: *Good morning.* Abby and Maggie were blowing up my phone, too—still fishing for details about last night's dinner with Roman's family. I ignored them for now. My brain couldn't handle the postmortem.

I made it into the office early and went straight to my desk. The place was blissfully quiet, giving me time to catch up on email and start digging into that neighborhood research I'd been putting off. I also had a five o'clock meeting with the Santoros to discuss the two properties they toured last week—back when I was a little preoccupied with my gas tank and Roman's Greek god distractions.

I shook him from my thoughts and opened a few tabs, focusing on the neighborhood Ella had brought to my attention. I'd closed my office door for peace, and no one had interrupted me—until I got up for more coffee and opened the door to find Grant standing there, hand mid-knock.

"Jesus!" I jumped back. "One more second and you would've caught a right hook."

He laughed and held out a cup. "I come in peace—with caffeine."

I took the coffee gratefully and we exchanged quick hellos. He eyed me curiously. "What's got you so deep in concentration this morning?"

"Digging into Burrow Township. Ella Jackson gave me a few breadcrumbs, and I started following them. A politician's been sniffing around down there—talking to investors—and apparently the police have no interest in patrolling the area."

Grant frowned and dropped into the chair across from my desk. "That combination makes me uneasy. Police and politicians only mix well in court."

"Right? I'm with you. But I've got actual work to do today, so I'm taking a break for now. The Santoros are coming in later, and I want to be prepped."

He offered his help, then left me to it. I refocused, but by lunchtime, I needed air—and company that wasn't steeped in zoning records and tax history.

"Shay," I called across the front office, "want to grab lunch?"

She popped up like a jack-in-the-box, purse in hand, already excited.

She'd been unofficially training as my assistant for weeks. Once our new receptionist started next week, Shay would be shadowing me full-time—while also starting her licensing courses, which I'd offered to sponsor. She was bright, hungry, and genuinely sweet. I loved helping women like her build something for themselves.

"So," I asked once we were in the car, "how's Owen? Any updates?"

Her cheeks flushed instantly.

"We went on our first official date last night," she beamed.

"That's great! Where'd he take you?" I paused but interrupted before she could answer. "Hang on, tell me once we're seated."

We pulled into a sunny little bistro with a shaded patio. The breeze was warm, not stifling, and I requested a table under one of the umbrellas. We ordered ice water with lemon and fresh salads.

"Okay, spill."

"He took me to this cute pizza spot near my place. Alex... he opened the car door for me."

She looked completely baffled.

"No one's ever done that before. Is that weird?"

"Yes, it's weird no one's ever done that before," I said, smiling. "It's called being a gentleman. Who *have* you been dating?"

She giggled. "Not gentlemen, apparently. But Owen... he held my hand after dinner. Told me I was beautiful."

She hesitated then, suddenly shy.

"He also told me about you."

My stomach dropped. "Oh no. Shay, I'm sorry. I had no idea you liked him or I would've stayed a hundred feet away."

She waved me off. "I didn't *really* know him back then. It was just a little crush. And honestly, I admire you. I wish I had your confidence."

I barked out a laugh. "Shay, is that what you think this is? Confidence?"

She nodded. "Absolutely. You're fearless."

I reached across the table and rested my hand over hers.

"Well, what if I told you I wish I was more like *you*?"

She blinked, surprised. "Why?"

"Because no one's ever accused you of being a man-eating psycho bitch." I cringed just thinking about it.

That did it. She laughed so hard I nearly spit my water.

The rest of lunch was lighthearted. We talked about her new role and what she'd be learning. I could already picture her running her own show one day, and I couldn't wait to help her get there.

Back at the office, I threw myself into more research on the Burrow Township area. Something about it kept gnawing at me, like I was missing a critical piece. I started pulling tax records, zoning changes, and court filings on the vacant properties.

Then—*bam*.

"Bingo!" I shouted, slamming my fist on the desk.

Grant rushed in like I'd triggered an alarm. "Jesus, what happened?"

"Oops," I said sheepishly. "Forgot the door was open."

"Pretty sure the whole floor heard you."

I turned the screen toward him. "You see this neighborhood? The one stuck in a time capsule while everything around it's been developed?"

"Yeah, what about it?"

"It was protected under the Historical Preservation Law—until six months ago."

Grant's brows lifted. "They reversed it?"

"Yep. Which never happens. And guess who pushed the reversal through?"

"Tell me."

"Marcus Ellington. Burrow Township's rep. The same guy Ella saw chatting with the cops."

Grant's mouth tightened. "I've heard some shady things about him. There's talk of him holding up developments unless investors pay 'expedited fees.'"

Something cold slithered down my spine. What if the Kings were tangled up in this?

"I've got calls to make," I told him. "Thanks for the insight."

"Be careful, Alex. Seriously."

I nodded but knew I wouldn't let this go. I had to see it through. First call—Ella.

When she answered, her voice was breathy, like she'd been rushing.

"Hey Ms. Alex. You ready to meet Darius?"

"Not today," I said gently. "I actually need to ask you about something else."

"Go ahead."

"Did you know your neighborhood was under Historical Preservation status until six months ago?"

"No. Is that... important?"

"It's *very* important. And the guy who overturned the designation? Marcus Ellington. The same politician you saw near your house."

She was quiet, then added, "He's been back—talking to those same officers."

I swallowed my worry. "Ella, I want to help you. Let's get you into my office this week to sign the listing agreement. That way, any inquiries about your house go through me. And I'll make sure, if we can't stop this, that you get the best deal possible."

She sniffled. "Thank you, Ms. Alex. I'll come by tomorrow. Darius will drive me."

We said our goodbyes, and I hung up with a pit in my stomach. I needed answers. And there was only one person I trusted to tell me the truth—even if it hurt.

I texted Roman: *Call me when you're free.*

My phone rang a few minutes later. His name lit up the screen in bold caps—ROMAN—and I realized I must've saved it that way. I couldn't help the goofy smile that spread across my face.

"Hello there. What a pleasant surprise," he said, his voice all rich and low. "You texting me during work hours? Must be serious."

"Well, you know me. I don't like revealing my secrets, but I figured you could probably hear them through the phone anyway."

He laughed, and my heart skipped.

"Fair enough. What's on your mind?"

"There's a small matter I wanted to discuss, Mr. King."

He made a sound. "Hmm. Mr. King? That's my father's name."

"It's yours too," I said sweetly. "And I'd like to schedule a meeting—with you and Harrison."

There was a pause. Long enough to make me second-guess myself.

"Harrison too? Okay. This is business, then. What's it about?"

I didn't tiptoe. "Did you know that the section of Burrow Township I've been working on was a protected historical district until six months ago?"

Another pause. Then: "No, I didn't. Is there a reason I *should* have?"

"Well, your brother's investing in that area. And protected districts can't be developed. So... yeah."

He exhaled slowly. "I feel like I'm being accused of something."

"Just trying to understand," I said. "Are you involved?"

"I've got a meeting this week with Harrison and Matt Stevens—come to it. I'll have Amelia add you."

Matt Stevens? That was unexpected.

"Wait—why's Matt involved?"

"He's got some insight, I think. Also... I'll be in Texas for a few days. Dinner when I get back?"

"Sounds good. When?"

"Thursday night. I land late afternoon. I'll pick you up at seven."

"What if your flight's delayed?"

"It won't be. I tell it when to take off."

I blinked. "You're *flying* the plane?"

He laughed. "No, but I own it."

Of course he does.

"Must be nice," I said, grinning. "Skipping airport lines."

"Very. Hey, I've got to run to another meeting. Can I call you later?"

"Sure."

I ended the call and stared at my phone.

Matt Stevens. Harrison. Roman.

This thing was deeper than I thought.

And I was nowhere near done unraveling it.

***

ROMAN

She said yes. Thank God.

I checked my watch—shit. I'd lost track of time and had to sprint across the hotel to my next meeting. I walked in slightly winded, scanning the room. Small groups were clustered in quiet huddles, speaking in hushed tones. Not a great sign.

I spotted my architect, Mike, and our foreman waving me over.

"What is all this?" I asked, frustration creeping in.

Mike shrugged. "I don't know. I brought all the blueprints and topography plans—there's no reason we shouldn't have zoning approval."

"Then who's in charge of this meeting?"

He pointed to a group of suits in the corner. I pushed my way through the cluster, already irritated.

"Excuse me," I said. "Who's heading this meeting and what's it about?"

One of the men turned, a smug smirk planted firmly on his face. He looked vaguely familiar.

"That would be me. It's about your zoning issue."

I stared at him, trying to place the face. Bruised and arrogant.

"I'm Roman King, King Construction. And you are?"

He gave me a look like I'd insulted him by breathing. "Tanner Ellington. Aide and brother to Ohio Representative Marcus Ellington."

What the...

"Did I get on the wrong plane? Pretty sure this is Texas."

He didn't flinch. "You're very observant. Must be the smart one."

The migraine started as a low throb behind my right eye.

And then it hit me. The bar. That's the prick I elbowed in the face. No wonder he looked familiar. I tried not to smirk unsuccessfully.

"I don't understand what you or your brother have to do with real estate down here."

He smiled wider—smug and irritating. "Let's just say we have interests in Texas as well."

I pushed further. "Did your brother remove the Historical Preservation designation from Burrow Township?"

"Oh yeah. That one. Made a lot of money off that deal." His voice oozed satisfaction.

"And what part of that real estate did he own?" I asked tightly.

He slapped me on the shoulder like we were old pals. "Let's get this meeting started. We've all got things to do."

I wiped his handprint off my jacket, jaw clenched. This guy was going to push me too far.

By the end of the meeting, I was boiling. Nothing about this made sense, and everything reeked. Marcus Ellington was knee-deep in corruption—taking kickbacks, greasing palms, and gutting communities like Burrow Township without a second thought.

And I was involved.

Worse, so was my company. My name.

Alex had been right to dig deeper. Now I had to do the same.

Back in my hotel room, I poured a bourbon from the minibar and dialed my father. He answered on the first ring.

"Hello, son."

I exhaled slowly, rolling my shoulders. "Hey, Dad."

I placed the call on speaker, sat down, and unbuttoned my cuffs. "I'm in Texas," I started, "and something's not sitting right. You ever hear of a guy named Marcus Ellington?"

Silence.

That wasn't good.

"Yeah," he said finally. "But the guy I knew was his father. Marcus Ellington Sr. He worked for me as a foreman—ten years. I had to let him go. He was selling properties he didn't own, using political connections, even the courts. Got messy."

Jesus.

"And his son?"

"Came to see me after the funeral. Told me his dad's last words were, *'Never forget what the Kings did to our family.'*"

Perfect.

"Dad, is this guy coming after me?"

"You need to watch your back. And don't do business with them."

"Too late. We're already halfway into the Burrow Township project."

"You might have to make some hard decisions."

"I don't even know how deep this goes."

We talked for another twenty minutes. He offered wisdom, support—but not solutions. I knew I'd have to fix this myself.

Harrison was too reckless. He saw opportunity and jumped in without looking. I couldn't let him steer this company into ruin because of blind ambition and dollar signs. If Marcus Ellington was coming for us, I needed to be two steps ahead.

When I finally hung up, I poured another bourbon, popped two aspirin, and stared out at the skyline.

Then I reached for my phone.

I needed Alex.

***

ALEX

The intercom buzzed.

"Mr. and Mrs. Santoro are waiting in the lobby for you," Shay said, her voice bright.

"You can send them in," I replied, standing.

Shay escorted them in herself. As she slipped out of the room, she mouthed, *Wow*, eyes wide, and quietly closed the door behind her.

And wow was right.

The Santoros were... stunning. Effortlessly elegant in that old-world European way that didn't try too hard. Lucia wore a sleek black Gucci dress and enough gold to stop traffic—including a diamond ring so big it could double as a skating rink. Alessandro looked equally regal in a tailored black Armani suit, crisp white shirt, and gold cufflinks dotted with diamonds. His Rolex was so massive it probably had its own security detail.

But despite their red carpet appearance, their energy was soft, warm—even gracious. I'd spoken with them briefly over the phone, but in person, they were far more down-to-earth than I expected.

They were relocating from Italy to Ohio, of all places. Apparently, they'd sold their vineyard back home and were planning to start a new winery here. They'd mentioned two large properties north of Cincinnati, and I'd lined up options with enough acreage for their new venture. I was disappointed I couldn't show them personally, but they didn't seem to mind.

"Mr. and Mrs. Santoro, it's a pleasure to finally meet you," I said, stepping forward to shake hands. "I'm sorry I couldn't be at the showings myself, but I'm here to help in any way I can."

Before I could extend my hand, Lucia pulled me into a warm hug, followed by her husband.

"Oh my goodness, dear," she said, her voice soft with concern. "We heard about what happened. How frightening! We're so glad you're all right."

Wait—*what*?

Alessandro nodded. "It must've been terrifying. We're grateful you're okay—and thrilled to finally meet you. We've heard nothing but glowing reviews."

I smiled, a little stunned. I hadn't realized word had spread beyond the "ran-out-of-gas" version.

Their thick Italian accents made every word sound like music. We chatted about the two properties they saw, and I scheduled another set of showings for Saturday—noon and three o'clock, with lunch in between so we could get to know each other better. They were currently staying with friends nearby, but they also had properties in Napa Valley and North Carolina's Yadkin Valley.

Wine, beautiful land, gracious people—I was genuinely excited about this project.

They had four kids, all school-aged. Two girls, two boys. I made a mental note to prepare some family-friendly options too. I had a feeling their manners would be just as polished as their parents'.

As they left, we exchanged goodbyes and promises to talk soon. I walked them to the elevator and, once back in my office, sat down to follow up with Matt—only to see Roman's name light up my screen.

My heart jumped.

"Alex Kennedy speaking," I said, trying—and failing—to sound completely professional.

"Hey, Ms. Kennedy. Mr. Perfect here," came Roman's smooth reply.

I laughed. "I'm never living that down, am I?"

"Not a chance. But I did call for a reason. You were right—there's definitely something weird going on. I don't want to get into it on the phone, but I wanted to give you a heads-up."

A chill ran down my spine. I wanted to be right... but not like this.

"Is everything okay?" I asked softly.

"I hope so. But I've got a feeling things are going to get complicated."

He sounded tired—more than tired. Worn thin.

"Well, I guess we'll compare notes at the meeting, then?" I offered gently.

"Yeah. Hopefully, between the two of us, we'll have enough to make sense of this."

His voice was laced with something I hadn't heard from him before: uncertainty. It made my chest tighten.

"I have a dinner meeting to cancel the project," he added. "But I'll call you in the morning, if that's all right?"

"Of course. I'm heading home, heating up leftovers, and having a glass of wine. Actually, speaking of—do you think your mom would mind a call this late? I'd like to schedule a session with her."

"She'd love to hear from you."

We said our goodnights, and I dialed Lisette.

"Hello?" she answered on the first ring—a kind soul and unmistakably Roman's mother.

"Hi Dr. King, it's Alex Kennedy. I hope I'm not calling too late."

"Not at all. And call me Lisette, please."

"I was hoping to schedule an appointment... maybe become a client?"

"Of course. Is everything all right?"

"I think so. I just have something coming up and could use a little guidance."

Family vacations: the real mental health gauntlet.

We settled on Tuesday at four. Home office. Perfect.

After we hung up, I called my aunt.

"Hello?" she answered breathlessly, like I'd made her day.

"Well, hello, my sweetest Auntie D," I said, wine in hand, sinking into my couch.

"Ali girl, what's going on?" She said enthusiastically.

Only she called me that. Ali girl. To my parents I'm Ali Marie. To the world, I'm Alex.

I chewed my thumbnail. "I was just wondering what you think about me bringing... a friend on our vacation?"

"A *friend*?" Her voice sparkled. "Like a *girlfriend* or a *boyfriend*?"

I sighed. "It's a man. But he doesn't have a label."

"Is he gay?"

I choked on my wine, laughing. "I don't think so. But he is *hot*. So let's go with that."

"Ohhh," she sang. "So, *friend* with *benefits*?"

I could barely breathe through the laughter. "I don't know what the benefits are, but sure, why not."

She chuckled in that dry, mischievous way that told me she was humoring me—but absolutely not letting this go.

"If there's no benefit, why bring him?"

Fair question.

"He makes me feel calm. And I need that right now."

That stopped her. Silence settled between us for a beat before her voice softened.

"Well. So you're finally getting in touch with those feelings you pretend you don't have?"

I blinked at the ceiling. "Maybe."

"You'll have to talk to your mom."

Ugh. The words alone gave me hives.

"I know. But I can tell her *you* approve. Do you?"

"I think it's *wonderful*, Ali girl. It's about damn time. That creep you married—he never made you calm."

I winced. "Let's not go there."

"Well, then," she said, brightening. "Bring him to meet the family first."

My stomach twisted. *Meet the parents.* The final boss level of dating.

I mumbled, "If no one likes him—or he doesn't like them—then no harm done, right?"

She laughed. "Exactly."

I said goodbye to my aunt, promising we'd catch up again soon, and ended the call. The screen went dark in my hand, but I didn't move right away. My thumb hovered over the next number, a familiar knot tightening in my stomach.

Calling my mom was different. It always was. I drew in a steadying breath before hitting dial, the phone already warm against my ear from the last conversation. When she picked up, her voice carried that bright edge of expectation, and I pushed a smile into mine. Dinner, she said, could be either Friday or Saturday. I told her I'd check with Roman and let her know.

The second the line clicked off, the silence pressed in heavier, the realization sliding in before I was ready for it.

I still hadn't called Matt.

Too late now.

The meeting would have to do.

Chapter 17

ALEX

The past couple of days blurred by, Roman lingering at the edge of every thought. Our conversations had been light, harmless—nothing remarkable except for the fact that they were with him. And somehow, even the ordinary felt different when it involved Roman King.

I planned to ask him tonight, over dinner, what day might work best to meet my parents. But I hadn't said a word yet about vacation—mostly because I wasn't sure I could handle hearing "no." We were leaving in a week. He ran an empire. Timing wasn't exactly on my side.

I got home around five, stripped off the day, and stepped into the shower. I let the water run hotter than necessary, hoping to rinse off the week's stress, but instead all I could think about was Roman—his voice, his eyes, the way he looked at me like he saw through the surface.

After drying off, I left my robe loosely tied and padded into the kitchen, still damp and barefoot. I poured a glass of wine, turned on some soft jazz, and sank into the couch. The music swirled around me like silk. I scrolled through emails, fingers mindlessly flicking until one caught my eye—an invite from Roman's assistant: a 4:00 p.m. meeting tomorrow.

I accepted it automatically and made a mental note to schedule dinner with my parents right after. Regardless of how the meeting went, I needed to get that over with. Saturday was already booked solid with the Santoros, and Sunday was sacred—brunch with the girls, no exceptions.

As I topped off my wine, there was a knock at the door.

I glanced at the clock. 6:15. Too early for Roman.

But when I checked the Ring cam, there he was, standing there like trouble in a perfectly tailored suit.

I looked down at myself—bare beneath my robe, hair still slightly damp, glass of wine in hand—and debated whether to throw on clothes or just own it.

I opened the door.

Roman's eyes traveled slowly from my bare legs up to my collarbone, lingering a little too long at the parted fabric. The heat in his gaze made my skin tighten.

"Well, hello," he said, voice low and teasing. "Is this what you're wearing to dinner? Because if it is, I might need to change our reservation."

I tilted my head and took a sip of wine, watching him over the rim of the glass. "Are you done yet?"

He laughed, stepping inside. Before I could move, he reached for the belt of my robe, tugging gently. The silk slid slightly, just enough to remind me how little I had on. His mouth brushed close to my ear.

"I'm only just getting started."

"Easy, big guy," I whispered, refusing to flinch. "You're early."

"And lucky," he said, glancing down at me like he might devour me. "This is a welcome surprise."

I pressed a hand to his chest, creating space I wasn't sure I actually wanted. "Would you like a drink while I change?"

"I'd love one," he said smoothly. "Can I drink it while watching you get dressed?"

I choked out a laugh. "How about you sit on that sofa and drink it like a gentleman."

He raised his hands in defeat. "Fine. Just crush my dreams."

I handed him a glass and smirked. "Dreams of watching me get dressed? I'd have thought you'd prefer the opposite. Maybe my aunt was right and you are gay."

He looked wounded, eyes twinkling. "Your aunt thinks I'm gay?"

I nearly spit out my wine.

"I talked to her today," I explained, still giggling. "Told her I might bring a friend on vacation. She asked if you were gay."

His brows shot up. "You told your aunt about me? Wait you want me to go on vacation with you?"

"I was...feeling things out."

"What things?"

"If everyone agreed." But the heat in my face betrayed me.

"Should I be flattered or worried?"

"You should be flattered," I said, leaning in just a little. "But don't get too comfortable. I'm inviting you to meet my parents first. Tomorrow night. After our meeting."

"Testing the waters before the big ask?" he teased, pulling me against his side with one arm while sipping his wine with the other.

"Exactly. I need to know you can survive my family for one night before I ask you to spend a week with them."

His lips brushed my temple. "When do you leave?"

"Next Friday. Back the following Saturday."

He nodded. "If you ask me, and they don't burn me at the stake, I'll be there. And if they don't want me in the house, I'll rent us our own."

I pulled back just enough to narrow my eyes. "We're just friends, remember?"

He sighed dramatically. "Then I'll rent myself a place nearby and pine from afar."

"You're impossible."

"And yet, here I am."

I turned toward the bedroom. "I'm getting dressed. Stay. Behave."

He gave me a playful slap on the rear as I walked away. "That was very romantic, don't you think?"

I tried not to let the way my body reacted show. I needed distance. And clothes.

He looked maddeningly good tonight—khaki linen suit, white shirt opened just enough to be dangerous, no socks, and brown leather shoes. How does he always manage to look like he just stepped off the pages of a fortune 500 magazine?

I chose a form-fitting green dress with a subtle V-neck, light enough for summer, just enough structure to feel put together. Strappy black heels, black clutch. The wine had settled into my limbs just enough to loosen me up, make my skin feel warm.

When I stepped back out, he stood and took my empty glass, placing it next to his.

His eyes darkened. "Wow. Just... wow."

I mirrored his gaze, letting the tension stretch between us.

"You always make me feel underdressed," I murmured.

"Trust me," he said, leaning in. "I'm the one who needs to keep up."

"Let's go," I said, voice low. "Before I change my mind and stay in."

He tucked me into his side in the elevator, hand warm on my lower back, thumb brushing just above the curve of my hip. By the time we reached the lobby, my entire body was humming.

The restaurant was dimly lit, all ambiance and shadows. The hostess greeted Roman like she knew him—of course—and led us to a private booth tucked in the corner. He sat across from me, eyes locked on mine like I was the only thing in the room.

When the waitress came, he ordered my favorite bottle of wine—*How did he know?* I suddenly had a strong suspicion he was the one who paid that tab at Sabastian's that night.

When she left, he leaned forward, voice low. "So... you want to invite me on vacation. As your friend."

I tilted my head. "Was that a question?"

"That depends."

I sipped my wine, letting the silence tease him. "Well, we are friends. Aren't we?"

"We are," he said slowly. "But I'd like to think we're more than that. Too presumptuous?"

"I like it when you presume things."

He smiled, slow and delicious. "Are you dodging the question?"

"I'm agreeing. In my own roundabout way."

He leaned back, victorious. I hated that he always got the last word. I also hated how much I loved it.

"Roman," I said, clearing my throat, "why don't you ever wear a tie?"

He raised an eyebrow. "That's your big question?"

"I'm serious. It's always the same—top two buttons undone, no socks, no tie. There's a pattern. I want to know why."

He smirked. "Would you like me to unbutton more? Maybe take something off? Would that help?"

I stared at him, trying not to let my cheeks give me away. "You're a menace."

He shrugged. "I'm just trying to be accommodating."

The waitress arrived just in time to keep me from saying something I'd regret—or enjoy too much. Roman ordered. I wasn't even listening. My mind was somewhere completely off-menu. I just murmured "same" and hoped it wasn't escargot.

As she walked away, he turned back to me, voice quiet.

"Was there something else?"

I smiled slowly, sipping my wine. "I was just wondering... is there something behind all this?" I said as I motioned my hand towards his attire.

His grin was devastating—I think I was about to find out.

***

ROMAN

I saw the color rise in her cheeks the second the words left her mouth. That pretty pink flush she always tried to hide. She knew—knew I wasn't going to give her the answer she wanted. Not yet, anyway. And maybe not in the way she expected.

I slid out of my side of the booth and pressed in beside her, letting my hip brush against hers. She didn't move to make room. Didn't even turn her head. But the heat coming off her body was undeniable—tight, pulsing, coiled. Whether it was embarrassment or desire, I couldn't say. But I had a guess.

She held her wine glass like it was a lifeline. Her knuckles were pale from the grip, her other hand limp at her side. I took it gently and pressed it against my chest, right over my heart. Her palm was warm, a little damp. I half-expected her to pull away.

She didn't.

Her touch lit something in me—warm at first, like the spark of a match, then spreading in slow waves beneath my skin. It wasn't loud or showy, just a pulse I could feel in my chest, steadying my breath and quickening it all at once.

I turned her hand over and brought it to my lips, brushing a soft kiss across her knuckles. Then I pressed it back against my chest and leaned in closer, so close I could feel her breath hitch. So close I could smell that mix of lavender and vanilla she always wore—delicate and intoxicating. Her hair slid against my cheek as I dipped into the curve of her neck.

"Yeah," I whispered, letting the words drag slow and deep. "There's something behind my clothes. And underneath them."

I closed my eyes, inhaling her. I shouldn't have done it. Not with the waitress due back at any second. Not with the state my body was in. But Alex had that effect on me—pulling me out of my own head and into a place where nothing else existed but this magical pull between us.

She still hadn't moved. Still hadn't opened her eyes. Her hand was trembling slightly on my chest, and I didn't know if it was from nerves or restraint. Maybe both.

"Hey," I said quietly, "you ready to hear why I dress like this all the time?"

She didn't speak. Just nodded, eyes still shut, whispering a shaky *"mhm"* that might've been the sexiest sound I'd ever heard.

Yeah. This backfired. Gloriously.

"Okay," I murmured, brushing a thumb across the back of her hand. "But maybe let go of the glass first. Or at least take a sip and put it down."

Her eyes fluttered open. She took a long drink, nearly draining it, and set the glass down with a clink. Then she turned her gaze on me.

God help me.

Those eyes— crystal green, warm and demanding—snapped something loose in me. It was like trying to speak while drowning.

"Are you done using your superpowers on me?" she asked. "I'd like to eat dinner at some point tonight."

She blinked. "Wait... what did I even order?"

I laughed, relieved. She'd pulled us both back from the edge with one snarky breath. She did that a lot—unraveled me, then stitched me back up like it was nothing.

"You ordered the filet," I said, still grinning. "Medium rare. With asparagus and truffle mashed potatoes."

She let out a soft moan that didn't help me recover at all. "God, that sounds amazing. I'm so glad you ordered that."

We both chuckled, tension bleeding out into something softer.

"You want me to go back to my side?" I asked. My body was finally under control again—barely.

She shook her head, sliding over to give me room. I stayed close anyway.

I topped off our glasses, buying myself a few seconds. I didn't want to say what I was about to say. Not because it was a secret, but because it felt... stupid. Personal. Vulnerable in a way I hadn't planned to be tonight.

"Okay," I started, clearing my throat, "so this is going to sound ridiculous, and I swear I'm not looking for sympathy..."

She tilted her head, waiting. No judgment. Just curiosity.

"I don't wear ties, or button up my shirt all the way, or wear socks... because I'm claustrophobic."

She blinked. "Wait—seriously?"

I nodded, already regretting it.

"How claustrophobic do you have to be to ditch socks?" she asked, eyes wide. "You still wear shoes. You're not out here in Crocs."

I laughed softly. "It's mostly the collar thing. Ties make me feel like I'm choking. Socks just make me... uncomfortable. Same with belts, but I make an exception when pants are non-negotiable."

She snorted. "So the whole 'sexy billionaire rebel' thing is really just trauma from socks?"

"Pretty much," I said, shrugging.

She stared at me for a beat, then smiled. "I thought it was just your thing. Trendy. Sexy."

I looked over at her. "You think I'm sexy?"

She shoved me with her shoulder, laughing. "I am not playing this game with you."

"Oh, come on. You said it."

She rolled her eyes. "You think it's a *superpower*, for God's sake. I'm not feeding your ego."

I smirked, leaning in just a little. "Too late."

That's when the waitress returned—timing, of course, impeccable.

She smiled like she knew exactly what kind of energy she was walking into and set our plates down.

Alex, always quick, lifted a hand and gestured toward me dramatically. "It's fine. We've all been his victims."

The waitress chuckled and nodded, retreating gracefully.

I looked over at Alex again.

She was blushing, beautiful, her laughter still lingering between us.

I reached for her wine glass, topped it off, and decided I'd never get tired of hearing her laugh—especially when I was the reason for it.

Especially when it made her lean just a little closer to me every time.

The food was incredible. The wine, even better. But what had my atten-tion—what always had my attention—was her.

Alex had that distant, glassy look in her eyes that told me her mind was somewhere else entirely. Somewhere warm. Private. Dangerous.

She'd had just enough wine to soften her edges, and I could tell by the way her lips parted ever so slightly when she looked at me that her thoughts weren't innocent. I imagined she was thinking about helping me out of these clothes—not just a few undone buttons, but all of them. And if I was right, that both thrilled and terrified me. Because if we crossed that line, there'd be no turning back. This wasn't some fling. This woman wasn't built for casual. And God help me, I didn't want her to be.

When dinner ended, I guided her outside, holding her hand lightly as we walked to the car. Her fingers were warm in mine, and I didn't want to let go.

"Do you have any appointments or meetings you have to be in the office for tomorrow?" I asked as casually as I could.

She pulled out her phone and scrolled through her calendar.

"Nope," she said. "Just our meeting at four."

I hesitated for a breath, then asked, "Can we stop at your place so you can grab whatever you might need for tomorrow and stay at my place tonight?"

She blinked, as if calculating her answer through the fog of wine. "I guess I can do that."

That "guess" hit me like a cold splash of water.

"You guess?" I tried to keep my tone light, but something in me pulled back. "You don't have to if you don't want to."

She shook her head quickly, correcting. "Sorry, I didn't mean it like that. I was just thinking through everything. Like... do I need to bring clothes for dinner with my parents? Or go home and change in between?"

That perked me right up.

"Just bring everything you need for the day," I said. "Do you have anything going on Saturday?"

She nodded. "Yeah, actually. A couple of showings and... exercise classes I signed up for."

I tried to hide the amused look on my face but failed. "Exercise classes? What more could you possibly need?"

She laughed. "Well... maybe exercise isn't the right word. I signed up for a self-defense class. And kickboxing to control my anger issues. Someone said I put myself in dangerous situations" She winked before continuing, "and I figured it's time I learned to stop doing that—or at least fight back if I do."

Something about the way she said it—half serious, half trying to play it off—sent a slow chill through me.

Kickboxing. Self-defense. Of course I called her reckless.

"I didn't realize you had anger issues," I said, trying not to sound too concerned. "You always seem calm to me."

She turned her head, voice quieter now. "I work hard to be calm. Some days, it takes more effort."

And just like that, I knew not to push. So I didn't.

When we got to her place, I waited in the living room while she gathered a few things. I checked my phone—nothing urgent. Good. When she came out, she had a sleek little satchel over one shoulder. I took it from her and slung it over mine.

In the elevator, I slipped my arm around her waist. She leaned her head against my shoulder, and I closed my eyes for just a second. Whatever storm might be brewing inside her, she let herself rest on me in that moment. And I didn't take that lightly.

"Is everything okay?" I asked as we drove.

She smiled sleepily. "Yeah. Just a little wine-drowsy."

I took her hand, brought it to my lips, and kissed each fingertip. She relaxed, completely.

"Feel free to go straight to bed when we get there."

She gave a soft laugh. "What about a tour first?"

Ah, the realtor in her was still alive and well.

"I'd love to give you a tour." I rubbed the back of her hand absently, pulling into the private garage beneath my building.

When the elevator doors opened into my penthouse foyer, she froze. Like she was seeing something magical.

"You okay?" I asked, glancing around. "Do you see monkeys flying?"

She blinked at me and then burst out laughing. The sound echoed off the stone floors, light and unfiltered. That laugh could knock the wind out of me.

"I'm sorry," she said. "It's just... wow. I've seen nice places, but this..."

"I helped design it," I said, proud but trying not to sound like it.

Her eyebrows shot up. "You did?"

"Worked with one of the architects in the firm downstairs. Designed most of it myself."

She looked at me like I'd just revealed another secret superpower. "You're seriously talented."

I grinned. "Were you questioning that before?"

"Maybe a little," she teased, and I tugged her hand, leading her down the hall.

As we passed my bedroom, I dropped her bag just inside the door. The room lit automatically.

"It's okay if you sleep in here, right?" I asked, already knowing I wanted her here, beside me.

She nodded, glancing into the room.

We moved through the rest of the tour quickly—she asked about design choices, architectural materials, layout flow—but her yawns were getting more frequent. When she stifled another one, I reached for her hand.

"Okay," I said. "Let's finish this in the morning. You look exhausted."

She turned to me suddenly. "Do you have a gym in the building?"

"There's one downstairs, with a lap pool and a sauna. Yoga studio too."

Her eyes lit up like Christmas. "Is it busy in the morning?"

"No one lives in the building but me. And it's locked to the public until 8 a.m. So... just us."

"There aren't any other apartments?"

"There's one other unit, but it's empty. I built it for Harrison. He didn't want it."

She went quiet for a moment, and something flickered in her eyes.

"What's wrong?" I asked, gently lifting her chin.

"I didn't bring a swimsuit."

I exhaled, relieved. "I'll lock the gym. Swim in whatever you want... or nothing at all."

Her expression shifted into a wicked little smile. "I'll think about it."

"Let's go sleep on it," I said, brushing her hair back from her cheek. "You can use my bathroom. I'll take the guest bath."

"Do you want me to sleep in the guest room?" I added, hating the question as it left my mouth.

She looked at me like I'd grown two heads. "Absolutely not. I'm not kicking you out of your own bed."

I smiled. Something tight inside me finally relaxed.

"Good," I whispered, nudging her gently into my room. "Then stay."

And maybe—just maybe—don't leave.

***

ALEX

I slipped into Roman's ensuite with my bag and shut the door behind me, letting the silence settle around me like steam. The bathroom was a dream—more spa than space. White marble glistened across every surface, and the soaker tub looked deep enough to disappear into. The shower, framed in glass and veined stone, could easily fit five people. Multiple showerheads pointed in every direction. The mirror stretched the entire wall above the stone double vanity, and the soft rugs beneath my feet were warm—plush clouds against the cold tile.

It smelled faintly of eucalyptus and something clean and masculine. Probably him.

I stood there for a moment, just absorbing it, until my reflection pulled me back. I looked tired. Not just sleepy—but soul-tired. Like someone who had too many thoughts behind her eyes and not enough silence between them.

I washed my face and slipped into an oversized sleep shirt that hit just below mid-thigh, tossed my hair into a loose knot, and padded out into the bedroom—only to walk straight into Roman.

He didn't say a word. Just wrapped his arms around me and pulled me in, firm but gentle, like he'd been waiting to do it all along. His cheek settled against the top of my head, the faint rasp of stubble brushing my hairline, and I melted into his chest. His heartbeat thudded steady beneath my ear, a low drum I could have matched my own to if it wasn't racing so fast.

His warmth enveloped me, the clean spice of his cologne mixing with the salt of his skin, the soft hum of his breath stirring against my temple. It unraveled me piece by piece, loosening the knots I'd tied so tightly inside.

If I closed my eyes, I could almost believe none of it scared me. Almost. But it did.

His touch was so safe, so grounding, and still my insides trembled, a fine quiver running through me no matter how still I tried to stand. And he felt it. I know he did—the faint tightening of his arms told me he wasn't oblivious.

"What are you afraid of?" he murmured into my hair, his raspy voice, vibrating against my skull like a secret meant only for me.

I tensed, the sound of it lodging deep inside me, and pulled back just enough to meet his eyes. "You don't want to be in my head. It's a mess in there."

His expression darkened—not with anger, but with something softer. "I hate that you feel you can't trust me enough to let me in."

I looked up at him. "I trust you... right now. That's the best I can do."

He nodded slowly. "Then that's enough."

There was a pause, the kind that stretches out and invites something deeper. I found myself asking, "Have you ever been in love?"

He smiled. "Yeah. In third grade. Her name was Faith. She used to steal my pencils and giggle when I couldn't find them."

I laughed, shaking my head as I crawled into the bed. "How about as a big boy?" I teased, my voice pitched playfully.

He climbed in next to me, sliding close and resting his head on my stomach. I instinctively ran my fingers through his hair.

"I've tried, was even engaged once," he said, voice muffled against me. "But my mom—she's always had this way of peeling back layers I didn't know I had. She told me once I didn't know the difference between my feelings and someone else's... and sometimes, I still wonder if she's right. I've kept most women at arm's length because I didn't trust their intentions—or mine."

His honesty stunned me. I traced his hairline, smoothing it back gently.

"What didn't your mom like about the one woman you almost married?"

"She didn't like anyone. But that one... she went out of her way to get rid of her."

"That's weird," I whispered. "I didn't feel like that with her at all. Your mom was kind to me. I felt... safe with her."

He lifted his head, smiling as he looked into my eyes. "You went to her for help. That made all the difference."

Something in the way he said it struck a nerve. That ache—the one I'd carried for years—rose up again.

"I'm sorry," I whispered.

"For what?"

"For anything I might do that ends up hurting you."

He pushed up onto his elbows, studying me. "How would you feel if I said that to you?"

I blinked. "I wouldn't feel much. I already expect to get hurt."

He sat up, fully now. I followed, and he cupped my face like I was something fragile.

"Let me be very clear. I don't know who hurt you, or why you expect it from everyone, but the last thing I could ever do is hurt you. It's not even in me when it comes to you."

A tear escaped down my cheek. "That's nice to hear. But I've heard it before. It's never about intention, Roman. It's just... it always happens. Maybe I expect too much. Maybe I love too hard or hope too much. But distance feels safer—for everyone."

He shook his head slowly. "Well, what if I don't want to keep my distance?"

I looked down, stared at his hands as I held them in mine, searching for answers I'd never find written in his palms.

"You have no idea how much I want to feel the way you do."

He didn't try to fix it. He just pulled me into his arms and held me like he meant it. Like he wasn't afraid of my sharp edges or my softness. My tears soaked into his shirt, and he said nothing—just let me be.

"I feel like such a whiner," I mumbled into his chest.

He kissed my forehead, lips feather-light. "How about we go to sleep and figure it all out in the morning?"

I gave a little laugh. "I'm still planning on that swim, by the way. So you better lock that gym door, because I need to cry it all out in peace."

He grinned—one of those crooked, sexy ones that made my insides melt.

"You realize you didn't bring a swimsuit, right?"

I stretched out beside him with a dramatic yawn. "I'm so sleepy. Guess I'll just have to sleep now..."

He chuckled, his voice low and warm in the dark. "You really are going to be the death of me."

I curled into him, let the weight of the day fall away, and for the first time in a long time, I slipped into sleep feeling safe—still terrified, still unsure—but safe.

And completely wrapped in him.

Chapter 18

ALEX

S ome obnoxious music built to an irritating crescendo—my alarm.

I groaned and reached to shut it off, but Roman's arms tightened around me like a vice. His chest pressed against my back, the steady rise and fall of his breathing warm against my neck. The rough scrape of his morning stubble brushed my shoulder, and his hand slid lower on my waist, anchoring me in place. Heat radiated off him, the weight of his body heavy and unyielding, and the faint scent of soap and cedar clung to his skin. I stilled, caught between the urge to wriggle free and the pull of wanting to stay right there, wrapped up in him.

"I'm trying to turn off my alarm," I giggled, squirming in his grip.

"Come back here for just a little longer," he murmured against my neck.

I sighed dramatically. "Fine. But only five minutes."

"Yes. I win again." He pulled me in closer, one leg thrown over mine. "Now I'm happy." He said victoriously.

I let myself melt into him for a minute, my hand resting over the steady thud of his heartbeat. His scent wrapped around me like a familiar memory I didn't ever want to let go of.

"I'm counting the minutes," I warned, jokingly.

"Okay, but tell me something..." He kissed my shoulder, slow and warm. "What are you wearing in the pool?"

I smirked. "It's a secret." I whispered in his ear then felt the goosebumps ripple across his skin. A second later, he groaned and pressed himself into me, the hardness of his arousal undeniable.

"This is all your fault," he muttered, grinding his hips with a low, frustrated growl.

I rolled my eyes, smiling despite myself. "I think we can share the blame."

I tried to free myself, but he tickled me until I shrieked and begged for mercy, laughing so hard I threatened to pee myself. He finally let me go, and I stumbled to the bathroom with hair sticking up and adrenaline buzzing through my veins.

I changed into workout clothes and tossed a sports bra and underwear into a pouch. They'd work for the pool. No need to overcomplicate things.

When I stepped into the kitchen, Roman was already there—shirtless, of course—making coffee like some domestic dream I never realized I wanted.

"Good morning," he said, smiling as he leaned in for a soft, lingering kiss.

"Do you usually eat or drink anything before working out?" he asked.

That simple question hit me harder than it should have. No one had ever asked me that before. My ex used to roll his eyes when I laced up my sneakers. Roman's question felt like care.

"I usually do a pre-workout mix. You don't happen to have any?"

He grinned. "Strawberry-kiwi, grape, or lemonade?"

"You're joking."

"Nope. They were on sale if you bought three. I stocked up."

I shook my head, smiling. "Strawberry-kiwi, please."

He handed me a shaker and we sat at the kitchen island, sipping in silence, trading smiles like secrets. It felt... normal. Easy. Maybe something worth getting used to.

In the elevator, he gave me a sly look. "So... what are you wearing in the pool?" He asked again.

I smirked. "Still a secret."

"That bag looks suspiciously empty."

"What are you going to do—gawk at me while I swim?"

He didn't even try to deny it. "Maybe."

His gym was ridiculous—spotless, sleek, and private. I cycled through my routine: weights, yoga, cardio. Roman hovered for a while, then vanished. When I finished, I slipped into the locker room, stripped down, wrapped a towel around myself, and walked to the pool.

He was already there lounging at the edge.

I held my arms out dramatically. "Prepare yourself."

He took in every inch of me as I dropped the towel, revealing my sports bra and high-cut black underwear. My skin heated under his gaze.

"Nice." he said, voice reverent.

I laughed. "You need a better eyesight."

Before I could say more, he stood, scooped me up like I weighed nothing, and cannonballed us both into the pool.

We came up gasping and laughing, tangled in each other's arms. His touch was playful, but there was something else—something that made my heart pound faster than it should.

"You really need to stop with the negative self-talk," he said, brushing my wet hair back. "You're gorgeous. And smart. And sweet. And confident."

"That's the second time someone's called me confident this week. I don't feel that way."

He backed me against the pool wall, arms caging me in. "Then we'll work on that. Because I see it. And I'm not the only one."

Goosebumps spread across my skin.

I needed distance. I needed to stop falling.

"Do you have other meetings today besides the one at four?" I asked.

"Yes. Why?"

"Because I need to swim laps, and you need to get ready."

His smirk said he heard the unspoken part of that sentence.

"Will you be working from the apartment?"

I nodded. "And snooping through your things."

"You can snoop anywhere you want."

"Lunch plans?"

"You're free from twelve to two, right?"

"Yes." He remembered my schedule.

"Then we're going out."

With a wink, he swam away, giving me the space I desperately needed.

After laps, we sat in the sauna. I leaned back, eyes closed, sweat slipping down my spine. But peace was short-lived.

Roman's voice was soft. "Can I ask you something?"

"Sure."

"Last night... you said something about needing to step up your game to go out with me. Why?"

My stomach clenched, the question vibrating against my spine where his chest rested. The heat in the room had nothing on the pressure coiling inside me. My voice came out low, uneven.

"It's not you," I murmured, every word catching in my throat. "It's... him. My ex."

And then it all came out. "He didn't like how I dressed. Said I needed to look more polished. Impressive. I had to 'fit in' with his people—designer everything, always put together. Meanwhile, I wasn't allowed access to the bank account and had to 'make it work.' I still don't know if he could even afford what he wore."

Roman listened without interrupting. Then he pulled me closer.

"All that? That was his issues. Not yours."

I nodded, not trusting myself to speak.

"You're so damn beautiful. That bathing suit? Devastating."

I laughed through a tear.

"Don't ever feel like you have to impress me."

I melted into his chest and let the silence say thank you.

***

The rest of the day crawled. Lunch helped—Roman took me to a quiet bistro where we sat on the patio, sunlight catching the red in my hair and the corner of his smile. It was warm. Real. Something I didn't want to jinx by naming.

By 3:55, I was stepping into his office building again, heels clicking, heart hammering.

I'd worn a white pantsuit and nude heels, my hair down, red lipstick on. Not for him. Not for anyone. For me. Because after everything he said in the sauna, I needed to remind myself I could be powerful and soft, composed and chaotic. All at once.

Roman stood in the doorway when I walked in, his eyes dragging over every inch of me before he said, low and close, "Did you wear that for my benefit?"

"Nope," I replied without even glancing at him. "Someone told me to wear whatever I wanted. So, I wore this for me."

The groan that slipped out of him was barely audible—but it made my thighs clench.

"Good girl," he murmured.

My breath caught. My body reacted before my mind could. I shifted, heart thudding against my ribs. His gaze was fire. And then—knock, knock.

Matt.

Roman exhaled like he'd been holding his breath. I darted toward the door just as Matt walked in, casual and friendly. He kissed my cheek and gave me one of those brotherly hugs that had always felt like a security blanket.

"Roman," he said, shaking his hand. "Good to see you again. Looking forward to hanging out more."

"Same," Roman replied, keeping it cool, collected.

Matt turned back to me. "Harder to get her to bring herself," he said with a smirk.

Roman raised a brow. "How many points are you down?"

"None," I said, biting my lip.

"Damn cheater," Roman muttered, as Matt looked between us like he'd stumbled into a silent game neither of us admitted we were playing.

Harrison showed up late. He looked like a walking hangover, one hand in his pocket, the other lazily holding his phone. Roman's jaw ticked as he watched his brother stroll in like the world owed him something.

We all sat down, and the room went still.

Roman opened. "Thanks for coming. I know we've all been circling this deal from different angles, and it's clear now that there's more going on than we thought. So, I'd like to get everyone on the same page."

Matt nodded. "Roman, I appreciate that. I want to keep this as cordial as possible. My friendship with Alex is important, and I'm getting to know you now, too."

Roman glanced at me, then back at Matt. "That matters to me, too."

I took a breath. "I know I can get emotional. So, if I come off strong, it's only because I care."

Roman offered me a reassuring smile. "Understood. And I'll be mindful of how I say things. I know this project means a lot to you."

Then Harrison—because of course he did—yawned. Loudly.

Roman turned to him, ice in his voice. "Harrison, do you have anything to add?"

"Not really. I don't even know why I'm here."

Roman's eyes narrowed. "Because you're about to learn what it means to separate business from personal."

"Already heard that speech from Dad," Harrison said, smirking.

Roman leaned forward. "And maybe it's time you listened."

I braced myself.

Roman held up three fingers. "Here are your options: One, sit and listen like a professional. Two, keep mouthing off and I'll match your energy. Or three, get out."

Harrison held up a single finger with a flick. Option one. His smug expression didn't budge. I think I heard Roman groan, an explicative under his breath.

Roman turned back to Matt. "I was in Texas recently, sorting out a zoning issue on one of our smart home sites." He glared at his brother. "While I was there, I met a man named Tanner Ellington—brother of Marcus Ellington, who's heading up the Burrow Township project."

Matt tensed. "I've been trying to reach Marcus for weeks. No response."

"Because he's busy lining his pockets," Roman said flatly. "Turns out, he removed the historical preservation status from that section six months ago and sold it off piece by piece to investors. Fast, and shady and apparently our investors donated to that transaction."

Harrison's face went sheet white.

Roman looked at me. "You have more context."

I nodded, my jaw tight. "I'm representing one of the last homeowners still fighting. The others were pushed out or priced out. There was no real notice, just 60 days."

"Tanner told me Marcus saw an opportunity and took it," Roman added. "Same patterns in Texas. When I asked what Marcus actually owns, he dodged the question."

He met my eyes. "And just so you know—Tanner Ellington? He's the one I elbowed at the bar that night."

I blinked. "No f'ing way." I blurted before I could think to stop myself.

Harrison grinned. "Nice mouth. Do you kiss your mother with that?"

I ignored him. "Sorry," I muttered, dragging my hands over my face. "It's just... that complicates things."

Matt looked confused. "Why? What's going on?"

"Remember the 'protecting me' conversation at your house?"

"Yeah. Roman elbowed some guy for being gross. What about it?"

I closed my eyes for a second. "He assaulted me, Matt. So, I returned the favor."

Matt stared. "You what?"

"I grabbed his favorite part until he dropped. Told him to keep his hands to himself."

Matt laughed, then covered his mouth. "Does Maggie know about this?"

"No. I figured one assault disclosure per evening was enough."

"Well, it's not enough now," Matt said. "If we're in this, we need full transparency."

I nodded. "No one here's at risk of seeing that side of me. But if Marcus and Tanner find out I'm involved in this... it's going to be a problem."

Roman turned to Harrison. "Who brought you this deal?"

Harrison shifted. "A friend's brother. He's a cop in Burrow Township. Said something big was coming. I didn't ask questions. I should've. I didn't know the land was protected. Or that the people were being forced out."

Roman nodded slowly. "From now on, every deal goes through me. Full transparency."

Then he turned to me again. "Alex, would you be open to helping us research future investments? You clearly spot things we don't."

That... I hadn't expected.

"Yes," I said, surprised by how much I meant it. "I'd love that."

"And the buyers?" I asked. "Do we know what agency is selling off the properties? Maybe I can negotiate with them."

Harrison hesitated. "You're not going to like it."

"Try me."

"Tanner Ellington."

I looked to the ceiling, mouthing obscenities repeatedly, praying someone would offer divine intervention.

Roman added, "There's more."

I groaned. "Of course there is. What now?"

"This is the boogeyman part," he said. "Marcus and Tanner's father used to work for my dad. He was fired seven years ago—for real estate fraud. Political bribes. Forged deeds. After he died, Marcus came to my father and said his dad's dying words were that the King family would pay for ruining him."

My stomach dropped.

Roman looked at me. "Seems he passed the con down like a family heirloom."

I couldn't breathe. Couldn't sit.

"I need air."

I stood and walked out before anyone could stop me.
I didn't even realize I was moving until the door clicked shut behind me.

I kept going—I had to. The hallway outside Roman's office stretched long and empty, every step hollow, every breath too shallow. The silence pressed in, amplifying the thrum of my pulse in my ears. By the time I reached the end, the tightness in my chest stole the air from my lungs.

My palm slapped against the wall without thought. The surface was cool, unyielding, a sharp contrast to the heat burning under my skin. I leaned into it, eyes squeezed shut, trying to hold myself together as the panic rattled loose inside me.

Breathe.

In for four. Hold. Out for seven.

Again.

It wasn't working.

Marcus Ellington. Tanner. Their father. Roman's family. My name and face entangled in a web I never intended to touch, much less fall into. How the hell had I gone from sipping coffee in his kitchen to setting off landmines in his boardroom?

I'd meant to do good. To help. But what if I just made everything worse?

My chest tightened. My skin flushed hot, then cold. I closed my eyes, trying not to fall apart. This wasn't just another real estate deal. This was blood money, and I'd just dragged Roman King into the middle of it with me.

Footsteps approached. I didn't look. Not until a soft voice cut through the hum in my ears.

"Alex?"

I turned. Amelia was standing near the front desk, gathering her things. Her brows pinched, lips tugged down in concern.

"You okay?"

I wanted to say yes.

Instead, I gave her the same weak smile I'd been handing out like breath mints lately. "I hope so."

She stepped a little closer, her tone kind but careful. "Rough meeting?"

That almost made me laugh. "Let's just say I wasn't expecting to find out my ex-groper is the brother of the guy we're investigating... or that the whole family has a vendetta against Roman's."

Her face softened with something like compassion—and maybe something more. Loyalty or concern, I'm not sure which.

"Sweetie... I don't know what's going on exactly, but I do know Roman doesn't bring just anyone in like this. If he's letting you close, that means something."

I blinked fast, trying to keep the burn behind my eyes from turning into tears. "I want to lean on him. I do. But I think I'm the one who just lit a match under his entire company."

She stepped closer, her hand light on my arm. "Then I'll pray it works out. Roman has a way of making things right. And more than that—he knows how to choose the people he believes in." The certainty in her voice carried the weight of someone who'd lived it.

"I'll take all the prayers I can get," I whispered to myself not knowing if I even believed there was anyone to answer them.

She smiled then she walked away and left me standing there, heart still racing, hands still shaking.

But not for long.

Matt came barreling out of the office and wrapped me in a hug without saying a word...I didn't even try to hold it together.

"Jesus, Matt," I mumbled into his chest, my voice thick. "What the hell am I going to do?"

He gently pulled me back, hands gripping my shoulders just firm enough to anchor me. His eyes locked on mine.

"Alex, listen to me. You are *not* alone in this. We're going to help you help those people—do you hear me? Don't think for one second that you're carrying this by yourself."

And just like that, the floodgates opened again.

I threw my arms around his neck and pressed my face against him, letting the pressure of it all roll through me—the anger, the fear, the exhaustion. Every emotion I'd been trying to keep in a neat little box spilled out and soaked into the shoulder of his jacket.

"I'm so angry right now," I hissed, pulling back just enough to see his face.

Matt offered a smile that turned serious. "I can tell. That's why I'm coming at this two ways. First, I'm pushing for a fraud investigation into the Ellingtons. Second, I'm calling in some favors—quiet ones—to start undermining them politically."

My stomach dropped. That wasn't a small move. He had Maggie. Kids. A life that didn't need to be dragged into this.

"Matt, be careful. Please. I don't want anything happening to you, or Maggie, or the kids. We both know what people like the Ellingtons are capable of."

It wasn't until I felt the pressure in my fingers that I realized I was gripping the lapel of his blazer like a lifeline. He reached up and covered my hand.

"I promise," he said. "Nothing is going to happen to any of us. Including you."

I let out a long breath and released my grip, nodding.

We hugged again, just as Roman stepped into the hallway.

The worried expression on his face was twisting me up inside.

I stood a little straighter, wiped beneath my eyes, and pushed the emotions down far enough to speak clearly.

"Let's meet again next week—before I go on vacation. We'll come up with a solid game plan. How does that sound?"

They both looked surprised for a second—then they grinned, that same crooked, we're-in-this kind of grin.

"Hell yeah," they said in unison.

That was the thing about me—I could spiral. I could fall apart. But I always came back ready to fight.

Once Harrison had slinked off to wherever Harrison slinks off to, Roman and I walked Matt to the garage. He and Roman shook hands, and then Matt turned and gave me a tight hug, his hand patting the back of my head like a big brother who knew I needed it.

After he drove off, I lingered by the car, my phone buzzing like it had a personal vendetta. One glance at the screen made me laugh under my breath.

"Someone harassing you?" Roman asked, tipping his chin toward it.

"Yeah. Maggie and Abby. Tag-teaming me." I flashed him the screen.

He smirked. "Let me guess—Matt told Maggie what's going on?"

"Not exactly. He only told Maggie about Tanner. You know, my little bar-room moment."

Roman arched a brow, and I groaned. "Yeah, I know. I never told them. I figured dropping the whole 'Roman broke Tanner's nose' thing was enough excitement for one night. No need to add my antics on top. They worry."

He didn't say anything at first. Didn't move to get in the car either. He stayed where he was, leaning against the passenger side with a far-off look in his eyes—until they found mine again.

"You know we're going to be early for dinner if we leave now," he said, his tone was filled with unease. "Do you want to stop and get a glass of wine? That was... a lot, back there. I'm sorry, truly. I feel like I've put you in a really bad position."

I stared at him like he'd lost his mind.

"First, yes—I could very much use that drink. And second... how exactly did *you* put me in a bad position? Roman, if anyone's to blame, it's me. If I'd just kept my head down and minded my business..."

"No." His tone cut through my spiral before it could take root. "Don't do that."

I turned toward the car to avoid the heat crawling up my neck, but he moved faster. One second, I was facing the door, and the next, his hands were at my waist, gently spinning me to face him. He stepped close—too close—backing me up to the car door and looked me dead in the eye, grounding me the way only he could.

"This is not your fault," he said, slow and sure. "These are bad people doing bad things. This would've come out eventually. You just lit the match a little earlier. And that's a good thing."

I opened my mouth, but he wasn't done.

"I know some good cops. Matt and Jack do too. We'll get them involved. But I don't want you doing anything more than helping those people sell their homes. Just that. Let us handle the rest."

The way he said it—like I was worth protecting—knocked the breath right out of me. I slid my arms around his neck and buried my face in his chest, inhaling the quiet comfort of him.

"I'll talk to Grant too," I muttered. "He's going to lose his mind when he finds out someone's messing with me. He's pretty protective of me."

Roman chuckled, arms tightening around me.

"I'm glad you've got people looking out for you," he murmured. "You're a very lucky woman."

"Lucky seems to be the word of the week," I whispered, rolling my forehead against his collarbone. "I just don't know how much of it I have left."

And the truth in that statement—it settled in my bones like smoke after fire. I felt scorched, stripped down, but somehow... still standing.

Still ready.

***

ROMAN

We stopped for a drink—something to take the edge off the tension still clinging to her shoulders. She was quiet. Deep in thought. I let her be. Some silences say more than words ever could.

Then we headed to her parents' house.

They lived on the west side of town, way out near a golf course, surrounded by trees and open sky. Peaceful and quiet, except for the storm of nerves I could feel radiating off Alex as we pulled into the driveway.

I caught the flicker of hesitation in her expression as she glanced toward the front door.

"You okay?" I asked.

She nodded, but not convincingly. "Yeah. Just... brace yourself. They're a lot."

Noted.

We stepped inside, and Alex paused, frowning.

"They have a dog—Sadie. She's usually all over everyone the second they walk in." She said before looking around some more.

I followed her through the hallway toward a bright, open-concept living room, and there she was—Sadie, I'm assuming, on the other side of the sliding glass door, losing her mind trying to get inside. Alex sighed in relief and opened the door just enough to let her in.

The moment the door cracked, the rest of the house came alive. Laughter, clinking glasses, voices raised over one another in a cheerful kind of chaos. Her family was out on the back deck, soaking up the last bit of sunlight while the grill sizzled nearby.

Alex turned to me, smirking. "Get ready. They're all nuts."

I leaned in a little, amused. "I like nuts."

As soon as she opened the back door, a tall guy with a drink in hand—her oldest brother, she explained in a rush—grinned wide and shouted, "Well, it's about damn time!" Before Alex could react, he slung an arm around her and spun her off the ground as if she weighed nothing.

"It's 6:55," she said flatly, shaking him off.

A woman followed up with a warm hug for Alex and a handshake for me. "Ignore him" she instructed, smiling. Then, under her breath, while still hugging Alex, she added, "Bianca," just for me.

Alex grinned. "I know. I just don't know how you put up with him."

They laughed, and I was already starting to piece together the family dynamic—loud, fast-talking, fiercely loyal.

The other brother, Patrick, walked over and raised an eyebrow. "Did you pick this guy up off the street, or were you planning to introduce him?"

Alex held up a hand. "Can we get through the door first, please?"

Sadie trotted out beside us as I followed her across the deck, where everyone was seated.

"This is Roman," Alex said, gesturing vaguely in my direction. "Roman, this is everyone."

They all stood and came over, one by one—introductions, handshakes, a few lingering looks. I could feel them sizing me up, deciding if I was worth their sister's time. I didn't blame them.

At one point, I caught her mother glancing at me with a tilted head and narrowed eyes. She pulled Alex aside, not exactly subtle. I couldn't hear the words, but I caught the expression on Alex's face—something between disbelief and barely-contained laughter.

Later, she whispered to me, "She asked how much plastic surgery you've had."

I blinked. "Excuse me?"

Alex giggled. "I told her you were like a Ken doll. Only prettier."

Not sure whether to be flattered or concerned.

I spent some time talking to her dad, checking in on how he was doing post-heart attack. He seemed good—healthy, tired of being fussed over, maybe. I liked him. No nonsense. The kind of man who probably knows how to read a room without saying much or he just didn't get in the middle of the rest of them.

For the rest of the night, I barely saw Alex. Her family had me moving from one chair to another, one conversation to the next. Everyone wanted to know what I did, what I drank, if I could cook, if I golfed. It felt like an informal interview—one I didn't mind passing.

When I finally made my way back to her, she looked up at me with a mixture of amusement and exhaustion.

"Your family's fun," I said honestly. "Not nuts."

She smiled, one brow arched. "Trust me, that was their best behavior. Enjoy it while you can—it won't last."

I believed her.

"You ready to go?" I asked.

"Yes. God, yes," she breathed out.

We got in the car, and once we were alone, the energy between us shifted. to something more relaxed.

I glanced over. "I've been wanting to ask you something."

She raised an eyebrow. "Yeah?"

"Your place or mine?"

She laughed. "Well, I don't have any more clothes to wear at your house."

I shrugged. "That's fine. You don't have to wear any."

She rolled her eyes, but I saw the smirk pulling at her lips.

"Without all this ammo I give you, you'd have nothing."

"On the contrary," I said. "You're giving me everything."

She turned to the window, pretending not to smile.

"We can go to your place, but I don't have clothes there either," I teased.

She tilted her head. "Okay, here's an idea—you drop me at my place, then you can go to yours." Her tone dripped with all the snark she could muster.

I caught her face in the corner of my eye, her reflection in the window lit with mischief.

"Yeah," I said finally. "I've got nothing for that one. So instead—I'm staying at your place. And no clothes it is."

Her laughter filled the car as we drove into the night. And just like that, I knew I was in deep.

Chapter 19

ALEX

Saturday morning, the alarm buzzed at 5:00 a.m. as usual. I slipped out of bed carefully, trying not to wake Roman, and tiptoed into my running gear. In the kitchen, I prepared my pre-workout drink as quietly as possible.

Apparently, I wasn't as quiet as I'd hoped. Suddenly, a pair of arms wrapped around my waist, and Roman rested his head on my shoulder.

"Good morning," he whispered, pressing a gentle kiss to my cheek. Then, with a sleepy grin, he asked, "What's for breakfast?"

"Anything you want," I said with a smile, "but first, I'm heading out for my run."

He let out a dramatic sigh and dropped his arms. "Right. I must've forgotten. And clearly, I can't go with you—I've got nothing to wear. Mind if I meet you at the coffee shop after I run home and change?"

"Sure," I said, heading toward the door. "But don't even think about offering me a ride home."

Roman held up his hands in surrender, backing away with a playful grin. "Okay, okay. I promise—no ride offers."

He pulled me in for one last hug, smooshing a kiss against my cheek before letting me go.

***

I walked longer than usual, lost in thought about the conversation—well, interrogation—I'd had with Roman's mom. On the surface, we'd gotten along fine. But after talking to Roman, I couldn't shake the feeling she'd been probing for something—some excuse to push me away like she had with all his other girlfriends.

Maybe I was just being paranoid. Again.

I had too much on my plate today to spiral into that. This kind of emotional chaos was exactly why I'd sworn off *relationships*. Ugh.

I jogged the rest of the way to the coffee shop, spotting Roman outside with two coffees and a blueberry muffin. My stomach flipped—he remembered. The butterflies were annoying, but I couldn't help smiling.

"Thank you," I said, sliding into the chair across from him, careful not to brush him with my sweat-drenched self.

He gave a slight nod. "How was your run?"

"Productive, as well as my walk."

"A *productive* walk? Do tell." He asked to make conversation, I guess.

"I like to think when I walk. Got a lot of that done today."

"That's good," he said. "Anything you want to share?"

About your mom? Ha. Yeah, no.

"Not really." I deflected with a bite of muffin, letting the blueberry sweetness melt on my tongue.

Roman watched me closely, like he was trying to read between the crumbs. I could tell he was working hard to get past my walls. But why? How could he not see the obvious trainwreck I was?

He asked about my schedule today. I told him I had appointments the majority of the day and a self-defense class at four, followed by kickboxing at five.

"You must be a glutton for punishment. Aren't you going to be sore tomorrow?"

I laughed. "Oh, I'll be sore tonight. Guaranteed."

"Well," he said, leaning back, "I'll leave you be. I'm having dinner with my parents and Harrison. Dad and I are planning to talk to him about his particular brand of business practices."

He exhaled slowly, raising his eyebrows. I could tell it wasn't going to be a light-hearted family meal.

"I won't be up for anything tonight anyway," I said. "I'm planning to abuse myself into oblivion."

"I can only imagine."

We said our goodbyes, and I jogged home.

***

Saturday showings were usually casual. Since I'd be walking a lot, I picked a flowy white cotton maxi dress with long sleeves and a deep V-neck—breezy but elegant. I added a tan wide-brim hat, some gold jewelry, and finished it off with thick-soled brown leather sandals.

Before heading out, I called Mr. Santoro to confirm our first stop. We met at the property and toured the grounds: ten acres, a 10,000-square-foot house that looked like it was plucked straight from the Italian countryside.

"This reminds us of home," Mr. Santoro said. "We're even planning to transport our vineyard grapes from Italy to replant here."

The logistics sounded wild, but I nodded, impressed. I told them both properties were zoned for residential and commercial use, so setting up a winery wouldn't be an issue.

Afterward, we settled at a café down the street, the kind with open windows and soft instrumental music drifting between tables. The air was warm, the kind of day that made you want to linger, and conversation came easily.

Curious, I asked why they'd chosen Ohio when they already had vineyards in California and North Carolina.

Mr. Santoro rested his elbows on the table, thoughtful. "The weather here is better suited to the grapes. And the people—we like the culture in the Midwest. Honest. Grounded. And the private schools here reflect our values."

I sat back, surprised. They weren't just testing the waters. They were intentional. Strategic. These were people who knew exactly what they were doing.

"Sounds like you've really thought this through," I said. "Makes my job easier."

Mrs. Santoro smiled, then surprised me with: "So, Alex, is there someone special in your life?"

I blinked. Kind of a strange question, but they were clearly family-oriented, so maybe not *too* weird.

"I'm keeping my options open," I replied. "I made a bad choice in my first marriage. I'm not in a hurry to repeat that mistake." My mind drifted quickly from Luke to Roman and I had to stifle a smile.

They exchanged a look, then Mr. Santoro nodded. "Very wise."

We toured the second property—every bit as stunning as the first, with details that could have sealed the deal for most buyers. Afterward, we said our goodbyes at the curb, their smiles warm and polite. They promised to let me know soon whether one of the houses felt right, or if we'd keep searching.

As I watched them drive away, my gut tugged in a familiar way. I had a hunch the first property had already captured their interest. And my instincts in these matters were rarely wrong.

On the drive to the MMA studio, my phone buzzed with a notification. The zoning had changed—*no longer commercial* on either property. My blood boiled. I didn't have time to deal with it now, but I had a pretty good idea who pulled the strings. This wasn't over.

I slammed Betty's door and stormed into the studio like a woman possessed.

"Whoa. What happened to you?" Bruce asked from behind the desk.

"Don't ask. Just let me hit something," I grumbled, tossing my bag.

He smirked. "Should I be worried you'll hurt *someone*?"

"Probably. Though it'll likely just be me." We both laughed. He handed me my bag that landed somewhere behind the desk with him.

"Go get changed and join the group."

The first class was beginner self-defense. I asked to be paired with a man—I wanted realism without doing any real damage. By the end, I was already sore.

During my break, I gulped water and tried to sweat out my rage.

Bruce helped me wrap my hands for the next class, the fabric pulling snug across my knuckles, scratchy and tight enough to bite into my skin. The smell of rubber mats and sweat hung heavy in the air, mixing with the faint smell of disinfectant.

An hour of kickboxing—no breaks. By the halfway mark my lungs burned like fire, my mouth dry with the taste of salt. My stomach rolled, threatening to turn inside out. I paused, bent at the waist with my hands braced on my thighs, sweat dripping off my jaw and splattering onto the mat.

But each time, I straightened, gloves up, heart hammering in my ears. The sting of impact vibrated through my arms with every strike. My legs shook, jelly under me, but I forced them to keep moving. By the final round, I was running on nothing but willpower—shaky breaths, aching muscles, and a stubborn refusal to quit.

After class, I collapsed on the mat. Bruce sat down beside me.

"Why are you doing this to yourself?" he asked, nudging me.

"I'm angry. A lot. And I don't want to take it out on anyone else. I need to keep that in check."

"What are you angry about?"

"Where do I start?" I exhaled. "My failed marriage. My alcoholic mother. Her selfishness. How I let people treat me. How I treat myself, you know the self-loathing."

He was quiet. Then he said, "We've never really talked before, have we?"

"Nope. You caught me at my weakest. Too tired to guard the gates."

He laughed and nudged me again. "Alex, we all have demons. You're dealing with yours better than most. But the 'self-loathing' part—that worries me. What do you have to hate about yourself?"

I hesitated, then said, "I feel like a fraud. Like I've just gotten lucky and eventually everyone will figure it out. My ex—he wasn't like the guys my friends picked. I chose wrong. And now, I want to avoid relationships entirely. But Roman? He's not letting me."

Bruce leaned back with a laugh. "You mean, you *like* him and you're getting comfortable. Let me guess—this is the guy who broke that jerk's nose last week?"

I groaned. "You're terrible at this. You're supposed to tell me to run."

"I don't give that advice unless it's necessary. This? Doesn't sound like one of those times."

"Thanks, O wise one. But I prefer wine to wisdom." I paused. "Actually, both would be great right now." With Wine Comes Wisdom, I thought. "One last thing..."

He raised an eyebrow. "Yeah?"

"Help me up off this floor, please."

Chuckling, he pulled me to my feet, handed me an electrolyte drink, and patted my shoulder. I told him I'd be back next week before my vacation.

In the car, I noticed a new message on my phone: *"You've been gifted a one-hour massage from Roman King. We will arrive at 8:00 p.m. Please confirm."*

I called him, forgetting he was with his family. He still picked up.

"Hey, did you send me a massage?"

"I did. Thought you'd need it after all that training."

"That's... so thoughtful. Seriously, thank you. I might need a full body cast instead, but I'll enjoy every minute."

"You're welcome. You deserve it."

I almost wished he'd stop being so nice. It was making it harder to believe I was the mess I thought I was or that when he finally saw it, he'd run, and I'd be in deep by then and get my heart ripped out.

Stop getting ahead of yourself Alex.

"I'll let you get back to your family. Tell them I said hello." We hung up and I confirmed the appointment.

That evening, the masseuse arrived—with a bouquet of African daisies and a lavender candle.

"Courtesy of Mr. King" the lady said.

He really was leading me straight up the garden path, and I was starting to forget why I ever wanted to avoid it.

***

ROMAN

I smiled as I hung up the phone with Alex. The massage and flowers were the least I could do. Honestly, I would've preferred to give her that massage myself, but for now, this would have to do.

Lately, I'd been thinking about what my mom said—about needing patience. She was right. Alex was doing everything she could to keep me at a distance. And still, she invited me on this family vacation. I knew that meant something. I just wasn't sure what.

Maybe Mom could help. She had a way of seeing people—especially women—that I didn't always catch right away.

"Mom, can we talk for a minute?"

"Of course," she said, smiling. "Do we need to swing?"

I laughed. "No swings required this time. Just some advice... about the trip with Alex next week."

"I'm so glad she invited you. That's exciting. What's on your mind?" she asked, resting a hand on my arm like she used to when I was nervous as a kid.

"I'm starting to feel like maybe she doesn't want me around as much as she says. Do you think there's something she's not telling me? Could she cancel on me last-minute?"

"Roman," she said, her voice gentle, "I told you before—Alex is a complex woman. How much time have you two been spending together lately?"

"A lot," I admitted. "Maybe too much? I don't know. I just... worry about her. She doesn't seem to care much about her own safety. She takes risks. I try to point things out, but I think she resents it."

My mom's look told me everything before she even spoke. "And what does *she* say about that?"

I sighed. "She says she never used to worry until I started listing all the things she should be worried about."

She nodded slowly. "Then maybe it's time to ease up. You can't protect someone who doesn't want protection. You'll only push her away."

Right. Message received. The words landed heavy, like a weight pressing against my chest. I wanted to be helpful—but instead I could feel the tension building around me, sharp as static in the air. My stomach tightened, my pulse kicking up, the sting of being more burden than blessing cutting deep. Not exactly the plan.

"She's not pushing you away because she doesn't care," my mom added. "She's doing it because she *does*. You're close enough to matter now—and that's scary for someone who's been hurt."

That hit harder than I expected. I didn't say anything, just nodded and we rejoined Harrison and dad.

After dinner, my dad caught my eye and gave a subtle wave of his hand. That was the signal. Time for a talk—with him *and* Harrison. This wasn't going to be a pleasant one.

Harrison had no idea what was coming.

Mom quietly left the patio, already knowing what was about to go down.

Dad poured a drink and started casual, which meant the blow was going to be hard. "Boys, I couldn't be prouder of everything you've built together. The way you've grown this company—hell, it's every father's dream. But..." He paused, his jaw tightening. "If you two don't start making better business decisions, you're going to drive it into the ground."

He slammed his glass on the table.

Harrison and I exchanged a glance. So much for casual.

I tried to play it straight. "Alright. What do I need to do differently?"

"Yeah, same here," Harrison said. I was a little surprised by how agreeable he sounded—especially since he hadn't realized yet that the criticism was about to land squarely in his lap.

Dad narrowed his eyes. "An old enemy of mine—someone I fired years ago—seems to be creeping back into our business through his kids. And you two rolled out the damn red carpet for them."

"What?" I said, taken aback. "I didn't have anything to do with those deals." I edged slightly away from Harrison, subtly throwing him under the bus.

Dad gave me *that* look—the one that used to shut me up cold as a kid.

"Roman, you may not handle the investment side, but you're not off the hook. Everything in this company is connected. You had just as much opportunity to do your homework on who was involved."

He spun the top off the bourbon bottle with one flick of his thumb—another bad sign. Dad didn't usually drink like this unless he was really upset.

I straightened in my seat. "You're right, sir. I should've looked closer."

"Cut the 'sir' crap," he snapped.

I bit back a smirk and took a sip of my drink instead.

"Okay, fair enough. I told Harrison after our last meeting that I wanted to be looped in on all future deals."

Harrison scoffed. "Yeah, and that's going to slow everything down because Roman has to inspect every detail with a microscope."

Dad turned his glare on Harrison now. *Game on.*

"Smart business, son. Unless you *want* some shady politician screwing up your projects."

Then Dad leaned in. "So, Harrison—what the hell were you thinking, getting involved with those people?"

"I didn't know anything shady was going on!" Harrison snapped. "He's a state rep!"

"Exactly. The worst kind of crook," Dad said, his voice rising. "Zoning kickbacks? You didn't even check?"

Harrison looked ready to explode. "How was I supposed to know?!"

"Did you investigate? Did you ask someone who *does* know?"

Harrison's jaw locked. "You mean Roman?" he practically growled.

"Yes, Roman. He knows how to pull zoning permits; he's a builder for God's sake."

Harrison looked down, clearly pissed, then threw out a snide, "Fine. I'll remember that next time. Sorry I'm still the family screw-up."

There it was.

He shoved back from the table, snatched up his drink, and threw it back in one swallow. The glass hit the bar with a rough smack, teetered, then toppled to the floor with a sharp shatter. He didn't so much as glance at the mess—just turned on his heel and stormed out, leaving everyone else to clean up his mess. Classic Harrison.

I was ready to call him out again, but Dad held up a hand to stop me.

"He's a tough nut to crack," he said quietly. "I don't know if I'll ever get through to him. He doesn't respond to tough love, but I can't coddle him either. I just hope something sticks—and maybe some of *you* rubs off on him."

Pretty sure Harrison prided himself on being the *opposite* of me.

"Dad," I said, "I know it doesn't always seem like it, but I think he listens. He just stores it away. In that thick skull of his."

Dad laughed. We both did.

A few minutes later, Mom reappeared with a dish towel in hand. She crouched to gather the shards of glass, her movements careful, her sigh almost lost under the clink of pieces hitting the trash. Concern flickered across her face, but she didn't say a word—just straightened, smoothed the apron she must've put on to protect her dress and carried on as if this wasn't the first time she'd had to tidy up after one of Harrison's storms.

We shared one last drink in silence before calling it a night

Chapter 20

ALEX

I don't think I'll be running this morning.

The thought came quietly as I laid still, taking a slow, almost cautious inventory of every muscle in my body. Everything hurt. Not in a sharp, alarming way—but in that deep, slow-throb kind of way that reminds you you've been pushing too hard. That your body isn't just a machine to be fixed with coffee and willpower.

Maybe I should rest. Maybe just this once I should let myself off the hook. I've heard you're supposed to take a day off. Recovery and all that.

I rolled onto my side, careful not to wince out loud. This was the first Sunday morning in a long time where I hadn't woken up foggy-headed, dehydrated, or piecing together slurred memories from the night before. No wine haze. No regret clinging to my ribs. I blinked at the ceiling and actually laughed—a dry, brittle laugh—because even without the alcohol, I still managed to wreck myself last night. Turns out you don't need a bottle to beat yourself up. You just need a pair of gloves and a chip on your shoulder.

My phone buzzed next to me.

MAGGIE: *Hey jerk face, you coming to brunch?*

God, I've got to talk to her about my nickname.

ME: *Damn, I went from jerk to jerk face?*

MAGGIE: *LOL!!! Yeah, before you were a whole jerk, now it's just your face. Progress!!!*

ME: *OMG, if I didn't love you, I'd smack you."*

ABBY: *Should we bring boxing gloves to brunch today?*

ME: *NO NO NO! Please don't say boxing gloves!!!*

ABBY: *Um, what's wrong with saying that?*

ME: *I'll tell you when I see you. 11:30 on the nose, don't be late this time girls!!!*

MAGGIE: *You beat us to the restaurant once in how many years, and all of a sudden we're the ones not showing up on time?*

I let out a little laugh and left it there, heart warmed by their usual banter. These girls—they're home. They don't even know it, but they keep me anchored when the world starts spinning.

Dragging the dress over my head took everything I had. My arms protested. My back protested louder. The soft blue mandala print maxi dress felt like the only option—long sleeves to hide the bruises I didn't want to explain, breathable fabric that didn't cling to every tender spot. Even putting on shoes was a production. I spotted some old platform sandals on the closet floor and thanked the universe I didn't have to reach for the sandals on the top shelf.

I moved gingerly getting into my car. I leaned into the seat with a sigh and whispered, "Let's do this."

Five minutes early. A record.

MAGGIE: *Hey jerk face, we saved you a seat. LOL.*

Of course they beat me here. Probably just to throw me off my texting game.

I spotted the mimosas first—one already sitting at my place. The girls stood to hug me, and I braced myself.

"Girl, you look amazing," Maggie said, pulling back to study me. "Are you doing something different?"

I laughed—except it wasn't really a laugh. More like a groan disguised as amusement. "Yes. I'm purposefully kicking the crap out of myself."

The mimosa was cold, fizzy, and went down half in one gulp. I needed it—not for a buzz, but as a kind of soft reprieve. A buffer between me and the ache.

Abby's brows knit together. "What? Like...at the gym?"

"Yes and no." I set the glass down gently. "I'm doing a self-defense class. And kickboxing. First classes were yesterday. I hit the floor and just...laid there. For, like, thirty minutes."

Their laughter cracked like thunder, and I couldn't help but smile through the soreness. We talked schedules. They actually wanted to join me for self-defense. That meant more than I had words for—safety in numbers, maybe. Solidarity. Or maybe I just didn't want to do this alone anymore.

The conversation had been light, easy—until my mind circled back to the one thing I hadn't told them yet. My pulse quickened just thinking about it. They were going to have opinions, no question. I took a deep breath and decided to rip the Band-Aid off.

"I don't know if I told you this already...but I invited Roman to join my family on vacation."

I barely got the words out before Maggie let out a screech that made me shield my ears. "Let's not get carried away," I said quickly. "We're still very...platonic."

She blinked. "You haven't slept with him yet? Is that what I'm hearing?"

"That's..." I replied, but before I could say more, she turned to Abby.

"Is that what you heard?"

Abby nodded, eyes wide. "Loud and clear."

I laughed, shaking my head. "Seriously, what kind of girl do you think I am?" I asked, then took a quick sip of my drink, letting my gaze slip away before they could read too much in my expression.

Maggie dropped her fork with theatrical flair. "Please. You've done something with him."

"We've kissed. That's it. One on the cheek, one on the lips." I lifted my hands in mock surrender. "Honestly."

Maggie stared at me. "I don't know whether to be proud of you or commit you. The man is literally a walking statue of Zeus."

"Tell me how you *really* feel," I said, eyebrows raised.

More laughter. Another round of mimosas appeared like magic. But under it all, I felt it—the tension humming quietly under my skin when I spoke his name.

"It feels intense with him. That's the only way I can explain it. It's like...every time I get close, I want to run, but I also want to stay. I talked to his mom about it—she said to take my time, feel it out."

Maggie raised a skeptical brow. "Of course she did. I'll bet no one's good enough for her baby."

"Maybe," I murmured. "But I don't think that's what this is. I think he feels it too. That weight. That pull. But he's grounded in it, and I'm just...not. This trip to Florida is going to test that. I won't be able to send him away when I get overwhelmed. No more escape hatches."

They were quiet for a moment, nodding gently as they listened.

We shifted gears after that—talking about sleepovers with the kids. I joked about being the favorite godmother and they immediately pulled out their calendars like it was a life-or-death situation. We settled on a Saturday a few weeks away.

As we stood outside the restaurant, hugging goodbye, I felt something lift. No judgment. No lectures. Just love.

Back home, I slipped into my favorite loungewear, the fabric brushing against me with that lived-in ease I always craved at the end of the day. A few candles flickered to life, their warm glow casting shadows that swayed with the rhythm of the flame. Soft meditation music drifted through the apartment, each note easing the knots in my chest. I didn't even glance out the window—I didn't want the outside world pressing in. Not yet. The hush inside these walls felt sacred, like a fragile cocoon.

Little by little, my shoulders loosened. I almost let go. Almost.

Then my phone lit up.

ROMAN.

The name alone stole the air from my lungs, catching hard in my throat. My heart stuttered, then raced, the fragile calm shattering in an instant.

***

ROMAN

I laced up my shoes before the sun had fully claimed the sky. I didn't really know why I was doing it—running down to the river like she did—but I guess I wanted to feel what Alex felt. She'd described it as peaceful, like it cleared her head, and God knows I needed that this morning.

I hit play on one of her classical playlists she shared. The strings and piano softened the edges of the city as I jogged through it. It was quiet this early—just the rustle of wind and the occasional dog walker. Down by the river, it was still and wide, brown and ugly, but strangely calming.

I slowed my pace to a walk and drifted toward the railing. Planting my palms on the warm metal, I leaned forward, letting the view settle over me while my thoughts churned. Sweat trickled down my temples, stinging my eyes, the rise and fall of my shoulders uneven as I fought to catch my breath. My heart pounded hard, each beat pushing against the weight of everything I'd been processing from last night. For a long moment, I just stood there, staring at the water, letting the air burn in my lungs and the music try to make sense of it all before *she* took over my thoughts again.

I didn't expect to see her, not really. Maybe I hoped to. But I also knew if she caught me out here, she'd give me that pointed look and accuse me of stalking. And hell, maybe she'd be right. I just wanted to understand her world—this calm place she created in the middle of all the chaos.

Afterward, I stopped by her coffee shop, the one she swears makes the best blueberry muffins. I don't even eat that crap, but I ordered one and a black coffee, sat by the window, and watched the street like some idiot in a rom-com. She never showed, and I was relieved.

Back at the penthouse, I showered, dressed, and debated ignoring Harrison's text altogether. He wanted to talk. Which meant complain. Which meant I'd need beer. I texted him to meet me at the Rooftop Brewery, told them to save me the corner table with the best view, then waited. Harrison's 1:00 was more like 1:45.

When I got there, Dominick—owner and old friend—greeted me with a grin and a slap on the back. The place had been an old, dilapidated warehouse once. I'd helped turn it into what it was now: exposed beams, steel accents, warm lighting, and the best rooftop in the city. Packed, as always.

"You need anything, it's yours," Dom said as he walked me up. "Saved your spot with that view you like."

"Perfect."

Harrison finally showed, looking annoyed at the air itself. Dominick brought over two of their specialty drafts and clapped Harrison's back. "Good to see you, Harry."

Harrison's expression soured. "Why the hell does he call me Harry?" he growled as Dominick walked away.

"Maybe because you've never corrected him."

"Well, I will now."

He took a long pull from the bottle, already setting the tone.

"What do you want to talk about?" I asked. "And let's not make it a therapy session."

He didn't listen. "Dad was way out of line last night. I'm twenty-seven, Roman. He still treats me like I'm fifteen. He doesn't pull that crap with you."

"False," I said, leaning back. "He lit me up too. Told me we were careless. Told me I should've been watching you. You just don't like criticism. I use it."

Harrison sneered. "Of course. The golden boy. Doing everything Daddy says."

I clenched my jaw, the muscle ticking as I forced the anger back down where it belonged. My hands stayed flat on the table, steady, even while the air between us tightened. This was going downhill fast.

"You want to talk like an adult or act like a brat?"

He ignored me, signaling to the waitress with his beer bottle. "Another one. Tall. And just keep 'em coming."

The waitress glanced at me like I had the final say.

"Another round is fine," I said. "But don't keep them coming. One at a time, please."

She nodded, grateful someone wasn't being a jerk.

"Did you all want to order food?" she asked.

"I'm drinking mine," Harrison muttered.

"Could you ask Dominick to pick out a few appetizers and two entrees?" I asked, polite and clear.

"Of course," she said, throwing me a thankful look before walking off.

I rubbed my forehead. "Harrison—or should I say Harry—what the hell is your problem today?"

He flipped me off and ignored the question, retreating into his drink with all the petulance of a sulking child.

The food arrived. He started eating. Of course. I didn't say a word. I'd known he'd fold like this. Everyone's always picking up his pieces. He gets to screw up, and I get to make sure we don't all go down with him.

When lunch was over, I took him home. No way he was driving anywhere. Then I drove back in silence, the hum of the tires loud against the weight in my chest. I kept wondering how long I could keep this up—picking up his slack, managing the fallout, pretending I wasn't burning out.

Back home, I changed and headed to the gym. Alex's words echoed in my head: *"It's not about exercising every day—it's about control."* That stuck.

The pool air hit me damp and heavy, the faint sting of chlorine in my nose. I slid into the water, the shock of cold biting at my skin, and pushed off the wall. Stroke after stroke, lap after lap, my body took over where my thoughts had run dry. Muscles burned, lungs tightened, shoulders strained, but I welcomed it—it drowned everything else out. I lost count, lost track, until I surfaced at last, chest heaving, water streaming down my face.

When I finally dragged myself out, the clock read close to five.

I showered, toweled off, and stared at my phone. I'd left her alone all day. Maybe that was enough.

I hit call.

She answered on the first ring.

"I was wondering when I might be hearing from you," she said, her voice warm and a little teasing.

"I was trying not to bug you."

"Bug me? Why would you say that?"

"I don't know," I said. "Sometimes I get the sense you need space. I don't want to be that guy."

She exhaled softly. "I don't want you to be that guy either. So... what kept you so occupied?"

Here goes.

"Well, don't get mad, but I went for a run... down to the river. Took a walk. Had earbuds in. Classical music. Then I stopped by your coffee shop. Had a muffin."

There was a pause.

"Did you enjoy it?" she asked gently. "Was it as peaceful to you as it is to me?"

I smiled. She wasn't mad.

"It was," I said. "But I probably need a better post-run snack."

She laughed, and something in me unraveled. "Were you hoping to run into me?" she asked, her tone curious rather than accusing.

"No. Not exactly. Maybe. I don't know. I just... wanted to understand it. The way you talk about that place. You inspire me to try new things."

"I didn't run today," she said, amused. "I feel like I need a walker."

"You inspired me anyway. I swam laps later too," I said, a smile tugging at my mouth. Thank God she couldn't see just how smitten I really was.

"See? It's not about fitness. It's about clearing your mind. Gaining back some control."

"I needed that. Especially after lunch with Harrison."

"How'd it go?" she asked.

"Awful. He got drunk. I had to drive him home. Dad chewed us both out last night, and Harrison took it personally. I didn't disagree with Dad, so now I'm the enemy too."

"I'm sorry," she said softly. "Is there anything I can do to help?"

"You can be our realtor," I said. "That would be enough. I want to keep you away from the other stuff—it's too messy."

"I'd be honored," she said, her voice edged with enthusiasm. "I want to do more than just sell real estate. I want to create something. I thought Burrow Township would be my breakthrough, but..."

I caught the pause, the faint waver she tried to bury. She wanted to sound confident, but I could feel the fear threaded through her words.

"We'll find something better," I promised.

And I meant it.

We said goodnight soon after. I stayed on the line a few seconds longer, just listening to the quiet.

Chapter 21

ALEX

Monday was a mess.

I'd planned to get ahead of everything—to comb through zoning records, identify the shell companies involved, connect the dots between what Roman found in Texas and what I suspected here. I even got to the office early, coffee in hand, hair pulled back like I meant business. I told myself I was going to fix this.

But by noon, I'd been staring at the same public records database for over an hour, blinking at parcel IDs and PDF download links like they were written in a language I didn't speak. Every file led to another dead end—contracts signed with LLCs that didn't trace back to any real name, permits "approved" by city officials whose signatures looked copy-pasted. The deeper I dug, the more it felt like I was sinking.

By midafternoon, I had four browser tabs frozen and a highlighter cap in my mouth. My desk was covered in sticky notes I kept rewording and then discarding, as if a better version of the truth might appear if I just phrased it differently.

My jaw was tight. My brain buzzed with static. I felt like I was trying to solve a jigsaw puzzle that someone had purposely thrown into the wind.

I stood up too fast from my desk at one point and knocked over my water bottle. It soaked the corner of my notebook—pages of half-finished thoughts bleeding together into a soggy mess that somehow summed up my entire day. I actually laughed. It was either that or cry.

I wanted to call Roman but didn't. I didn't want to sound like I was unraveling. I wanted to be competent. Useful. Not the woman who couldn't crack a city zoning problem and needed comfort. I chewed on the inside of my cheek until it stung and told myself I'd figure it out tomorrow.

But the truth? It felt like failure.

Still, I dragged myself to the self-defense studio that night, each step across the cracked parking lot like moving through wet cement. The glass door gave a soft squeal as I pulled it open, and the now familiar scent of sanitizing cleaner felt almost homey. Fluorescent lights buzzed overhead, casting pale stripes across the scuffed mats.

My legs still ached from Saturday's drills, muscles tight and heavy like wet rope. My arms trembled from too much caffeine and not enough food, a fine tremor I tried to hide as I tightened my wraps. But I showed up. I showed up because I needed to hit something—anything—to quiet the static rattling around in my head.

I needed to sweat out all the noise. I needed the slap of my gloves against the pad, the dull thud echoing back like a heartbeat I could finally control. I needed to feel my body coil and uncoil, to hear the low grunt in my throat with each strike and know the sound belonged to me.

The instructor might not have realized just how much I needed this, but it didn't matter. Every jab, every knee, every breath stripped off a thin layer of helplessness, like peeling away old paint to get at raw wood.

By the end, my hair clung damp to my neck, my shirt plastered to my back. My lungs burned. My hands ached inside the wraps. Sweat dripped from my jaw and darkened the mat beneath me. And for once the ache in my muscles made sense—clean, honest pain.

I got home and showered with the lights dimmed low, the water sliding down my back in steady streams, washing away the ache of hours spent chasing invisible ghosts through city records. By the time I slipped into bed, Roman's call lit up my phone.

His voice was soft, easy, warm—like slipping under a favorite blanket. We didn't talk long. He didn't press, didn't pry. He just told me he missed me, wished me a good night, and hinted at a surprise later in the week—said it in a way, like he knew I needed something waiting for me on the horizon.

When we hung up, the quiet of the room felt different—less sharp, more settled. I tucked into the sheets, the faint scent of clean cotton wrapping around me. My chest was still tight, but my heart eased, just enough to let the darkness take me.

***

Today was the first time I'd be alone with Roman's mother, Lisette. No family dinner. No buffer of noise or laughter or wine. Just me and her—face to face.

I told myself it was fine. I told myself she wasn't here as Roman's mother, but as a psychologist. A guide. Someone to help me understand myself... even if I wasn't entirely sure I wanted to.

Still, I was nervous in a way I didn't know how to explain. Nervous in my ribs. In my hands. In the way I played soothing classical music during the entire drive to her home, trying to calm my breath like I'd read about in mindfulness blogs I never finished.

By the time I pulled into the driveway, it was almost 4:00. No other cars. No distractions.

I sat there for a beat longer than I needed to, gripping the steering wheel and reminding myself I was here to understand what the hell was going on with me—not to impress her. Not to win points with Roman. Not to get dragged into something I wasn't ready for.

I knocked once. The door opened a second later to Lisette's warm smile and open arms.

"Hello, Alex," she said, pulling me in for a soft, maternal hug. "It's so good to see you again. Come in."

"Hi," I said, my voice wobbling a little. "Thanks for seeing me. I really appreciate it... any insight you can offer."

"Of course," she said, already leading me through the foyer. "Let's go to my office where it's quiet."

I don't know what I expected—mahogany paneling, a big brown desk, maybe some intimidating diplomas framed like warning signs—but this room was none of that.

It felt like someone's soul lived here.

Dr. King's office didn't look anything like I expected. I'd braced myself for something cold and clinical. But the moment I stepped through the doorway, I felt like I'd wandered into a storybook.

The space was softly lit, not by overhead fluorescents, but by warm table lamps and scattered candles that cast golden flickers across the room like it was always on the edge of twilight. Plush beige sofas faced each other, ready for conversation. Their oversized cushions inviting you to sink in and stay a while. Between them sat a wide, rustic cocktail table with scuff marks and character—stories etched in its grain.

Floor-to-ceiling bookshelves lined the back wall, overfilled and gloriously messy—not chaotic, but lived-in. Some books leaned sideways, others were stacked horizontally like little forts. Tucked between them were framed photographs, tiny stone statues, and little brass trinkets that perhaps came alive after dark. Candles were scattered in between, each in mismatched holders—glass, wood, ceramic—none of them uniform, all of them glowing with intention.

A whitewashed stone fireplace took up one wall, and the mantle was crowded with family photos in vintage frames. None of them matched. Some were polished and gold-trimmed, others chipped and charmingly faded. Mixed in were short taper candles, dried eucalyptus, and a delicate chain of copper fairy lights that twinkled like stars in daylight.

The far window was a bay cut-out, and in it sat a cushioned chaise lounge draped with a woven blanket in soft lavender and cream. More books were stacked beneath the window, their spines cracked and familiar. A few notebooks rested beside them, along with a mug of pens and—yes—more candles. The curtains were pulled open just enough to let late afternoon sunlight spill across the chaise like a spotlight, casting long shadows on the pale wood floors.

The rugs—plural—were all different. Bright and woven, Turkish and tasseled, bold patterns and soft textures layered over each other like they'd been collected from her travels or thrift stores or maybe both. They didn't clash. They danced.

And the art on the walls—God, the art. Not stiff portraits or somber prints. These were bursts of color and joy. Abstract florals, dancing figures, a watercolor of a woman with wild hair and a crown of sunflowers. One corner held a cluster of tiny canvases, each painted in a different shade of blue, like windows into someone's imagination. The room didn't just feel safe—it felt *enchanted*. Like anything could happen in here. Like healing might not be clinical after all. It might be warm. It might be soft. It might even be beautiful.

I stood there for a moment longer than I meant to, caught in the hum of it all. It felt like a place made to hold people gently—without judgment or pressure. A place that didn't ask you to fix yourself, just to sit down and *feel*.

Lisette smiled at me like she already knew what the room was doing. "I love color, if you couldn't tell."

I exhaled a breath I didn't realize I'd been holding. "Me too," I said. "This room is... magic."

And I meant it.

She motioned for me to sit. "This is my space to think, read, dream... whatever I need. Therapy doesn't have to feel clinical to be effective."

I nodded, still absorbing it all. The scent of something herbal—lavender maybe—lingered in the air. The lighting was soft. There wasn't a screen or clipboard in sight. Just presence.

Then came the shift. The silence between us thickened slightly, and I knew she was waiting for me to speak.

Before I could, she cut in gently. "Alex, before we begin, I want to ask you something."

Here it comes. *What are your intentions with my son?*

"Sure," I said carefully.

"What do you hope to get out of today's session?"

Oh. That wasn't what I expected.

I looked down at my hands. "I think... I just want to understand what this empath thing is. What it really means. I don't know how to separate what's mine from what's everyone else's. And I think it's starting to consume me."

She smiled like she'd been waiting for that answer.

"That's a very wise place to start," she said. "And yes, we'll take it slow."

I let out a long exhale. "And can you explain it like I'm five? Because if you say the word 'aura,' I might bolt."

She laughed. "I won't. And I think you'll surprise yourself with how much you understand."

She handed me a glass of water with a lemon wedge. I sipped it slowly as we sat down on the couches facing each other. My nerves buzzed, but her presence dulled the edge.

"Alex, I suspected you were an empath from the first moment I saw you," she said softly. "But not just because of what you feel. It's what you *hold*. Empaths absorb everything around them—not just the emotions, but the weight of them. The room changes when they walk in, because they *carry* it all. Sometimes without knowing it."

I swallowed hard.

"The definition of an empath is someone with the paranormal ability to apprehend the mental or emotional state of another. But don't let that word scare you. 'Paranormal' just means it isn't easily explained yet."

I sat up straighter. "So... you're not about to do a candle ritual and summon spirits or anything?"

She laughed again. "No summoning today."

I relaxed a little. "Good. Because I have pepper spray in my bag."

Her eyes sparkled. "I wouldn't expect anything less."

She went on.

"Roman's always been highly sensitive—especially to animals. We called him Dr. Doolittle when he was younger. We stopped having pets for a while because their illness and loss hit him so hard. He never just 'had' feelings—he lived inside them."

My chest ached at the thought. "Yeah... I get that."

We drifted into small conversation about pets, and I admitted I loved dogs but didn't feel right keeping one cooped up in my apartment. She called that unselfish. I called it selfish. She countered, gently, that it was what empaths do—see both sides and blame themselves anyway.

Then I blurted, "If I'm feeling everyone else's emotions... then why don't I ever feel good? Why am I always angry? Or sad? Or overwhelmed?"

Lisette tilted her head, her expression pure empathy. "Because you haven't learned how to let go. You've built a wall, but it's keeping *everything* in. You're not protected. You're stuck in a room with every emotion you've ever absorbed—and it's exhausting you."

My throat tightened. "How do I get out of the room?"

"You start by recognizing what isn't yours. Then, you give yourself permission to stop holding it. Meditation helps. So does silence. Stillness."

I groaned. "I knew you were going to say meditation."

She smiled. "You already do a version of it. Roman told me about Lookout Park."

I blinked. "That's my quiet place."

"How do you feel when you're there?"

"Peaceful. Safe."

"And when Roman was there with you?"

That was harder to answer. I stared at my hands. "Freaked out."

"What happened?"

"He told me it wasn't safe. That if something happened to me up there, no one would know."

Lisette frowned. "I'm sorry he took your peace. I don't think he meant to—but that's the thing about being close to someone who feels so much. His worry overpowers your stillness."

I nodded slowly. "It took a couple of days to feel normal again."

"Did you see him during that time?"

"No... and I was calmer when I didn't."

She sat back thoughtfully. "That's something worth paying attention to. You're learning your boundaries. That's a good thing."

We moved into more conversation—about anger in crowds, bar energy, and eventually the Ellingtons.

She knew the name. Of course she did.

"Alex," she said gently. "Don't carry the burden of their toxicity. And don't apologize for the way you stood up for yourself."

I cringed. "I wish Roman hadn't told you about what I did at the bar..."

"I'm glad he did. Because if you two had been together then, that man wouldn't have left on his own."

I laughed, dry and surprised. "Well, he still left with a parting gift."

We both laughed, and something inside me finally—*finally*—settled.

Afterward, she invited me to sit on the patio with a glass of wine. We talked. Not about therapy. Just about life. It was restorative.

Before I left, we scheduled another session for after vacation. And I realized... I was looking forward to it. Maybe even more than the kickboxing class.

That night, I took a long, hot bath.

No phone. No distractions. Just candles, a soft playlist of meditation music I barely remembered queuing up, and steam curling from the surface of the water like it was trying to lift something off of me—something invisible, heavy, and long overdue for release.

The tub filled higher than usual. I didn't stop it. I wanted to feel weightless, submerged. Wanted to float so fully that even my thoughts would lose their footing.

I sank in slow, letting the warmth kiss my skin. My knees surfaced, then dipped again. My fingers traced idle shapes in the water. My breath began to steady.

And for once—just once—I didn't feel crowded.

The invisible crowd I always carried—expectations, regrets, the sharp-edged thoughts that jabbed at me when I tried to sleep—was finally gone. For the first time in days, the voice in my head wasn't asking me to perform, fix, or control anything. It wasn't shouting about zoning permits or ethics violations or how I should've kept my mouth shut. It wasn't whispering doubts about Roman or dragging me back to old conversations I wish I'd handled differently.

It was just... quiet.

My mind started to wander, but not in the usual direction. Not to worry or panic or fix-it mode. It wandered into weightlessness.

I imagined what it would be like to live in a place like Lisette's. Not just her house, but her *energy*. That kind of peace. That kind of rootedness. A sunroom for journaling. A fireplace just for rainy afternoons. A kitchen that smelled like fresh herbs and patience.

I imagined Roman, barefoot and sleepy, coming in to kiss me from behind while I made tea. Wrapping his arms around my waist, whispering something smug and low that made me roll my eyes while secretly melting.

I imagined us slow dancing in the kitchen to a record neither of us remembered buying. His chin tucked over my shoulder. His breath warm against my neck. No deadline. No damage control. Just music and breath and him.

And then I imagined none of it ever happening.

I imagined pushing him away. I imagined saying the wrong thing, again. I imagined whatever this was between us dissolving the second real life demanded more from either of us.

I blinked hard.

That's the trouble with peace—it's fragile. You start to trust it, and your brain wants to test it. Wants to shake it, poke at it, see if it'll hold.

Still, I didn't get out.

I stayed. Let the heat soak into my muscles and settle behind my ribs. Let the flicker of candlelight blur the edges of the room until everything felt dreamy, not real. Let myself feel the rare, sacred fullness of simply being okay for no one but myself.

By the time I climbed out, the water had gone tepid, my fingers were shriveled, and the candles were nothing but soft, sleepy glows of wax and smoke. I wrapped myself in a towel and padded into my bedroom like I was moving through a dream.

My phone lit up.

ROMAN: *Hope today was kind to you. Can't wait to see you tomorrow. Sleep well, beautiful.*

I smiled, involuntarily.

Then my imagination picked up again—this time gentler. I pictured him reading that message over and over, wondering if I'd respond. I imagined him lying in bed, arm behind his head, thinking about me. Or maybe not thinking at all. Maybe just feeling it.

I wondered what his sheets smelled like.

I wondered what it would be like to fall asleep with his breath on the back of my neck.

I wondered if he meant what he said.

If any of it was real.

I texted him back—just a simple: *Goodnight. Today was kind because of you.*

Then I slid under the covers, turned out the lights, and curled into myself like I was finally something whole.

And I fell asleep without needing anything more than that small, impossible hope...

That maybe the calm was mine to keep this time.

Chapter 22

ROMAN

I had plenty to keep me occupied at work today—most of it frustrating. Trying to untangle the zoning issues tied to the Burrow Township project felt like playing chess against an invisible opponent who kept moving the pieces when I wasn't looking. Matt and I were narrowing down a shortlist of police officers, investigators, and zoning officials we *could* trust—people not already knee-deep in backdoor deals or kickbacks. Thank God he knew a lot of decent ones. I was starting to realize how few I actually trusted.

Turns out, the network of people I thought I could rely on was a little too cozy with the Ellingtons. I had to tread carefully, watch my words. Some of them were still useful—but only because they could point me toward where the next shady deal was brewing. I didn't realize how deep this went. Or how close to home it really was.

At least I was back to my usual pace—working straight through the day, except for lunch.

Today, I called Amelia into my office for it. First time in over three years, apparently. She walked in with takeout in hand, narrowed her eyes, and said flatly, "What's this about?"

"What do you mean? Can't I have lunch with my assistant?" I asked, smirking.

She crossed her arms and let out a long-suffering sigh that almost made me laugh.

"You *can*, you just *haven't*."

Oof. "Why didn't you tell me I was being a...never mind."

"I do. Frequently." She figured it out anyway.

I barked out a laugh and tossed a French fry at her. She ducked it, grinning, and I felt the tension ease between us. I needed this kind of honesty in my life. Especially today.

"You know," I said, sobering, "I actually wanted to ask you something."

She speared a bite of her salad and didn't look up. "Does it have to do with someone named Alex?"

Jesus. "Is it that obvious?"

She raised an eyebrow, still chewing. "You've mentioned her in literally every other sentence for the past two weeks."

"Should I ask the question or just let you guess the answer, then?"

"Shoot," she said, finally looking up.

I leaned back in my chair, arms crossed. "It's been a long time since I've wanted to really spend time with someone. Alex is... different. She's sharp, funny, strong as hell, and somehow still soft around the edges. I'm used to the princess types—the kind that need a handler. Alex doesn't want anything from me... she's always pulling away."

Amelia studied me. "That was a beautiful monologue. Was there a question in there?"

I blinked, pulling out of my thoughts. "Right. Why do you think she's pushing me away?"

She tilted her head. "Why do *you* think she is?"

"I don't know. Maybe she's just being honest—she's said more than once that she likes being alone."

Now she looked genuinely baffled. "You have got to be the dumbest smart man I know. Do you realize how rare that is? A woman who enjoys solitude but still chooses to spend time with *you*?"

I frowned. "You think that's a *good* thing?"

"She spends time with you. That's the part you're missing. If she really wanted to be left alone, you'd already be blocked, deleted, and ghosted."

I blinked. "Damn. I sound like one of those needy Instagram girls."

"Bingo." She took a long sip of water. "Get your self together. If you want to keep seeing her, stop obsessing. Don't try to own her. She's not that type. She's a free spirit— independent. You cage her, she'll run."

I nodded slowly, letting it settle. "Alright. From now on, we're having lunch at least twice a week."

She smirked. "I'll be here to slap sense into you anytime."

The rest of the afternoon flew by. Meetings stacked up, emails pinged nonstop, but I felt lighter than I had in days. Sometimes you just need someone to look you in the eye and tell you to quit acting like a lovesick idiot.

Just before I was supposed to leave for dinner with Alex, her message came through:

ALEX: *Hi, hope you had a good day. My kickboxing class just ended, so I'm headed home to shower. Just come on up when you get here—push the ring button.*

ME: *Sounds good. Productive day. Can't believe you already took another class—you're a beast. LOL. See you soon.*

When I got to her building, the door buzzed open like magic. Her place was secure—sophisticated security, automatic locks. She didn't need me to protect her, but I was glad she had the tools anyway.

I stepped inside to find two wine glasses on the counter, a bottle of cab already breathing, and a handwritten note that made me smile.

Please pour us a cocktail before dinner. Thanks, A.

I poured the wine and sat on the barstool closest to the hallway, half-nervous anticipation, half mental pep talk. She had a habit of walking out and leaving me speechless.

Tonight was no exception.

She came down the hallway in a fitted white T-shirt that clung to her curves like a second skin and a pair of torn jeans that fit like a glove. Her hair was still damp from the shower. Effortless and beautiful.

My mouth went dry.

"Hi," she said, lifting a brow and taking the glass I handed her. She sipped, her eyes locked on mine, head slightly tilted like she was trying to read my thoughts.

She probably could.

"Hi to you," I managed.

"Everything okay?"

"Better than okay. Honestly, I think I like you better like this than when you're dressed up."

Relief flickered across her features. "Good. This is definitely more comfortable. The dresses—they're fun, but not all the time."

"Then maybe we skip the fine dining from now on and hit some pubs instead."

Her eyes lit up. "Can we go to Rooftop? I haven't been yet. I heard it's got a great vibe."

"Absolutely. I know the owner. Did the renovations when it was just an old warehouse."

Her jaw dropped a little. "No way. That must've been so rewarding. Turning such a clean slate into something so beautiful."

That hit me harder than it should've. Since that's what I love so much about what I do. Construction not destruction. I thought about Burrow Township. I thought I was making it better by constructing new "better" things when in fact I was destructing an entire neighborhood to do it.

"I'll see if Dominick can give us a tour." I shifted my thoughts back to Alex and her excitement about this place.

As expected, Rooftop was packed when we arrived—music thumping, glasses clinking, the buzz of conversation spilling into the stairwell. But Dominick had our table ready. No wait. No stress. Just a knowing grin as he waved us past the crowd.

He led us through the belly of the brewery—past polished copper tanks and warm oak barrels, down low-lit corridors with floors that hummed beneath our feet—then up a narrow stairwell that opened into the rooftop garden patio.

And that's when she lit up.

Alex didn't just *look* around. She absorbed it. Eyes wide, hands trailing along the reclaimed wood beams like they were relics in a museum. She leaned in close to the copper tap lines, tracing them with her fingers as she asked question after question, her voice soft and curious and full of that wonder she didn't even try to hide.

I stayed a step behind the entire time—and I didn't mind. Not one bit.

There was something about watching her discover new places that made the world feel new to me, too. Like I was seeing it through her—like her excitement rewrote the blueprint of the space itself.

And with the way she moved ahead of me, talking with her hands, spinning on her heels to point something out—well, let's just say I had no complaints about the view.

Dinner was on the house. Dominick liked her immediately, and I didn't blame him. She had that quiet magnetism—the kind that pulled people in without effort. She didn't need to perform. She just *was*. And somehow that was more captivating than anything rehearsed.

On the drive back, we couldn't stop laughing. About the food. The brewery dog that licked her sandal. Her obsession with the mason jars hung from twine like fireflies. Her joy had this way of spilling into everything around her—and that joy was contagious.

When we pulled up to her building, I stayed behind the wheel while she got out. She leaned in through the window, hair falling forward in soft waves, her perfume mixing with the warm summer air.

"I'll see you tomorrow," she said. "Just need to pack tonight."

I nodded, eyes still on her. "We're staying at my place, right?"

"Yes. Makes more sense. The meeting's at your office in the morning, and then we fly out."

She smiled, gave a little wave, and disappeared into the glow of the lobby.

I didn't drive off right away.

I just sat there, staring at the spot where she'd stood, that stupid grin still pulling at my mouth.

One more night apart. Then a full week. Just us. No clients. No zoning boards. No distractions.

I had no idea what the week would look like. And for the first time in longer than I cared to admit... that unknown didn't scare me.

It felt like possibility.

Because wherever she was—that's where I wanted to be.

***

ALEX

Thursday morning at the gym was... humbling. I barely had the energy for yoga, and even that felt like too much. My muscles ached from head to toe, a quiet rebellion from the week's chaos. I let myself melt into the sauna for fifteen slow minutes before I practically crawled back upstairs to the apartment, my body begging me for grace.

After a long, hot shower that did little more than take the edge off, I slipped into black pants and a fuchsia halter-neck top—one of my favorites. Black heels, a swipe of gloss, and I was ready. Today was the last day I'd have to dress like this for at least a week. After this? Swimsuits and cover-ups. Just thinking about it loosened something in my chest.

All I had to do was tie up a few loose ends at the office. Make sure my clients were taken care of and trust my team to do the rest.

Shay would be training the new receptionist next week, then transitioning to my assistant the week after. That promotion couldn't come fast enough. I didn't just need support—I wanted someone I could mentor. Someone I could trust.

I grabbed my bags and headed to the elevator, looking like I was about to board a cargo ship, not catch a flight. I don't care how low-maintenance you think you are—when women travel, we bring our lives in those suit-cases. And don't let anyone shame us for it. The valet helped me get my bags in the car.

At the office, I headed straight to Shay's desk. She was mid-call, so I leaned over her counter, scrolling through emails. The moment she hung up, she shot out of her chair and threw her arms around me.

"Only two more weeks and I'm yours!" she squealed, bouncing like a kid at Christmas.

I laughed, barely keeping hold of my coffee. "Oh my God, it sounds like we're getting married."

"I didn't know that was an option," she teased, hands on my shoulders like she was steadying me and her excitement at the same time.

"You never know," I said, smirking, throwing my arm around her.

We moved into my office and went over my client list. She took notes, asked all the right questions, and when we finished, I had her send Grant in.

Emails, calls, follow-ups. The Santoros were gracious, telling me to enjoy my vacation. I packed up my laptop, tied up my files, and headed out.

I called Roman from the car.

He answered like he'd been waiting for me. "Well, hello there. Perfect timing. I was just turning out the lights in my office."

"At three o'clock?" I asked, suspicious.

"I've got better things to do today."

"Like what?" I asked, already smiling. I could feel the butterflies starting their usual warm-up routine.

"Working out."

I snorted. "You're so full of it."

He laughed—God, that sound. "Alright, fine. I had plans to take a walk down to the river with you. Maybe swing on the swings."

"That actually sounds perfect," I said, softening. "What about dinner?"

"I'm cooking."

Freaking total package. Don't screw this up, Kennedy.

"This night just keeps getting better."

I pulled into the garage and parked next to his car, but the second I stepped out, a shiver ran down my spine. That uneasy feeling—like someone was watching me. I glanced around, trying to play it cool. Nothing. No one. Still, the air felt heavy, off.

I slipped into the elevator and texted Roman so he could unlock the penthouse access. The doors closed, and I sagged against the back wall, letting out a breath I hadn't realized I was holding. But even as the elevator climbed, my anxiety crept higher. Every glass panel in the walls made me feel like I was being exposed.

When the doors opened, Roman was waiting. He didn't say a word—just stepped forward, took my bags like it was the most natural thing in the world, and that quiet calm that only he seemed to offer swept through me. I glanced over my shoulder one last time, then followed him inside.

I was still in my work clothes and wanted out of them immediately. I grabbed a change of clothes from my suitcase and was on my way to the bathroom when he caught me by the waist.

"Hey there. I didn't even get a proper hello."

His voice was warm and low, and his touch sent a shock of awareness through me. My nerves were still firing from that parking garage weirdness.

"Hi," I whispered. "Sorry. Just want to get out of these clothes and into something comfy before our river stroll."

He smirked. "I really like it when you say you're getting out of your clothes."

My knees actually buckled. The scent of his cologne, the heat of his body behind mine—Jesus.

"Mmm." My eyes fluttered shut.

He chuckled and the sound vibrated right through me.

"Go get changed," he said, smacking my behind gently before nudging me toward the door.

I peered back with fake outrage.

I changed into black running shorts, a soft white t-shirt that read *"I love Jesus, but I curse a little,"* and my black-and-white sneakers. My hair went up in a high ponytail. Easy and comfortable, before stepping into the kitchen.

"I didn't know you were a Jesus girl," he said, reading my shirt.

The subject always made me squirm. I gave him just enough to end it.

"Maggie's kids got it for me one Christmas. We used to go to church together when they were little. One day they asked, 'Why does Aunt Ali get to say the bad words you told us not to?'"

He laughed so hard I thought he might choke.

"What happened with the church thing?"

I shrugged. "I got too busy."

"If you ever want to go back, I'd go with you."

I scrunched my nose. "I don't think so, but if you ever want to, Maggie and Abby's families go. They really like you." God hadn't done anything good for me in a long time, so why bother.

He smiled but didn't respond.

"Let's go before walking is the last thing we end up doing," I teased, eyeing him head to toe to try and divert his attention from all this God talk. I was thankful it worked.

His eyes darkened. "Careful."

He grabbed my hand and twirled me into the elevator.

Outside, it was overcast—gorgeous in its own way. The air was thick with that pre-storm feeling, but we took our chances.

Five minutes in, the skies opened up. A full-blown summer downpour. We sprinted toward the nearest shelter, laughing so hard my sides hurt. My clothes stuck to me in seconds. I should've been annoyed—my hair, my makeup, my outfit—but instead, I was buzzing. Alive.

"Let's just walk in the rain," I said, grabbing both his hands and tugging.

"I'm game if you are."

I let go of him, spun in the rain, arms wide. "I just want to be free for a minute."

He grinned, grabbed my hand again, and we strolled—soaked and laughing along the river path. Just us. The path was void of any people since the rains came.

We walked straight through the front doors of his building—dripping, disheveled, and unapologetic. No one dared stop us. Everyone knew who

Roman was, even if they didn't say a word. Still, I could practically hear the front-desk girls already lining up their whispers, ready to spin our arrival into tomorrow's gossip.

After my shower, I slipped into one of his robes. When he came out, it was his turn to steal the breath right out of me—nothing but gray sweatpants hanging low on his hips, a walking violation. My brain short-circuited, and judging by the heat rushing to my face, I was certain it showed.

"I like that robe on you," he said, eyes blazing. "But I'd like it better off."

I swallowed hard, knees weak. "I feel the same about those sweatpants."

He smirked, but then—just like that—the moment shifted and came to an abrupt halt.

"Well," he said, voice teasing but a little too composed. "Now that we got that out of the way, let's go make dinner."

I blinked. *What the hell just happened?*

We moved to the kitchen—me perched on a stool with a glass of wine, him barefoot and gorgeous, sautéing something on the stove. I watched him, silently battling the need to say something.

Finally, I broke. "Roman... you said something earlier that stuck with me. 'Now that we got that out of the way.' What did you mean by that?"

He didn't look at me at first. Just kept stirring. "I was fishing."

"For what?"

"For a sign. That I'm not crazy. That you feel it too."

I froze. "You can't read me?" I asked playfully as my nerves started to get the best of me.

"I can't," he said, finally turning, "but I can feel you. And it's intense. It's not like anything I've felt before."

That unlocked something in me. "It's overwhelming," I finally felt like I could admit. "And... it feels too important to rush. I don't want to screw it up."

He came around the counter slowly and wrapped his arms around me from behind, resting his chin on my shoulder.

"I feel the same," he whispered. "I'm not used to waiting. But this? You? I'd wait."

I melted into his chest, into his words.

After dinner, I changed into pajamas—soft cotton shorts and an old tank top. Nothing sexy. Nothing clingy. Just enough fabric to remind myself we had a full week together in the same orbit starting tomorrow. The thought made my stomach flip.

I lingered in front of the bathroom mirror, brushing my hair slower than necessary, trying to tame both the strands and my breathing. The dinner had been perfect—candlelight softening every edge, the faint clink of glasses punctuating laughter that flowed easily between us. Roman had been all warmth and patience, answering every question, his gaze steady, intent—like I was the most fascinating thing in the room. And maybe that's what unnerved me. The way he looked at me. Like he saw me. Like he liked what he saw.

Not just my body. Not just the spark I gave him.

Me.

I cupped cool water into my palms and let it wash over my face. Droplets slid down my cheeks, beading along my jaw, trailing to my collarbone before I blotted them away with a towel. My skin was warm, too warm, my reflection flushed. The wine left my pulse low and steady, but beneath that calm was a restless hum. A thrum in my blood. An ache I couldn't shake.

It wasn't just desire. It was deeper. Hungrier. I wanted him in a way that felt cellular, as if the pull came from bone and marrow. As if surrendering—even for a moment—would mean losing myself inside whatever this was.

And maybe I wanted that.

Maybe I wanted him.

But not tonight.

Not yet..

When I walked out, Roman was already stretched out on the bed, shirtless, flipping through something on his phone.
He looked up at me like he'd been waiting—not impatient, not demanding—just *there* in that steady way he always was when I needed anchoring.

He didn't say a word. Just smiled, soft and slow, like he was letting me set the tone.

I climbed in next to him, careful not to touch too much skin. My body had other ideas—warmth pooling low, thoughts flickering to places I'd spent all week trying not to go. But I curled under the covers and kept a few inches between us. Not because I didn't want him.

But because I *wanted* him too much.

And God help me, I was finally starting to believe this might be the beginning of something real. The kind of real that doesn't just burn bright—but lasts. And I didn't want to risk rushing it. I didn't want to break it before it had a chance to become whatever it was meant to be.

So I laid there in the dark beside him, heartbeat steadying, breath syncing with his, and let the quiet hold us.

And for once, I didn't feel like I needed to run.

Chapter 23

ALEX

Every time I spend the night with him, the world just... softens. Colors seem warmer. Sounds quieter. Even the chaos in my own head hushes a little when I wake up next to him. Roman made coffee this morning before I could even roll out of bed—without asking, without a word. Just set it on the nightstand next to me like this wasn't something totally new for us. Like knowing what I needed before I needed it was second nature.

We moved through the rhythm of our morning easily. A workout and then breakfast at the counter, knees brushing under the bar. I kept catching myself watching him in small moments, like brushing his hair back while he read an email, or the way he ran his thumb along the rim of his coffee cup while he listened. Mundane things. But God, I was smitten. Helplessly, stupidly smitten.

And now, here we were. Sitting side by side in the conference room, waiting for the others to arrive, pretending this was just another meeting.

But my heart didn't get the memo.

I didn't know what I was even bringing to the table today. I had concerns—not solutions. Warnings, not strategy. I was hoping—no, *needing*—Matt to come in with more than just a sense of justice. I needed him to have facts. Tools. Leverage. Because all I had was gut instinct and a rapidly growing belief that something terrible was unfolding beneath all this glossy paperwork, ruining the easy feel of the morning.

Roman, for his part, looked maddeningly composed. Crisp white but-ton-down. Khakis. Brown loafers—no socks, of course. That one detail always got to me. It was just so *him*. But this morning, his jaw was tight. His brow furrowed. His eyes distant, locked on something outside the window that I couldn't see, tracking a storm on the horizon, one only he could feel rumbling beneath the surface.

I wanted to reach for his hand. Tell him we'd figure it out. But I didn't. Not here. Not yet.

Instead, I memorized the way the morning light hit the slope of his neck. The way the fabric of his shirt pulled slightly across his back when he leaned forward. I let myself fall a little harder.

And if today fell apart—if the meeting spiraled or the truth got uglier—I knew I'd still remember this moment. The stillness before it all began. Sitting beside him, not knowing what came next... but wanting to face it anyway.

With him.

"You look a bit serious," I said gently. "Care to share?"

He shook his head slowly, almost like it weighed more than usual. "Sor-ry. I'm just having trouble processing all of this. I don't get it—they're pissed because they got caught doing something illegal. Following in dad's footsteps and rather than learning from his mistakes, they doubled down. Made it worse."

"That's exactly what it sounds like," I agreed.

"It just feels like such a waste of time. Everyone knows it's illegal. It's obvious. But here we are."

"Don't you think they've already accounted for that?" I asked. "I mean, who does something *this* blatant unless they believe they're untouchable? What if it's not just the Ellington brothers? What if this goes deeper than we thought—beyond some disgruntled former employee of your dad's?"

He turned to me, that worried expression darkening his whole face.

"If that's true, you're out. I won't let you get caught up in this mess."

There he goes again trying to protect me, like a savior of some kind.

I laughed, though there wasn't a trace of amusement in it. "Number one—you don't get to make that call. Number two—this mess came after *me* too. One brother put his hands on me. The other revoked commercial zoning on a property I was showing to a client."

He froze. The shift in his energy was instant.

"What do you mean? He went after your client's business?" His voice was low, but the anger vibrated beneath it.

Shoot. I should've eased him into that.

"I've been working with a family—trying to help them buy a commercial property. The two they liked best were zoned residential and commercial when we booked the showings. But the morning of the second visit, zoning had been changed. Revoked. By Marcus Ellington."

His hands flew through his hair, wild with disbelief. "That motherf…" He trailed off—holding back on finishing that word.

I'd never seen him like this—genuinely angry, rattled to the core. It scared me a little, but more than that, it made me ache for him.

"I invited Grant to this meeting," I offered, trying to de-escalate the temperature in the room.

"Good." He exhaled, but his voice was still tense. "I don't want you doing this alone. But it's like you don't even *want* me to help."

"That's because your idea of help is locking me up in a tower so no one can touch me," I said with a frustrated chuckle. "That's not what I need."

"But it's what makes me feel better," he said softly. Afraid, even.

I let out a sigh. "Roman, I'm sorry all of this is happening. How about this: I'll stay in my lane. I'll handle the real estate part. Grant can back me up in any negotiation. Will that make you feel better?"

He shoved his hands into his pockets and started pacing. "Maybe. The builders and investors don't typically attend negotiations—we just fund the deal and do the renovations. But now? Now I think we need to be there too." He said staring out over the city.

I wanted more than anything to somehow fix this, but it just seemed like things were continuing to get worse no matter what we did.

"Then let's talk about that once everyone's here," I said, hoping he'd hear the calm in my voice and let it carry him.

When he stopped trying to wear out the floor, his eyes met mine with a flicker of regret.

"I'm sorry for lashing out. I just—hate feeling helpless."

Oh, trust me. I *know* that feeling.

"That's why I work out so much," I said, shrugging. "Why I keep throwing myself into classes that leave me in a heap on the floor. It's the only way to drain the noise out of me."

He chuckled faintly and wrapped his arms around me, pulling me in like *I* was his calm now. My cheek rested against his chest, his heartbeat steady beneath my ear.

"By the way," he murmured near my temple, "I have a surprise for you today."

His words were low and warm, laced with just enough tease to make me forget everything else.

"You do?" I tilted my head up, arms still wrapped around his waist. "And what might that be?"

"If I told you, it wouldn't be a surprise," he said, brushing his lips across my forehead.

"Well, you *kind of* took the surprise out of it by telling me there *was* one," I teased.

He laughed and I could feel the tension finally leaving his body.

"I doubt I ruined anything."

"It better be good," I said, squeezing him once more before letting go.

"Oh, I think you'll like it."

With Roman calmer and the energy finally shifting into something manageable, I turned my focus to prepping for the meeting. Slowly, the others filtered in. Matt showed up with a folder full of names and notes, and the weight I'd been carrying around all week started to lift.

The meeting turned out better than I expected. Matt had recruited officers and investigators who weren't on anyone's payroll—good people. Smart people. They were already combing through zoning files and backdoor transfers. There was no denying it now: the Burrow Township deal was going through. Too much money had already changed hands. But that didn't mean we couldn't fight for those who hadn't been bought.

Ella, her family, and everyone else who wanted our help—we'd do everything we could. The plan was to relocate as many as possible, under better terms. More transparency. A cleaner deal.

When Harrison offered up the name of his "buddy" in the police department, Matt promised to dig deeper, to see if we could track down who exactly had been shielding the Ellington brothers.

That's when it hit me—I was just supposed to be a realtor. I sold houses. Condos. The occasional commercial property. I wasn't trained for this. I wasn't *supposed* to be in meetings that involved corrupt police officers and real estate racketeering. But here I was.

And strangely, I didn't feel like I wanted out.

***

ROMAN

The meeting went better than expected—on paper, at least. No yelling, no surprises, no one flipping a table. We laid out what we knew, Matt stayed levelheaded, even Harrison managed to keep his smartassery to a low simmer. If anyone had walked in halfway through, they might've thought we were just four professionals strategizing a project—not standing at the edge of something that could get very ugly, very fast.

But beneath the surface, I was unraveling.

Because Alex was involved now. Not just tangentially. *Directly.*

And I hated that.

I watched her across the table—sharp, composed, that fire in her eyes when she laid out the facts about the homeowners and what was being taken from them. She was brilliant. Brave. Fiercely moral in a way that made people like the Ellingtons flinch. And yet, all I could think about was how much danger that kind of integrity attracts.

I'd told myself I didn't go for the princess types. And I meant it. I didn't want someone who needed saving every time things got hard. But in this moment, God help me, I *wished* she had a little princess in her. Just enough to pull back. To let someone else fight this fight. To let *me* protect her without her diving headfirst into the fire.

It didn't bother her at all anymore when she talked about Tanner. About the bar. About what he did. Her voice didn't waver, but mine did—internally. Because I knew what men like that were capable of. I'd watched men like that destroy things just to prove they could.

And now they knew her name.

That terrified me in a way I didn't have words for. Not because I didn't think she could handle herself. But because I knew she *would try*—and she'd do it alone if she had to. She'd throw herself in the line of fire to protect other people, without even considering that she had people now too. People who'd bleed for her if it came to that.

I clenched my jaw and let the others talk while my thoughts spun. All I could think about was how to get her out of this mess without making her feel like I didn't believe she could stand in it.

Because I did. I just didn't want her to have to.

She deserved to be treated like a lady. Quiet mornings, coffee in bed and a life free of politics and land deals and men like Tanner Ellington. She deserved peace.

But she kept choosing war and I hated that I couldn't keep the shrapnel from hitting her.

After we said our goodbyes, Alex looked like a completely different person. She looked happy and excited.

"Did something happen?"

"What?" She asked— eyes sparkling with excitement.

"A minute ago, you were ready to bite someone's head off. Now, you're smiling. Should I be worried?" She laughed.

"Nope. The meeting is over and I'm ready to get to the beach. I'm planning to forget about everything except sun and fun for an entire week."

"Now that sounds incredible." Her smile spread as I called down to the front desk to have one of the drivers come pick us up. We grabbed our bags then took the elevator to the lobby.

Harrison was at the door when they opened. He took Alex's bags, even though she tried to insist she could do it herself. We walked out to the front where the car was waiting.

"Damn, this is a lot of bags. Do you think the plane can handle all this crap?" Harrison teased with a chuckle.

"I told you I could carry it myself, you big baby."

Alex bumped Harrison with her shoulder, laughing when he exaggerated a grunt and nearly dropped a small bag balancing on top. The two of them moved around each other like siblings already—easy, unguarded, no tension in sight. It was strange to see her like that, open and carefree, teasing someone who wasn't me.

I stood a few steps back, pretending to check my phone while I watched them. The sun caught the copper in her hair, the breeze tugged a loose strand across her cheek, and she didn't even notice—too busy laughing at something stupid my brother said.

I should've been annoyed. Maybe jealous. But instead, there was this quiet pull in my chest. The kind of feeling that made the noise in my head settle into something more like peace.

Then the thought came, uninvited but impossible to shake: Alex, in white. Walking toward me. Smiling like that.

I blinked away the thought as Harrison helped put the bags in the trunk and Alex got in the car then he pulled me aside before I got in.

"Roman, we'll talk when you get back, but I'm going to work on this issue while you're gone. I could've done better. I need to do better. Things were good and I screwed it up."

"You're right, we need to talk. It's my fault too— we need to find a good way to work together on this, okay?" I gave my brother a hug and slap on the back, then he headed inside the building.

"What was all that about?" She looked at me curiously and I wanted to kiss the cute little furrow between her brows.

"Dad hoped he could hear through all the noise he was making. Looks like he can after all."

"Well, that's good to know." she responded.

And a good start to this vacation, I thought.

"Where are we going? I don't remember this being the way to the airport." She side-eyed me skeptically.

"I told you I had a surprise for you." Her mouth fell open as realization hit.

"You canceled our plane tickets, didn't you?" I smiled and kept my mouth shut. She shook her head, slipping her hand in mine, returning her curious gaze to the window as we pulled off the interstate to the private airport.

The plane was already out of the hangar, fueled and ready to go when we pulled up.

"This was so sweet of you. I really hate the lines at the airport not to mention the frisking and taking off your shoes." she wiggled her toes in her flip flops, running my gaze up her long legs to the bottom of her very short cut off shorts. "Thank you." I leaned over and kissed her gently on the cheek knowing I had more surprises than this for her.

The driver helped us get our luggage over to the plane, then we climbed the steps as the crew, two pilots and one flight attendant, got us situated.

Chapter 24

ALEX

Yep. I totally forgot about Roman's over-the-top air travel habit.

I should've known. Private jet? Of course. The man owns half the skyline.

I wasn't mad, just... mildly irritated with myself for not seeing it coming. If I had, I wouldn't have shown up looking like I'd just rolled out of a Southwest gate lounge. I had dressed for TSA battle—t-shirt, shorts, flip-flops. Easy to strip down for those jerks, easy to slip back into afterward, post-frisking and pre-shoe-hunting. Ugh. Airport checkpoints were the worst. Nothing killed vacation joy faster than being scanned, questioned, and patted down for existing.

If I had known we were skipping that circus entirely, I would've dressed like someone who didn't pack her dignity in her carry-on.

But the moment I stepped on that plane, all my annoyance evaporated.

The jet was gorgeous. Black and white, just like his penthouse. Sleek, modern and expensive. White leather seats with matte black tables, with a black and grey chevron patterned carpeting. I reached out instinctively and brushed my fingers across one of the seats—soft, buttery, and way too luxurious for the likes of me. Could I get used to this? God help me, I already was. How would I ever fly commercial again?

There were cozy spots to relax, wide chairs for dining, actual legroom. *So much legroom.* I stretched on my toes just imagining how good it would feel not to land in Florida shaped like a pretzel.

Toward the back, there was a bathroom and another closed door that I assumed led to a cargo hold. I didn't have time to ponder it long—Roman was already giving me a tour.

"You really like your surprise?" he asked in a soft whisper, glancing toward the flight crew like he was sharing a scandal.

"It's actually a very nice surprise," I admitted, a little breathless. "It's a little much... but it's perfect."

He gave me a mock gasp, placing a hand over his heart like I'd insulted his honor. I shoved his shoulder playfully and he caught my hand mid-swing, holding it.

"If you get tired," he said, guiding me toward the back, "there's a bedroom."

Bedroom?

He opened the door I thought was for storage. My jaw dropped.

A king-sized bed dominated the small space—silky white sheets, down comforter, and enough fluffy pillows to drown in. It looked like a cloud with mood lighting.

I walked over and pressed down on it gently. Ridiculously soft. My fingers lingered. If I wasn't so wired, I would've flopped face-first into it.

"No," I said, shaking my head with a small grin. "I'm way too excited to sleep. But this is *definitely* happening on the way home."

He looked a little disappointed as he closed the door behind us. I didn't dare ask what he'd *hoped* would happen back there. But my mind? Oh, my mind was already writing a dozen possibilities.

"Lunch before takeoff?" he offered.

"Perfect," I said quickly, clinging to the normalcy.

We sat down at a small table, already set for two. I placed the napkin in my lap like I was on my best behavior, plus I didn't want to get anything on these white seats. He sat across from me, like confidence came as naturally to him as breathing.

The flight attendant brought out sandwiches and a tray of fruit. She asked if we'd like anything to drink.

"Yes," Roman said smoothly. "Can you bring the bottle of Perrier Jouët I requested—and a couple champagne flutes?"

She blushed, then nodded. "Of course, sir."

I cleared my throat. "Could I also get a water with lemon?"

She didn't even look at me. Her eyes never left Roman's face.

Roman shot me a quick look and shook his head with a smirk. I pressed my lips together, trying not to laugh. Another one under his spell.

"What's the occasion?" I asked, folding my hands in my lap to hide the irritation bubbling under my skin. Jealousy wasn't my thing—or at least, it hadn't been before. But after being cheated on, those old reflexes had a way of creeping back in. Watching her all but swoon over him while I sat there in my travel-wrinkled clothes, hair a little too messy from the rush, it was impossible not to feel it. That sharp, familiar pinch of insecurity. The quiet thought that maybe beautiful men like him always had options. And maybe women like me were foolish to forget that.

"Nothing," he said, eyes locked on mine. "But I think going on vacation is enough reason to pop a bottle, don't you?"

Honestly? You're damn right it is.

"Look at you," I teased. "Just full of surprises."

"And I've got more up my sleeve," he replied.

I raised a brow. "Let's not blow through all of them before takeoff."

He chuckled. "Not possible. One of them has to wait until we're in the air."

Oh, God. That look on his face. Mischievous. Calculated.

"You know, your ability to take things *slow* is uncanny," I said, studying him.

He didn't so much as blink—just smiled while the champagne was poured, then lifted his glass with easy confidence. "To vacation."

We toasted. The champagne was light and bubbly—elegant. It settled my nerves in a way water never could. Not that I got my water. The flight attendant had long forgotten I existed.

By the time we were taxiing down the runway, I was already two glasses deep and swirling a third. Plates were cleared, lights were dimmed, and Roman was holding his glass in one hand, my hand in the other.

Takeoff was smooth. I barely felt the lift. The plane seemed to glide. I'd never flown private before, but if this was what it felt like—I understood the appeal. Outside the window, all I could see were clouds. Puffy, weightless and perfect.

For a moment, everything inside me stilled.

The flight attendant stepped into the cockpit. I heard the click of the door locking behind her.

Roman turned toward me slowly, setting his glass down.

"Do you trust me?" he asked.

The question should've been innocent. But it wasn't. Not with that glint in his eye.

"I did," I said cautiously, narrowing my gaze. "I'm not so sure now."

"That's fair." His voice dipped an octave, rich and teasing. "What aren't you sure about?"

I tilted my head toward the cockpit. "The fact that I just heard the door lock. That I have no exit. And that you have *that* look."

He leaned closer, his scent warm and spicy and so intoxicating.

"What look?"

"You know the one. Where you're trying to use your superpowers on me."

He smiled lazily. "Is it working?"

I shifted in my seat, already too warm. "Depends. Are you trying to seduce me or scare me?"

"Neither," he said calmly. "I want to play a game."

Oh no. A game. In the air. Trapped.

"What kind of game?" I tried to sound neutral, but my voice cracked a little. "Is it a drinking game? Because I feel like I need another drink."

A slow, velvet sound slipped from his throat. That sound could melt granite.

"No, it's a game of trust." He assured me.

Trust. The word scraped against my skepticism, unfamiliar and almost foreign on my tongue. I took a slow sip of champagne, letting the bubbles sting before meeting his gaze. "Alright," I said lightly. "Now I trust you."

But the truth was, I didn't. Not yet.

"I'm being serious."

"So am I," I deadpanned. "What's the game?"

He looked at me with that same intense focus he wore when he was making a deal. It made my stomach flutter.

"I want to blindfold you. Tie your hands and ankles to the chair."

My breath caught. I blinked. Once. Twice.

"You want to... tie me up?" I repeated, trying to gauge if I'd misheard.

"Yes."

My fight-or-flight instincts screamed. But my body? My body hummed. I shifted again, heat blooming low in my belly. *Betrayer.*

"Mhm," was all I managed.

He caught that. "So, is that a yes?"

I couldn't speak. I nodded.

He pulled out a small velvet pouch from under the seat. Red. Of course. Inside were five black silk scarves.

"You're serious."

He nodded. "Dead serious. But you can stop me anytime."

My heart pounded as he crouched and tied one scarf gently around my ankle.

"How does that feel?"

I tested it. Soft. Secure. Not tight.

"Okay," I admitted quietly.

He repeated the same with the other ankle, then moved to my wrists.

"I don't usually do this," I blurted, my words tumbling out faster than I meant. "Just so you know. Like—ever," I added, needing him to understand that somehow.

He grinned. "Me either. I was researching trust-building exercises. This one just seemed like the most fun."

"Jesus," I whispered, unsure if I meant it as a prayer or an expletive.

He laughed again, low and effortless, then moved behind me. My nerves sparked—excitement or fear, I couldn't tell anymore. It was all starting to blur together.

"I'm not going to do anything that makes you uncomfortable. But I *am* going to make you feel."

And suddenly, being tied to a chair 30,000 feet in the air didn't seem like such a bad idea—but feel what?

***

ROMAN

Watching her surrender like that—it undid something in me.

Not because I needed control. Hell, I spend most of my life trying *not* to control things. But with her? With Alex? It was different. This wasn't about power. It was about *trust*. About showing her she didn't always have to fight, to carry it all on her own.

And she *never* let go. Not until now.

As I tied the last silk scarf around her wrist, she tested it, tugging soft-ly—just enough to let me know she wasn't helpless, just... willing.

My voice dropped low, rough around the edges. "I'll let you out whenever you say the word." She seemed unsure. "Too tight?"

She gave the faintest shake of her head, a small smile tugging at the corners of her mouth. That smile—equal parts nerves and anticipation—sent a rush through me I could barely control.

She was breathing faster, and so was I. I needed to settle us both.

"Are you ready for the blindfold?" I asked, meeting her eyes like it might be the last time I'd see them for a while. "I hate to cover those up, but... I want you to *feel* this. Really feel it. Not think. Just *be*. You tell me if anything gets too intense, alright?"

She nodded, her voice a quiet tease. "What kind of touching are we talking about here?"

I almost laughed. "Not that kind," I assured her. The idea that she might think I had some ulterior motive—something purely physical—almost made me stop right there. But I didn't. Because as much as this was about her learning to trust me, it was also about me learning to stay in control when every instinct wanted to give in.

Her expression fell somewhere between relieved and disappointed. That playful pout lit a fire I wasn't sure I could contain much longer.

"Just relax," I murmured, stepping behind her. "You're safe."

She wiggled her hands a little. "Looks like I'm completely in your hands, then."

Jesus, help me. Don't let me mess this up.

I tied the scarf gently over her eyes. The moment I did, a low rumble escaped my throat—half groan, half growl. She was so still. So exposed. So damn *beautiful.*

Her breath hitched. She shifted in the seat, and I could tell—she was getting turned on. And I was barely keeping it together, myself, and the game hadn't even started yet.

I swallowed, my throat tight. "Alright. I'm going to turn on some music now. Something soft."

I queued up our favorite instrumental playlist—something slow and ambient. Nothing distracting. Just enough to fill the silence without overwhelming it.

Then I moved to her feet.

When I touched her, she flinched.

"Just your shoes," I whispered. "Didn't mean to startle you."

She exhaled. "Okay. Wasn't ready."

"I'll narrate from now on, if that helps."

"You don't have to... if it's not part of the game."

That vulnerability in her voice? That was what I was after and it was bringing me to my knees in a way I never imagined. I had to steady myself just to answer.

"This game's whatever you need it to be. It's not about rules—it's about you."

She unclenched slightly. Her hands relaxed around the armrests. She was slowly letting go.

"I'm going to massage your feet now, alright?"

Another soft smile. "That's fine."

I slipped her shoes off slowly. Her feet were perfect. Soft. Manicured in a pale pink polish that looked fresh. *Too* fresh. No calluses. No signs of wear. And yet I *knew* she was a runner. That she wore heels for hours and worked long hours in them. These feet shouldn't have looked this good.

And still, here I was, getting turned on by her *feet*.

I rolled my neck, trying to snap myself out of it.

She tilted her head back, a soft, almost reverent breath leaving her lips as my thumbs pressed into the delicate arch of her foot. Her body melted into the cushions—unguarded and trusting. I moved slowly, deliberately tracing every dip and curve from her ankle to each tender toe. She didn't say a word. She didn't have to.

The room seemed to shrink, the silence thick with heat. My fingers swept up along her calf, not out of necessity but because I *had* to. I needed to feel more of her. The way her skin responded beneath my hands—the way she gave in to the sensation without flinching or second-guessing—unraveled something deep in me. Watching goosebumps rise in the wake of my touch sent a thrill through me.

But I wasn't in control anymore. Not of this moment. Not of the rhythm of my breath or the thoughts running wild behind my eyes.

She was softness and heat and surrender all wrapped into one perfect ache.

All I could think about was how far she'd let me go if I kept touching her like this—how much of her she'd give if I just kept asking with my hands instead of my mouth.

God help me, I was drowning. Willingly. Slowly. And I never wanted to come up for air.

"How're you feeling?" I asked, barely trusting my voice.

"Hmmm..." she moaned softly.

I pressed my eyes shut, willing God to rein me back to the task at hand—back to trust.

"Should I keep going?"

"Mhmm."

My self-control frayed.

I moved to her hands next. The silk scarf I'd tied around her wrist slipped free, and I let it fall to the floor without looking away from her. My fingers found her palm, tracing the soft lines there like they held a map I'd spent years searching for.

I worked each knuckle carefully, rubbing slow circles until I felt her exhale again—like every part of her was loosening under my touch. When I reached her wrist, I lingered. The delicate flutter of her pulse there made my own heart stutter, made something low in my chest tighten.

I lifted her hand to my mouth without thinking. Pressed a kiss to the center—light at first, then deeper, letting my lips drag against her skin as I inhaled her. She shivered. Just a breath. But I felt it everywhere.

Her fingers curled slightly, not pulling away but curling *into* me. Like she needed something from me I wasn't sure I could hold back anymore.

She didn't speak. Didn't ask for more. But her body was already telling me everything.

And God, I was listening.

She moaned again.

I froze.

One kiss, and I was already coming apart.

I wrapped the scarf back around that hand, then did the same with the other, her fingers wiggling playfully as I worked.

She was glowing. Vulnerable. Radiant in her restraint.

I couldn't breathe.

"You okay?" she asked, that rasp in her voice driving the edge deeper into me.

"Yeah," I lied. "Yes. Just... didn't expect this to *feel* like this."

She giggled. Like I'd just confessed to something harmless. But it wasn't harmless. It was dangerous. For me. For her. For my self-control.

"How about you?" I asked. "How are you feeling?"

"Heavenly," she breathed.

I nearly choked on it. Heavenly wasn't the adjective I would've used for my own feelings.

She went on, and her voice got even softer, deeper. "It's like an out-of-body experience. I'm not even picturing anything. Just... sensation."

My body was screaming. *Try it*, it said. *Feel it*. But if I gave in, I wasn't sure I'd be able to come back from it.

Instead, I whispered, "Shoulders next."

Her head tipped slightly, bracing for it. I stepped behind her, placing my hands on her shoulders, and felt the tightness there. I kneaded gently—circles, pressure points—my thumbs working their way into the muscle.

She was so strong. But not bulky. Just perfectly lean. A body built from tension and release.

I moved down her back, then reached up, sweeping her hair over her right shoulder. My lips brushed her neck. Not kissing—just breathing her in.

Pheromones. Perfume. The pure scent of her skin. I was intoxicated, and the thought of God pressed in like an uninvited witness. Why did it feel like treachery to think of Him now?

I pushed the thought reluctantly from my mind.

My mouth found the base of her neck, and I kissed. Slowly. Intentionally.

She exhaled sharply, her head tipping back.

I moved to the other side, repeating it. I couldn't stop. I didn't *want* to stop.

"Forgive me," I murmured into her skin. "I lost myself for a moment." An invisible tether tightened, reining me in before I crossed a line.

She didn't flinch. Her voice was barely more than a plea. "Don't worry about it." But I did—I worried about being just another man she couldn't trust.

She tilted her neck farther, offering more.

And that was it.

I broke.

I pulled away, heart pounding, and dropped into the chair beside her, burying my head in my hands.

"Looks like you win," I muttered, exhausted by the simple act of restraint.

"What? How did I win?" she asked, voice still soft, still floating somewhere between pleasure and concern.

I started untying the scarves with trembling hands.

"You did what you were supposed to do—just feel. I was the one meant to lead. To stay in control." I shook my head, frustration tightening my voice. "I lost it." I was overwhelmed.

Lead. The word echoed in my mind—something I'd heard in church once. The man is supposed to lead. But here I was, guiding her straight into something reckless. Something that felt good but wasn't right.

When I got the last scarf undone, she reached out and cupped my face, guiding me to look at her.

"You were incredible," she said. "That was the most intimate experience I've ever had. And you gave it to me."

Her smile undid the rest of me.

"You guided my mind to places I didn't know existed. There's no way this game has losers."

I couldn't speak. I just pulled her into me, arms around her, forehead tucked into her shoulder, like maybe she could hold all the fractured parts of me together.

She rested her head on mine.

Peace. It was peace.

And for the first time in a long time, I let myself believe I deserved it.

The pilot's voice broke through the cabin: *"We'll be landing in about thirty minutes."*

And all I could think was—thirty more minutes of this? Please. Let time stop.

***

ALEX

Holy crap. I hadn't been prepared for it. My mind wandered to every sensation.

It hadn't felt like a game at all—it had been a surrender. A stripping away of everything I once thought I needed to survive; control, distance, power. I remember bracing myself for discomfort, for fear, maybe even embarrassment. But when he tied that second scarf, something in me cracked open.

I'd expected restraint to feel like confinement. Instead, it was release. Every knot he tied seemed to undo something in me.

There hadn't been anything to see, nothing to do, nowhere to run. Just sensation. Just him. Just that moment.

And if love is real—not the kind that shatters you, not the kind that tries to fix you, but the kind that's sacred, rooted, safe—I think that's what I felt then.

It went deeper than the physical. My body would've given him anything—it ached for more—but that hadn't been the point. It had been about being seen in a way I never knew I wanted. Being held in a way I never realized I needed.

"Thank you," I whispered, when my thoughts allowed. "I don't know if I'll ever be able to explain what just happened to me. But... I think a brick or two fell. If that means anything to you."

His head lifted at that—fast, like he wasn't sure he heard me right. Something like relief flitted across his expression.

His arms came around me again, this time tight and urgent. Like he needed my words to hold him together.

Eventually, he exhaled, and we started to gather our things as the plane was making its final decent. The silence between us thick but comfortable. I settled into the seat beside him, fingers brushing his thigh before I reached for his hand. I didn't ask permission—I just took it.

He glanced at me, smile tight, eyes a little glassy. Then he turned to the window like he needed distance, but didn't want to let go.

I looked down at our linked hands. "Can I ask you something?"

"Sure. Anything."

"What happened to *you* during the game?"

He gave a small, strangled laugh. Perhaps he wasn't sure how to share his feelings. "Hmmm, maybe I shouldn't have said anything."

"You don't have to tell me. I was just wondering... was it a good kind of overwhelming? Or the bad kind?"

He drew in a slow breath, his fingers tightening around mine for just a second before easing again. His gaze stayed fixed on the sky beyond the window, like he was searching for something out there.

"It's hard to describe," he said, his voice low and thoughtful. "I think I was feeling *everything*. You. Me. All of it at once. And it hit me harder than I expected. You were so open, so vulnerable... and I was having a hard time not crossing the line. The kiss on your neck wasn't planned. But it felt—"

"Necessary," I finished for him.

He glanced over. The tension in his shoulders seemed to ease slightly.

"It's not like I'm a virgin, Roman. I understand desire. I've felt lust before. But this?" I shook my head. "This is different. What we have is so intense, it's almost painful. And I think... I think that was the first time I've ever really let someone touch me without my guard up. Something your mom said I should do in our recent session..."

His brows lifted, clearly caught off guard as he hurried to interrupt me.

"Wait—did my *mom* tell you to do this?" His face cracked into something halfway between teasing and horror.

I burst out laughing. "Uh, *no*. Your mom did *not* tell me to play sensual massage bondage games with her son, thank you very much."

He smiled, relieved as I saw the color flush his face a little pinker than before.

"But she *did* tell me I needed to learn how to meditate." I left out the part where she told me to meditate on God's word. I don't even know what that means. "To slow down. To feel what's mine and let go of what isn't. That's what this was. A total reset. I didn't have to *see* anything or *say* anything or even *think*. I just had to feel. I let go of everything I couldn't control and focused on the only thing that felt true."

His gaze was steady now. The heat was back—but tempered by something reverent.

"I didn't even realize you were losing control," I admitted. "Maybe I did, deep down, but I chose to trust you anyway. And... I'm really glad I did."

He leaned in and kissed me—soft and warm. Not a claiming. A gift. And when he pulled away, I was breathless.

Not from the kiss, but from the connection.

I wasn't inhaling air anymore. I was inhaling *him*.

The door to the cabin creaked open, and the flight attendant appeared. She headed straight for the champagne bottle, her tone suddenly more professional.

"How was your flight, Ms. Kennedy? Mr. King?"

"It was incredible," I said honestly, still dazed.

Roman turned to her, but his eyes stayed on me. "What she said."

And just like that, the butterflies were back. My whole body flushed with awareness.

I was about to get lost in him again when the attendant held up the champagne bottle with a gentle interruption. "There's still enough champagne for two more glasses. Would you like a refill?"

We both nodded, still staring at each other like we hadn't just been wrecked and remade in the same hour.

We sipped the last of the champagne as we prepared to land—his hand still holding mine, as if letting go now might dismantle the magic of what we'd just created.

Chapter 25

ROMAN

At least I'd made some headway with her—though I couldn't shake the sense I'd stumbled backward, too. Empathy was still difficult to navigate for me. I'd been grappling with it for years, yet she had just discovered it and already wielded more control than I ever could.

The plane touched down, luggage loaded into the waiting car, and before I'd caught my bearings, we were pulling up to two houses pressed so close together they might as well have been one. Her family had already arrived, eager to get the grill started, and the moment the driver carried our bags to the front door, the crowd descended. Hugs, voices, hands tugging at luggage—it was chaos I wasn't ready for.

I tipped the driver, took his card for the ride back in a week, and braced myself. Too many introductions. Too many faces. The anxiety bled in sharp around the edges, though I kept it buried where no one could see.

Except Alex.

"Hey everyone, this is Roman," she announced, cutting through the swarm. "Let us get in and settled first, then the great inquisition can resume." A chorus of reluctant *fines* followed, and finally I could breathe.

I gave her a weak smile. *"Thanks."* She caught the weight beneath it without me needing to explain.

"Of course. Come on—let's unpack and change. Want a shower?"

"Yeah, just a quick one."

"Just a quickie, huh?" She winked, easing the tension with silly innuendo.

Still, I nearly choked on the comeback I didn't dare voice. She was rubbing off on me more than I cared to admit.

Upstairs, the routine helped. Bags opened. Shower taken. Anxiety rinsed away. I dressed in navy shorts, a white short-sleeved button-down scattered with blue fish, and brown leather flip-flops—my attempt at Florida festive. The mattress welcomed me, and I nearly drifted off while Alex finished in the bathroom.

The bed dipped hard. I opened my eyes to find her grinning, lying on her side, gaze fixed on me.

"You wanted to come," she teased.

I rolled toward her, arm snapping around her waist, tugging her close. "Yes, I did. And I'm not even going to respond in the childish way I'd like to."

"Oh my God, you're such an adolescent." Her breathless laugh told me she was half-serious, half-delighted as she tried to wriggle free.

I held fast, nose buried in her hair, inhaling that familiar lavender-vanilla fragrance—the same one she'd worn the night we met. One of the best moments of my life.

"You have no idea." I pulled her on top of me, meeting her eyes. Her palms pressed into my shoulders, holding herself up, and I traced my fingers down her cheek, her throat, lingering at the dip of her blouse, just enough to tempt myself. *Perfect.*

"Okay," she said, smiling but breathless, "let's get out of here before they send a search party."

I groaned. "Good idea. Because I'd love nothing more than to lock that door and never leave."

Self-control? Hers had never been the issue. Looking back, I realized she'd played me all along. The one losing control now—the one undone—was me.

***

ALEX

"For the love of all that's holy, would you please be quiet and let's go get a drink—or do I need to push you in the pool to cool off?"

"I dare you," he said, a wicked gleam sparking in his eyes.

"Oh, so now you want to play my kind of games, huh?"

He nodded slowly, the corner of his mouth tilting into mischief.

"I'm ready for all kinds of games now."

That side of him felt new. Roman, playful and unguarded.

"Then let the games begin. We can make up the rules as we go. One rule I'm establishing now—no drunk mistakes. If anything ever happens between us, I want it remembered clearly." I planted my hands on my hips, standing firm.

He smiled. "So, sober fun is on the table?" He wiggled his brows, and I rolled my eyes.

"What? " He said in response. "I wasn't going to say anything scandalous." His lips twitched, though his eyes betrayed the thought.

"Really?" I asked, tipping my head innocently, trying to hide the flush that betrayed me.

"I'm going to take you in that pool with me." He responded with mischievous eyes as he lightened the mood.

I giggled before darting out of the room before he could catch me. His footsteps thundered behind me, and before I could reach the stairs, his arms wrapped around my waist, his fingers digging playfully into my sides. I gasped from the sudden grip.

"This game is fun," he laughed into my ear.

"Yes, it is. And this is just day one." I nudged him with my hips in retaliation before wriggling free.

By the time we made it outside, everyone was settled near the grill. While Roman chatted with the men, my aunt Diana pulled me aside. Roman glanced over his shoulder and winked, and I shrugged before being led away.

"Where did you find this man?" she asked, sipping her beer, her tone daring me to lie.

"He was in one of those mail-order magazines. What do you think?"

She shoved my shoulder, and I laughed.

"Oh, shut up. I'm serious. He looks like he really might have walked out of one of those magazines."

"I know—and he knows it too. Don't puff his head up any bigger than it already is. He thinks it's a superpower."

She nearly spit out her drink, laughing.

"I'm not kidding. He's as charming as he is gorgeous. Have you had a chance to talk to him yet and look into those eyes?" I whispered sharply, lowering my voice so only she could hear.

"No. Tell him to get over here. I want to see if those eyes are full of it or not."

I grinned. My aunt never minced words. "I'll grab him when I get us another drink."

"I bet you will."

My mouth dropped open. "Can I say anything without innuendo? What is wrong with all of you?"

She waved me off. "I'm thirsty. Go."

My aunt was my favorite—blunt, discerning, and protective. If Roman wasn't the real deal, she'd see it in an instant. I returned with a seltzer for myself and another beer for her, breaking up the circle of men Roman was standing in.

"Roman, come with me," I said, tapping him with my elbow since my hands were full. "Your presence has been requested by Princess Diana."

The men chorused, "Uh oh!"

Roman looked at me, then at them. "What did I do?" He seemed genuinely nervous.

"Nothing," I assured him as we walked. "She just wants a word without all the riffraff around."

He arched a brow. "Why do you call her Princess?"

"Because she is. You'll see."

I brought him over. "Auntie, this is Roman King. Careful—your title's only Princess, but you're about to meet a King." I leaned closer and whispered, "Though really, he's more like a Greek god."

My aunt laughed while Roman nudged me with his shoulder.

"Diana, it's a pleasure to meet you. I don't think you should be intimidated by anything as far as I'm concerned." He reached out his hand, waiting.

She eyed it for a moment, then clasped it firmly. "Oh, I'm not worried about you. But you should be worried about me if you hurt my niece."

His eyes widened, darting toward me. I smiled to reassure him.

"Then we're both safe," he said. "Because hurting her isn't an option. I think she's amazing, though she doesn't believe I've got much potential."

I shot him a look for the jab, but he winked and gave himself a point in our silent game.

"Well, my niece is a very intelligent woman," my aunt countered.

I beamed and held up a finger for my own point, making Roman laugh.

"Touché," he conceded.

"What are you two even keeping score about?" she asked.

We both shrugged, laughing because neither of us really knew.

Diana shook her head. "Whatever it is, it looks like you're having fun. Roman, so far so good. Just enjoy each other." She lifted her beer toward him.

"Thank you," he said, though the mischievous glint in his eyes was back and set me on edge.

Before I could react, he scooped me over his shoulder and marched toward the pool.

"Roman!" I squealed, pounding his back.

"I think it's time we both cooled off," he said, patting my leg for good measure.

"You wouldn't dare."

"Didn't you say this was your kind of game? Then why not play?"

"I'm going to drown you," I threatened between laughter.

"I'm sure you'll try," he said—and then he leapt in with me.

***

ROMAN

As we swam toward the shallow end, I felt like I'd won the dare when I asked, "So... does this mean we have to go take a shower?" I stood, pushing my wet hair back and wiping the water from my eyes—ready to turn this game into an excuse to sneak upstairs.

"Nope," she choked out, coughing from all the water she'd swallowed during her screaming entrance. "It means we now have to hang out with everyone in our soaking wet clothes." She splashed me, water landing harmlessly against my chest.

"Party pooper," I muttered, feigning irritation. She laughed, and just like that, my plan failed miserably.

"Do you want to go for a walk on the beach?" she asked, batting her lashes playfully as she tightened the elastic band holding back her dripping hair.

"Right now? Like this?" I gestured to both of us, clothes clinging.

"It's eighty-five degrees out—we'll dry. Besides, I want to see the sunset. And you're the one who threw us in the pool."

"Well, I didn't know you wanted a beach walk." I shook my head, wiping the rest of the water from my face before slicking my hair back with both hands.

She smirked. "We can always take our clothes off and walk the beach naked."

I didn't give her time to backpedal. I knew she was joking. I caught her hand with a grin. "Fine. Naked sunset it is."

Her laughter trailed behind me as I tugged her toward the sand. I pulled my shirt off with one hand, tossing it aside and kicking off my flip-flops at the edge of the property. She followed suit, flinging her sandals in the same direction as she hurried to keep up.

The sky was already painted in streaks of gold and rose, and for a moment I forgot about everything else—except her hand in mine, and the beauty God had stretched across the horizon just for us.

***

ALEX

We stopped in our tracks, the sight stilling us both.

Red, gold, and orange bled together across the horizon, their reflection rippling over the glassy water. Warmth clung to the air as the sun made its slow descent, painting the sky in strokes too vivid to ignore. We stood hand in hand at the edge of the tide, toes in the surf, eyes closed, soaking in the last of the day's heat before it vanished into night.

For the moment, the beach was quiet. But I knew the stillness wouldn't last—soon my family and the rest of the vacationers would pour down to witness the sunset. I wanted to be sure he was truly okay before the chaos began. I gave his hand a soft squeeze.

"Tell me how you're feeling. Is it a little much up there?"

"Maybe a little." His honesty twisted a knot in my stomach. "I like every-one—it's just a lot of people, a lot of questions. I'm not used to big families."

I'd never asked much about his family, beyond what I already knew. My fingers threaded with his, my nod slow and understanding. My family had never been known for their subtlety.

"I'm sure they're done after today. I've never seen you so..." I trailed off, searching for the right word.

"Like Harrison?" he supplied.

I laughed. He was usually all confidence and business, but here he seemed uncertain, almost shy with a side of reckless abandon.

"Yeah, a little like that."

"I'm just trying to figure out this immature fun you all seem to love."

"And how do you like it?" I teased, wringing water from my hair. "I look like a drowned rat because of your fun."

He grinned. "Actually, you look incredible—all wet and sparkly."

The compliment made me squirm, even though he was always generous with them. Around my family, who loved pointing out flaws, I struggled to accept his words. So I pushed the focus back to him.

"Other than the attention, are you okay?"

He drew our joined hands behind my back, pulling me flush against him. "Yeah. I think it's going to be a lot of fun. Do we have a schedule of events?"

"As a matter of fact, we do. And while we don't have to do everything, I usually do."

"What's on the list?" He swayed with me in his arms, and it felt natural.

"Deep sea fishing, a sunset cruise, surfing lessons... plenty of beach days."

"All that sounds great."

The waves lapped against our legs, steady and soothing. It was the perfect backdrop for the conversation—until I saw my family approaching.

"Well, here comes the crew." I sighed as he pulled me down onto the sand between his legs, his body a shield, our eyes fixed on the fading sun.

"Anyone up for ghost stories? I'll build a fire tomorrow night," Edward suggested.

"Can we skip the ghost stories?" I muttered. "I've had enough scary crap lately." Burrow Township flashed through my mind, and I rolled my eyes. No one in my family knew what Roman and I had been dealing with.

"What scary stuff?" Edward pressed, flicking his gaze from me to Roman.

"Nothing to worry about." My tone was clipped, my smile forced. He didn't push further, but I knew my brother—this wasn't over.

Later, on the porch, drinks in hand, Edward cornered me while Roman slipped away.

"Everything okay?" he asked.

"Yeah, why wouldn't it be?"

"You called me about self-defense. Did something else happen?"

"No. I'm fine." The words were automatic. We both knew I wasn't.

"Okay, if you say you're fine, I believe you." He didn't. His smirk as Roman reappeared told me he planned to get answers elsewhere.

By the time the night dwindled, my parents had gone to bed, leaving me with Roman, my brothers, and their partners. The girls pulled me aside.

"Did he make a deal with the devil for that face?" Rose whispered, wide-eyed.

"No," I said, smirking. "He asked me to go to church with him."

She arched a brow, unconvinced. "Wow. He's so good-looking. Is he actually nice too?" She avoided the church talk just like the rest of my family. I wonder why it's so taboo in my family. I let the thought fade.

"He's more than nice. He's smart, talented, thoughtful..." My own words hit me like a jolt. *What's wrong with me? He's everything I've ever wanted.*

"So, when's the wedding?" Bianca shot back.

I gawked at her. "Are you insane?"

"If you don't get that man off the market, someone else will—and you'll end up with another Luke."

The heat in my chest flared at the memory of Luke, and I must've shown it. Roman's smile faltered across the patio, worry flickering in his eyes. I forced my face into something softer, returning his smile.

"Roman's great. You're right. Maybe I'm the one who's not."

Later, in our room, I showered until the tears blended with the spray. Her words echoed through the water—the thought of losing Roman, of repeating old mistakes, made something deep inside me ache.

I shut off the water and stood there for a minute, willing the thoughts to fade. Then I grabbed a towel, swore under my breath for forgetting clothes, and prayed Roman was asleep.

He wasn't. He sat waiting on the bench at the foot of the bed.

I tried to tiptoe past him, but his hand shot out, catching mine, tugging me forward with a force that nearly unraveled the towel. His eyes burned, dark with intent.

"I forgot my clothes," I whispered, pointing toward the dresser. "I'll just—"

He shook his head, that sun-tired kind of slow, but when his gaze lifted to me, the energy shifted. His eyes traced the towel, the drops still clinging to my skin, and in an instant, fatigue gave way to something hotter, heavier. "That won't be necessary."

The timbre of his voice sent fire racing through me. My breath hitched. He drew me onto his lap, my back against his chest, his arms caging me in.

"Don't say a word," he murmured against my ear.

Music played softly somewhere in the room, but all I could hear was my heartbeat. His hands traced down my arms, back up, then lingered on my shoulders as his lips began a deliberate path of kisses from one side to the other—butterflies swarming.

Every touch was fire. Every pause, torture. I clutched his hair to keep from moving, his command echoing in my head.

He teased, tested, restrained—until the restraint broke. His mouth claimed every inch of my neck as his hand slid higher, then lower, until I could no longer contain the sound clawing out of me.

And he smiled against my skin, satisfied, before silencing me with his hand as wave after wave of release tore through me.

When the storm subsided, he kissed me—slow, grounding, reverent. Then, with a pained smile, he whispered against my skin:

"I'm going to shower. Then we're going to sleep."

"If that's what you want." I asked sadly, wondering why he didn't want me to touch him back.

He nodded his head helping me off his lap then left me trembling in more ways than one, wondering if restraint had been his greatest act of intimacy yet.

***

ROMAN

Damn, she's like a drug.

I only meant to tease, to mess around a little—but I lost all control. Even under this cold spray, I could feel her hands in my hair, her mouth moaning against my palm as she came apart. I could still taste her, smell her, hear her. It clung to me.

Yeah, this shower isn't worth a damn. I cranked the heat and finished off the ache myself—hardly satisfying, but necessary. She'd have gladly reciprocated, but tonight wasn't about me. I was supposed to be patient, deliberate. Slow. Apparently, I'm terrible at all three.

Towel slung low around my waist, I stepped back into the room. The cool air hit my skin, carrying her scent with it. She sat propped against the pillows now, tank top on, glowing. Smiling. Exactly what I'd wanted to see.

I grinned, grabbed a pair of briefs from the dresser, and let the towel drop right in front of her. If I was falling off this wagon I was going out in style.

"Jesus," she whispered—and the thought of defying what He'd actually want me to do sent a thin blade of shame through me. I pushed it down, trying to reason with myself. This isn't that bad... right?

I turned, smug. "Did you say something?"

Her lips twitched. "I was praying."

A laugh slipped out of me. I pulled on the briefs, adjusting as her eyes followed.

"Coming to bed like that?" she asked.

"Is it too much?" I made a point of shifting just to keep her attention. She choked on a laugh until she coughed.

"What the hell are you trying to do to me? You're going to break me."

I leaned on the mattress beside her, savoring the dramatics. "I thought you liked games."

"I have issues with this game," she pouted. "The lines are a little blurry, don't you think."

"I thought we only had one rule."

Her chin tilted up. "Correction—two. Rule number two: no giving without receiving."

I stretched out beside her, head on her stomach. "Didn't break that rule."

She shoved my shoulder. "Cheater."

I laughed, rolling to my back so her lap became my pillow. "How can you cheat when we're making it up as we go?"

"Fine. Then all bets are off."

I pushed up on my elbows, meeting her face-to-face. "Funny. For someone who just had an out-of-body experience, you sound like a sore loser. And if sore's what you're looking for..." I said jokingly as I wiggled my brows, hand sliding up her thigh until she swatted it away.

She grew serious, biting her lip. "I feel selfish when you give and I don't. I like to give too."

I studied her, then softened my voice. "I know. But maybe it's time you learn it's okay to just... receive. No rules. No debts." This wasn't supposed to be the way things went, and I was losing my battle with restraint.

Her eyes sparked. "Am I being taught a lesson?"

"Depends," I murmured. "Do you need one? Because I'm picturing you bent over my knee."

She blinked. "Okay."

My body flared hot at that single word. For heaven's sake, this woman had me completely flustered and as far from God as I could get.

"No lesson," I admitted quickly. "I just got caught up. Out of control. I want to take things slow, but when you're this close—half-naked—it's damn near impossible." I felt the need to be as truthful as I could.

She laughed, breathless. "Same. So, what do you suggest we do?"

"I'm going to check into a hotel."

Her head snapped up. "Like hell you are."

I cracked up. "Relax, it was a joke."

She groaned, flopping onto her side. "Oh my God, you've turned me into one of those desperate needy women."

I leaned in close, whispering against her ear. "Good. Because I'm already ruined."

Chapter 26

ROMAN

I ran into Patrick's girlfriend, Rose, in the kitchen. She was already making coffee, hair pulled back, when she turned with a grin.

"Yeah, definitely." She lifted a mug that read *First Coffee Then I Do the Things* "Coffee first in this house." nodding like it was gospel.

"Good morning. My thoughts exactly." I poured my own into a travel mug and gestured toward the deck. "Want to join me outside?"

"Sure. I'm an early riser—even on vacation. Nice to have someone else up this time of day."

I pulled out a chair for her, settling in beside her with the salt air on my face. "Alex doesn't wake up early?"

Rose laughed. "Oh, she does. But she runs on the beach at sunrise. Not much talking happening then."

I nodded, leaning back. Figures.

In true Alex fashion, the moment her name came up, she appeared—already in running gear.

"Well, hello you two." She brushed her lips over mine as she passed. "Back in half an hour."

"Beach run?" I caught her around the waist.

"Of course. Where else?"

"Sidewalk? Grass? Running on sand's brutal on your calves."

She smirked like I was clueless, and I shut myself up with a laugh.

"Never mind. Go run." I patted her backside, earning a wicked grin.

"You can rub the cramps out later," she tossed over her shoulder.

Damn that girl. I watched her head toward the water, then glanced back at Rose, who was laughing and blushing.

"Am I in trouble with this one?" I asked.

Rose shrugged. "Depends on what you call trouble. Personally, I think she's awesome. Better than when she was with that asshole. I know I'll have a great sister-in-law when Patrick and I marry." She smiled toward the beach.

That guy had clearly left his mark on everyone—not just Alex. I filed it away for another time.

I asked how she and Patrick met, mostly to cut the silence, and she'd just started when Patrick himself walked out with coffee in hand.

"Morning," he said, gaze fixed on the surf. "Did Alex already hit the sand?"

We both nodded.

"Can't keep up with her, can you, Roman?" His tone was sharp enough to feel like a jab.

I shook my head, unsure what he meant, until he added, "That girl's addicted to exercise. Did you know she added self-defense and kickboxing to her routine?"

"I did, yes." I studied him. "You seem worried."

Patrick gave me the same look Alex did when she thought I was missing something obvious. "Well, aren't you?"

I kept my tone even. "Patrick, is there more I should be worried about than exercise?"

His smirk made me want to punch him. He was baiting me.

"Too much of anything is too much." His voice dripped with self-satisfaction. Alex had warned me he was the angry brother. I decided to let him have the last word.

Before things could escalate, Alex returned from her run just as Edward and Bianca joined us with their coffees. Edward wasted no time.

"So, Roman, our sister still doesn't care about asking for help, does she?"

I laughed lightly. "On my end, that's a yes. I'm guessing you've got your own reasons."

He gave me a measured look. "Yes, and I'd be glad to share them anytime." He lifted his mug in a toast.

I let out a breath. This family was protective, competitive, and relentless. Now I knew exactly where Alex got it.

***

ALEX

The morning was clear, the air thick with salt. My favorite smell. The sand was soft and white, the water glittering as sun sparkles danced across the waves. Every step sank into serenity. The rhythm of the surf felt like it vibrated with my soul. Why did I limit myself to half an hour on mornings like this? Running here was therapy—better than a thousand sessions. Maybe I should move closer to the ocean.

Halfway through, my buzz broke. Thoughts of everything that needed doing for beach day crowded in. And then Roman crept into my head—his hands on me, his mouth, his refusal to let me return the favor. Heat tore through me so fast I had to stop, bent over with my hands on my knees. *There's no way I can hold out on this man. Not for him, not for me.*

I forced my mind back to the day ahead. Beach chairs. Umbrellas. Coolers stuffed with alcohol, water, Gatorade. Towels, books, sunscreen. Snacks in a sand-sprinkled bag. Passing out in the sun, getting burned, swimming in the pool before Mom and Diana made dinner. And at least one day where I'd have to apologize for my mother's behavior. Maybe that's why I ran every morning—get a head start on the chaos.

My thoughts tangled: Roman's touch and my mom's drunken rants. The good with the bad. I stopped again, stretching tall into the sun, then bending down to rake my fingers through the sand. Keep what feels good, let go of what doesn't. Last night was worth remembering forever. My mother's fights? Not so much.

This was the longest run I'd ever pushed myself through out here. My lungs burned, my legs ached, and every breath came sharp and uneven. I needed to get back before someone started to worry.

When I reached the house, everyone seemed to be awake. I caught sight of Mom and Dad heading out as Roman and Edward talked on the deck. They both looked straight at me. Obviously, I was the topic. I smiled, shook my head, pretending not to care. Let them talk. I had plans to make Roman squirm today. I'd packed swimsuits that barely covered anything, and he was going to put sunscreen on me where he couldn't do a thing about it.

Sweaty and sticky from the humidity, I brushed past the crowd with my arms raised, avoiding contact, and kicked my sandy shoes off at the door. Straight upstairs. Shower, swimsuit, cover-up. No distractions. Well—fewer, anyway.

Roman was right—running on sand always wrecked my legs. Maybe, on some level, I liked the punishment without even realizing it. But for what? My calves burned as I braced against the towel rack to stretch them out, quads taut, hamstrings aching. I held each pose until the tension eased, then shook out my legs, dressed quickly, twisted my hair into a messy bun, swiped on sunscreen, and slid into my flip-flops.

When I came out, hat in hand, Roman was exactly where I found him last night—smiling like he expected a repeat.

"Yeah, I learned from my mistakes," I teased. "Got dressed in the bathroom this time."

He laughed. "Figured you wouldn't fall for it again."

I tilted his chin up to meet my eyes. "Oh, I'll fall again. I'm just going to be ready for you. Maybe *you'll* be on the receiving end."

His teeth caught his bottom lip, fighting a smile. "I'd never let you go without."

"Sometimes we just need to be grateful," I mocked in his own tone, pinching his cheek.

He leapt up, wrapped me tight, saving me from stumbling backward. His voice was low, teasing against my ear. "What kind of trouble am I in when that cover-up comes off?"

"Let's just say I hate tan lines."

His frown was immediate. "So... really big trouble."

***

ROMAN

Once outside, she showed me where everything was—umbrella, Adirondack chairs with cushions, bags of towels and sunblock. The beach was only a hundred feet from the back door, but lugging all this gear made it feel like a mile. After setting up our spot, we trudged back for the cooler and snacks.

By the time we hauled it all down, I was winded. *All this work for one day at the beach? And we have to repeat it tomorrow? There's got to be a better system.*

"I can't drink all day without eating," she said matter-of-factly while she looked through the refrigerator. "I love food more than I love alcohol. I put OJ and champagne in our cooler, plus vodka and Bloody Mary mix. Should be celery in there too."

I arched a brow, hoping she was scanning for *real* food, because she couldn't be serious—celery and tomato juice did not count.

"You guys are serious about your beach days, aren't you?" I asked. I was used to full-service resorts, not DIY vacations.

"That's 100% fact." She tapped her hips thoughtfully, then spun around with a grin. "Breakfast?"

Real food. Good. I nodded, though my appetite was pointed at what she wore under that cover-up.

She made us eggs, bacon, hashbrowns, and toast with blackberry jam. We sat at the kitchen island, coffee steaming between us. She sipped her orange juice, then tucked supplements and a couple packets of Liquid IV into her shirt pocket, pulling out extra bottles of water as she did.

Smart, prepared and sexy as hell.

***

ALEX

Once everything was set up under our umbrella, I poured a Liquid IV into a water bottle, shook it, and tucked it back in the cooler. I filled my Yeti with ice water, set it by my chair, then made the real priority: a Bloody Mary. Celery stalk, a couple olives, a long stir, and the first sip pulled a satisfied moan straight out of me.

Priorities, right?

I dragged an oversized raft through the sand for us to float in the ocean. No water sports today—my body needed a break. Just floating. Roman cracked open a beer, slipped a koozie on, and stretched back in his chair, eyes locked on me the whole time.

Even through my cover-up, his stare felt hot enough to scorch. I pulled my sunglasses down, smirking at him. He tilted his head to the sun, then asked out of nowhere, "Can I take you on an island vacation? Just the two of us."

First day of vacation and he's already planning another?

"Maybe," I said. "When?"

"I don't know. Whenever. Just think it'd be fun. No tan lines."

I giggled. "That does sound nice."

He rolled onto his side, elbow propped, beer in hand. "So when are you taking that shirt off?"

I sipped my drink. "As soon as I'm done with this. Then I'll need help with sunblock."

His brow arched. "Can I help?"

"Who else did you think I had in mind?"

"I don't know. You seem to plan everything."

"Normally, yes. But with you here? Of course I want *you* rubbing me down."

His grin turned wicked. "I can't wait to get you in the water."

My head whipped toward him, mouth open. "Get me in the water to do what?"

"Oh, I'll think of something."

"Just remember the rules," I warned. "We have one in particular—"

"And the other's bullshit. Doesn't count," he cut me off.

"Fine. All bets are off. No more games." I laughed, crossing my arms.

"Looks like we have a quitter." His tone carried that smug edge that always made me want to knock him down a peg.

So I did. I rose slowly, meeting his gaze as I worked each button loose, one by one. The humid air slid beneath the fabric, brushing against my skin as the shirt fell open. His eyes didn't move—just stayed locked on me, the teasing replaced by something heavier. I slipped the cover-up from my shoulders, folded it with careful precision, and leaned down to tuck it into the beach bag. The sun warmed my bare back, the salt in the breeze clinging to my skin, and I could feel his attention like heat—steady, unblinking, impossible to ignore.

He choked on his beer. "Can I get another towel, please?" he sputtered, coughing through laughter.

I bent again, grabbed a towel, and he growled, "You need to stop doing that." His throat worked as he cleared it.

I spun, tossing it at him. "Or what?"

"Or I'm going to poke some kid's eye out." He slapped the towel over the front of his swim shorts.

I doubled over laughing. "Oh my God. We're going to kill each other for sure."

Chapter 27

ROMAN

I sat up, leaving the towel in place until things settled down. I killed the last sip of beer and swapped the empty can for a fresh one. Normally I didn't drink this much, but it felt necessary on this trip—and hell, it was vacation. Harrison and Amelia had the company under control; I could let go a little.

"Can you get my back, please?" Alex handed me suntan lotion, undoing her bikini strap but holding the top in place with her arms.

I bit my lip, closed my eyes a second for composure. "Sure, no problem."

The lotion was cool against my hands, her skin warm and soft. I rubbed slowly across her shoulders, circling lower, letting my fingers brush the edge of her bikini bottoms. My body reacted instantly. If I didn't stop, we were heading straight back to the house—and I'd gladly let the whole family wonder where we went.

"Okay, you're done." I gave her a playful smack on the butt. "Let's go in the water."

I grabbed the raft, holding it strategically in front of me, and raised my beer to her with a wink.

"Wait for me," she laughed, fumbling with her bikini top. She caught up quickly, drink in one hand, her other hooked into the waistband of my trunks to match my stride.

"Cheers," she grinned, reaching across me, clinking her cup against my can. I leaned down, kissing her just as the first warm wave splashed over our legs.

We waded deeper, her tugging at my arm like she couldn't get us out there fast enough. I noticed why when I caught sight of her family heading down. No complaints from me—we beat them to the water.

The raft was big enough for two, complete with cup holders. The gulf was calm, the water clear. Perfect.

But of course, Bianca and Edward floated over with their own raft. "Mind if we join you?" Bianca asked, as sweet and forward as ever.

"Sure," Alex said, all smiles. But I felt her hand slip into the hem of my trunks, fingers sliding higher. My pulse jumped.

I leaned in, whispering, "You really want to do that here?"

She nodded, grinning like the devil.

I needed a distraction before I lost it. "Edward, tell me something about Alex I should know."

Her hand snapped back out as she glared. "Really?"

Edward smirked. "How about the time she decided to play dress-up for a family photo shoot? Middle school Alex in a prairie dress, blue eyeshadow, bright pink lipstick—oh, and soccer cleats."

Alex splashed him square in the face. "That was middle school! Doesn't count."

Bianca leaned forward. "Wait—*with* the cleats?"

Edward raised his drink, grinning. "Tomboy Alex meets Little House on the Prairie. Classic."

She groaned, flipped him off, and kicked us farther out to sea. "Bianca, you can stay. Edward, get lost."

I chuckled, though I caught the flicker of sadness on her face. "Alex, it was just a sibling story. Harrison and I have plenty ready to fire when the mudslinging starts."

She avoided my eyes, sipping through her straw. I rubbed her back gently. "Hey. Look at me. Did that really bother you?"

She turned, sadness clouding her features. "No, I just feel like people have the worst memories of me."

"Why?"

"Because I have the worst memories of me. When someone brings them up, it just proves I'm right."

I shook my head. "Well, I don't have a single bad memory of you."

"You don't even know me yet." She sighed. "Give it time."

I smiled, sliding my hand over her sun-warmed skin. "I plan to get to know you. And I promise—I'm going to help you make better memories."

She wiggled against my hand, smiling at last. I gave her a playful pat—then tipped us both off the raft into the water.

***

ALEX

I splashed to the surface grabbing onto the raft laughing as I emerged. He came out right after me laughing at his handy work. Oh well, our drinks were almost empty anyway.

"What the heck did you do that for?" I sputtered, pushing wet hair out of my eyes. My guess? A distraction. And truthfully, I was grateful for it.

"Oops." Roman's laugh rumbled, unguarded and a little wicked. Before I could recover, his hand found the back of my head, fingers sliding deep into my soaked hair, tugging me toward him. The playful glint in his eyes had vanished, replaced with something feral. Needy.

His mouth crashed into mine.

The kiss was wild and urgent—his lips devouring mine as his tongue swept past my parted lips, drawing a gasp out of me. He nipped my bottom lip, sucked it into his mouth, released it only to deepen the kiss further. I clung to him, dizzy from more than just the salt water.

He anchored us with one hand gripping the raft, the other holding me so tight I could feel the tremor of strength in his arm. My legs wound around his waist on instinct, my body fitting against his like it had been waiting for this moment. The water lifted and dropped us in slow, dizzying rhythm, tugging me just far enough to feel the pull—then back again, right into him. His grip didn't waver.

The world around us blurred to sunlight and salt, the steady slap of waves against the raft. Without him, without that tether, I knew I'd drift—swallowed by the tide and everything it carried. The thought sent a ripple of fear through me, sharp and fleeting, before dissolving into something else. Something that made me cling harder—one hand tangled in his wet hair, the other gripping the raft like it was the only thing keeping us from disappearing.

"Roman..." I finally tore my mouth from his, gasping for air. My chest heaved, my skin prickling with heat despite the cool water. I blinked toward the shoreline, half-panicked, half-thrilled at how far we'd drifted.

"Yes," he answered simply, his own breath ragged, like he knew exactly what I was about to ask.

"What was that?" My voice came out breathless, almost reverent.

He shook his head, water dripping down his sun-kissed face, his grin both boyish and wicked. "Pretty awesome, don't you think?"

Did he plan this? Pull me out far enough so it was just us—no curious eyes, no interruptions? If it was a trick, it worked.

"That was incredible," I breathed, still watching him like the rest of the world had dissolved into salt and sunlight. Water beaded down his face, tracing the hard lines of his jaw, his hair slicked back and dark from the sea. His eyes caught mine—steady, burning, unguarded—and something in my chest tightened.

He looked unreal. Mouthwatering. Mine.

The thought startled me. I'd never felt that kind of claim over anyone before—not even when I was married. It wasn't control. It was connection. Raw and consuming, like if I looked away for too long, I might lose him to the tide.

I still had my legs cinched around his waist, my ankles locked tight. He held me with one arm gripping the raft, the other firm on my ass, fingers digging in like he'd never let go. I slid one hand from the raft to his neck, dragging him back to me.

This kiss was slower, more deliberate. No frenzy, just deep, consuming pressure. My chest pressed into his, my hips rolling without thought, the heat between us impossible to ignore. I could feel him hard against me, the water doing nothing to cool the fire he stoked with every touch.

If only we could touch bottom, if only—

"Hey, you two, it's time for lunch!"

The shout shattered the moment. We ripped apart like kids caught red-handed, laughter bubbling up even as our cheeks burned.

We clung to the raft, paddling furiously back toward shore, kicking in rhythm. Every time our eyes met, we broke into another fit of giggles, like we'd just gotten away with something dangerous. Like we were teenagers again—reckless, breathless, and hungry for more.

***

ROMAN

Damn, the attraction I have to this woman is unreal. It feels like she was made just for me. The thought of anyone else ever having her—especially the man she was once married to—makes my chest ache. At some point

I'll need to talk to Edward, to learn the truth about what she endured, so I can spend my days filling her head with better memories.

We hauled everything back up to the house, both of us worn out from sun and alcohol. Alex looked ready to collapse.

"Why don't we take a quick nap after we shower?" I suggested, rubbing her back as we climbed the stairs.

"Sounds perfect," she murmured, nearly asleep on her feet.

I wasn't sure she'd make it through a shower, but I had sand in places sand shouldn't be. I needed one.

"Honey... Alex, can I start the shower for you?"

She looked more awake at that, her eyes glinting mischievously. Instead of answering, she tugged me with her, shutting the bathroom door behind us.

"Is this alright?" she asked, her voice low, her gaze playful but intent.

"That depends on what *this* is," I said carefully, turning the water on. I tested the stream with my hand. "How do you like your water temp?"

Her arms slid around my waist from behind, her front pressed into my back. Her lips grazed across my skin as she whispered, "However you like yours."

I turned to face her, still holding her close. "I like mine hot."

Her chin lifted, her eyes half-lidded as she hummed softly against me. Then she smiled faintly, tilting her head. "Can you help me out of this suit?"

My throat tightened. I hesitated just long enough to be sure she meant it, then eased the clasp free. Her hair tumbled loose, and I brushed it gently over her shoulders. She stood in front of me unguarded, and I could only breathe one word:

"Beautiful."

Her answering smile was soft. "Thank you... Are you coming?"

She stepped into the shower, looking back at me once with a teasing glance.

That was all the assurance I needed. Whatever guilt might come could wait. Right now, all I could think about was her—warm, breathless, and so close I could feel her heartbeat against mine. I'd deal with the consequences later.

I joined her, steam already filling the room. She tilted her face into the spray, letting the water cascade down, her posture relaxed and unhurried. I reached for the body wash and lathered it onto the loofah, the lavender scent curling through the steam.

Slowly, deliberately, I traced it over her shoulders and down her back, letting my touch stay just long enough to feel her melt beneath it. She leaned into me, trusting, her eyes closed as I cared for her.

I turned her gently to face me, sliding the lather across her stomach, her arms, her neck. She giggled when I pressed a kiss against her shoulder, and the sound nearly unraveled me.

The water rinsed the soap away, leaving only the heat between us. I cupped her face, kissed her deeply, hungrily, until there was nothing left but us. She clung tighter, pulling me impossibly close, and I thought I might never have enough of her.

The world outside vanished. There was no family, no past, no pain—only the two of us, steam curling around our bodies, hearts racing in unison.

And when she whispered yes against my mouth, it wasn't just permission. It was trust. It was everything.

***

ALEX

Spent. That was the only word that fit. My body felt like it had given every ounce of itself and still somehow wanted more. I'd been tired before the shower, but afterward—after *him*—I was wrecked in the best possible way. It was more than release, more than sex. It was transcendence.

I rolled onto my side, tracing the line of his arm as his hand drifted lazily across my stomach, stopping at my hip. One arm bent under his head, eyes closed, his chest rising and falling steady, the sheet tangled low around his waist. A low sound rumbled in his chest, and I realized he'd already drifted off.

I nestled against him, resting my cheek on his chest, letting the rhythm of his heartbeat guide mine. My fingers wandered across the ridges of his abdomen, not to wake him, but to feel something solid, grounding. His warmth and the steady rhythm of his breaths were all I needed to let go. Sleep pulled me under.

***

"Hi."

His lips brushed my forehead, coaxing me back awake. I blinked until his face came into focus—Roman, dressed, sitting at the edge of the bed.

"Oh no, did I sleep through dinner?" I rubbed my eyes, still sore in the sweetest way from what had happened before we collapsed.

He smiled. "No. Everyone's just starting to emerge. We weren't the only ones who needed a nap."

We shared a knowing look. A nap, sure.

"Good. I'll get dressed." I stretched, reaching for my clothes, but he caught my hands in his and drew me up instead.

He stretched my arms out wide, his gaze sweeping over me like he was memorizing every inch. "So beautiful," he hummed, his eyes lighting a trail of chills across my skin.

I smiled, embarrassed and grateful all at once. He let one hand go, spun me slowly back toward him, and pressed a soft kiss to my lips—just lips, no urgency. The kind of kiss that made me believe the word he'd just said.

I slipped into a pink shorts-and-tank set, pulled on flip-flops, and grabbed the light hoodie draped over the chair. Together we headed downstairs.

Dinner was casual, noisy, the usual with my family. Afterward, we carried blankets down to the fire Edward had built on the beach. I laid ours out, brushing away as much sand as I could, and Roman dropped onto it, stretching his legs wide enough for me to slide between. I fit myself against him easily, knees pulled up, his arms wrapping around me. The fire's warmth pressed against the ocean breeze— the perfect balance.

Patrick leaned forward across the flames. "So, are we telling ghost stories tonight or what?"

The kids were perched on laps, already yawning. Their parents shook their heads.

Edward's eyes narrowed at me across the flames. I rolled mine back, pretending not to notice. Roman must have, though, because his hand cupped my chin, turning me up toward him for a kiss. Sweet. Protective. His way of grounding me.

Drinks passed around—wine, beer, cocktails. My family never traveled without a bar's worth of alcohol. Bianca handed me a canned white wine; Roman grabbed a light beer. The first sip was cool and fruity, but it stung a little, too, the way alcohol threaded through everything in my life. Brunch mimosas, bourbon after work, Friday cocktails, family coolers on the beach. *Is there ever a day I don't drink?* I tucked the thought away, leaning back against Roman, letting the fire and his arms soothe me.

Our parents stayed up at the house. Diana came down and spirited the grandkids away so their parents could actually breathe. Once the kids were gone, filters dropped fast. Too much booze and too many siblings—that always meant trouble.

"Alex," Edward called out, his voice sharp. "Tell us about your death wish."

My eyes flew open. Roman's fingers tightened on my hips, the warning in his touch almost painful.

He leaned in, whispering through clenched teeth, "What is he talking about?" His tone was low but anxious, protective, and I could feel his unease pulsing through me.

I glared across the flames at Edward, who only smirked, squinting back at me like he had the upper hand.

"What death wish would that be, *Eddie*?" I shot back, drawing out the nickname he hated most. If he was going to poke, I was going to scratch.

"Cute," he said. "I believe you were the one who called me, talking about serial killers and crime-ridden neighborhoods."

Roman's grip eased—he understood now—but my blood still simmered.

"Oh, so you want a scary story." I raised my wine like a toast. "Everyone get ready to be scared out of your minds."

I took a dramatic sip, letting the pause drag before glaring at my brother. "I ran out of gas. Oooh, terrifying." I waved my hands in mock horror.

Silence. My laugh rang out alone.

"I know, I know—you're stunned into silence," I added, stretching the joke. Still no laughter.

"Is that it?" Patrick finally asked, confused.

"Yep, that's it. Sorry to disappoint. Eddie probably has better stories than me. I mean, looking in the mirror every morning has to be the scariest thing of all." *For him.*

That landed. Laughter rippled around the fire, and Edward leaned back, lips tight. I exhaled, relief loosening my chest. For now, at least, I was off the hook.

Chapter 28

ROMAN

After everyone had woken up and Alex came back from her run, we met on the deck for breakfast. She slid into my lap, stealing a piece of toast from the plate I'd made her, while Patrick went over the day's plan.

"Today is deep sea fishing day," he announced. The women barely reacted—some even groaned. I grinned. I loved fishing.

Patrick continued, "Whoever's going, I need a head count so I can call the marina. We've got a charter, just need to make sure we'll fit."

I raised my hand, but Alex didn't move. "You're not going?" I asked, rubbing my hand up her thigh.

She shook her head with a laugh. "Nope. Happens every year. The guys fish. The ladies get a free day."

Great. That meant I'd be trapped on a boat with her brothers for what I could only imagine would be a private interrogation. Still, it was the perfect chance to talk to Edward about her ex.

"So, what do you mice do when the cats are away?" I teased.

She smirked. "We play, of course. Maybe gossip a little."

I kissed her cheek and helped her off my lap. "I'll see you later then." Better to get out the door before I changed my mind.

The marina was crawling with charters when we arrived. Edward passed out Dramamine. Patrick declined, puffing his chest like he had something to prove. The ocean is something that deserves respect. Rookie move.

I dressed practical—board shorts, a t-shirt, slip-proof shoes. Wallet sealed in a waterproof bag, extra shirt inside. Phone in a waterproof case but tucked in my pocket in case the moment called for a picture.

I found a spot next to Edward. He wasted no time.

"Nice of you to come with us, Roman. Thought you'd stay glued to Alex's side."

I smirked. "She's great. I'm surprised she didn't want to come."

He chuckled knowingly. "She never does. This is when she spends time with our aunt alone. They're thick as thieves—nobody's invited."

That was news. "Why?"

He shrugged. "D'know. They slip away and come back with no stories. That's just their thing."

Interesting. Another layer to unravel later.

As we motored farther out, Edward and I talked about life in general. I made sure he knew I was genuinely interested in the family, not just Alex. The truth was, this was new territory for me. Big families. My world had always been just my parents and Harrison. Business associates filled the rest. Grandparents gone early, no cousins or uncles.

Still, there was one subject I couldn't leave alone.

"Edward, what can you tell me about Alex's ex?"

He snorted. "Oh, Peckerhead?"

I raised a brow. "If that's what you call him, sure."

"Luke. His name's Luke."

Patrick groaned. "Why the hell are we talking about that asshole on vacation?" His contempt dripped like venom.

"I just want to understand the history," I said evenly. "You can tell a lot about someone by how they were treated in past relationships."

Edward ignored Patrick and continued. "They married right out of college. Luke was finishing law school, Alex finishing her business degree. She was young, trusting. Had these fairytale ideas—best friends marrying best friends, raising kids side by side. Worked for Abby and Maggie. Not for Alex."

Patrick grunted. "Yeah, guys aren't into women like her."

My head snapped toward him. "What kind of woman is that?"

"A tomboy. Too independent. She emasculates men. We called her 'the great emasculator.'"

Edward and I exchanged a look before both of us cracked a laugh. I couldn't help it. If Patrick thought that was an insult, he was an idiot.

"I may use that," I said with a grin.

Patrick bristled, pushing up out of his seat. "You think that's funny?"

I stayed seated, calm. "I think Alex being strong and independent is the best thing about her." Although I had hoped she'd lean on me a little more than she does.

Edward shoved an arm out, holding Patrick back.

Patrick's face went pale green. He clutched his stomach, stumbled to the rail, and emptied himself into the ocean. Guess Dramamine wasn't such a bad idea after all.

Edward sighed. "Sorry about him. Rose isn't a pushover—she just picks her battles."

I nodded, though I couldn't figure out what kind of woman would willingly deal with Patrick's moods. Still, not my problem.

"So, back to Luke. What was he like with Alex?"

Edward's jaw clenched. "I knew from the start he wasn't right for her. The way he touched her—always on her arm, like he owned her. The way he looked at her..." He shook his head. "It was off."

I ground my teeth. "And she married him anyway."

"She was naive. Too forgiving. He chipped away at her confidence, said things that cut deep. We wanted to step in, but she'd tell us to back off—that it was none of our business. Told me if I didn't like it, I should try standing up to our mom sometime." Edward let out a bitter laugh. "She was right. Alex was the only one who ever stood up to her."

His gaze darkened. "That son of a bitch had affairs. Let her know about them too. Told her she wasn't enough, that he had to go elsewhere. In truth, he was just too weak to be with a woman like her. So he tore her down instead."

My stomach twisted. I hated Luke without ever meeting him.

Edward's voice softened, guilt lining the edges. "Maybe we should've done more. But Maggie and Abby were the ones who finally got in the middle of it."

I nodded slowly, understanding more now than I had before. No wonder Alex kept walls up.

"Thanks for telling me. I'm sorry about your mom," I added. "Alex mentioned a little."

Edward shrugged, resigned. "We've learned to live with it."

The captain's voice boomed over the intercom, announcing we'd reached our first stop. Edward and I stood, reaching for the poles. But my mind stayed on Alex, and how badly I wanted to replace every one of those memories with something better.

***

ALEX

"Thank God. Finally, away from the riff raff," my aunt said as we sidled up to our favorite bar on the beach. It was a twenty-minute cab ride, but worth every second. This was our tradition: one afternoon carved out for us alone, no brothers, no parents, no kids, no judgment. Just us.

"Welcome back, ladies. What can I get you?" Marco leaned across the bar, grinning. He'd been here for years and never forgot us. Every summer it became our spot, and usually by the second round we turned the whole place into a party.

"Frozen piña colada with a dark rum float," I said automatically. My aunt ordered her light beer. Marco nodded.

"Coming right up."

My aunt turned to me, eyebrow raised. "So. How are things, Alex—honestly?"

I stalled. "Good, I think."

"You *think*?"

"I just mean... so far, so good. Work is great."

She smirked. "We're playing that game? Fine. Work's great, money's fine, you look fabulous. Now—" she leaned in conspiratorially "—have you seen him naked yet?"

My eyes nearly popped out of my head. "What?" It came out way too loud, half the bar turned. I slapped a hand over my mouth. Marco slid our drinks over, shaking his head, laughing.

"Don't act like a prude. He's gorgeous. And don't bother pretending you haven't noticed."

I gulped down half my drink, brain freeze stabbing behind my eyes.

"Wow," I muttered. "Here I thought we were going to gossip about Mom."

She chuckled. "We're having fun. But I hope you're having *more* fun than the rest of us. And if you're not—sweetheart, with a man like that? Someone else will be."

There it was. The family belief, loud and clear: Alex is only enough if she keeps a man like Roman interested. I clenched my glass a little too hard.

"Okay. And so what?" My voice came out sharper than I meant. "What if I don't keep him?"

Her smile softened. She put her hand over mine. "You're right. So what. I just meant—if you're going to be with someone, he seems like a catch. That's all."

I sighed, forcing a smile. "Sure. I think he's great. We have fun. That's the best I can do right now. Is that okay?"

"Of course it is." She pulled me into a hug. "I just want the best for you, sweet girl."

And just like that, we let the subject go. We laughed, we danced, we sang karaoke until our voices cracked. For a while, it was the two of us again. No men, no pasts, no pressure.

By the time night pressed in, the bar was packed and we were three sheets to the wind. Drinks kept appearing—half of them bought for us—and Marco let us lead the place in a rowdy round of "Don't Stop Believin'."

"I'll be right back," I slurred, sliding off the stool and nearly missing the floor. I swayed my way to the bathroom, giggling to myself.

On the way back, my pocket buzzed so hard I thought a bee had gotten trapped in there. I fumbled my phone out, blinking at the screen until Roman's name came into focus. A text.

ROMAN: *How's it going?*

ME: *giid*

ROMAN: *What? Was that supposed to say good?*

I snorted. Talk-to-text would save me.

ME: *eye ant n eye are dunk*

I stared at it for a second, shrugged, and hit send. Good enough.

ROMAN: *Where are you?*

I gave up. Too much work. He'd see me later. I shoved the phone on the bar, laughing as I nearly toppled off the stool.

"Roman's calling," my aunt sing-songed, pointing at my phone. I turned my face away, mistake number one. She grabbed it, mistake number two.

"Hello, Diana speaking," she answered brightly.

Oh God.

"Mhm, pretty plastered," she said into the phone, shooting me a wicked grin. "We're at the Pink Panda."

I slapped my forehead. The mascot. The stupid giant pink stuffed panda that sat at the end of the bar.

Marco shook his head, laughing. "It's the *Pink Cabana.*" He pointed to the sign above us.

My aunt shoved the phone into his hand. "Here, tell him."

"Pink Cabana," Marco said into the receiver. "I'll give you the address." He rattled it off, handed the phone back.

"Okay, see you soon," my aunt chirped, hanging up.

I groaned, face in my hands. "You gave up our hideout."

She laughed, patting my back. "Sweetheart, if he's coming to find you, that's not a hideout. That's a rescue mission."

***

ROMAN

"The Pink Panda?" I repeated, half-snorting. Where the hell were they? In the background, I could hear loud music, the unmistakable noise of a bar in full swing.

"Hey man, this is Marco," a voice came through the line. "I'm the bartender at the Pink *Cabana* on Oceanfront Drive, off Main. The ladies are good—just a bit tipsy."

From the sound of it, "a bit" was generous. Still, Alex was with her aunt, so I decided not to panic. "Thanks, Marco. I'll come by."

I looked around at the group. "Edward, want to take a trip to the Pink Cabana with me?"

His brows lifted, interest sparking. "Sure. That place is a blast. Bianca, want to go?"

She nodded eagerly. The others begged off—kids in the pool, parents exhausted from the long day on the water.

"What's going on at the bar?" Bianca asked as she slipped her hand into Edward's.

"Alex and Diana need a ride home."

Edward gave a low whistle. "So *that's* where they've been sneaking off all these years."

Bianca tilted her head. "How do they usually get home?"

"They take a cab," I said. "Apparently, they always come back like this." I looked towards Edward, since he's the one that told me.

I reminded myself this was vacation. Letting loose was part of it... still, I wasn't thrilled with "three sheets to the wind Alex."

The Cabana's parking lot was jammed, neon lights casting pink and blue reflections across car hoods. We ended up parking way off to the side and walking. The thump of bass and the rise and fall of laughter hit us before we even opened the door.

Inside, the place was chaos that somehow looked like fun—music thumping, bodies packed shoulder to shoulder, bartenders moving with practiced speed. And then I saw her. Alex, perched at the bar with Diana and Marco, I'm guessing, laughing so hard she nearly tipped off her stool. A glass of water sat in front of her, which—given her usual choices—was its own kind of miracle.

Edward threaded Bianca through the crowd, taking the lead. I hung back, deciding it was smarter not to be the first face Alex saw. Better she unleash her *tipsy* wrath on her brother than me.

"Hey, you two. So, this is where the party's at?" Bianca beamed as we reached them.

"This is it. You found us," Diana said, lifting her glass with a glassy-eyed grin. From the look she gave me, I knew she'd given away their hideout on purpose.

Alex turned, and my chest loosened at the sight of her—definitely drunk but smiling and seemingly happy. She slid off the stool and wrapped her arms around my waist. I kissed the top of her head, reaching over her shoulder to shake Marco's hand.

"Can I get you anything, man?" Marco asked.

"No thanks. Just the bill."

He smirked, shaking his head. "These two have barely paid for a drink here in seven years. Tonight's no exception."

I scanned the room, taking in how many eyes were on them, how many guys were grinning like they'd been the ones buying rounds. My jaw tightened, but Alex burrowed into my side, and I forced myself to focus on her.

That's when a woman appeared—short pink mini skirt, bleach-blonde hair teased sky-high, skin leathered from too many summers under the sun.

"You must be Roman."

"Yep." I leaned back slightly, pulling Alex closer, planting an elbow on the bar like I wasn't rattled.

Her eyes raked over me, slowly. "Alex told us all about you. And honey—you do *not* disappoint."

I resisted the urge to shudder. Her gaze made me feel like I needed a shower.

"See? I told you he's freaking gorgeous," Alex slurred, proud as if she'd just won an award. I bit back a laugh, knowing she'd regret saying that out loud later.

"Alright, time to head home. Alex, honey, you ready?"

She nodded against my chest, then went slack, arms falling uselessly at her sides. Perfect. Out cold.

I scooped her up in my arms. Edward looped his arm through Diana's, and the crowd parted without complaint, offering pats on the back and cheers as we made our way out.

I slid into the backseat with Alex still cradled against me, Diana next to her. Edward and Bianca climbed into the front, already laughing about the spectacle. Alex snored softly, her head tucked under my chin. I brushed her hair from her face, chuckling.

I lowered my voice so only Diana could hear. "Why did you give away your location?"

Her smile softened, just for a moment. "Because she needs to know she's worth it."

The words landed heavy in my chest.

"She's worth it to me," I murmured, rubbing a strand of her hair between my fingers. "I just hope I can get her to see that."

"You keep doing what you're doing, Roman. She's coming around."

I nodded, meeting her eyes. "Thanks."

At the house, I carried Alex upstairs. I eased her onto the bed, slipped her shoes off, then stripped her down to her underwear so she'd be comfortable. Tucking the covers around her, I lingered for a moment, watching her sleep. Even drunk, even vulnerable, she was beautiful.

I checked my phone.

AMELIA: *Hope you're enjoying vacation. Work is good, nothing to report. Anything major went to Harrison. He's done a good job filling in.*

I smiled. She rarely gave Harrison credit.

ME: *Vacation's great. Went fishing today. Glad you two are getting along.*

AMELIA: *Act like a grown man and I don't have a problem.*

I laughed quietly. Classic Amelia.

ME: *Good night.*

AMELIA: *Goodnight.*

I plugged the phone in, undressed, and slipped under the covers beside Alex. I kissed the crown of her head, whispering against her hair.

"Goodnight, beautiful."

Chapter 29

ALEX

"License plate. Did someone get the license plate?" My voice came out like gravel—barely audible and still too loud for my pounding head.

Ugh. Where am I?

One eye cracked open, the other refusing to cooperate. My face hurt when I touched it. Even blinking felt like a felony. God, how much did I drink last night? And how the hell did we get home?

A shadow stirred beside me in the bed. Roman. Relief trickled through me like water on parched soil.

"Good morning," he murmured, propping himself on an elbow. A smile tugged at his lips—thank God he wasn't mad. "What's this about a license plate?"

"The car that hit me. Did you get the plate?"

He chuckled, low and warm, as his hand found my arm. His touch was careful, like I might break.

"Yeah. I think it was Rum 2000."

I squinted at him. "Rum... what?"

"That's how many piña coladas I think you had."

If my brain weren't sloshing like a half-full fish tank, I would've laughed. Instead, I groaned. "Funny."

He smirked. "Are you feeling okay? Do you ladies get this drunk every time you go there?"

Here comes the judgement. I flopped an arm across my eyes to avoid his gaze. "Maybe. But I usually remember the ride home. What happened this time?"

"You passed out at the bar. Your brother and I came to get you."

A low groan escaped me as I rolled away, mortified. Of course Roman saw me like that.

"How did you even find us?"

Roman's hand didn't leave me. It slid up and down my arm, brushing hair back from my shoulder, pressing gentle squeezes into my muscles before working into the knots. My body betrayed me with a moan that nearly erased the shame.

"Your aunt answered when I called. I tried texting you, but I couldn't make sense of your replies. The bartender told me where you were."

I stifled a laugh. "Was she drunk too?"

"She seemed more with it than you, that's for sure."

Great. Two grown women, drunk as teenagers. We'd been pulling this Pink Cabana stunt for years, and nobody cared—until Roman. He actually came. That thought hit somewhere deep, uncomfortable in its tenderness.

"Good," I muttered, surrendering to the pillow. "I'm going back to sleep."

His lips pressed against my shoulder, then my temple. The bed shifted as he slipped out, leaving me to sink gratefully back into oblivion.

When I woke again, the smell of coffee lured me downstairs. Roman was in the living room, laptop open, focus sharp.

"Hey," I croaked.

His head lifted. "How do you feel?"

I braced myself for a lecture, but instead of a raised brow or pointed tone, he just smiled.

"I'm good. Just need some coffee and orange juice. Maybe food."

"I made you a sandwich. It's in the fridge." He gestured toward the kitchen and turned back to his emails.

Something twisted in my chest. I'd expected judgment. Instead, he'd been quietly... good to me.

"Thank you." I moaned. "What are you working on?" I forced out to make conversation, but the words almost made me nauseous.

I opened the fridge and found the sandwich—turkey, lettuce, tomato, mayo, stacked neatly on thick bread. My stomach growled as it needed nourishment but maybe wasn't going to be accepting of it. I poured coffee, OJ, and shook up a liquid IV with careful precision, determined not to jostle my fragile head.

Roman kept typing. "Just catching up on emails so I'm not buried when we get home. Harrison's handled most of it. Got some great feedback on him."

The pride in his voice softened his features. Just a week ago, those two could barely be in a room together.

"Yeah," I said softly. "Funny how things change."

I ate while he finished work. After cleaning up the counter, I felt him come up behind me. His arms slid around my waist, his chin resting on my shoulder. The warmth of him, the easy intimacy, sent shivers dancing across my skin.

"What's on the agenda for today?" he asked, lips brushing my neck. His breath tickled my ear, and I gripped the sink for balance.

"The... uh... pool." Smooth, Alex. Real smooth.

"Just the pool? No swimming with sharks with a steak around your neck?"

I barked a laugh, remembering that diner conversation after Lookout Park. "No sharks this trip. Just the pool."

He pulled back, and I hated the emptiness he left behind.

"You need anything out there?" His voice was casual, but I caught the flicker in his eyes—wondering if I'd pour another drink before noon.

"Nope. Just water."

Relief eased his shoulders, but mine sank under a weight I didn't want to name. Since when did I make people worry about my drinking? It was supposed to be harmless fun—something to take the edge off. Yet even as I tried to tell myself that, a small, uneasy truth stirred beneath the surface. Maybe I was starting to wonder about it too.

He picked up my water bottle, threading his fingers through mine. "Shall we?" He said as he ushered us out the door.

And just like that, we walked out together into the sun—me with my coffee, my Liquid IV water, and the man who cared enough to come find me when everyone else had just laughed it off.

***

ROMAN

Only one more day after tonight. The thought left a strange weight in my chest. This week had flown by in a blur of saltwater, sun, and laughter. We'd gone deep sea fishing—which I thoroughly enjoyed—spent lazy hours on the sand, braved a sunset cruise, and even tried surfing. All in all, it was tame compared to what Alex had warned me about. The only real drama had been picking her and her aunt up from that bar. I chuckled to myself, remembering her slurred texts and her aunt giving up their hideout without hesitation. But she hadn't gone that far again. Maybe tipsy here and there, but not blackout drunk. Just vacation fun.

The house behind me was quiet, the chatter of her siblings muted by closed doors and the distance. I stood near the waterline, shoes dangling from my hand, toes sinking into cool sand while I waited for her. The night air was heavy with salt, but soft, almost sweet. The sky was clear, the stars brighter than I'd ever seen, and the moon stretched a silver road across the surface of the ocean like it was laid out just for us.

"I'm ready now." She called out from the top of the sandy steps.

Her voice pulled me around. She padded down the steps of the deck barefoot, a lightweight hoodie draped over her tank top, sleeves pulled over her hands. She carried a can tucked into a koozie, but it was the glowing smile that struck me hardest—like the stars above had nothing on her.

I leaned down, kissed her softly, savoring the taste of salt and sweetness. "Me too." I said and wondered if that had more meaning than just a walk on the beach.

We strolled hand in hand along the shoreline. The waves curled and broke gently, whispering against the sand. Palm trees rustled at the edge of the property, swaying in rhythm with the breeze. Above us, the moon shimmered across the water, glassy and endless.

I tugged her in front of me, wrapping my arms around her middle, pressing her back to my chest. Together we looked out at the ocean, the quiet hum of nature swallowing us whole. I closed my eyes, inhaling deeply, and let the moment sink in.

"Can you feel that?" I asked, curious if she was starting to notice the undercurrent I'd been trying to explain.

"Feel what in particular?"

She swayed side to side, almost unconsciously, the way the tide lifts and lowers your body if you're waist-deep in it. She didn't even realize she already understood.

"Exactly this. The pull of the tide. Do you feel it?"

She tilted her head back toward the moon, a low sound escaping her. "I feel like I'm dancing to music I can't hear. I just feel it. Does that make sense?"

I smiled and bent down to press my lips to her forehead. "Yes, baby. That makes perfect sense."

I turned her gently to face me, my palm finding the small of her back as my other hand slid into her hair, fingers threading through the wind swept strands. The air between us seemed to still, thick with salt and anticipation. Her koozie slipped soundlessly to the sand, forgotten, as she moved closer—arms wrapping around my waist, fists curling into my shirt like she needed something solid to hold on to.

When our mouths met, the world narrowed to warmth and breath and the steady rush of the ocean beside us. The kiss deepened, slow and hungry, tasting of salt and sun and something I hadn't realized I'd been starving for. Her body melted against mine, fitting perfectly, as if the tide itself had drawn us together and refused to let go.

When I finally broke away, she stood breathless, eyes closed, lips parted. The moonlight spilled across her face, painting her in silver, and I was caught in awe.

"Hmm. That was nice," she murmured, opening her eyes slowly.

Nice didn't even begin to cover it.

"Yes. Nice," I teased, chuckling as I laced my fingers with hers again. Together we walked back toward the house, the sound of the waves trailing us like applause.

Chapter 30

ALEX

Everything had gone so well up until the very last night. I should have known better. Mom had gotten drunk every night, but until then she kept to herself, hovering in the background with her glass of wine like a storm cloud we all pretended not to see. But tonight? She came in swinging. No one at the table was spared—except Roman. She tried, but I cut her off before she could land the first blow.

Bianca's face flushed bright red, and she shoved back her chair so hard it nearly toppled. "I'm done." She didn't even look at my mother before storming out.

"What the hell is her problem?" Mom sneered, her voice thick with vodka and venom. She didn't even glance at Bianca's retreating back. Classic. Always flipping the script so the person reacting became the problem.

Edward's jaw tightened as he followed after Bianca, but not before he gave me a look. The kind of look that said *hang tight, we all know you're about to handle this*. Per usual.

Roman stayed silent beside me, his hand clamped over mine under the table. That steady grip—firm and grounding—kept me from detonating the way I usually did. The blood pounded in my head, the rage bubbling hot in my chest, but his presence was a dam. Still, part of me wanted to shove him away before he had to see me at my ugliest.

Diana tried to step in, with gentle persuasion. "Patty, maybe it's time to—"

"Oh, shut up, Diana," Mom snapped, waving her hand like she was swatting a gnat. The sting in my aunt's eyes nearly broke me. She got up quietly, my uncle right behind her, both of them too tired to stay for another round.

By then the cousins and their kids had already slipped out—no way they were letting their children soak in this circus.

That left the core of us. And Rose. Sweet, timid Rose, usually quiet as a mouse.

But when Mom turned her sights on her, I braced myself for tears. Instead, Patrick tried to step between them, which was a first in itself. He couldn't stop her tongue, though.

"You sit your sorry ass down," Mom snarled at him before zeroing in on Rose.

I don't even remember what she said to her. The words blurred. What I *do* remember is Rose's chair scraping violently against the floor and her voice, sharp and shaking but fierce:

"You know what, Patty? Go screw yourself."

My mouth fell open. Rose—sweet little Rose—just lit the grenade and lobbed it. She stormed out, Patrick scrambling after her.

Not a little mouse at all.

I sat back in my chair, blinking. *Good for you, Patrick. Finally picked a woman strong enough to stand toe-to-toe with Mom.*

I turned to Dad, shrugged, and muttered, "Well, we almost made it out unscathed."

His face collapsed in on itself, agony etched in every line. He reached for Mom's hand. "Patty, please don't do this." His voice cracked on the plea.

She slapped his hand away like it burned her. "I'm not done."

And then she turned her sights on Roman.

Not tonight. Not him.

"Mom, enough is enough." I pulled my hand from Roman's grip and planted both palms flat on the table. I closed my eyes, sucked in a breath. Held it. The anger filled every inch of me, clawing at my ribs, begging to be unleashed. I opened my eyes slowly, locking onto hers.

It was like the whole room went black, a spotlight on just her. Her glassy, cold eyes.

"We get it. Everyone here is a piece of shit. Thanks for the reminder. But Roman? He's off limits. Do you understand me?"

A chill swept the table. Even drunk, even slurring, her glare was like acid. Pure evil radiated off her. The alcohol twisted her into something unrecognizable. The thought hit me like a sucker punch: *Could that ever be me? Could that poison take root in me too?* The fear was almost worse than the anger.

"I don't give a damn what you think," she spit out, her words slick and jagged. I'd heard them too many times to count.

And then came the knife twist: "You should've stayed married to that lawyer. Instead, you're out galivanting with this...construction worker." She jabbed her finger toward Roman. "That pretty face will only get you so far before you're just a used-up old maid. Maybe you'll marry him. At least you'll have *something*."

I gripped the edge of the table so tight my knuckles ached. Focus on breathing. In. Out. Roman didn't need to see me explode. He didn't need to see what I was capable of when I snapped.

"Yeah, I know, Mom. You've told me enough. Get married or die alone. Heard it all before." My voice was steady, but my insides were quaking. "We're going back to the house. We'll head out early in the morning."

I pushed back from the table, tossed my napkin down.

"Well isn't that nice for you," she slurred at my back.

I didn't turn. Couldn't. One glance would've been the end of my restraint. I caught Dad's eyes instead. His heartbreak was almost worse than her words. He knew how deep the cuts went, and he was powerless to stop them.

I grabbed Roman's hand and walked out. Fast.

Back at the house, the silence was loud. Everyone knew why I was last to return. They knew I was always the one who said what no one else had the guts to say. Words she'd never remember. Words that tore me apart. This time, though, Roman's steady presence kept my demons chained.

Edward broke the silence. "Sorry, Roman. I don't know what generous compliment Mom left you with tonight, but you didn't deserve it."

"She didn't say anything to me." Roman's arm wrapped around me. His lips brushed my cheek, a gesture so tender it made Edward raise his brows.

"You must really like this guy, huh?" Edward probed.

The closeness suddenly burned. I wriggled free of Roman's arm. "What does that mean?"

"She didn't leave him alone out of kindness. You protected him."

My jaw clenched. "You all protect Rose and Bianca too."

"Yeah, but she still gets a jab in at them. If she skipped him, you stopped her."

If even one of them stepped up like I did, maybe Mom would finally get the picture. Maybe I wouldn't always have to be the villain.

"Well, someone had to. I'm done with this shit. These vacations are supposed to take stress away, not pile more on." My chest was tight, my head pounding. If I didn't get out, I'd say something I couldn't take back.

I bolted. Down to the beach. Fell to my knees in the sand. The sobs came hard and fast, drowned only by the crash of waves.

Why couldn't she just love us enough to stop?

Strong arms enveloped me. Not Roman's. My father's.

I buried my face in his shoulder. "How can you live with that? How can you stay? She hates us, Dad. I can't take it anymore. I'm not as strong as you."

His arms tightened, his voice soft but sure. "You're stronger than I am. You stand up to her. I never can. I vowed to love her in sickness and in health. That vow means something to me. And you kids...you mean everything to me. One day you'll understand."

I gave a bitter laugh. "Doubt it. I'm divorced, remember?"

He chuckled, squeezing me tighter. "Your ex doesn't count. That was an exception."

For a man of few words, his effort hit me like a lifeline.

When he left, Roman and Diana took his place, sitting on either side of me.

"Ali Marie," Diana said softly, "you know your mother's sick. That's not her, that's the booze. She loves you."

"Knowing doesn't make it easier," I whispered.

"No. But holding on to it will destroy you. You have to forgive her, or let it go."

"Do I have to forgive her every time?" My voice cracked. "Do I have to keep walking into these ambushes?"

"No," she said gently. "You don't have to go back. That's your choice. But you love her, and she loves you. That won't change."

Her arms wrapped around me. "I love you, Alexandra. My door is always open. My phone is always on."

Thank God for her. Why am I thanking God for anything, if this is what I always get.

"I know. And I'm so grateful. You'll never know how much that means."

When she left, Roman stayed. Silent. Steady. His arm around my shoulders like a fortress.

"I'm sorry you had to see that," I murmured, looking up at him through tear-swollen eyes.

"I'm fine. I'm worried about you."

"I've lived with it for almost twenty-nine years. I'm used to it."

"Is this typical?" he asked gently, pulling me closer.

"Yep. Drunken stupor. We're all pieces of shit. Sometimes assholes. Always the same."

He smoothed my hair, his voice low. "Alcohol changes people. My mom's told me stories from her patients."

"Maybe I should talk to her."

"She'd listen," he said, kissing my temple.

And for the first time in years, I felt safe.

Chapter 31

ROMAN

The ride to the airport was silent in that heavy, unspoken way. We'd slipped out of the house at dawn, footsteps muffled on the wooden floor, careful not to wake anyone. No cheerful send-off, no hugs in the driveway—just a quick escape.

"Are you sure you don't want to wait and say goodbye to everyone?" I whispered, already knowing the answer.

She shook her head, her jaw set, her eyes ringed with exhaustion. Without a word she slid across the seat to press herself against me. I draped an arm around her shoulders, knowing she wasn't looking for conversation—just quiet, just something steady to lean into.

At the plane, I guided her up the narrow stairs, her hand limp in mine, the weight of the world written in every slow step she took. The crew had already stowed the luggage, the hum of the engines barely rising over the quiet between us. She looked fragile—eyes glassy, shoulders slumped, her strength worn thin. I was grateful the jet had a small bedroom tucked in the back.

I led her there gently, easing her down onto the bed and pulling the blanket over her. The fabric swallowed her small frame, and I pressed a kiss to her forehead, tasting the salt of dried tears on her skin. She turned onto her side, drawing the blanket up to her chin, and let out the faintest sound—something between a sigh and a whimper—that cut straight through me.

No words. Just that tiny, broken sound.

I stood there longer than I should have, watching her chest rise and fall, brushing a hand through her tangled hair once, twice, as if that small touch might make up for everything I couldn't fix. Then I forced myself to step back and close the door softly, leaving her to whatever fragile peace sleep could offer.

Out in the cabin, I pulled my phone and dialed my mom before takeoff.

"Hi, honey! How was your trip?" Her voice was bright and steady.

I closed my eyes, pinching the bridge of my nose. "It was really good until last night. I was introduced to some of Alex's demons."

There was a pause, then her soft intake of breath. "Oh dear. Is Alex okay?"

I almost laughed, but it caught somewhere in my throat and came out rough. "I don't know. I think she's... broken."

The word hung there, heavy and wrong, but I couldn't take it back. It wasn't the word I wanted—it was just the only one that came close to what I saw in her eyes. Something cracked deep down, holding itself together by sheer will. And somehow, the more I said it, the more it felt like I was talking about both of us.

"Broken? Did she get hurt? What happened?"

"She's not hurt. Not physically. It was her mom. She's awful. Every night she drank, but she kept to herself. Last night, though? At dinner she tore into everyone. Except me. And the only reason she didn't is because Alex stood between us. She took every ounce of her mother's rage on herself."

Silence, then a ragged sigh. "Oh dear Lord, Roman. That poor girl. She must be in so much pain." Dear Lord, is right. We could use a little bit of him right about now.

"She hasn't spoken much this morning. She's asleep now. She'll probably sleep through."

The stewardess passed, and I mouthed *bourbon*. She nodded.

"Good," Mom said. "She probably needs the rest. I have an appointment with her Tuesday. Hopefully she'll open up and tell me what happened."

Relief loosened the knot in my chest. "I think she will. She wanted to last night, I could tell." I rubbed at my jaw, my nerves twitching. "Hey Mom, Harrison's calling. I'll talk to you soon."

"Okay, sweetie. I love you."

"Love you too."

I hung up and immediately answered Harrison, bracing myself.

"Hey man, did you get yourself some finally?" His voice dripped with smug amusement.

I pinched the bridge of my nose again. "If this is what this call is about, it's over."

He barked out a laugh. "Wait—wait. It's not. Geez, you're no fun anymore. Just wanted you to know Amelia and I took care of everything while you were gone. Projects are fine. Nothing new with the Ellingtons either. Matt might be waiting on you, though."

I exhaled slowly, letting his chatter roll past me. "I appreciate it, Harrison."

"Hey man, is everything good? You don't sound like yourself."

The stewardess returned with my drink, and I mouthed *thank you*. I tipped back a long swallow, the bourbon burning its way down, finally dulling the sharp edges inside me.

"Yeah. Fine. Just tired. Too much sun," I lied.

We said our goodbyes, and I turned to my emails. Poor Wi-Fi. Matt's message barely loaded. I texted him.

ME: *Can't open your file. Important?*
MATT: *It's a list of permits Marcus revoked. Who's affected, where, and who's on the hook.*
ME: *You home tonight?*

MATT: *Yeah, why?*
ME: *Might stop over. Alex needs the girls.*
MATT: *Patty strikes again, huh?*
ME: *Guess I'm new to this.*
MATT: *Sorry you had to be introduced at all. Bring her. I'll call Abby.*
ME: *Thanks. She's lucky to have you.*
MATT: *Sounds like she's lucky to have you too.*

I set my phone aside and stared at the closed bedroom door. She was behind it, sleeping, or maybe just hiding from the weight of her world. Either way, I wasn't letting her carry it alone anymore.

***

ALEX

Oh my God, this bed is so comfortable. The sheets were like silk, cool and smooth against my overheated skin. My head felt like it was buried in a cloud, the pillow swallowing me whole. For a blissful few seconds, I rubbed my hands across the fabric, sighing as I burrowed deeper. Heaven. This had to be heaven.

Then my eyes opened.

Wait. Where the hell am I?

The space was small—walls close, low ceiling—just a box with a bed filling it. My chest tightened, air thinning. I sat bolt upright, heart jackhammering. *Oh my God. Maybe I really am dead. Maybe this is a coffin.*

The door creaked open. A shadow filled the frame.

Roman.

Relief whooshed out of me in a gasp as I slapped a hand to my chest. "Holy crap, I woke up and had no idea where I was. I thought I was dead—in a coffin."

He smiled, strolling in with maddening calm, and sat on the edge of the mattress. "Nope. Not dead."

"Good to know." I exhaled hard, sinking back into the pillows and yanking the covers to my chin like a security blanket. "This bed is really comfy though. Did I sleep the whole ride home?" My voice was scratchy, my eyes still half-blurred from fatigue.

"No, we've got about forty-five minutes left. I was sure you'd sleep the whole way. Do you even remember me tucking you in?"

I tried, but the memory wouldn't come. "I barely remember the car ride this morning. I must've been tired, I guess."

"I'm sure that's what it was," he said, though his doubtful glance lingered as he reached to rub at my foot under the covers.

The guilt crept in. "Hey, I'm really sorry about last night. That's not how I was hoping the trip would end. It's hard to be a part of my family." My throat tightened as I reached for his hand, staring down at it because I couldn't bear to meet his eyes.

"Yeah, that seemed tough. You seem to be the only one willing to stand up to her."

That's because I am.

"Well, what can she really do to me? My feelings don't get hurt when it's directed at me. It bothers me when she goes after other people."

Roman slid into the bed behind me, arms circling my waist, his breath warm against my neck. "I agree, you're tough. The strongest woman I've ever met. But I wonder if at some point taking all that abuse isn't going to have some kind of effect on you. I'm not trying to shrink you—I just know there's only so much anyone can take."

I let out a dry laugh. "Your mom told me something at our meeting that made a lot of sense. She said I'm taking in all these negative emotions and building a wall—holding them all in. She said I'm not using it to keep people out as much as to keep all the bad stuff in. And by keeping it all locked up, I'm not leaving much room for anything good."

The words hung heavy, even though I'd been turning them over since I heard them. Speaking them out loud now made the truth sting sharper.

Roman leaned back against the wall, guiding me so I reclined against his chest. His heartbeat was steady against my shoulder blade, anchoring me. I closed my eyes, letting myself melt into him. For once, I felt safe.

"Thank you for sharing that," he murmured, pressing his lips briefly to the crown of my head. "That makes a lot of sense. And one of the reasons I came in to bug you is to ask if you'd like to join me tonight at Matt and Maggie's house. Abby will be there too."

I tilted my head, squinting at him. "You did that for me, didn't you?"

"I thought you could use some time with your friends. And..." his hand slid down my arm, squeezing lightly, "I didn't want to leave you just yet."

I curled closer, tucking myself deeper into the circle of his arms. The hum of the plane faded, the hurt of last night softened. Maybe we could make this work. Maybe this was how it started—letting myself lean, letting myself believe.

We stayed like that, wrapped together, the rest of the ride home.

***

ROMAN

Once at the penthouse, I ran a hot bath and poured in lavender oil, watching the steam float through the air. I lit a few candles around the tub, dimming the lights so she could sink into the calm after everything that had happened. We came home earlier than planned, and I thought pampering her a little might help before heading to Maggie's later.

While she soaked, I busied myself in the kitchen. I grilled chicken, tossed it with pasta, olives, peppers, feta, and a light vinaigrette. I set Pellegrino with lime over ice on the counter—no wine, no cocktails. We both needed a break.

I heard the shuffle of feet down the hall. When she rounded the corner, I froze. She was wearing my robe and slippers, sleeves hanging long on her arms, the hem brushing the floor. Her hair was damp, curling slightly at the ends, her cheeks pink from the heat of the bath. And that smile—small, sheepish, like she'd been caught sneaking into something forbidden—nearly undid me.

I crossed the space, wrapping her in a hug. "Are you hungry?"

She nodded, and I lifted her easily, setting her down on the kitchen stool. She looked so small, so fragile. Vulnerable in a way I hadn't seen her before. It tugged at something deep in me, protective and fierce. And yet, the other part of me—the part that noticed the way she looked me up and down—was already fighting to keep in check.

"Starving," she said, voice soft but edged with something else.

That glance wasn't innocent. I looked away, my throat tight.

"Good. Because I made something special for you." I cleared my throat. "Mediterranean pasta salad with grilled chicken." I focused on the words like they were a lifeline. Food. Safety. Normalcy.

She tilted her head. "You made this while I was in the bath? I'm very impressed."

I nodded, glancing back at her. She ran her tongue over her bottom lip, and my resolve wavered.

Focus, Roman. She's just hungry. Feed her first.

"Thank you," I said lightly. "I love to eat, so I figure learning how to cook is a useful survival skill."

She giggled softly, and the sound settled my nerves. At least for a moment.

"I should be the one thanking you. For lunch. And...for going to the beach with me."

Her voice faltered, the humor fading. Her face crumpled, eyes glossing like she was holding back tears.

I circled the counter again quickly, turning her stool toward me. I brushed her damp hair from her face, searching her eyes. The spark was still there, but shadowed now. I didn't want her to lose that light.

"You're welcome," I said firmly. "I'm glad you asked me to go. I enjoyed it. It was a good time."

She leaned her forehead against my chest, groaning quietly.

"Hey," I whispered, hand gentle under her chin as I lifted her face to mine. Her smile flickered back, soft and sad.

"Just...everything was going so good," she breathed.

I bent closer, smiling back, hoping it might anchor her. "Then let's concentrate on the good parts. How does that sound?"

She nodded. Relief loosened in my chest. I brushed my lips gently over hers, a kiss meant to reassure more than anything. "You ready for lunch?"

Her answer was a slow shake of her head. Her hands moved to the belt of my robe around her waist. She pulled the knot loose, the fabric sliding open across her shoulders before falling away completely.

For a moment, I just stared at her. I'd tried to draw the line, to be the steady one—but somewhere along the way, she'd drawn her own. Vulnerability had shifted into something else. Choice. Hers, not mine, or at least that's what I told myself.

When I lifted her from the stool, her legs wrapped around me instinctively, her breath catching against my neck. The feel of her—the trust in that small surrender—sent my pulse racing as I carried her down the hall. The sound of her heartbeat seemed to echo against mine, quick and uneven, like we were both falling toward something we didn't fully understand.

In the quiet of the bedroom, I laid her down carefully, tracing a hand over her cheek before leaning in. What happened next wasn't about escape or forgetting—it was about remembering. About giving her something gentle when the world had been anything but. Still, as I held her afterward, the question pressed hard against my chest.

Was this mercy? Or a mistake I'd spend forever trying to justify?

Chapter 32

ALEX

Why did I get the feeling this elevator ride was going to be more than a way to get to the first floor? I swung my head in his direction, and our eyes connected.

"What?" he asked, all innocence.
I wasn't buying it. I narrowed my eyes.
"What?" he repeated.
"You're up to something, aren't you?" I crossed my arms, chin lifted.
"No. How could I be up to something in here? What can I possibly do in here?"

Yep. Definitely something. Meanwhile, we weren't moving. The elevator hung in its glass cage, suspended twenty-four stories above the atrium. My gaze caught the sweep of green and steel below—tiny walkways, specks of benches—and my stomach lurched. Too high. Far, far too high.

"Uh, I don't know, maybe because no one's here on the weekends and you haven't hit the garage button yet." I nodded toward the panel, casual on the outside, frantic on the inside.

His smile turned mischievous. "You're very perceptive."

I tried to fight nerves with humor. "So...glass walls for your claustrophobia?"

The curve of his mouth told me he knew I was deflecting. "That's one reason. And the view, of course."

The view. My pulse spiked. I glued my eyes to him instead of the dizzying plunge outside the walls.

"I really am impressed with what you've done here," I said quickly, words tumbling over themselves. "The greenspace—you thought about your employees, right? Or am I making that up?"

He laughed, easy, unaware of the way my skin prickled with sweat. Should I admit it? That I could barely breathe? That the glass might as well be air? No. He already worried about me too much.

Heat climbed my throat, my heart hammering. Even talking couldn't slow it down.

"No, you're right," he said. "Happy employees are more productive."

"It really is beautiful," I managed. "Now—do you want to push the button, or should I?"

"You go ahead."

I tried. I really did. But my legs were lead. When I finally stretched for the G, he caught my hand and drew me against him, pivoting me so my back pressed to the glass wall.

My breath hitched. The atrium fell away behind me, twenty-four stories of nothing but air and plants and steel beams that looked flimsy from up here. The glass felt thin, humming under my spine, as if it could give way at any second. My chest locked.

He must have seen the terror in my eyes because he spun me again, his body blocking the view. But it didn't help—I could still *feel* the height, like gravity tugging harder at me alone.

"Are you okay?" he asked.

"I'm better now," I lied, the words rasping.

"Good," he said softly. "Because I'm going to kiss you."

His hands framed my face. I wanted the steadiness of his touch, but the world tilted. My vision wavered, the atrium bleeding into streaks of light. My ears roared with the rush of blood, my chest refused to rise, and just as his lips neared mine, the glass, the height, the air itself collapsed into black.

***

ROMAN

What the hell just happened? One second I was telling her I was going to kiss her—the next, she was crumpling to the ground.

I lowered us both to the floor of the cabin, cradling her against me, and jabbed the button for the garage with one hand. My pulse was hammering in my throat. I tapped her cheek lightly, terrified that might not be enough.

"Alex, are you okay, honey?" My voice cracked, softer than I meant it to be.

Her eyes fluttered open right before the elevator reached the garage. They rolled slightly, unfocused, like she was fighting her way back. Relief hit me so hard I almost sagged against the wall.

"Hey there," I said carefully. "Do we need to go to the hospital?"

"For what? Why are we on the floor?" she mumbled, dazed, trying to piece things together.

"You fainted." My gut twisted. "You scared the hell out of me."

She blinked at me, still foggy. I forced a grin, trying to keep it light for her sake. "Guess my kissing skills are lethal. Knocked you out cold."

That finally drew a laugh out of her, and only then did I breathe easier. Still, I wasn't convinced. Something was wrong, and the concern gnawed at me. Maybe I'd pushed her too far. Maybe she was overloaded. Maybe I needed to back the hell off.

"Do you feel okay?" I asked.

"Yeah, I feel fine," she said, more herself now. "That was like the most intense feeling I've ever had with you. Does that sound crazy or what?"

"Considering some of the things we've already done?" I arched a brow. "Yeah. That sounds crazy."

Her eyes searched mine, suddenly serious. "Do you think we're somehow becoming more connected?"

I helped her up, keeping my arm tight around her waist in case she decided to fold again. "Damn, I hope not."

She laughed, the sound lighter now, and I clung to it like proof she was really okay.

"I'm willing to explore it," she added, thoughtful again. "I feel more just being around you than pretty much anything else in my life."

She meant it. I could tell. But my head was still reeling, trying to reconcile what just happened with the woman in front of me. Maybe it tied back to what went down on vacation. I wasn't sure and I doubt it was going to get answered tonight, so I let it go.

I got her settled in the car and drove us to Maggie's. When we arrived, I let her drift off toward the girls while I gravitated to the guys. I didn't normally do this—I spent most of my time buried in work, surrounded by associates, not friends. Trust wasn't a luxury I handed out easily.

"What happened that brought you over tonight?" Matt asked, his tone casual but knowing. Jack's eyes were on me too. Maybe they knew something I didn't.

"Do you guys know her mom very well?" I asked, hoping for context.

They both nodded, each taking a sip of their drinks.

"Yeah," Jack said flatly. "A real piece of work. Maggie and Abby have been the only ones who've stuck with Alex since childhood. We met them in college. Interestingly enough, her ex, Luke, actually got along with her mom."

Not a shock. Probably drinking buddies, maybe even tag-teaming her when they were blitzed. My jaw tightened.

"I could see how being around her mother would make relationships of any kind difficult," I said. It explained a lot, and it made me wonder what Edward and Patrick had endured being tied into all that family mess.

Matt leaned forward. "Alex is worried about stuff like that. Don't let her fool you. Abby's told me she doesn't date because she dreads having to bring anyone around her mom. She sees it as an albatross."

That word landed heavy. An albatross. Suddenly, all her dismissive behavior about relationships clicked into place.

"So," I said slowly, looking between them, "what's the best way to help her shake that weight off her neck?"

"Maybe she just needs space," Jack offered.

Space. Maybe. But if I gave her nothing but space, then she'd have nothing but her old fears to fill it.

"Yeah," I said, rubbing my jaw. "I guess I could give her some space. But if I don't show her what I actually want, she'll only keep believing the same thing—that pushing people away is safer."

Jack didn't strike me as the fight-for-your-woman type. He kept everything neat and controlled, engineered so he'd never have to fight. Maybe I thought that's what I wanted too. But Alex wasn't neat or controlled.

She made me want to fight. She made me want to protect. All the things she seemed to believe she didn't want at all.

***

ALEX

Time with my friends is exactly what I need. Brunch tomorrow should help me reset, and I've saved the real conversation for then. I'll talk to them about my mom—it always helps more when I say things out loud, when I can see their faces and feel that kind of support you can't get through a screen.

I'm definitely not mentioning the elevator ride, though. The girls would just tell Roman I'm afraid of heights, and I can't stand giving him more reasons to see me as fragile. I hate having a weakness, especially one I can't reason my way out of.

Still, I think tonight will be the last night I spend with him for a while. As much as I love being near him, I need to find my footing again. My routine. Work starts back Monday, and I'll have a new assistant to train. The guilt of not checking in all week sits heavy—I hate falling behind, hate the way it makes me short-tempered. Distraction has never looked good on me.

Roman reached over the console, laying his hand on mine, rubbing the back of it with his thumb. *Mm, that's so relaxing.* I thought as I stared at our connection in a daze.

"So, what're you thinking about?" That snapped me back to reality.

"Work stuff, actually."

"Yeah, me too." I couldn't tell if he meant that or not, but I wanted to rip this band aid off as far as spending some time apart— focusing on work was a good motivator for that.

"The beach was nice even though it ended on a sour note, but I'm glad to be home and getting back to work. I'm taking on an assistant in a week and I can't wait to train her to be me."

I guess warming him up is good also. Let him know I'm focusing on work now.

"You're going to train your competition?"

What? I never even thought of it like that.

"No, my successor."

"How long will that take and once she or he is trained what will you be doing?"

As soon as I find my niche, I'll be doing whatever that is. "I don't plan on doing this forever. I don't know when I'm planning to end my real estate career, I just know someday I am."

We pulled into the garage, and he came around, helping me out of the car. I don't know if knowing about my fear of heights even makes a difference. He's so overprotective.

"I know I fainted in the elevator earlier, but there's nothing wrong with me. I'm just recovering from vacation. Lots of partying, maybe a dry week will do me some good?" I shrugged my shoulders hoping to convince him with my most angelic expression—if I even had one. His curious look told me he wasn't buying it.

"Nonetheless, I'm going to help you out of the car and we're not going to mess around in the elevator anymore."

Oh well, I guess that didn't work. He's still planning to treat me like I'm fragile.

"If you say so." I shrugged, brushing past him to hit the button to call the elevator.

As soon as the doors opened, he pushed me in, pressing me against the back wall. He held both of my hands behind my back, staring into my eyes. He brushed his lips across my neck, breathing heavily into my ear.

"Are you feeling lightheaded or dizzy?" Oh hell, this was heaven—doesn't get any higher than this.

"Yes, but this is just how I feel every time you do this to me." I breathed out a sigh.

"Good. Then you must be feeling better since you didn't faint." He let me go, putting the code in for the penthouse then leaned his back against the glass. I turned around, leaning against him so I wasn't touching the glass, then he wouldn't have to try and guess my little phobia.

I gathered my senses before getting off the elevator and went straight to the bedroom to collect my things. Roman followed me in and saw what I was doing.

"Are you going somewhere?" I nodded nervously, wondering if he was going to try and stop me.

"Do you mind if I spend the week at my place?" I was having flashbacks of asking Luke permission to go out with my friends and I cringed, dropping my bag to the floor.

"Of course, you can stay at your place. I just thought you'd like to stay the night since it's already so late." My hands started to shake as I reached for the bag. I can't figure out if he's really this nice or if this is some kind of manipulation tactic. *How late is it? Will he really let me go home if I decide to leave?*

"You know what? You're right, you haven't been home in over a week. I'm sure you miss your bed and having your stuff handy. I know I did. Are you okay to drive?" I took a deep breath, letting it out with an audible sigh. I'm fine. This is good.

"Yeah, I'm good. I'm just going to get my stuff together and go." I walked into the bathroom, gathering up my hairbrush and toothpaste that I took out when I had a bath earlier. I turned on the sink, splashing some cold water on my face to try and get the thoughts of Luke out of my head. Even after all this time he still had too much control.

"I'll carry your bags to the car."

I nodded trying not to cry. He didn't deserve to be treated like this. I don't know if I can be the woman he needs. He picked up my bags, helping me get everything in my car.

"Thanks, Roman. For everything." He opened the driver's side door for me, and I hoisted myself in trying not to let him see how affected I was by everything that transpired this week. Roman reached across me with the seatbelt, clicking it in place. He ran his fingers over my hand, up my arm then cupped my face in his hand, as I leaned into it. He was warm and safe. Everything I needed and more. He gently turned my face towards him, planting a lingering kiss on my cheek. Don't cry, don't cry. I repeated to myself over and over.

"You're welcome." He said as he pulled away. His voice was low and gravely. It sounded like he was in pain. I nodded while looking straight ahead, hands firmly gripping the steering wheel. "And Alex?" I turned to look at him. There was sadness in his eyes. "I'm not them." He took a step back, closing the door. I watched him walk to the elevator and get on. He turned around and our eyes stayed connected until the doors closed. I laid my head down on the steering wheel as tears spilled over.

***

ROMAN

The look on her face when I asked if she was going to spend the night— God. I'll never forget it.

It wasn't hesitation, it wasn't annoyance. It was terror. Wide-eyed, sharp as a knife, like I'd just dragged her back to some place she'd sworn she'd never go again.

What the hell did I say? One simple question, and it gutted her. It had to trace back to her past—the ex who broke her down, the mother who hollowed her out until she couldn't trust her own worth. And now I was the one holding the match, lumped in with the people who'd hurt her most.

The thought makes me sick.

Am I doing something to warrant that kind of reaction? Am I pushing too hard, even when I swear I'm trying to hold back? I don't know anymore. All I know is I can't stand the way she looks at me—like I'm another man waiting to cage her.

Jack told me I should give her space. Maybe he's right. But space feels like silence, like walking away when every part of me is screaming to stay.

And the worst part? I don't think I've made it clear enough, how much I feel for her, how deep this thing already runs in me. She doesn't know. Maybe she can't know.

I stretched out on my bed, phone in hand, screen glowing against the dark. My thumb scrolled over nothing, aimless. My chest ached, tight, restless. She must be home by now. Alone. Telling herself she doesn't need me.

Finally, I typed the only thing I could manage.

ME: *Hope you made it home safe. Sweet dreams.*

The minutes stretched. My pulse drummed. Then her reply came, short, polite, a wall hidden behind words:

ALEX: *I did, thanks. You too.*

Two lines. Not cold, but not close. Not what I wanted.

I stared at them until the screen blurred. My throat burned. I set the phone down on my chest and shut my eyes, whispering the lie I've been telling myself since the moment she walked out the door—

I guess for now that's enough.

Chapter 33

ALEX

That's two days in a row my alarm didn't go off.

I already knew who the culprit was—Roman, silencing it while I slept. I rolled over, hand reaching for him, and gasped when my palm hit cool sheets. He wasn't there.

My chest seized. I bolted upright, eyes darting around, until reality landed like a slap. My own room. My own bed. I'd forgotten I'd gone home last night.

I sank onto the edge of the mattress, head in my hands, forcing my heart rate down. The silence of my condo wrapped around me, heavier than it should have been. My phone read 6:00 a.m. Not too late for a run, but the rain streaking the windows decided for me.

Workout clothes on. Bathing suit packed. Kitchen light humming overhead. I mixed my pre-workout, the sharp tang of powder filling the air. Sunday mornings in the gym were blessedly empty. The pool would be mine and I was grateful for the peace it would bring.

I leaned on the counter, scrolling through emails while I drank. Tomorrow's schedule stared back: paperwork with my penthouse clients. Negotiations done, inspections pending, closing in three weeks. Another payday—another stack for the savings fund.

I thought about those first three years, the flood of money. How easily it had come. Grant tossing me deals when he was overloaded, introducing me to Bradley the financial advisor. I'd nearly stuffed the cash under my mattress back then, terrified to let anyone touch it. Worried that if Luke found out he would take it all. Bradley turned out to be solid—ethical, sharp, cautious. He doubled what I trusted him with. And even then, a part of me still felt safer hoarding it, waiting for the other shoe to drop, but it never did and Luke never came after it.

Maybe one day I'd use it for more than myself. For that neighborhood. For something real. The thought flickered and faded as I slung my bag over my shoulder.

The gym was a cavern of echoes. Chlorine hung sharp in the air. I dropped my things on the bench, grabbed a towel, and sat at the pool's edge. My toes skimmed the water, ripples spreading outward, and my mind went straight to Roman. His voice, low and certain: *"I'm not them."*

Not who? Luke. My mother. The ghosts of every betrayal that gutted me. He wasn't either of them, I knew that. But knowing and believing were different things. If my own mother couldn't love me, if my husband couldn't stay, how could Roman possibly mean it when he said he cared?

The water was cold, a shock against overheated thoughts. I slid in slowly, inch by inch, letting the chill climb my body until it gripped my chest. Finally, I ducked under. Silence. Darkness. Just me, lungs burning, thoughts scattering.

When I broke the surface, hair plastered to my cheeks, I swore I heard movement—shoes against tile, a door clicking shut. I froze, scanning the pool deck. Empty. The air felt heavier though, like someone had been watching. The unease coiled low in my stomach, squeezing my chest. I shook it off, one last glance over my shoulder before I started my laps.

Stroke after stroke, the tension bled out. I skipped the weights, heading straight for the sauna. The cedar heat wrapped around me, sweat already prickling at my temples. I slipped in my earbuds and let classical strings pour over me. My body melted into the bench, but my mind refused to quiet.

Pros and cons. Roman. The mental list unrolled whether I wanted it to or not. Cons: his overprotectiveness, the way he scared me sometimes just by caring too much. Pros: his steadiness, his touch, the safety I hated admitting I craved.

My phone buzzed, startling me. Maggie's name lit the screen.

MAGGIE: *You're still coming to brunch today, aren't you jerkface?*

I smirked, typing back:

ME: *Yes. But I'm all talked out, so don't expect me to have anything to say.*

The phone started vibrating almost immediately, her name flashing again. I let it go to voicemail, leaning back against the hot wood, music swelling in my ears.

She wanted gossip. She wanted me to spill about Roman. But I wasn't ready. Not yet. The sweat stung my eyes as I breathed deep and tallied my list.

So far? The pros were winning.

***

"What the hell was that text message bullshit? And sending my call to voicemail?" Maggie glared as I slid into the booth.

I blew her a kiss and laughed. "You need to give me a better nickname."

I winked, and Abby laughed softly, but Maggie wasn't having it.

"I'm sorry, but if the shoe fits..." Maggie raised her mimosa.

I shook my head, refusing to clink. "No, that shoe definitely doesn't fit."

"Okay, okay," she relented. "I'll think of something else. But no promises."

The waitress appeared, took our orders, and as soon as she walked away Abby leaned in.

"Besides the mama drama, what else happened? Did you two finally..."

"Do the deed?" Maggie cut her off without hesitation. Abby rolled her eyes and sank in her seat like a kid caught cursing in church.

I couldn't help it — I laughed. "If you're asking if we had sex, then yes. We had sex."

The words fell flat. Neither of them reacted the way I expected. Relief? Excitement? Nothing.

"That's it?" Maggie looked appalled. "You've been going on and on about your *freaky connection* with this guy, and you expect me to believe you just had boring vanilla sex?"

I burst out laughing, almost spilling my drink. "You should see your face. You look so disappointed. Is everything okay with you and Matt? What's with the fascination?"

Her eyes narrowed. She wasn't playing anymore. "Matt and I are fine. *You're* the one I'm worried about. You've been out there messing around with everyone you can get your hands on, and now you finally have this amazing guy you seem to like... and I want to know if it means something to you."

The words landed like a punch. Heat flooded my face. I stared at her, stunned.

"I'm out there doing what with everyone?" My voice dropped, sharp and hushed. Abby shifted uncomfortably, her cheeks pink.

"How would I know? You don't tell us anything anymore," Maggie shot back. "What's happened to you?"

I thought this brunch would be fun, easy, familiar. Instead, my chest squeezed with anger and shame. The last thing I wanted was to feel like I was losing them too.

I pressed my hands to my face, drew in a shaky breath. "You're right. I've been distant. That's on me. I created a mess."

The waitress returned. I ordered a martini. Abby stuck with water. Odd — she usually matched Maggie drink for drink. I made a note to check on her later.

"What mess, Alex?" Abby's voice was quiet and motherly.

I dropped my hands, meeting their eyes. "Letting you believe I've been sleeping around."

Confusion flickered across their faces.

"You mean you haven't?" Maggie leaned forward. "You go out every weekend. You're seen with a different guy almost every time."

My stomach turned. "How do you know that? Better yet, who told you?"

"Matt told me." Her pause was a knife. "Luke keeps in touch."

The blood roared in my ears. Luke. Watching. Reporting. Still trying to control the narrative of my life.

"What the hell has he been telling Matt?" My voice shook with fury.

Maggie reached across the table, squeezing my hand. "Don't worry. We believe you over him. He's just been trying to convince Matt to get you back together."

The waitress set down my drink. I lifted it, drained it in one swallow, and handed her the empty glass to order another.

"Why didn't someone tell me?" My voice cracked. I scanned between them, searching for betrayal.

"Matt told him to go to hell. He didn't want you upset. He thought he was protecting you."

Protecting me. Everyone always protecting me with silence, with secrets. Meanwhile, I was drowning in them. I lowered my head to the table, eyes shut against the burn.

"Girls," I whispered, voice raw. "I'm a total mess."

I lifted my head, staring past them, through them, at nothing.

"No, you're not." Abby's voice steadied me. "You just need a little positive reinforcement."

"Maybe a little Jesus, too." Maggie said as her voice trailed off.

Do I need Jesus?

Right then the waitress slid my second martini onto the table along with our food. I smiled faintly, lifted my glass and pushed Jesus as far out of my head as I could get him.

"Cheers to reinforcements."

Glass tapped glass — Maggie's martini, Abby's water.

For one small second, it almost felt like enough.

After that brunch I was certain the prickling, watched feeling was Luke. Bulletproof from the drinks and pissed off, I decided to answer him once I was outside.

ME: *Leave my friends alone, asshole, and quit following me — you stalker.*
LUKE: *What the hell are you talking about? Who's following you? I just asked Matt to help me talk to you. I don't know anything about a stalker. Where are you? Are you in trouble?*
ME: *Right. Like I believe you. I'm not telling you shit about where I am ever.*
LUKE: *Nice language Alex. You sound like a truck stop hooker. Why don't I come get you and we can talk like adults.*
ME: *No thanks. I'll take my chances with the deranged stalker if it's between you and him. Since you say you're not it.*
LUKE: *Have you been drinking? I know you girls like to get sloshed on Sunday. Shouldn't you be in church instead? You could use some holy water splashed in that dirty mouth of yours.*

My fingers trembled as I typed the last line. I wanted to drop my phone and stomp on it. I wanted to find him and shove the truth down his throat. Instead I ground my teeth until the ache moved behind my eyes. I'm going to strangle that creep if I ever see him again.

ME: *Get lost Luke and leave me the hell alone.*
LUKE: *Bye Alex. I'll see you later.*

A cold shiver crawled across my skin. I jammed the apartment door open and nearly knocked the new front-desk guy off his stool with my thunderous entrance. He gave me that deer-in-headlights look like I was a hurricane. I didn't bother to apologize. I slammed my bag on the rug and hit the elevator button so hard the light flickered.

"Who the hell does he think he is?" I said aloud, to the ceiling in the empty hall as I padded down the corridor to my apartment. The question landed hollow.

I stood in my kitchen holding a bottle of red like it was a grenade. Two in the afternoon and he'd already had me considering opening it. The corkscrew was in my other hand, cold metal pressing into my palm. I could feel the chemical tug of wine in my blood — an easy fix, a small erasure. For a second my fingers toyed with the screw, and I imagined the warm buzz smoothing the edges of everything Luke had touched.

Instead, I set the bottle down gently as an apology, slid the corkscrew back in the drawer, and closed my fists until the tremor passed. Breathe in. Breathe out. Count to ten until the burn in my chest softened.

If it wasn't Luke watching me, then who in hell was it? The thought that someone else might be trailing me made my scalp prickle—an animal's fear that won't be soothed with reason. And then his last words echoed at me like a thrown knife: *I'll see you later.*

Did he mean it as a promise or a threat?

***

Chapter 34

ALEX

Monday, the girls came with me to self-defense class. Bruce's eyes nearly popped out of his head when I walked in with my lifelong partners in crime.

"These girls are kind of delicate, don't you think?" he said with a smirk, like he'd already written them off.

The three of us exchanged a look. Maggie rolled her eyes, Abby sighed, and I folded my arms.

"Bruce, these girls have been my friends since we were six years old. Looks can be deceiving, don't you think?"

He chuckled, but I saw him watching as class went on, sizing them up differently every time they landed a hit.

By the end, he was shaking his head in disbelief. He walked right up to Maggie and Abby.

"You fooled me," he admitted. "Designer bags, fancy shoes, Lululemon matching sets — I thought you were here for selfies. But after watching you today? I'd be scared stiff of the three of you in a dark alley. You're like Charlie's Angels."

We all burst out laughing. His big bear hug nearly crushed my ribs.

"We'll be back for kickboxing on Wednesday," I promised as we waved goodbye.

***

Tuesday dragged at work. By four, I was exhausted and already dreading therapy. My mind was cluttered, buzzing with all the things I hadn't said, and I worried I'd bury Lisette under my baggage. She deserved hazard pay just for listening.

When I pulled under her carport, she was already at the door, warm smile and arms open. That hug almost broke me before we'd even started.

In her office, I curled up on the sofa, flip-flops kicked aside, knees tucked under me. Words poured out before I could stop them — everything about my mom on vacation, every raw nerve exposed.

"Why do you think you defended Roman like that?" she asked gently.

I stared down at my hands, fingers knotting. "Because he didn't deserve it."

Her brows lifted. "Do you defend other family members or their spouses like that?"

I hesitated. "Usually I wait until she's run everyone off, then I let her have it." Saying it out loud made me wince. It sounded cold, even if it was true.

"So why did you think everyone else could handle it, but Roman couldn't?"

The answer pressed hot against my chest. "It's not that I thought he couldn't handle it. It's that I know what it's like to have that garbage in your head. I didn't want him carrying it too. I invited him. He didn't know what she's capable of. And honestly? That wasn't even the worst I've seen her."

Her smile was small but knowing. "You care about Roman more than you admit, don't you?"

I tilted my head. "Are you asking as a therapist or as his mother?"

"Maybe a little of both."

"At least you're honest," I said, voice breaking with something close to relief. "I care about him. I'm terrified I'll hurt him. Or that my family will be too much."

She leaned forward. "In here I'll do my best to keep the two separate. But Alex, Roman is a grown man. No matter how much I want to protect him, he'll make his own choices—with or without me."

The words cracked something inside me. I'd been clinging to this illusion of control—of saving him from me, from my mother, from my mess.

"You don't get to decide what's best for him," she said firmly. "Only what's best for you. But don't just assume you're not what's best for him."

I fell back on the sofa, staring at the ceiling like it held answers. Her words seared into me, impossible to forget.

Afterward, we sat on the patio with wine, sunlight glinting off the pool. We talked about safe, easy things — vacation stories edited down to PG. Her laugh was a balm.

By the time I left, I felt lighter. I even smiled when I called Roman on the drive home.

"Hi there." His voice was warm enough to make me almost invite him over. Almost.

"Hi. How are you?"

"Good. Were you with Mom?"

Ugh. Therapy with his mother. Freud would have a field day.

"I saw Dr. King for an hour, then hung out with your mom for another."

He laughed. "How's Mom?"

"Wonderful as ever. Dr. King was helpful too."

"I'm glad. What's your week look like? Can we do lunch?"

I hesitated, heart tripping over itself. Lunch was harmless, right? "Maybe Thursday or Friday. I'll check. The crew's going out Friday night to Sebastians to celebrate Shay's promotion—want to join?"

He paused, then: "It's not my favorite place, but if you're there, I'd love to."

That caught me. He'd endure Sebastian's just for me.

"Wonderful. I'll call you about lunch on Thursday, so you don't get Alex-overload on Friday."

He chuckled. "Not possible. Two days in a row with you is a win."

By the time I pulled into my building, I was smiling. "Thank you for being you, Roman. Good night."

"Good night, Alex. I'll see you Thursday."

I hung up and sat in the quiet, his mother's words still echoing: *Don't assume you're not what's best for him.*

If I walked away now, claiming I was protecting him, I'd be lying. And if there's one thing I can't stomach—it's a liar.

***

ROMAN

Come on, you just saw her—she said she needed space. Leave her alone. She'll figure this out.

That was the mantra, looping in my head long after she left. Even after I finally heard from her. Would she keep our lunch date? Would she cancel? I told myself I couldn't put myself through this. Not again. Not even for her. But here I was anyway, consumed with all things Alex.

I moved through the office like a ghost. Amelia handled the details—took notes in meetings I barely heard, fielded calls from the politician and his sleazy brother about the Texas project I'd frozen. Their secretaries kept circling, trying to force me back to the table, and Harrison kept deflecting them right back at me. I wanted them angry. I wanted them desperate enough to make a mistake I could tear apart. If there was dirty money in those contracts, I was going to find it and drag every last cent back for the families already bruised by their schemes.

Still, none of it cut through the fog. The week came and went, each day indistinguishable from the last, my chest tight with the question I wouldn't let myself ask: *Is she pulling away for good?*

By the time I made it home Wednesday night, I was spent. I cracked a bottle of water and collapsed onto the couch. The Bible sat on the table beside me, a fixture I'd set out days ago and hadn't touched. My mom used to read me stories from it when I was a kid. Back then it quieted me, gave me a kind of peace I didn't understand but clung to. Maybe it could do the same now.

I thumbed it open at random. Job. Somewhere in the middle. I huffed out a laugh. *Figures.* Loving Alex felt like my own private trial—one long, grinding test of endurance. Still, I was grateful it was nothing compared to what Job endured.

My eyes fell on the words:

"What I feared has come upon me; what I dreaded has happened to me.
I have no peace, no quietness;
I have no rest, but only turmoil." —Job 3:25–26

The verse hit harder than I wanted to admit. I wasn't Job, but I knew what it was to dread losing someone before I'd even truly had them. To feel turmoil coil in my gut, no matter what I did to hold it at bay.

I leaned back against the couch, exhaling slow. For the first time all week, the silence didn't press so heavy. She was home. She was safe. And for tonight, that was enough.

Chapter 35

ALEX

I love these Wednesday night kickboxing classes with the girls. There was an MMA training session scheduled these nights as well. I don't know what it is about the sounds of aggression that gets me going. I can hear the fighters in the ring grunting. The sounds of kicks landing on flesh instead of a sandbag is thrilling. I feel like a masochist enjoying it. I walked over to the ring, watching the fighters move like they were in a choreographed dance. Seems almost poetic. I nodded to the guys in the ring and headed back over to get ready for class.

As for the kickboxing class, I didn't need to take as many breaks as I did when I first started. You would think with all the exercise I do; I wouldn't have needed to take any breaks. In all fairness, I had just taken a self-defense class right before that first kickboxing class. I high fived the girls at the door because we were a sweaty mess and headed back inside to talk to Bruce.

I walked up to the counter, leaning on it like a crutch. One because I was tired, and two because he was on the phone and I couldn't hold myself up while I waited on him.

"Thanks, see you on Friday." He said to whoever was on the other end of the line and hung up. "Alex. What's up? How was class?"

"It was good. I felt strong. I feel a lot stronger than I did when I started despite how I look at the moment."

"Good. I like to hear that. So why are you still here then?" He smiled, tipping his head waiting for something profound to come out of my mouth or maybe sarcastic, but I was all out of wit and sarcasm at the moment.

"Bruce, I think I have a stalker." His eyes widened and he stood up, coming around the desk with concern in his eyes. He leaned against the desk next to me— still towering over me and pretty much everyone else.

"Why do you think that? Has someone contacted you or been bothering you?" Good question. Luke swears it isn't him but he's the one that's been telling my friends what I'm doing and where I'm going. It has to be him.

"Maggie told me my ex has been trying to get back together with me via her husband. His ex-best friend."

"Ok, so how does that equate to stalking?"

"It doesn't but the fact that he's told them where I've been and who I've been with is a bit concerning."

"Have you confronted him?"

"Yes, and he's denied it vehemently." I rolled my eyes thinking how much of a liar Luke is and that this has to be him.

"Do you have any correspondence with him that the authorities could use to bring him in and maybe have a word with him? Scare him a little?" The text messages all deny my allegations and make me sound like a raving lunatic.

"No, I don't think the texts could prove anything."

"I have a friend who does security. I could ask him to look into it for you."

"Maybe it's nothing. Would you just read the texts and let me know what you think? I don't want to cause any drama or get him in trouble if he's telling the truth."

"Sure. I can do that for you." Bruce read through the texts. I watched as his face cracked a few times with a smile, and I shook my head only imagining what crazy rant he was reading.

"Not sure that proves anything in those texts other than the fact you really don't like that dude." I laughed, thinking what an understatement that is.

"Ok, well, like I said I don't want to start something for no reason." I couldn't understand what the bad vibes were that I couldn't shake. If it wasn't him, who else could it be?

***

On Thursday I got lots of work done at the office in the morning before lunch with Roman.

ME: *Hey, I'm almost done here then I'll be heading your way.*

I sent an email to Ella's grandson to set up an appointment to talk to him. I had a feeling he was going to be an ally with this whole neighborhood debacle. As I was finishing up the email, I saw a text come in from Roman.

ROMAN: *Hi there. Sounds good. Did you want to have lunch at the office, out, or in the penthouse?*

ME: *Oh, there are options? How about your penthouse, that way you can cook for me again. How much time do you have? I'm done for the day. Decided to take the rest of my work home.*

He was a good cook and being in the penthouse meant alone time.

ROMAN: *I have a couple hours. A meeting was rescheduled, and I'd love to cook for you.*

ME: *Awesome. I'll see you in about fifteen minutes. Should I just come up or meet you in the lobby?*

ROMAN: *I'll meet you in the lobby and ride the elevator up with you. That way I'm there to catch you if you pass out again.*

ME: *OMG I feel like I do a lot of stuff you get to hang over my head.*

ROMAN: *I promise I won't mention it again.*

Yeah right.

ME: *I'll see you soon.*

I was dressed casually today, wearing a black and white striped tee shirt dress that came just above my knees, a thin jean jacket and black sandals. My hair was down in large beachy waves, and I had my very large purse draped over my arm because my laptop was in it. I didn't feel like leaving that in the car for some reason. I'm still unsure of this stalkerish feeling I'm getting. I needed to tell someone about this. Maybe there were cameras in the parking garage that picked up if someone was creeping around. I should at least let Roman know.

I sat down on one of the open sofas in the middle of the lobby, sending a text to Roman. I didn't have an appointment, so I didn't want to bother the receptionist with giving me a name badge in the building. She already gave me a dirty look when I sat down.

ME: *I'm here.*

ROMAN: *I'm on my way down now. Got held up by a phone call.*

The elevator doors opened and there stood Roman, looking like Mr. Perfect, wearing a tailor-made black suit with a white button up shirt with the top two buttons undone and no socks with his shiny black shoes. Damn, this guy makes it difficult to just be chill around him. He walked over with one hand in his pocket and his beautiful white toothy grin. I couldn't help but smile back and probably had a flushed face to go with it. I stood up before he got to me, putting my hand out to shake his. He looked surprised as his eyebrows shot up.

"Yeah right," he announced, tugging me into his strong arms. I wasn't comfortable with his employees witnessing any sort of PDA. Especially the look I'm getting right now from his not so pleasant receptionists. I guess he doesn't care, so why should I. It's not like I work here, I just have a thing about PDA in the workplace and petty women.

"You look great. I feel like I haven't seen you in forever." His arm was still around me almost possessively. Maybe he really did think I was going to pass out again.

"I know, it's kind of weird, maybe that's why I tried to shake your hand." None of these people need to know I'm dating Roman, if that's even what we're calling it—especially the unfriendly receptionist.

"I was wondering about that." He brushed his lips over my temple, and I relaxed into him. I should try not to worry about all these people and just enjoy it. I do feel better when he's around, especially his calming touch. I've missed this the past few days.

"So, how's your week been so far?" I did my best to keep up some sort of communication, so I didn't lose focus and swoon.

"It's been productive. We've gotten some traction on the zoning projects. It seems I've pissed off the right people. They've been calling, trying to connect with me but I'm not taking a meeting with those assholes until I find out more information about how they managed to become so involved in this."

That's troublesome information. Maybe he should set up a meeting and ask them directly what they're involvement is.

"Let me know what you find out. I'm going to do my best not to get too involved myself. It just seems like it's way out of my comfort zone." I'm already worried that I've gotten in over my head.

"I like that idea." He nodded his agreement.

I smiled at him as the doors opened then realized how much I like this place. It's so clean and stark. It makes me feel calm because there's nothing to pull the emotions out of me. I used to think all this clean white was antiseptic and cold. I set my purse down on the chair by the front door. Roman grabbed my wrist, spinning me to face him and kissed me. Not the usual peck on the lips, top of the head or cheek, but a full-on, open-mouthed tongue exploration that was overwhelming all my senses.

I don't know how we got here. One minute I was standing by the front door, and the next, I was on the couch in his arms, lost in a kiss that stole the air right out of my lungs. His mouth was soft and warm, his five o'clock shadow just rough enough to make my skin tingle without leaving a mark.

At some point, he must've taken off my jacket—I could feel the cool air from the vent brushing over my bare arms as they looped around the back of his neck, my fingers tangled in his hair, pulling him closer.

When we finally came up for air, I was flat on my back across the chaise, gasping. He lay beside me, propped on one elbow, his head resting in his hand, a small, knowing smile playing at his lips as his other hand traced slow, gentle lines up and down my leg.

How the hell does he do that to me, every freaking time? I've got to learn the trick to this because he has some weird voodoo control over me.

"I'm so glad you didn't do that in the lobby downstairs." I said between gasps of air.

His chuckle was low, vibrating deep in his chest— sexy.

"I thought about it, but I don't like people staring at you. I mean, you'd have to be a blind idiot not to look at you, but staring isn't okay."

There's that possessiveness again. It worries me so much. I decided to change the subject.

"Now that we've gotten that out of the way, what's for lunch?"

"What did we get out of the way? Maybe I'm not done yet."

Oh shit, he really needs to stop that, my insides are full of butterflies and the need to jump his bones right now. The loss of control is something I'm not ok with.

"Oh yes you are." I jumped up off the couch, scooting out of his reach. He slowly stalked over to me like a predator.

"I am?" He looked so serious. I was trying to hold in a laugh shaking my head. He was so much fun when he acted with abandon instead of with all that control he seemed to exude.

I stopped abruptly, stood up straight and said, "Should I assume that you want to test my new self-defense skills?" That stopped him in his tracks. I thought his look was one of intimidation then it turned to that devilish smirk again.

"I was hoping you'd just let me attack you, but it sounds rather sexy to have you *try* and take me down."

I put my hands on my hips in mock insult.

"So, you don't really think I can?"

He shook his head slowly.

"I'm a head taller and I can bench press at least double your weight, so I'm going to say, no."

He seemed so sure of himself but now I was feeling competitive. I took a deep breath, inhaling his amazing cologne. Maybe competitiveness is the wrong feeling as my legs started to shake and arousal took over.

"I'm game if you are," I said as confidently as I could.

He chuckled.

"Ok, so we're back to the games again. Can we take this game to the bedroom where it's softer?"

I laughed. That sounded like a good idea but something felt too intense.

"What, are you afraid to get hurt?" He shook his head with that damn sexy grin still plastered on his face, crushing my resolve.

"Should I tell you what I'm going to do before I do it, so I don't freak you out?" he teased.

"Would you like to blindfold me, so you have an advantage?"

He relaxed his posture as he slowly approached me.

"I don't really want to wrestle or fight or whatever we were planning to do." He wrapped his arms around my waist, pulling me to his firm body. I slipped my arms inside his jacket around his waist, staring up into his eyes.

"Me either." He put his head down to kiss me again and this time it was just a peck.

"I'm making grilled cheese sandwiches with tomato basil soup."

"You're too much." I gave him a little shove on his chest to push him away, but he didn't let me go.

"I've missed you."

I knew he had— I could feel it emanating off him. It mimicked my own feelings, but I was too stubborn to tell him.

"I know." I swallowed the lump in my throat. These are the feelings that are the hardest for me to express.

"You do? Were you going to tell me you missed me too?"

"Probably not. You know how I feel about being a needy, sad girl."

"Does that make me a needy, sad boy?" He sounded insulted.

"I don't know, does it? From here you just look like a freaking million bucks." He started laughing, spinning me around by one hand over to the kitchen counter then pulling the stool out for me. I sat down, watching, intently, as he gathered all the ingredients for making lunch. The tension in the air seemed to dissipate after that.

Without turning around, he assured me, "You know it's not a weakness to tell someone how you feel even if they don't feel the same way. I said I missed you because I was being me and that's how I feel."

Feelings, ugh. Please just let it go.

"I know but it's complicated. I've spent a lot of time burying certain feelings behind a big wall and it's hard to distinguish one from another these days because there's a lot of chaos in there. But I do love that you tell me how you feel. It helps me to see that it's okay to talk about them, I guess." Please let that be enough about it for him. I can't handle this conversation right now.

"That's the best thing I've heard from you in a while."

"You're very easy to please." He quickly glanced over his shoulder, smiling like he had a secret.

"Oh, you'd be surprised how easy I am to please, Ms. Kennedy."

I freaking knew it, what a damn pain in the neck. Now I'm just sitting here thinking of him naked and all the ways I can enjoy that amazing body of his. The ass on that man is something of a national treasure.

"No, I don't think I'd be surprised at all. I've imagined several different scenarios in the past ten minutes alone." These non-mushy feelings however seem to be fair game.

He stopped moving, clearing his throat. Throwing his suit jacket to the sofa, he slowly untucked and unbuttoned his shirt. He glanced back as he undid the cuffs on his sleeves, taking it off, tossing it over the jacket. I couldn't help but stare. My head was tilted to the side— I was chewing mindlessly on my bottom lip. The muscles on his back that I want to reach out and touch—rippled to perfection. The base of his spine where his waistband hits precisely on his hips, just above that amazing backside, is causing my mouth to go dry as the throbbing between my legs intensifies.

Without turning around, he acknowledged, "Sorry, I forgot to change out of that, I didn't want to get anything on it."

Uh huh.

"Yeah, it would've been a shame to mess up those clothes." I know I'm completely glassy eyed right now. I can feel the arrogant smile beaming on his God-like face without even seeing it, but I needed to pull myself together.

***

ROMAN

"How long were you staring at my... ehem?" I asked, glancing toward my rear. Alex wasn't even embarrassed. Not one bit.

"I guess the entire time after you took off your shirt. Right after I got a good look at your sexy naked back."

Her honesty made me laugh. Bold, unfiltered honesty—God, it was refreshing.

"What can I get you to drink?" I asked, trying to cool both of us off.

"Tequila would be good, but I think some ice water would be better."

That was... an interesting answer. I poured her a glass. "What did you want the tequila for?"

She groaned, throwing her hands over her face before smacking them against the counter.

"To do body shots off your stomach. I mean, come on, Roman. I'm freaking dying here. How the hell do you look like that?" She flailed an arm at my abs. "No one looks like that. Are you airbrushed or something?"

I laughed so hard I almost choked. She was nuts. Completely nuts.

"You're more than welcome to check and see if I'm airbrushed, anytime."

She ducked her head, biting into her sandwich instead of answering. Silence held until we finished eating.

"That was actually perfect," she whispered.

"It's one of my specialties." I grinned. "Grilled cheese and soup—it's an art."

"I bet there isn't much you aren't good at, is there?" she muttered, rolling her eyes.

I almost teased her more, but she cut me off. "Don't answer that. I can't take anymore right now."

I tugged her off the stool, sliding her between my knees and giving her hips a squeeze. "What's going on with you? Why are you acting like we haven't been down this road already?"

She leaned into me, breath shaky. "Uhhh. What the hell is wrong with me? I totally want you—in every way I can think of—but something's stopping me. And I don't know what it is!"

Always dramatic. Always breaking my chest open with it. I stood, gesturing to the sofa. She looked wary but finally sighed and lowered herself onto the cushion between my legs. I wrapped my arms around her waist, grounding her.

"Nothing's wrong with you. You're overthinking it. I want you. That's obvious. But I want you ready on your terms, not mine."

She moaned, frustrated. "I'm trying. I keep being told I must really like you. Doesn't that make it easier? Shouldn't it?" Her face dropped into her hands.

I chuckled softly. "Look, you went through a brutal divorce. That's bound to mess with you. I can't imagine you ever being with a guy like that, but it happened. And yeah—maybe I sounded jealous calling him a loser. I shouldn't have."

"It's okay. It says more about me than him."

My stomach sank. I'd pushed her into a spiral. "Alex, stop. It does not. Don't talk down about yourself. You don't see what I see. What so many people see. You're adored, more than you realize."

She pulled away, spinning to face me on her knees, hands on my shoulders, eyes blazing.

"What time do you get off work tonight?" she asked, breathless, inches from my lips.

"One more meeting. Then I'm done. Why?" My pulse quickened just having her that close.

"Can I stay with you tonight? Watch a movie, eat popcorn, something normal?"

Like she even needed to ask. "Hell yes. Pick the movie. Anything special you want me to grab?"

"No, I'll bring it. Do you have Netflix or Prime?"

"I do. Both. What movie?"

"I don't know yet. What do you like?"

"I don't watch much TV or movies. Your pick."

Her grin was wicked. "Okay, *Pretty Woman* it is."

I raised a brow. "You serious?"

"Absolutely. I kind of identify with the main character."

Uh oh. "Wasn't she a hooker?" I blurted before I could stop myself.

She burst out laughing, smacking my arm. "That's not the part I identify with, alright?"

"Thank God," I muttered, but the smile pulling at my lips wouldn't quit.

Chapter 36

ALEX

"Text me when you're done with work," I said, kissing him quickly before bolting to the elevator.

The second I got in my car, I called Maggie and Abby on three-way.

"This must be serious," Abby said. "A call, not a text?"

"Girls, it *is* serious. I asked Roman to do a movie-night sleepover."

Maggie laughed. "See, Abby? I told you she's in love."

Love? My stomach dropped. Abby immediately started singing *Alex and Roman sitting in a tree.*

"Wait, who said anything about love?" I snapped, catching a glimpse of my own wide-eyed reflection in the rearview. I looked insane.

"Me," Maggie said. "Because this is how a normal girl in love acts. Don't you dare get mad at me, jerkface."

"Good for you," Abby added. "You picked an amazing specimen."

I had no reply. My mouth just hung open.

"I only wanted movie and snack suggestions!" I protested.

They squealed with laughter, then Maggie chimed in, "My suggestion? *Fifty Shades*, wine, and condoms."

"Switch that order," Abby said, "condoms first, then wine."

"You're both ridiculous," I groaned. "Totally team Roman."

"Wrong," Maggie corrected. "We're team Alex. We just think Roman's good for you."

And then Abby casually dropped a bomb: "By the way, I'm pregnant!"

Maggie and I screamed in unison. We chattered all the way until I reached my apartment, thrilled for her—but once I hung up, my joy cracked into sadness. My best friends lived in the same neighborhood, raising their kids together, while I was still the odd one out. Godmother, not mother. Not married and not living in the neighborhood.

I shook the thoughts off as I punched in my door code, texting Lisette for a quick talk. She called me back instantly.

"Hi Lisette, thanks for taking my call. I just had an argument with myself in the hallway. Is that normal?"

She laughed gently. "Depends on the argument. Did something happen?"

"Yes. My friends accused me of being in love with Roman... then one of them announced she's pregnant."

"Which bothers you more?"

The word *bothered* fit perfectly. Confused, sad, overwhelmed—yes.

"I think I already knew the first answer," I admitted. "We're having movie night tonight."

"Do you think it's love?" she asked.

"I don't know. What if it's infatuation? What if I say it and he doesn't feel the same?"

"Quiet your mind. You'll figure it out. Stop overthinking. And Alex—don't fill yourself with so much negative energy. Maybe telling him will make room for the good stuff. Have you talked to you know who yet? Like I suggested?"

Tears slid down my face as I thought about what Lisette's reaction could have been and what it actually was. She was talking about God again. That I needed to talk to him. At least she didn't tell me to stay away from her son.

She shifted the conversation. "And your friend's pregnancy—what about that makes you sad?"

"We made a pact, years ago, to all marry and raise our kids together. Now they're both onto their second child, and I haven't even started."

"Children aren't like groceries," she said softly. "It's permanent, whether the marriage lasts or not. And not having kids with your ex? That was a blessing. Sometimes God's plans take longer."

Her words sank in like warm tea. "Thank you, Lisette. Truly."

"Have fun tonight. Pick a happy ending—you both deserve it."

I hung up, wiped my face, then focused on practical things. I packed yoga pants, a smiley-face tee, a maxi dress for tomorrow, popcorn, chocolate. Ordered pizza and beer for delivery. Then called Amelia for help hauling it all upstairs.

By the time Roman texted that he was done, Amelia and I were in the lobby juggling bags, laughing as she carried the beer and pizza. She swiped us up to the penthouse, where Roman stood waiting. His eyes flicked between us.

"Relax," Amelia teased. "I'm not staying. Just helping a girl out."

Roman chuckled, taking the food. "Amelia's like a sister." He said as the doors to the elevator closed. "But I'm not sure I want her telling you *everything* about me."

"Too late," I shot back, grinning.

He tickled me mercilessly until I shrieked for him to stop, then he eyed the pile of food and bags.

"What is all this?"

"Movie night essentials—pizza, beer, popcorn, and chocolate."

"Is that a rule?"

"No rules tonight," I said. "Just go with the flow."

His smile softened. "Best game we've played yet."

***

ROMAN

"Okay, so which streamer is the movie on?" No more of this shy business.

"I think it's on Amazon Prime."

I found the movie and hit play. We ate pizza, chased it with a couple beers, half-watching the screen.

"How do you like it so far?" she asked, peeking at me before turning back.

"Is this like a hooker Cinderella story?" I tossed popcorn in my mouth.

She laughed, nudging my shoulder. "Exactly."

"Then I love it."

"So, do you like Cinderella—or hookers?"

Not hookers. Not Cinderella either. Truth was, I didn't even care for the movie. All I could focus on was figuring out why Alex related to a character who happened to be a prostitute.

"Neither," I said finally. "I like it because you like it." Best worst answer ever.

She smiled faintly. "Want to know how I identify with her?"

"I've been trying to figure that out all night. Can I guess?"

"I'd like that." She said, smiling genuinely.

Alright. Here goes. I turned toward her, giving it my best shot.

"She's beautiful but hides behind sarcasm and low self-esteem. Closed herself off to love. Thinks kissing is more intimate than sex. And now she's falling for the guy next to her but doesn't believe she deserves it—because of all the losers who convinced her otherwise."

Her face fell as her eyes filled instantly. Tears shimmered before she could blink them away. That was not the reaction I expected.

She bolted upright, slipping from my arms, and ran down the hall. Leaping to the sofa as he redirected to the kitchen.

I sat back, breath tight in my chest, bracing for her to come storming out with her bags packed. Looked like I'd just pushed my luck straight off a cliff.

***

ALEX

How did he know me better than I knew myself? The tears came without warning, hot and unstoppable. Was this what it felt like when the wall began to crumble? Did everything I'd tucked away have to break free before I could finally breathe?

I shut myself in the bathroom, locking the door before he had to witness the mess I'd become. I leaned over the sink and sobbed until my chest ached. When my legs gave out, I sat on the edge of the tub, careful not to fall in. Tears streamed relentlessly down my face. *What a disaster.* Please let this be quick. The last thing I needed was him breaking the door down.

At last the storm passed. A soft knock followed.
"Alex?"

"Just a minute." I splashed water on my face and repaired what I could of my makeup. To my surprise, I didn't look ruined. If anything, the tears had sharpened my eyes, made them greener. The reflection staring back carried something new—determination. For a fleeting moment, I thought maybe I could even tell him I loved him.

I opened the door. He didn't speak; he just pulled me into his arms, holding me as though he'd been waiting there the whole time.
"I paused the movie for you," he murmured against my neck.

"Thank you." The truth was, the movie was the last thing on my mind.

He eased back, cupping my face in his hands. "I didn't mean to upset you. Are you okay?" His voice was careful, almost anxious.

"I'm better now. Maybe after the movie we can talk. I don't think we should talk through it anymore."

He laughed and hugged me tighter, probably assuming he'd done something wrong. "Sorry. You do know what my mom does for a living, right? I was trying to impress you."

"I called her today." I shouldn't have told him that, he didn't need to know I was worried about this.

His brows lifted. "You called my mom? Were you digging for intel on me?"

"She's the one who told me you liked *Pretty Woman.*" I deflected.

"No, she didn't!"

"It's none of your business why I called her—because I didn't. I called my doctor, not your mommy." I tried to push away, but he caught my hand.

"Alright, get out here. You've earned a spanking."

I shrieked, pulled free, and ran back down the hall.

He returned with two fresh beers and another bowl of popcorn, dropping it on his lap so I'd have to reach between his legs to grab any. *What an ass. Why is this childish streak so damn sexy on him, though?*

"You do remember what happened the last time I reached into that vicinity on someone, don't you?" I teased, smirking.

He chuckled, though a beat late. "If you don't want popcorn, you can always have some nuts."

I pressed my lips together, dead. *I can't with this guy. He's got an answer for everything. I've totally met my match.*

"You win. I quit."

He pumped a fist in victory. "Yes!"

I laughed as he pulled me onto his lap, wrapped those strong arms around me, and kissed my temple. His voice softened against my ear. "Let's finish the movie, then talk—and then go to bed. Sound good?"

I kissed his cheek. "Yeah. Perfect."

And for once, I believed it.

When the credits rolled, I stood and stretched the stiffness from my body. We tidied the living room and the kitchen, and he asked if I wanted another beer.

"No, thanks. Can I have some water, though?" He came back with two bottles and settled beside me on the sofa.

"I don't want to get too deep tonight, but I know something happened earlier, and I want you to know you're in a safe place if you want to talk about it."

I swallowed a big sip to soothe the sudden dryness in my throat. After what had happened before, I wasn't sure I wanted to say anything.

"I think I may have lost a few more bricks," I admitted. "When you said what you said, it was like ripping a Band-Aid off."

We've been needing that a lot lately.

"In my head, I was only thinking about the kissing and the sex part and how she had that completely backwards—like, just wrong. But when I thought about everything you said, you were right. Hearing it out loud from someone else opened my eyes. I was able to feel it and let it go. It felt like a weight lifted."

He looked sorry. "I'm glad that was the outcome. I'm sorry for the way I said it. That was brutal."

"Have you met me?" I said. "I can take it. I dish it out enough."

He reached for my hands. "It just upsets me that you'd ever think so little of yourself or let anyone make you believe those things. I think so highly of you. Knowing what I do— even in this short time— I wouldn't care if you told me you were a hooker." The smile spreading across his face was ridiculous and warm.

I choked out a laugh. "Well, now that's fantastic, because I have something to tell you... I'm—" The words snagged; I took another drink.

"You're what?" He cupped my face. "Are you feeling the same way I am? Because you're not going to tell me you're a hooker."

Say it, I wanted to scream. Don't make me. This is torture. Then I had an idea.

"I think I do. Close your eyes for a minute. I want to play that game we played on the plane..."

His eyes widened. I remembered his claustrophobia. "I'm not going to tie you up," I added to ease him.

He closed his eyes and exhaled, throwing his arms across the back of the sofa.

I whispered in his ear, "Do you want me to tell you what I'm going to do as I do it?"

"Surprise me." His voice was husky and inviting.

Touching him didn't seem to make him nervous the way it did me. I straddled his lap, facing him, wanting some control. His hands came off the back of the sofa quicker than I expected, urgent and firm on my hips—an electric surprise. After that first claim, he rested them there, lighter but steady.

I stroked my fingers over his cheek and through his hair, kissed both sides of his neck, and inhaled his woodsy cologne. I could feel his grip tighten and the hardness at his waist.

"Tell me what you feel," I whispered into his ear.

"I feel an overwhelming sense of peace," he said.

That was one of the things I'd felt, too. I sighed at the memory.

"Exactly. What about love? Do you know what love feels like?" I needed to know if we were on the same page.

"I thought I knew once, but what I feel for you is stronger than that. The Bible talks about love—patience, kindness, not being proud." He hesitated, searching for words.

Back to God again, I thought. Those are good words, but is now the time to bring Him up while we're sinning?

"That experience on the plane taught me what love was," I continued. "That's the only way I can describe it—complete, total peace and content- ment. In that moment I didn't need anything else. Not food, not water, not sex." He glanced at me, and for a second I worried he'd misunderstand. I did still need food and water and sex—just not then. "I only knew what I was experiencing in that moment, and it was because of you. I found love because of you.

He opened his eyes, brown and endless, searing a hole straight into my soul. "Are you saying what I think you're saying?" His voice was rough and sensual.

I rolled my lips, pulling in a shaky breath. "Are you feeling what I'm feeling?" My words came out breathless, desperate for him to say what I couldn't.

"Yes. Since the moment I laid eyes on you." The playfulness had left his face; he was serious, and my stomach fluttered with equal parts nerves and excitement.

"Roman, I don't know how easy this is going to be for me. What I feel is so intense, overwhelming sometimes, and I may still need space. But I know—deep in my heart—you're the one."

He pulled me into his arms. "It's been torture waiting for this moment. I held out for you to say it first because I didn't want to scare you away. I was trying to be patient. Alexandra Marie Kennedy, I love you. I know it. Honestly, I may have known since the day we met. I've made myself do things I'd never do for anyone else—like begging you to unblock me." He laughed.

Speechless, I felt tears prick my eyes. For the first time in my life, I believed someone could love me—flaws and all.

"Or wait forever for a kiss," he continued, as if he'd been rehearsing. "Or stand at a door you slammed and locked, only to come back anyway. Or show up at a bar I hate just hoping you'd be there. And thank heaven you were. Not to mention whining to my assistant about you. She didn't tell you I did that, did she?"

I laughed through the tears threatening to fall. "No. But can you tell me all of that again?"

He didn't answer. Instead, he crushed his lips to mine, giving me all the proof I needed.

In one fluid motion, he pulled me up and hurried me down the hall toward his bedroom. My heart knew there was no going back—I wanted him in every possible way. My heart was his.

At the bedside, he cupped my face, kissing me so gently I thought I might shatter. Electricity coursed through me, sparking from my lips to my toes. As much as I wanted this, the intensity unnerved me. His kisses trailed down my neck, his arms tightening at my waist. I clung to his shoulders, whispering into his ear, "I'm scared."

He froze and pulled back. "That's the last thing I want you to be right now."

"I know. I'm just so overwhelmed I feel like I'm going to be sick. The room's spinning."

"Alex." His voice softened. "Come lie down before you fall."

Bent over and breathless, I let him guide me to the bed. I collapsed face down, gasping for air. He chuckled when I moaned into the blanket, mortified.

"Oh my God. Why can't I just enjoy this? I must be driving you crazy," I muttered.

He stretched out beside me, fingers sliding gently through my hair, down my arm. "Yes, you're driving me crazy," he said with a smile in his voice, "but in a good way. The intensity is overwhelming. Clearly more for you than for me." His hand smoothed over my back until my breathing slowed.

"How about we play that game again—just touch and feel?"

I nodded against the pillow. *Love. Was that what made it different? We'd had sex before. The only new factor was love.*

He leaned close, whispering. "I'm going to give you a massage." He brushed my hair aside and rubbed my neck and shoulders, then threaded his fingers through my hair, kneading lightly.

Relief swept over me. The anxiety drained away, replaced by something warm and steady. I didn't want to think, didn't want to anticipate. I wanted only to feel.

"Surprise me," I whispered, hoping he understood.

He stilled, then resumed—slower, deliberate. My only job was to surrender, to stay in the moment. I'd never had to concentrate so hard during something as simple as this. His touch was pure electricity. It had to be the love factor. That was the difference.

He shifted, straddling the backs of my legs without putting his weight on me. His broad hands massaged lower across my spine. Then he eased up the hem of my shirt and slid his hands against bare skin, warm and sure.

I sucked in a breath. His touch was searing, not painful, but so hot it left me aching for more.

He lifted the hem of my shirt and eased it over my head. With one hand he unhooked my bra, sliding it away as his palms skimmed my breasts. My nipples hardened beneath his touch and I gasped—not from the contact itself but from what it did to me. I was terrified to turn and see him. I could imagine how much it would take just to look into those dark eyes. He had total control over me; the thought both thrilled and frightened me.

He paused for a second, and I felt the bed dip as he removed his shirt and laid down beside me. Our bodies touched; my heart hammered, and my breath came quick and shallow. He threaded his fingers through my hair and brought a strand to his face, inhaling it. Slowly, I began to calm. Maybe I was finding a comfortable place after all.

His hand hovered at my waistband, his thumb rubbing just beneath the edge. Anticipation rolled me inward until my eyes rolled back. He slipped his fingers into my pants at my hips and, in one swift movement, pulled them down, leaving only the thin band of my underwear.

There's no way, but this was better than the first time.

I heard him undo his pants and pictured him clearly—the beach, the towel, the shower—images that only fed my arousal until I felt ready. He folded the covers down and, patting my butt and commanded, "Scoot."

I wriggled under the blanket and he climbed in beside me, pressing his body to mine while still in his boxers. I summoned the courage to roll toward him and opened my eyes to find him dark and hungry. He looked worn from everything we'd been through tonight.

He wrapped his arms around me, his hands firm on my ass. I slipped a leg between his, breathed deep as he pulled my thigh over his hip, and felt a surge of something electric. My eyes fluttered closed again as I soaked in the connection.

I traced my hand along the sculpt of his arm—strong, solid—and memorized the feel before I dared to look at him. When I opened my eyes, he was staring at me, seeing straight through to whatever I tried to hide. Peace and warmth radiated from him; in that instant I felt safe and certain this would be magical.

"You good?" he asked.

Good wasn't even close. I smiled. "Yes. Sorry. That was—" I breathed. "I feel like I ran a marathon trying to get my heart rate under control."

He laughed. "You drive me crazy." Then, with a wicked tilt to his mouth, he pulled me closer. "How about I make your heart race again?"

He licked his lips and hauled me on top of him. From here, the view was all mine—broad chest, powerful shoulders. I slid my hands across him until they rested beside his face and kissed him like the world might end. His hands found my hips and ground me down; I moaned, lost to the motion. In a flurry—where our undergarments went I couldn't say—we were suddenly skin to skin, entirely devoured by one another.

He surged up over me, kissing my neck, pinning my wrists above my head with feverish need. The urgency of him carried an assuring control; he wanted to lead.

"What are you thinking about?" he groaned.

"What do you think I'm thinking about?" I laughed through it, biting my lip to keep from saying too much. He looked at me, serious.

"I'm serious. You look like you're deep in thought." He watched my face.

"Nothing important," I replied, then smirked. "But shouldn't you be deep in something right now?"

He grinned and slipped off me, his lips tracing a slow path down my skin until my breath came uneven. My hands found his hair, the world shrinking to the heat between us. Every touch felt deliberate, every breath shared.

When his mouth found mine again, the kiss deepened—slow, steady, certain. It wasn't just want anymore. It was something deeper, something that made the rest of the world fade.

He drew me closer, and we moved together in a rhythm that felt inevitable, the kind that leaves no space for thought, only feeling. The quiet of the penthouse wrapped around us like a cocoon—just the sound of our breathing, the soft brush of skin, the faint creak of the sheets beneath us.

Later, when the stillness returned, I lay against him, tracing the edge of his jaw with my fingers. It was peaceful and terrifying all at once, the kind of moment you know can't last—but wish it would.

I laid there trembling and drunk on him. There'd never be enough. Who needs wine?

The room still spun in slow, dizzy circles when I realized he was beside me, his palm resting on my stomach, tracing soft spirals.

"Oh. My. God." The words tumbled out on a shaky breath, the only ones left to me.

"My sentiments exactly." His fingers brushed a damp strand of hair from my face. "How are you?"

"I don't know where you just transported me," I whispered. "But that was... beyond. Is it always going to be like that?"

He pressed his face into the hollow of my neck, a low sound escaping his throat as sweat ran down his temple. "If it is, we're in serious trouble." His hair stuck up in wild, damp waves.

"You're not kidding." I rolled to my side and exhaled a long, shaky breath. "Thank you."

"You're thanking me?"

"Yes. No one's ever taken me there before."

His brow knit slightly, though his touch stayed gentle. "Really?"

"Really." I said with a soft laugh.

I was ruined for anyone else. Was this what it felt like to finally find *the one*?

He brought me closer, thumb stroking my hip. "Honestly, I almost didn't. You looked so shaken. I didn't want to scare you. Then I remembered the plane—how calm you were—and thought if I could bring you back to that feeling, you'd feel safe again. I just followed your cues and hoped I wasn't wrong. Was I? This was nothing like the beach," he added quietly. "What do you think changed?"

I brushed my lips to his ear. "Love happened," I whispered. This must be what safe feels like. "And you were definitely not wrong."

His chuckle vibrated against my skin.

"I worry we'll lose so much time doing this instead of everything else," I teased, fingers tracing lazy lines over his ribs.

"What should we be doing?"

"Oh, you know—life, work, friends, food, coffee. Pretty much anything but this." I giggled as his fingers grazed a ticklish spot.

His eyes darkened with mischief. "We can work it around our schedules—pre-work workouts, long lunch breaks, appetizers before dinner, dessert after. You'd look perfect across my desk."

I shoved at him, laughing until I couldn't breathe.

"Come back here." I traced patterns over his chest like sketching on warm marble.

"What are you doing?"

"Checking for airbrushing."

He caught my hand and guided it lower, a grin curving his mouth. "Here's the brush."

I snorted with laughter. He was so at ease in his own skin—every inch of him a cavewoman's ideal.

"Do you think we could do that again in the morning?" I asked, half-dazed.

"We could do it again right now," he murmured, arching an eyebrow.

"I think I'd die," I whispered. "Let me just savor this."

He studied my face, thumb brushing my cheek. "You look beautiful. Love looks good on you."

Heat rose to my cheeks. *Love.* Such a big word. I hadn't expected it so soon.

"Ditto," I said softly, because everything already looked good on him.

Chapter 37

ALEX

What an incredible dream. It felt too vivid, too real — except it wasn't a dream at all. Roman's warmth surrounded me, his touch sending sparks across my skin, and for a moment I dreaded the alarm clock shattering the spell.

I blinked awake to find him already watching me, a wicked smile playing at his mouth. His hands slid up my sides, anchoring me to the moment. "Good morning," he murmured, voice still heavy with sleep.

My breath caught. "Good morning yourself."

He kissed me before I could say more, slow and deliberate, like we had all the time in the world. The rest of the morning blurred into heat and laughter and whispered promises, his body moving against mine in a rhythm as gentle as the tide, as relentless as the sunrise. By the time we finally stilled, the room was awash in soft light.

Roman brushed a thumb over my cheek. "Still think your phone alarm's better than this?"

I laughed, still breathless. "Not even close."

He rolled onto his back, one arm flung over his eyes. "Do you still need to go to the gym?"

"Yes," I said, though my muscles had turned to jelly. "But it'll be more sauna than squats today."

"Does that count as a workout?"

"Working out your mind totally counts. Did you miss how hard mine worked last night?"

He chuckled and pulled me close again. "Fair enough. Want to swim instead?"

"I might. I may only be able to float, though."

"I know what you mean." He brushed a kiss across my forehead. "What's on your schedule?"

"Couple of calls, a Zoom meeting, lunch with the crew to celebrate Shay's promotion."

"Okay, okay," he said, mock-pouting. "No mid-day rendezvous then."

"We can christen whatever surface you want tonight," I teased.

His eyes gleamed at the promise, but I slid out of bed, tugging on a T-shirt over my swimsuit. "First things first—coffee."

He groaned theatrically. "Not yet."

I laughed, pushing him back into the pillows. My body still hummed from our morning, but reality was calling. With flip-flops slapping softly against the floor, I headed to the kitchen to brew the coffee, already looking forward to tonight.

***

Saying goodbye to Roman that morning had been harder than I'd expected. By the time I was on the road to the office, the twenty-minute commute felt like a cool-down after a sprint — a chance to catch my breath and reflect on the morning's "mental workout" in the sauna.

Meditation after swimming laps had been helping me clear the noise out of my head. It was working, too, until Roman showed up. I could think of worse ways to be interrupted. Wrapped only in a towel, I'd been trying to center myself when he slipped in behind me, whispered "Don't mind me, just keep doing what you're doing," and kissed the back of my neck.

That was the end of any serious meditation. Let's just say my towel didn't stay put for long and the steam in the sauna had nothing on us. By the time we emerged, I was blissfully lightheaded and he had the kind of grin that would carry him through his day. I'd whispered in his ear, "Now you have plenty to visualize in your office today while you try to work," and darted out before he could tempt me into round two.

Work itself was unremarkable — a couple of leads to schedule, a string of phone calls, and finally a Zoom session. Shay's lunch celebration broke up the routine. We went to the hibachi place down the street, where the chef threw shrimp at us and poured sake while we toasted her promotion to my assistant and junior realtor. By Monday, I'd finally have someone to share the load.

That night was supposed to be our regular Friday meet-up at my place, only this time Roman would be part of it. Then he called to say a zoning issue had landed on his desk and he'd have to meet me at the bar later. Fine. I wasn't sure our little ritual was his scene anyway; he fit more naturally with Abby and Maggie than with my younger work friends.

Our Friday group had been growing as everyone's lives shifted. Landon was planning to propose to Piper. Shay had started bringing Owen. Ryan had met someone new and wanted to introduce her tonight. And now I had Roman.

Sometimes I barely recognized my own life compared to the day I'd run out of gas in Burrow Township. Everything was moving forward, reshaping itself. Change still scared me, even when it was good. I wasn't sure yet how I'd handle it, only that it was already happening.

***

The drink of the evening was supposed to be Tito's and soda with lime. Mine, however, was just soda water with lime — no vodka. I'd been feeling too good about things with Roman to risk blurring it with a drunken night. When I drank too much, I had a way of saying things I didn't mean, and tonight I wanted to be fully present. No one noticed the switch, so I poured everyone else's drinks and had no questions to answer.

I'd dressed for the occasion, and, if I was honest, for Roman. A strapless black bodycon dress skimmed mid-thigh, paired with strappy heels and a smoky eye. I'd swiped on his favorite red lipstick, thinking I might leave the faintest trace on his collar, a private signal for him alone. Jealousy flickered at the thought — who even was I, plotting lipstick warnings for invisible rivals? My phone buzzed: the Uber was already here. Too late to back out now.

The entrance line at the bar snaked toward the curb, but as usual Bruce waved us in. He refused my tip, claiming I gave him enough at his studio, so I slipped the cash to Steve instead with instructions to add it to Bruce's paycheck.

Inside was its usual Friday chaos — the main bar packed two layers deep, bartenders moving like clockwork, music thumping off the brick walls.

My drink was easy tonight: soda water on the rocks with lime. The barback handed it to me with a nod. I paused at the end of the bar, setting the glass down to fish my phone from my purse. It was buzzing with a text.

ROMAN: *Sorry, the meeting ran over. Shutting it down now, then a quick change at home. See you soon.*

I smiled. This place would still be humming by the time he arrived.

ME: *We'll be on the patio out back. Too crowded inside. See you soon. xo*

A moment later:

ROMAN: *Sounds good. BTW, what are you wearing?*

I almost laughed — I'd been expecting that.

ME: *Something that won't slow us down.*

I could practically picture him at his meeting table, trying to maintain composure while mentally herding everyone out the door.

ROMAN: *I'm speechless...*

I sipped my drink, smiling to myself, imagining him in a frenzy to get here.

The texting lasted longer than I thought. I gulped the rest of my drink — the heat and noise pressing down on me. As I motioned to Steve for a refill, a wave of dizziness hit. Lightheaded. Off-balance. Maybe from all the emotions swirling around Roman and me. Maybe from that sake at lunch. But this... this was different.

I needed water on my face. The room tilted slightly as I slid off my stool, one hand brushing the wall for balance. My skin felt too tight, my pulse too loud. Each step made the floor sway beneath me.

The crowd melted into shapes and shadows—faces blurring into streaks of light. The hallway ahead seemed to stretch and shrink all at once, the music muffled and distorted, like I was hearing it through glass. A thin sheen of sweat gathered along my spine, and the air felt too thick to breathe. I pressed my palm flat against the cool wall, willing the world to steady.

What is happening?

Hands gripped my waist. A solid body pressed behind me, guiding me through a doorway. Relief flickered—Roman. It had to be. This must be one of the quiet rooms where we'd hidden before. Thank God he's here.

"Roman?" The name came out slurred. Even to my own ears it didn't sound like me. His arms were too tight, too insistent. Not the gentle touch I knew.

"Roman King?" He responded sounding more like a question than an admission.

A low laugh. "Wow, you really are a beautiful little tease, aren't you?"

Confusion clawed up my throat. That didn't sound like Roman's voice, but nothing about this was right. My tongue felt thick, my limbs heavy. I tried to protest but nothing came.

Rough hands. A voice leaning close, words I couldn't process. Horror rushed in, cold and paralyzing. Why is Roman doing this. This isn't safe.

Inside my skull I was screaming—stop, please stop—but nothing came out. No sound. My throat felt locked, my voice gone. The self-defense classes I'd taken might as well have been a dream from another life. My body wouldn't move, wouldn't fight back.

Then the pain came—sharp, blinding—splintering across my cheekbone with a sickening crack. The world tilted, dropped out from under me, a dizzying freefall before another burst of agony bloomed at the back of my head. Everything blurred—sound, light, balance—until all that existed was the pain and the helplessness pressing in from every side.

Then another voice broke through, sharp and commanding: "Get off her!"

The pressure shifted. Yelling. A crash. Light seeping back in as the weight lifted from my body. I caught a glimpse of movement — Bruce? — before everything dissolved into blackness.

Chapter 38

ROMAN

S ebastian's was never my favorite place, but Alex hadn't gone out with her work friends in a while, and they were celebrating Shay's promotion. I wanted to be there for her.

Why is this meeting still going? It's already eight-thirty and I still need to get dressed.

"If no one has solutions to these complaints, then we're done," I snapped. "I'll work on it first thing Monday morning. Nothing else can be done tonight or this weekend. Meeting adjourned."

I left the office in a hurry, changed into jeans and a T-shirt, and headed for the bar. Reading her text over and over, I could only imagine what she was wearing, and the thought of her in that meat market without me had my gut clenched. She could wear whatever she wanted, of course. But there were men out there who didn't know how to treat a woman. Men like Tanner Ellington.

I had one of my drivers drop me off and told him to take the night off. When we pulled up, red and blue lights strobed across the street — an ambulance and two police cars out front. Bruce wasn't at his usual post.

I tried texting Alex again. No answer. Maybe she couldn't hear her phone over the noise, but the dread rose anyway.

Inside, the bar was chaos. Patrons pressed shoulder-to-shoulder, the music shut off mid-song, everyone craning to see. Steve wiped his hands on a bar towel, his eyes darting toward the back. "We're closing early tonight," he said when I asked what was happening.

"Steve, have you seen Alex?"

He shook his head. "Not sure where she is."

Not good.

I pushed toward the patio but was stopped by a line of police officers holding the crowd back. Bruce stepped forward, his face pale.

"You can't go in there, man!"

My stomach turned to stone. "Is it Alex?" My voice cracked on her name.

Bruce's eyes flicked away, then back. He didn't have to say the word.

Beyond the crowd, officers escorted a man in handcuffs — and even from here I recognized him. Tanner Ellington. A smile on his face.

Rage flooded my veins. Before I knew it, I was surging forward, ready to tear him apart, and Bruce had me by the shoulders.

"What did he do to her?" I growled through clenched teeth.

"I don't know," Bruce said, his voice low. "I called the police and held him until they got here. One of the waitresses stayed with Alex."

My chest tightened as paramedics wheeled Alex past on a gurney, her face pale and eyes closed. Bruce released me just as I grabbed at one of the EMT's sleeves, desperate for information. The medic shook me off.

"Sir, step back," someone barked, but the words blurred. All I could see was Alex disappearing into the ambulance, and all I could think was that I hadn't been there when she needed me most.

"Hey, this is her boyfriend—he needs to go with her," Bruce called out. The EMT gave a curt nod and waved me inside.

In the ambulance I fumbled for my phone, realizing I didn't have any of her family's numbers. I called Matt, asked him to tell Maggie, and hoped she could reach Alex's family.

At the hospital they moved quickly—ER room, monitors, IVs. They made me wait outside while they worked. I stood staring at the closed door, heart hammering.

When they finally let me back in, Alex lay still under a thin blanket. Machines blinked at her bedside. I wanted to hold her hand but they were both pinned under wires and cuffs.

"What's wrong with her?" I asked the doctor the second he stepped in.

"It looks like she's been drugged, judging by her pupils," he said, eyes on a tablet. "We won't know for certain until toxicology comes back. Whatever it was, it's potent. Her body's not handling it well."

"Is she going to be all right?" My voice cracked. Heat crawled up my face as tears burned my eyes.

"It could be an allergic reaction or her body rejecting whatever was in her system," he said quietly. "We'll know more soon. I'm sorry I don't have more for you right now."

"Mr. King," the doctor said, touching my shoulder. "Step into the hall with me. The nurses need room to work."

I followed him out, palms sweaty, mind spiraling.

"Do you have any idea what happened tonight?" he asked.

"No," I rasped. "I got there as they were wheeling her out."

The noise in the hallway dimmed until it felt like we were underwater. Through the door's small window I could see nurses moving around Alex.

The doctor placed a steadying hand on my shoulder. "They're performing an assault exam," he said gently. "We'll know more in about an hour."

I sagged against the wall as he walked away, the words echoing. A nurse came to explain what the exam entailed, her voice soft and practiced, but the details melted together. My stomach heaved. I pressed my elbows to my knees and buried my face in my hands.

"We've contacted her emergency contact, Patricia Kennedy," the nurse said. "She'll be here within the hour."

"Good," I murmured. "It might help if her mom is here when she wakes up."

An hour and a half later, Patricia still hadn't arrived. Abby and Maggie sat with me now in the harshly lit waiting room, the three of us waiting for any scrap of news.

"We called her dad and her brothers, but no one answered," Maggie said. "We had to leave messages."

Ten o'clock on a Friday night and no one could be reached. Where was everyone? No one had shown up yet. The only good news so far was the doctor telling us the assault exam had come back negative.

"Thank God," Abby whispered, rubbing my arm. I leaned back against the wall, palms over my face, letting out a breath I was pretty sure I'd been holding since I arrived.

Sirens wailed outside the ER. An ambulance screeched to a stop, and paramedics shouted updates as they wheeled in a patient. Nurses converged, calling for a surgeon.

"Car accident—critical," someone said as they raced past with the gurney. The attending doctor jogged alongside. "Get her to OR Two," he ordered before vanishing through a set of double doors.

The three of us glanced instinctively toward the commotion. It's hard not to look when catastrophe rushes by on wheels. I caught a flash of the woman on the gurney—dark hair, pale face—but Abby gasped as though struck.

"What is it? Who was it?" I grabbed her shoulders.

She broke free and hurried to the nurses' station. "Oh my God—can you tell me if the woman who just came in is Patty Kennedy? Patricia?" Her voice cracked. "She's Alex's emergency contact. We've been waiting more than two hours for her to arrive."

The nurse hesitated. "Are you a relative?"

"Yes," Abby lied without blinking. "Alex is my sister."

The nurse darted down the hall. When she returned a minute later, her expression told us before her words did.

"Yes. It was Patricia Kennedy. We've already notified her husband." She pressed a hand over her mouth.

Maggie's eyes filled with tears. "We only got voicemail when we tried to call..." Her voice trembled.

Abby stepped closer, her face draining of color. "Did you just say was Patricia? You mean is?"

The nurse swallowed hard. "They just called time of death."

Everything went still.

Abby let out a strangled sob. Maggie reached for her, but she looked as pale as Abby now.

My own knees gave out. I slid down the wall, hands locked behind my head. The words "time of death" echoed in the hallway, unreal, impossible. We'd been waiting for Patricia Kennedy to walk through the doors and instead she'd been wheeled past us under fluorescent lights.

***

Hank, Patrick, and Edward came rushing up to the nurses' station, faces flushed and eyes wild. By then, Alex's friends and I had managed to compose ourselves after what felt like hours. The staff had finished their tests and finally let us back in to see her. We were sitting at her bedside when the shouting started in the hallway.

I stepped out before the nurse could answer any questions and held up a hand. "It's okay," I said quietly. "I'll talk to them."

"Hank," I called. "Alex is in here."

He froze. "It's Alex? Where's Patty? I thought we got a call about Patty!"

I laid a hand on his shoulder. "Let's talk in the waiting room. Abby and Maggie are with Alex."

We walked down the hall to an empty row of chairs. Hank's steps slowed, Patrick's fists clenched, and Edward's jaw worked like he was holding something back.

"What the hell happened to Alex?" Hank asked.

I gave them the condensed version, the only way I could force the words out. Edward punched the wall. Patrick's face went red with tears, and Hank dropped into a chair, shaking.

I drew a breath, bracing myself for the next blow I had to deliver. "Patty was called as Alex's emergency contact," I said. "She never made it here. She was in an accident on the way."

My voice sounded flat, like it belonged to someone else.

Hank's eyes squeezed shut. "I couldn't understand her message," he murmured. "She must've been drinking... Oh my God. Was anyone else involved?"

They'd been at the golf course all day, they said — the reception at the clubhouse was poor, so none of the calls had come through until they stepped outside.

"I don't know any details," I said softly. "They haven't told us yet."

Hank surged out of his chair, striding back toward the nurses' station for answers. Patrick and Edward stayed rooted, stunned, while I stood there feeling like a shell, every sound in the hallway echoing around us.

Edward's eyes were red-rimmed, bright with fury. "Roman, did this piece of garbage hurt Alex? You know what I mean."

I did. My stomach twisted at the memory of the nurses moving around Alex's still body, the quiet urgency in the ER.

"He drugged her with something," I said carefully. "and hit her. She's got a concussion from where she fell and hit her head. They're working to stabilize her. The assault exam was negative." My voice cracked. Rage coiled through me, hotter than anything I'd ever felt.

"Who is he?" Edward's jaw clenched, grief and rage bleeding together.

"Tanner Ellington. We've had problems with him—both professionally and... personally."

"What kind of personal?"

I exhaled through my teeth. "He made an unwanted advance a few weeks ago. Alex made it clear she wasn't interested. I thought that was the end of it." Guilt burned at the edges of the memory. Why hadn't I been there tonight?

"Roman," Edward pressed, gripping my elbow, "just tell me what happened."

"He grabbed her inappropriately," I said, choosing my words with care. "And told her what else he wanted."

Edward's mouth twisted into a bitter half-smile. "And how did that end for him?"

"You know your sister," I said quietly.

He gave a dry laugh. "Were you dating her then?"

"No. But I saw it happen. Broke his nose for him."

Edward nodded once. "Thank you for that. Has he been arrested?"

"Yes," I said, though my mind flicked to the man's powerful brother. "But Marcus Ellington's a crooked politician. I'm worried Tanner won't stay behind bars for long."

Edward's voice dropped to a near whisper. "Then I guess I'll be paying him a visit."

We shook hands just as Hank returned, eyes swollen, asking to see Alex. Patrick still hadn't spoken a word. He followed his father into the room.

Edward and I stayed outside, listening as Abby and Maggie murmured comfort to Hank. Patrick stood behind his father with a hand on his shoulder, tears streaking down both their faces. In one night they'd lost a mother, a wife, and nearly a daughter and sister—all because of one man's violence.

***

ALEX

It was so quiet here. So impossibly quiet that silence itself seemed to glow. All around me stretched a boundless white expanse—no horizon, no ceiling, only light that shimmered like mist. The air felt warm but weightless, like standing inside a cloud.

I glanced down. A white gown draped from my shoulders to the floor, soft as moonlight, brushing over bare feet. I should have been terrified, but a hush of calm wrapped around me, steady and sure.

A ripple moved through the light. Someone was coming.

"Mama?" I whispered—except I didn't. My lips hadn't moved, yet the sound arrived full and clear, ringing through the space like a bell.

And then she was there. My mother.

She glowed with the same light but brighter, like sunlight caught in a prism. Her white gown moved without wind, and her hair shone with an iridescent halo. She looked younger, stronger, more luminous than any memory I had of her.

"Hi, Ali Marie," she said, and her voice landed directly inside my mind, not in my ears.

I pressed my hands to my heart. "Mama, you're perfect."

Warmth spilled over me in a tide of recognition, an ache and a balm at once. She reached toward me with her eyes, though not with her hands, and I understood—here, love required no touch.

"Mama, what's going on? Am I dreaming?"

A smile curved her lips. *Everything's fine, sweetheart. You're going to be okay. It's time to wake up now.* Her words bloomed in my chest rather than the air.

Wake up? I reached toward her. The white between us stretched, as though she were floating backward on an invisible current.

"No—wait, please," I cried without sound. "Wake up from what? Don't leave me yet."

Her gown shimmered like starlight as she receded. She turned once more, and for an instant our eyes met, the full weight of her love wrapping around me like a blanket.

Wake up, Ali Marie. I love you, sweet girl. It's going to be okay.

Her voice was the last thing left as the white world thinned, and I felt myself being pulled toward something heavier, darker—back to the place where breathing mattered.

Chapter 39

ROMAN

Alex had been unconscious for three days. The doctors still couldn't name the substance in her system, but her vitals were stable and her organs untouched. All she needed now, they said, was time and rest.

I lived at the hospital, going home only long enough to shower and change. I'd had her moved to a private room and arranged for a second bed so I could stay close. Each day I swore I could feel her inching back toward me — her skin warmer, her breathing stronger — like a tide turning beneath the surface. I kept telling myself she'd open her eyes soon.

Her friends and colleagues came and went in shifts. The room filled with flowers and cards, vases crowding every ledge, the air perfumed with lilies and roses. The hospital staff started calling it the garden room. Alex's mother's funeral was set for Friday, everyone hoping she'd be awake in time. I tried not to imagine her reaction when she learned her mother was gone.

My parents visited once. My mother lingered at Alex's bedside, fingertips hovering just above her arm as if she could will her awake. "She's getting stronger," she said softly. But then her eyes flicked to mine. "It won't be an easy return for her."

Anger still burned under my skin. I wanted to make Tanner Ellington pay. Every few hours I'd step outside to walk off the rage before it swallowed me whole.

One afternoon, after one of those cool-off walks, I returned to find two strangers standing in the hall outside her door. They were immaculately dressed — a man and woman in tailored suits, understated jewelry, the quiet confidence of old money. They didn't look like family, and they certainly didn't look like hospital visitors.

I hesitated, too drained to slip away, and pushed the door open. They followed, introducing themselves as Mr. and Mrs. Santoro. Important clients of Alex's, they said; the office had told them where she was. She'd been working to find them property for a new winery but kept running into zoning issues.

Their presence felt almost surreal in the antiseptic room — another reminder of Alex's life waiting just outside this suspended moment, a life full of plans and promises she'd made before everything stopped.

"Let me guess—Marcus Ellington?" My voice came out flatter and more tired than I intended.

Mr. Santoro's eyes flicked up in surprise. "How did you know? Did Alex tell you?"

"She told me she was having issues, yes," I said. "She didn't mention it was you. My construction company's been tangled up with the same zoning nightmares. Coming after me is one thing. Coming after her is something else entirely." I let out a slow breath. "Believe it or not, his brother is the reason she's in here."

Mr. Santoro leaned forward, brow furrowing. "What? How is he involved?"

I hesitated, then decided to give him the truth. "He drugged her at the bar Friday night and tried to assault her. People found her in time, but she reacted badly to whatever he gave her. She hasn't woken up yet."

Mrs. Santoro's hand flew to her chest. "Oh, dear Lord," she whispered in a thick Italian accent. "Why would he do such a thing?"

"She'd had a run-in with him a few weeks ago," I said, voice tight. "Another unwanted advance. It humiliated him, apparently."

A single tear slid down Mrs. Santoro's cheek. She closed her eyes, lips moving soundlessly. She clutched something in her fist against her heart, and it took me a moment to realize she was praying.

"You never harm a woman," Mr. Santoro said, shaking his head. "Alex is a remarkable person. I left Italy to escape certain...things. But I am still a protected member of my family. I have connections." His gaze fixed on mine. "It sounds like you may need my help to deal with predators like this."

I blinked, unsure I'd heard him correctly. Connected Italian family? That was the stuff of films, not hospitals. Surely he just meant he had influence, money. Right?

He leaned closer. "Let me give you my number. We will talk privately soon."

This is also a family matter for me—I thought.

I shook his hand, a strange heat running up my spine. In that moment, anger made the decision for me: I would do whatever it took to protect Alex and her family. Mrs. Santoro hugged me, then leaned over and kissed Alex's forehead, laying a small gold cross on her chest before leaving.

That night, after everyone had gone and I'd finished sorting through emails and Amelia's notes, the room went quiet. I glanced over at Alex. She was moving—hands twitching, her face shifting from joy to sadness to joy again as though she were dreaming.

Then, suddenly, she stilled. A faint, gentle smile broke across her lips. Slowly, her eyes opened.

It had been four days. My chair clattered back as I ran for the nurses' station. "She's awake!"

A team of nurses and a doctor swept into the room, checking vitals, asking questions, pushing me to the hall while they worked. My body ached from days of keeping vigil, and I stretched against the corridor wall, heart pounding, waiting for them to finish.

At last they cleared the room. I stepped back in, dropped into the chair beside her bed, and took her hand. "Hey there," I said softly. "Welcome back."

Her brow furrowed. "Welcome back from where?"

A fair question.

"Not sure, honey. You've been out for four days."

She looked at me, panic flickering across her face, as though she'd been somewhere far away and wasn't sure she wanted to be back.

"What happened to me?" Alex's voice was hoarse but sharp. She jerked her hand out of mine as though it burned.

I hesitated. "Do you want to hear it from me, or from the doctor?"

Her face drained of color. Terror flared in her eyes.

"Get away from me," she cried. "Don't touch me. Someone help me—"

The words knifed through me. What was happening? Why was she looking at me like I was the enemy?

The door burst open. Nurses, a doctor, and two uniformed officers surged inside.

"Get him away from me!" she screamed, voice rising and breaking. "How could you? How could you?"

My heart stopped. She thinks it was me.

The police moved in, steering me toward the hall. My own voice felt like a stranger's. "Alex, no—"

"Mr. King," one of the officers said, blocking my path. We'd already been over this. I thought it was clear I'd had nothing to do with what happened.

"Why does Ms. Kennedy think you were the one who assaulted her?" he demanded, face inches from mine.

"I have no idea. I wasn't even there."

He glanced at his notes. "We talked to the bouncer and the bartender. They say it was this Mr. Ellington. Are they covering for you?"

"Covering for me?" I stared at him. "I just met them. They're Alex's friends. Why would they cover for me?"

His partner shifted his weight, hand hovering near his weapon. "Sir, we need you to come down to the station for questioning."

"You're calling me a suspect?" I said, voice climbing. "You think I did this to her? My secretary can verify the time I left work. I'm not going anywhere."

The second officer's hand moved closer to his holster.

"Sir, don't make this—"

"Officer, I'll take it from here."

A new voice cut through the tension. A woman stepped forward — mid-thirties, long dark hair in a ponytail, plain blazer over a crisp shirt. She held out her badge.

"Mr. King?" she asked.

"Yes. Who are you, and what the hell is going on?"

"I'm Detective Danielle Lewis, CPD." She offered her hand. I took it reluctantly.

"What's happening?"

"Alex seems to think it was you in the room with her," she said gently. "She said the man identified himself as you. We know she was drugged with a hallucinogenic — it's been showing up on the street as a so-called 'designer date-rape' drug. It can cause confusion and false memories."

Bile rose in my throat. Designer date-rape. What kind of world was this?

"So you're aware it wasn't me?"

She nodded. "We know you weren't even in the building when the assault occurred."

"Then why were your guys trying to drag me to the station?"

"They're covering all bases," she said calmly. "The paperwork's ugly but it protects everyone. They weren't doing it for nothing."

I exhaled hard. "So what happens now?"

Detective Lewis's expression softened. "Mr. King, it's best if you go home and rest. The doctors will take good care of Alex. We'll make sure she's watched."

Watched. Why? If they'd arrested Ellington, was she still in danger?

"Fine," I said. "Is there any way for me to check on her? Can I call you at least?"

She nodded, handed me her card. I slipped it into my pocket, the weight of it feeling like a promise and a threat at once.

Then I stepped into the cool night air and called Harrison.

***

ALEX

The nurses held my arms as I thrashed, their palms like anchors against my trembling skin.

"Get him out of here!" I screamed. Pain knifed through my skull; nausea rose in my throat. I held my breath, trying not to throw up. The air itself hurt. I couldn't even look at him—being this close was unbearable.

The cops ushered him from the room. I caught a final glimpse of his shoulders as he vanished through the door. Watching him leave cracked something inside me. How could he? After everything. After telling me he loved me. He's just like Luke. Luke said he loved me, too, and look how that ended.

A pinch in my arm. My limbs went heavy, then nothing.

When I opened my eyes again, the room was hushed, low light glowing from a single lamp. My arms and legs felt like stone, my head still swimming. Why would they have sedated me? Why would they leave me vulnerable—with him here?

"Ms. Kennedy?"

I blinked at the woman standing in the shadows. No scrubs. No badge. Just a plain blazer and long dark hair pulled back in a ponytail.

"Who are you?" My voice cracked, barely a whisper.

"I'm Detective Lewis. I've been assigned to your case. How are you feeling?"

"My case," I murmured. "Victim." The word caught in my throat. Tears ran down my cheeks before I realized they'd started.

"Can you tell me anything about Friday night?" Her voice was gentle, not pushing.

Everything was foggy. Memories felt out of reach. "I remember being at my apartment. Vodka soda was the drink of the night. I wanted to see if being sober with Roman made things... better. So I left the vodka out of mine."

"What kind of drinks did you have?"

"Soda water," I said, my chest tightening.

"Nothing mixed in?"

"No. Just water. Did that not show up in the toxicology report? Did it say I was drunk?" My voice rose. "I thought I was drugged. Roman drugged me." The monitor beside me beeped faster.

"I'll review the doctor's report," Detective Lewis said, jotting a note. Her eyes flicked up at me, cautious.

"It was water," I repeated.

"Alex," she said slowly, "why do you think it was Roman who did this to you?"

"Because he said so." I tried to piece it together. "I couldn't see anything. I asked if it was him and he said yes—Roman King. He even said his last name. Who else would it be?"

She studied me, expression caught between pity and concern. "Alex..."

"Ali Marie—oh my God. Thank God you're awake."

My father's voice cut through the fog. He barreled into the room with my brothers on his heels.

"I'll come back later," Detective Lewis said quietly, retreating toward the door.

"How are you feeling, sweet pea?" Dad asked, his voice rough, eyes wet.

"I'm fine, Dad. It's not a big deal, I promise nothing is wrong with me." My voice sounded small and hoarse even to my own ears. "Did Mom come? Is she getting coffee or something?"

I scanned the room, searching for her familiar silhouette. I needed my mom to see I was okay—needed her to calm down before she used this as another excuse to drown her sorrows. But Dad just looked at me like he was holding his breath. His face flushed red, tears carving down his cheeks.

I blinked. "I said I'm fine. Why are you crying?"

He swallowed hard. "Yeah... let me go out to the nurse's station real quick."

A strange shiver passed through me. Why was he acting so weird? Where was Mom? She would've been the first one through the door. She never would have left my side—unless she was too drunk to function.

Dad returned a few minutes later with a nurse at his shoulder. A bad feeling coiled low in my gut. My chest tightened; beads of sweat gathered along my hairline. Dad reached for my hand, holding it so tight I couldn't tell if he was trying to steady me or himself.

"Sweet pea," he whispered, voice breaking, "the nurse is going to tell you something difficult. I'd tell you myself, but..." His hand trembled. "I can't bring myself to say it yet."

He looked shattered, as if a single word might undo him completely.

I turned to the nurse, my heart pounding. "Please," I said, more demand than request. "Tell me what's going on."

She hesitated, eyes soft with sympathy. "Alex..." Her voice dropped. "Your mother was in an accident on the way here. She... she didn't make it."

The words floated toward me but refused to land. "But that can't be," I whispered. "She was here with me before I woke up. She told me everything was going to be okay. She told me it was time to wake up."

My chest squeezed. The room spun. Bile surged up my throat. The nurse thrust a plastic basin into my hands just in time for me to vomit.

When I could finally lift my head, my father was doubled over, his forehead pressed to the mattress near my leg. His fingers clutched mine, shaking, refusing to let go.

What have I done? This is all my fault. If I'd never gotten out of my car that day, none of this would have happened. How do you fix this? How do you fix death?

Chapter 40

ROMAN

"Hello?" Harrison's voice came rough and low, like he'd been dragged from a dead sleep.

"Hey, it's me." My keys clattered onto the kitchen counter as I collapsed onto the sofa. I didn't even untie my shoes. The apartment smelled like stale coffee and rain from an open window, but I couldn't move to close it. Everything in me felt used up—especially now, with Alex believing I'd done the unthinkable.

"What time is it?" he asked, his words thick.

I stared at the ceiling, too hollow to guess. A glance at my watch blurred. "Five. Sorry, man. Five in the morning."

"No, it's fine." A pause, then a muffled rustle, like he'd sat up. "How's Alex? Is she awake yet?"

Somewhere behind his voice a woman murmured, but I ignored it. Whatever he was doing with his days didn't matter; mine had just fallen apart.

"Yeah. She's awake." My voice cracked. I pinched the bridge of my nose and threw my arm over my eyes, trying to hold myself together. The image of her face—eyes wide, voice trembling, screaming for me to get out—was seared into me.

"You don't sound too excited about that," he said, fully awake now. "What's going on?"

"She woke up thinking I attacked her."

Silence.

"Excuse me?" Harrison's voice snapped, electric now. "What did you just say?"

"You heard me." My throat tightened. "The drugs in her system were hallucinogens. She thought it was me."

"Christ." His voice went hoarse. "Did someone set her straight? The police know it's not you, right?"

"Yeah, they know. Detective Lewis said they're certain I wasn't even in the building." I pressed my fingers into my eye sockets, like pressure alone could stop the memory. "I don't know what they've told her. She threw me out before I could find out anything. The detective told me to go home."

"Are you home now?"

"Yes."

Another pause, softer this time. "Do you want me to come over? Is there something I can do for you?"

I stared at the far wall, where Alex's jacket still hung from a hook, like a ghost. My chest ached. "No. I'm probably going to take the day off and try to sleep. Can you handle the office?"

"Of course. Take tomorrow off too if you need to."

"Thanks, Harrison." My voice caught on his name.

"Roman," he said quietly, all the bluster gone. "I'm sorry, man."

I couldn't answer. The line went silent, only our breathing filling the space, and for the first time in days I felt the full weight of what had happened. The apartment seemed too big, the night too long, and the distance between Alex and me—unthinkably wide.

***

ALEX

I'd already talked to the police at the hospital, and a counselor too. But Dr. King? No. Not with my head still fogged by medication and fractured memories.

The police surprised me with their concern, especially Detective Danielle Lewis from CPD's Personal Crimes unit. She guided me through what happened, her tone steady and low. She swore Roman hadn't done this. I wanted to believe her. I'd heard him. Or thought I had. Maybe it was the drugs. Maybe it wasn't. That uncertainty lodged like a splinter I couldn't pull free.

Still, she was the only one I trusted. When I asked about the Burrow Township officers, she leaned in, gave me a clipped, off-the-record rundown. Her suspicions mirrored mine. At least one cop wasn't protecting the others. That tiny crack of light felt like oxygen.

The counselor, on the other hand, wanted me to book an appointment to "process my trauma." Not happening. Lisette was the only person I could talk to, and even with her, I needed to sort the noise in my own head first.

If Tanner really did this, why say he was Roman? Did he know about us? The thought kept looping, a slow-motion siren in my skull.

Dad came for me after discharge. Instead of taking me to his house, he drove me to my apartment. "I need my own space," I said, and he didn't argue. I promised to come over tomorrow. What I didn't say: tonight belonged to silence, wine, and trying to breathe without choking on memory.

My aunt was at my parents' place. I should have been there, but I couldn't. Not yet.

I let myself into my apartment, closed the door, and reached for a bottle. Wine into a glass. Glass to my lips. A toast to the memories. Another to forgetting.

***

The alarm never went off.

I woke on the couch still in yesterday's clothes, a wineglass slack in my hand and two empty bottles staring at me from the coffee table. This is where I'm at now. Eight a.m. instead of five. The gym wasn't happening. Not with the room tilting like this. I still tasted last night on my tongue.

I dragged myself to the bathroom, toothbrush in hand. The mint foam made me gag, my stomach heaving against it. One glance in the mirror told the truth—bloodshot eyes, bruised shadows under them, a face gone gray around the edges.

I stepped into the shower, hoping the heat might rinse off whatever clung to me. Instead the water only sharpened the nausea. I lurched out, dripping, and barely made it to the toilet. Everything in me came up at once until my eyes burned and my skull pulsed. I folded my arms on the rim, forehead pressed to porcelain, waiting for the spinning to stop.

When I woke again, I was on the bathroom floor. Somehow I crawled to the bedroom, curled into a ball on the edge of the bed, and passed out.

Hours later, I surfaced—lighter but empty, my body wrung out. Mentally, emotionally, spiritually shredded. The gold cross someone had left on my hospital bed flashed in my mind. Yellow gold with thorn-like filigree, delicate and strange. No one knew where it came from. I'd tossed it into my jewelry box the moment I got home. Out of sight, as if that would keep it from meaning anything.

I reached for my phone, a list of calls in my head, but stopped cold at the screen. Missed calls. Messages from Roman. My stomach clenched. I heard him. I know I did. His voice saying his name. I can't call him back. Not yet. Maybe not ever.

The tears came again, hot and unstoppable. "To hell with this day," I yelled, the words tearing out of me. It only sharpened the ache in my head.

By the time I reached the real estate office, I'd pieced myself together just enough to walk inside. A weak smile for anyone who looked up, eyes fixed on the hallway to Grant's office. He stood the moment he saw me, shutting the door behind us before pulling me into his arms. No questions. Just warmth. I pressed my face into his chest, sobs breaking loose and muffled against his shirt. He held me without speaking, one steady hand between my shoulder blades.

When the tears eased, he set a bottle of water and a box of tissues in front of me. We sat on the sofa, and I laid it out—everything I'd been told about that night, the doubts eating me alive. Then I told him I was handing all my clients over to him and wanted Shay to take over as his assistant. Train her. Run the office without me.

"You know how much we're going to miss you, sweetheart," he said softly, "but take all the time you need."

I sniffled into a tissue, my voice breaking. "Grant, I've been so blessed to be part of your team."

He caught my gaze, eyes full of concern. "We're the ones who've been blessed to have you, Alex and this is still your team."

Silent tears blurred the edges of the room. I could only nod, hug him one last time, and walk out without looking back.

Shay, Landon, and Ryan stood near reception, waiting. We shared quick, trembling hugs, tears sliding down their cheeks as I hurried for the door. Outside, in the car, I let my forehead drop to the steering wheel and gasped through another wave of sobs before forcing myself back onto the road.

When I pulled into Dad's driveway, my aunt was already on the front porch swing, a beer in her hand, watching me with quiet eyes.

"Hello, Ali girl. How you holding up?"
She was on the porch swing, sipping her beer, eyes fixed somewhere past the yard—glazed and unreadable.

"Not so good. You?"

She smirked, finally shifting her gaze toward me. "I'd say we're about the same."

I sat down beside her, let my head fall onto her shoulder. The swing creaked beneath us, back and forth, back and forth. For a few minutes, the motion almost calmed the noise inside my head.

Dad came out, rubbing his hands on a rag. "Ali Marie, I didn't know you were here."

I jumped up and wrapped my arms around him, grateful for the anchor he still was. "Just got here. Thought I'd check on you two," I teased, hugging tighter. Dad used to laugh at lines like that. I hoped some part of him still could.

"That's nice," he said, stepping back to study me, "but we should be the ones checking on you."

"I'm fine," I said, aiming for calm but feeling my face betray me.

"What happened to you was anything but fine." His voice had a new edge—anger twisting his features. Humor gone.

"It was a cheap shot. I'm going to press charges, don't worry, alright?"

My aunt's head snapped up. She stood, storming toward us. "Pressing charges against who? For what?"

I turned to Dad, stunned. "She doesn't know?"

Dad's face sagged. "I thought you should tell her. It makes me sick thinking about what could've happened to you."

Great. Another round of reliving this nightmare. Why was I always the one who had to say it?

"Dad, get that crazy shit out of your head. Nothing happened." Heat crawled up my neck.

"Nothing happened?" he roared. "You were unconscious for four days. That's not nothing."

So now he could yell, now he could stand up to me. Perfect.

"Okay, Dad, enough. I'm going inside to get a drink."

My aunt's footsteps followed. "Ali Marie, you stop right there and turn the hell around."

I exhaled hard, pasted on a smile, and rolled my eyes as I pivoted back. "Yes?"

Her face was cold as stone—she was the only one I couldn't snap at.

"Grab me a beer, get yourself a drink, and get your ass back out here. You're going to tell me what the hell is going on."

Another forced smile, another huff. I did as told.

When I finally laid it out, her face went ghost white. She was furious no one had told her sooner. I even confessed about seeing Mom when I'd been drifting awake in the hospital. For the first time all evening, she smiled—soft and small, like she understood something I didn't.

"I know she was there. She loved you so much. I know she had her issues, but she would've done anything for you. It's a shame her demons got the best of her. She was a wonderful person. Alexandra, don't let this deter you from having a good life, do you hear me? Don't let the demons win."

I wanted to tell her I thought they already had. Instead, I said nothing about Roman. When she asked, I only told her I needed space. She nodded, weary, like she understood that "space" meant he was out of the picture.

The funeral was set for Friday. Just thinking about it numbed me. I didn't know how to say goodbye. Mom had told me everything was going to be okay. Right now it didn't feel like it.

My phone rang. *Santoro* scrolled across the screen. Apparently no one had called them yet. I forced myself to answer. "Hello, Alex Kennedy." My smile felt brittle. The energy it took to sound normal was exhausting. Maybe that's why Mom drank so much.

"Alexandra, my dear, how are you? I'm so sorry to hear about your mother."

"Thank you. I truly appreciate your kind words." I took a breath. "Mr. Santoro, has Grant reached out to you yet?" Maybe they'd call him from now on.

"Yes, dear. We came to see you in the hospital. Roman was there. Very nice young man. He told us what happened. I am so sorry."

I blinked. They'd been there? What version had Roman given them?

"Roman told you?"

"No details. He just shared some interesting information about the person who did it."

So Roman had said something—out of anger, maybe. I could understand that. But why did Mr. Santoro sound angry? I barely knew him. And why did they feel they needed to visit me there?

"Mr. Santoro, you're in great hands with Grant. I'm sure he'll take care of everything and find the perfect spot for your new winery. I'm looking forward to patronizing the place." Hell, it's a winery. Of course I'll patronize the place—probably too often.

I think he got the hint that I wasn't up for more.

"Absolutely, Alexandra. We hope that you and Roman will be our first guests."

Maybe, but not together we won't. "Thank you. That's very sweet."

Before I could say goodbye he added, "Oh, did you get the gift my wife left you?"

"What gift?"

"A little gold cross. She said she felt like you might need it."

Relief loosened something in my chest. So it hadn't come from nowhere after my dream of Mom.

"Yes—please tell her thank you. She's probably right." It was exactly the kind of gesture I'd expect from them.

We said our goodbyes as I pulled into valet.

The elevator ride was heavy with memories of leaning against Roman's shoulder, his arms wrapped around me. This was going to be harder than I thought.

"Hey, Mags."

"Alex—oh God—are you okay? Are you still at the hospital?"

"No, I'm home."

"Hey girl."

"Hi, Abby." I paused, took a breath. "I'm going to take a break from brunch for a bit. Is that okay?"

"Yeah, that's fine. Whatever you need," Maggie said.

"Um, what about the kickboxing and self-defense classes? Are you still going to take them?" Abby asked.

"Yeah. I think that's a good idea."

"Do you care if we stay in them?" Abby pressed. She hated what she called my "silent treatment."

"No, of course not. I feel better knowing you girls can protect yourselves anyway."

I informed Matt I was out of the meetings about the neighborhood and told him to contact Grant for real estate matters.

The last thing on my list was meeting Bruce at the MMA studio to talk about what happened. He'd scheduled a police officer to teach a class on spotting drugs in drinks and reading the warning signs.

***

It was Friday morning—Mom's funeral.

I moved like an empty vessel, skin over stone. I could almost pretend we hadn't spoken in a while. We'd done that before—silent stretches after fights. But today was different. Today was final. We were burying her, and I'd never get another chance to apologize, forgive, or simply say I love you. The last words between us had been my anger in a restaurant on vacation. Now they were carved into the past, unchangeable.

In the shower I crumbled to the floor, water pounding down, sobs folding into steam.

Edward was picking everyone up in his big Suburban to take us to the funeral home. I didn't care who else would be there. The only person I wanted was gone, existing only in spirit.

My heart wasn't just broken; it was shattered, the pieces slicing through me like glass. Mom would've hated my outfit—black dress, black heels, black sunglasses, no makeup. She'd taught me color therapy. *When I die, you need to have a party. No black.* I couldn't do it. Not after the way she died—on her way to me—leaving me paralyzed with guilt.

The funeral service passed in a blur. Abby's face. Maggie's arms. Everything else dissolved into white noise.

At the cemetery, after the handfuls of dirt, I only wanted to leave. No condolences, no pity. I took off my glasses to wipe my eyes and felt it—a prickle along my spine. Someone watching.

Roman.

I hadn't known he was coming. After the hospital, I hadn't dared to expect him. Our eyes locked. My heart skittered out of rhythm. The pull between us still burned, alive and dangerous. I had to look away.

I hurried toward my brother's car, yanking my hand free from my aunt's grip. Edward stood with Bianca near the SUV. He reached for me as I stumbled up.

"Alex—"

He caught me and I shoved at his chest, panic and grief spilling into fury. I swung again, fists landing against muscle.

"Stop," he barked, catching my wrists. "Just stop."

He pulled my arms across my back, holding me until the fight went out of me. My wail broke loose against his shoulder, raw and unguarded. He said nothing, just held me steady while the sobs rattled through me. When I finally sagged, he guided me into the back seat.

I wiped at my face, staring out the tinted window. Across the cemetery, Roman was still there—and my aunt was already walking toward him.

***

ROMAN

My mom told me not to go to the funeral. So of course, I went.

I leaned against my car, hands in my pockets, watching Alex throw a handful of dirt onto her mother's grave, wiping her palms on the napkin her brother passed her. When she lifted her sunglasses, our eyes met.

Even swollen from grief, she was still the most beautiful woman I'd ever seen. Those eyes—my anchor and my undoing—still held the love I'd felt from her, and for one dizzy second, hope cracked open inside me. Then she dropped her glasses back into place and ran.

A gut punch. After everything we'd been through, how could she still believe I could do something like that to her? I watched her with her brother, then caught a glimpse of her aunt cutting across the grass with purpose.

Shit. I lowered my head. Did they all think I did this too? Should I leave before this turned into a scene—or stay and defend why I was here?

I stayed.

"Hi, Diana," I said as evenly as I could manage, forcing a calm I didn't feel.

"Hi, Roman. How are you, honey?" She reached out and rubbed my arm. Not the reaction I'd expected.

"Not so good," I admitted. "How is she?"

"She's having a rough time."

"Has she said anything about what happened? Why she still thinks it was me?"

Diana shook her head, her expression carrying sadness not only for Alex but for me.

"She hasn't been able to separate reality from fantasy," she said quietly. "She's refusing to speak with anyone except your mother, but says she won't go because she's afraid you'll be there."

I nodded, a lump forming at the base of my throat. "If you could please tell her I won't go anywhere near her or my mom if she wants to see Dr. King." I used the name deliberately—*Dr. King*—the only way Alex separated the two.

"I'll tell her. And Roman...I'm so sorry. We've been trying to help her see you didn't do this. None of us think you did."

That was a small relief. Maybe a reason to reach out to Edward soon. It was past time to find out exactly what Tanner Ellington and his brother were into.

I hugged Diana, my eyes drifting over her shoulder toward the SUV where Alex had disappeared. Even through the dark glass, I could feel her looking back at me.

I gave a nod to Edward standing by the car as their aunt crossed the grass. Then I slipped my phone from my pocket and typed:

ME: *I love you. I'm not going anywhere. I'll make sure Tanner pays for what he did.*

I hit send. One last glance at the blackened window—at the woman who still owned every part of me—then I started the engine and pulled away, heading toward Lookout Park, not realizing just how much everything was about to unravel.

Also by

JE JOHNSON

Acknowledgements

With Wine Comes Wisdom was born from a place I didn't fully understand at the time.

For years—nearly a decade—I had vivid dreams that didn't make sense to me then. I didn't know they were forming a story, or that one day I would feel so consumed by them that I wouldn't be able to stop until it was all out. When it finally began, it poured out of me—more than 2,000 pages of words spilling straight from my heart and soul.

What I thought was simply a story turned out to be something much deeper. It became my way of working through emotions I didn't yet have the words for—anger, confusion, and years of unresolved feelings. Writing this book became my form of therapy, even before I realized I needed it.

It took two years after the release of this book for me to fully understand what was happening beneath the surface. And while that realization wasn't easy, I am grateful for it.

To my family—thank you for loving me anyway, even as I navigated one of the most difficult and eye-opening seasons of my life. Growth isn't always graceful, and healing doesn't always come quietly, but your presence meant more than you may ever know.

To my lifelong friends, and to the new ones who have joined me along this journey—thank you for walking beside me, for supporting me, and for believing in something that started long before I even understood it.

And to my readers—if this story finds you, I hope it speaks to something within you. These books carry more than romance; they carry truth, healing, and a journey I didn't even realize I was on.

If it resonates with you, I would be so grateful if you shared your thoughts. Your reviews help these stories reach the people who may need them most.

Love, always,
JJ

About the author

JE Johnson

Just a believer who loves to write about extraordinary circumstances wrapped up in highly dramatic fashion with a hard fought for happily ever after bow— because a love worth having is worth fighting for!

www.jejohnsonauthor.com

www.ingramcontent.com/pod-product-compliance
Lightning Source LLC
Chambersburg PA
CBHW020922020726
47495CB00002B/303